The Guardian replied,
"By all that was. By all that will be."

"Yeah, that's helpful."

Though drawn here by the immense energies generated by the ageless time portal, Wesley had come seeking answers of his own. He guessed the portal, being one of but a handful of known temporal-based phenomena scattered across the galaxy, might attract his still-unidentified pursuers. Would it provide protection from his mysterious enemy? There was no way to be certain, given that the limits of the Guardian's powers remained a mystery even to him. At the very least he thought the temporal distortions caused by the artifact's obvious distress might shield him from detection and give him time to figure out the nature of his adversary.

You can run, he reminded himself, *but you can't hide.*

"Do you know how long you've been under attack?" he asked.

Its internal mechanisms still pulsing with power, the Guardian replied, *"The assault has not yet begun. The assault has continued since time immemorial. The assault will never begin, and yet will continue for eternity."*

Gritting his teeth, Wesley shook his head in frustration. "What the hell does that mean? How am I supposed to understand you?" The Guardian's penchant for speaking in conundrums was legendary, a practice that only lessened when asked direct questions about specific abilities it possessed. Why, then, did it persist with such obfuscation now? What was he missing? Perhaps the ancient portal simply did not know what menaced it. Considering this, Wesley groped for some query he could pose that might elicit more useful answers.

Wait, he thought. *What is . . . No!*

STAR TREK™
CODA

BOOK 1

MOMENTS ASUNDER

Dayton Ward

Story by
Dayton Ward, James Swallow, and David Mack
Based on
Star Trek and
Star Trek: The Next Generation
created by
Gene Roddenberry
Star Trek: Deep Space Nine
created by
Rick Berman & Michael Piller
Star Trek: Voyager
created by
Rick Berman & Michael Piller & Jeri Taylor

GALLERY BOOKS
New York   London   Toronto   Sydney   New Delhi

G

Gallery Books
An Imprint of Simon & Schuster, Inc.
1230 Avenue of the Americas
New York, NY 10020

First Gallery Books trade paperback edition September 2021

GALLERY BOOKS and colophon are registered trademarks of Simon & Schuster, Inc.

For information about special discounts for bulk purchases, please contact Simon & Schuster Special Sales at 1-866-506-1949 or business@simonandschuster.com.

The Simon & Schuster Speakers Bureau can bring authors to your live event. For more information or to book an event, contact the Simon & Schuster Speakers Bureau at 1-866-248-3049 or visit our website at www.simonspeakers.com.

Interior design by A. Kathryn Barrett

Manufactured in the United States of America

10 9 8 7 6 5 4 3 2 1

Library of Congress Cataloging-in-Publication Data is available.

ISBN 978-1-9821-5852-1
ISBN 978-1-9821-5853-8 (ebook)

Dedicated to the memory of
Dave Galanter
We miss you, Deet. And we love you.

PREVIOUSLY . . .

2376

- Captain Benjamin Sisko returns from his sojourn with the Bajoran Prophets, which began a year earlier following the conclusion of the Dominion War. (*Star Trek: Deep Space Nine*, "What You Leave Behind")
- Bajor joins the United Federation of Planets. (*Star Trek: Deep Space Nine* novel *Unity*)

2377

- After being marooned in the Delta Quadrant seven years earlier, Captain Kathryn Janeway and the crew of the *Starship Voyager* complete their 70,000-light-year journey home to Earth. (*Star Trek: Voyager*, "Endgame")

2378

- Wesley Crusher accompanies the Traveler, with whom he's been learning to grow and focus his emerging abilities, to his mentor's home planet, Tau Alpha C. There, he is "reborn" and becomes a Traveler. (*Star Trek: The Next Generation* novel *A Time to Be Born*)

2379

- Federation president Min Zife, guilty of selling to the independent world Tezwa illegal weapons that contribute to millions of deaths, is covertly removed from office by a group of Starfleet admirals with the assistance of Captain Jean-Luc Picard. Unknown to Picard, Zife is assassinated by Section 31. (*Star Trek* novels *A Time to Kill* and *A Time to Heal*)
- Shinzon, a cloned duplicate of Picard originally created to replace the captain as a Romulan spy within Starfleet, seizes control of the Romulan Star Empire following a *coup d'état*. He launches a bold plan to attack Earth and cripple the Federation, but Picard and the *Enterprise* defeat him. Diplomatic relations are renewed between the Federation and the Romulans. (*Star Trek Nemesis*)

- Captain William Riker takes command of *U.S.S. Titan*. His wife, Commander Deanna Troi, accompanies him as ship's counselor and first-contact specialist. (*Star Trek: Titan* novel series)

2380

- Picard marries Beverly Crusher. (*Star Trek: The Next Generation* novel *Greater Than the Sum*)
- During an incursion by the Borg, Admiral Kathryn Janeway gives her life in defense of the Federation. (*Star Trek: The Next Generation* novel *Before Dishonor*)

2381

- The Borg launch a massive invasion of the Federation, laying waste to numerous planets and billions of lives before Starfleet achieves final victory, forever ending the Collective's persistent threat. (*Star Trek: Destiny* novel trilogy)
- During the invasion, Ezri Dax, serving as *U.S.S. Aventine*'s second officer, takes command when her captain and first officer are killed.
- Riker and Troi have a daughter, Natasha Miana Riker-Troi, named in memory of deceased *Enterprise* crewmember and friend Natasha Yar, and the deceased sister of Aili Lavena, a member of the *Titan*'s crew. (*Star Trek: Titan* novel series)
- With the assistance of unlikely allies, Admiral Janeway's death is reversed. She takes command of Project Full Circle, with *U.S.S. Voyager* and an entire fleet assigned to further explore the Delta Quadrant. (*Star Trek: Voyager* novel *The Eternal Tide*)
- Picard and Crusher have a son, René Jacques Robert François Picard. The boy is named for Picard's nephew, René, and older brother, Robert, and for Crusher's first husband, Jack Crusher. (*Star Trek: Destiny–Lost Souls* novel, *Star Trek: Typhon Pact* novel *Paths of Disharmony*)
- Following the Borg Invasion, Sisko assumes command of *U.S.S. Robinson*. (*Star Trek: Typhon Pact* novel *Rough Beasts of Empire*)

2382

- Admiral Janeway, along with the crew of *U.S.S. Voyager*, agrees to help an alien race, the Edrehmaia, on their long journey out of our galaxy. They depart the Delta Quadrant for parts unknown. (*Star Trek: Voyager* novel *To Lose the Earth*)
- Andor secedes from the Federation over issues related to the Andorians' now-critical reproductive crisis. (*Star Trek: Typhon Pact* novel *Paths of Disharmony*)

2383

- Breen and Tzenkethi forces attack and destroy Federation station Deep Space 9. Over a thousand lives are lost. (*Star Trek: Typhon Pact* novel *Raise the Dawn*)

2384

- Years after sacrificing himself to save Picard, Data is "reincarnated" after his memories are removed from his brother, the android B-4, and transferred into the body of a new android created by Noonian Soong. His android daughter, Lal, is also repaired and reactivated. (*Star Trek: Cold Equations* novel trilogy)

2385

- Federation station Deep Space 9 (II) is declared operational, positioned like its predecessor near the Bajoran wormhole. At its commemoration, Federation President Nanietta Bacco is assassinated. Federation Council member Ishan Anjar of Bajor is appointed president pro tempore. (*Star Trek: The Fall, Book I: Revelation and Dust*)
- Julian Bashir defies Starfleet and President Pro Tempore Ishan to bring the Andorian people a cure for their reproductive crisis. He succeeds with help from Captain Dax. They are both imprisoned. (*Star Trek: The Fall, Book III: A Ceremony of Losses*)
- President Pro Tempore Ishan is exposed as a criminal. Andor rejoins the Federation. An Andorian wins the Federation's presiden-

tial election and pardons Bashir and Dax. (*Star Trek: The Fall, Book V: Peaceable Kingdoms*)

2386

- Exploring the Odyssean Pass, Picard and the *Enterprise* encounter an immense weapon, reverse-engineered by an alien race from a prototype "planet killer" device and sent back in time from the late twenty-fifth century. Investigating the weapon's onboard computer systems, Lieutenant Commander Taurik discovers information about future events he is not permitted to disclose. Taurik is debriefed by the Department of Temporal Investigations and sworn to secrecy in accordance with the Temporal Prime Directive. (*Star Trek: The Next Generation* novel *Armageddon's Arrow*)

- Picard and the *Enterprise* discover a rogue planet locked into a series of random jumps across multiple dimensions and points in time. They meet an alternate version of *U.S.S. Enterprise* NCC-1701-D from a reality in which Picard did not survive his capture and assimilation by the Borg. (*Star Trek: The Next Generation* novel *Headlong Flight*)

- Journalist Ozla Graniv, with the assistance of Bashir and Data, exposes Section 31's entire history and lengthy list of illegal activities spanning more than two centuries. All known Section 31 operatives are pursued and arrested, and Picard is implicated in the organization's assassination of Federation president Min Zife in 2379. (*Star Trek: Section 31* novel *Control*)

2387

- Exonerated from the fallout relating to the revelations about Section 31, Captain Picard prepares to return with the *Enterprise* to the Odyssean Pass to continue its exploration mission. (*Star Trek: The Next Generation* novel *Collateral Damage*)

AND NOW . . .

PART I

TIME'S SCYTHE

1

Like so many others he had seen in his travels, this was a dead world. Once, it teemed with life, but all of that ended uncounted millennia ago.

While much younger and learning to control his still burgeoning abilities, the Traveler had come to this planet to observe the civilization that called it home. Theirs was a society of peace, of arts and science, of wonder and awe. Using the same passion with which they scrutinized the stars above them, they also studied and learned about the world around them and—indeed—within each of them. He never discovered what ultimately had doomed this world, or even when that downfall had occurred. Like so much else about this planet, the final fate of its people remained shrouded in mystery, defying all efforts to draw the truth from darkness into the light.

Though the people were no more, long dead and gone, there was still life here. He could sense it—the faintest hints tugged at the very limit of his perceptions—but it existed. Life in its most basic, primeval form thrived. Perhaps over time, the simple amino acids struggling to survive long enough to form the first microscopic proteins would continue to evolve and advance toward other, higher-order forms of life. In another several billion years, a new civilization might well assert its dominance on this world. Then, the Traveler imagined, the cycle might even repeat itself all over again, just as it had on uncounted worlds throughout this universe and beyond.

Such was the nature of life, and of time.

Doing his best to battle the mounting fatigue weighing on

him, he knew this was but a temporary respite. Sooner or later, his pursuers—whoever or whatever they were—would find him. Whatever rest he managed to collect here would be at best fleeting, before the fight resumed once again. Even now and in this place, the Traveler did not possess the luxury of time. In point of fact and in so many ways, time was the true enemy.

The ground on which he stood was the very picture of desolation, doubtless unchanged to any meaningful degree since the previous civilization had long ago died and gone to dust. He could see where millennia of wind-driven sand had smoothed rock formations and other outcroppings littering the landscape in all directions. Snowcapped mountains in the distance suggested water was still in abundance. Heightened senses detected the presence of a nearby underground spring. Adjusting the strap of his worn leather satchel—itself an unnecessary affectation, a tangible reminder of a past life—so that it rested higher on his right shoulder, the Traveler walked toward the sound.

Water filled a depression near the base of a large rock formation jutting from the soil. Kneeling next to the pool, he cupped his hands and collected some of the water, noting how cold it was as he brought it to his lips. He knew before he tasted it that it was safe to drink, and savored its refreshing effects. The last of the ripples he had created began to subside and he bent closer to examine his reflection in the pool's surface. When had he last seen his own features?

Wesley Crusher stared at the deep lines in his face; at least, those portions of his face that were not covered by the full beard that was more gray than the brown he recalled from further in the past than he could easily remember. The same was true for his hair, which fell over his ears and forehead and rested atop the shoulders of his worn dark-leather jacket. Without thinking, he ran one hand through the thick locks, the pale color of which only served to make him appear far older than his actual age. Whatever that was anymore.

He had long ago quit bothering to keep track of such things, as they had ceased to have any real meaning with respect to his current existence. In one aspect, it had been over a quarter of a century since he began his travels. From another viewpoint, the years since leaving behind his life as a mere human mortal had passed within the blink of an eye. Both were true, along with the immutable fact that his journeys had traversed millions of years, both to the past and the future. No matter how keenly one might examine the span of his life or how small the unit of time used to measure it, he remembered its every aspect. He felt as young and full of hope and enthusiasm as he had at the beginning, while at the same time every particle of his being ached with the weight of time's passage. With force of thought he could push away the latter sensations, but Wesley had become acutely conscious of how much effort it seemed to take.

Was time finally catching up with him? How much longer might his travels continue? There was no way to be certain, and now more than ever there were factors in play that cast even greater weight upon his questions. Despite the abilities he had honed over the course of his strange yet extraordinary life, the only insight into future events he possessed was what he acquired during his travels. As he knew from lessons taught to him by his mentor as well as the Starfleet Academy instructors from a life forsaken long ago, that knowledge was dangerous for countless reasons. Wesley had always taken care not to allow the lure of foresight to influence his decisions or actions. To do so was too great a risk on a scale almost too massive for him to comprehend. The rules of temporal travel that he had respected in his former life, though almost naïve as observed by beings wholly incapable of fully understanding the ramifications at stake, at least were guided by a desire to do no harm. An element of that reasoning carried forward into the guidelines by which he now moved through the universe.

Precious little of that sentiment seemed to matter.

Moving along the desolate terrain, Wesley noticed that the rock formations flanking him seemed to grow in size as well as proximity. Even though he knew where he was going, he could not help feeling as though the outcroppings to either side of him seemed to guide him in a particular direction. He recalled experiencing similar sensations during his previous visits to this world, wondering each time if it was more than simply a fluke of nature or the result of deliberate design. It was just another of the many questions about this place for which he had never been able to obtain an answer.

A gap appeared among the rocks ahead, and with every step Wesley became more aware of the low, teasing, and almost musical whine permeating the air. By the time he emerged into another expanse of flat terrain, the drone was impossible to ignore. Was it his imagination, or was it even more pervasive and intense than he remembered from his last visit?

Doing his best to ignore the now quite omnipresent hum, Wesley directed his gaze to the ruins of the dead city sprawling in all directions into the distance across the austere plain. His point of arrival had placed him near the center of this ancient, deserted metropolis, allowing him to marvel at the tantalizing blend of form and function, of technical skill and artistic boldness, that had contributed to the city's construction. It never failed to amaze him that a people so skilled and capable of building such a thing of wonder had for reasons unknown allowed themselves to be swept from the face of this world. All that remained of their accomplishments was what had not yet succumbed to the elements as well as the relentless passage of time. Yet, what lingered here stood as mute testament to skill and beauty.

Then, there was the artifact.

Shrouded in a veil of mystery far more opaque than the fate suffered by this planet's extinct inhabitants, the odd construct seemed at home neither here nor anywhere else Wesley had visited. Couched among the ruins near the center of the dead city, it sat alone. Remnants of ancient architecture stood guard around it, indicating the artifact was an object of attention, not admiration. An asymmetrical ellipsoid perched on its edge as it sat atop the arid, dead soil, it appeared to be carved from stone, though Wesley could not identify its exact composition even with the powers he commanded. Attempts to define its age had also met with resistance. Records from Starfleet's initial encounter with the object indicated its construction or placement preceded the emergence of life on this world by billions of years. That meant it likely had been here long before life evolved on worlds throughout this galaxy, but all subsequent efforts to investigate and understand the artifact met with the same lack of progress. Standing before it, Wesley peered through its central opening, which for the moment allowed him to see more of the surrounding city ruins. Aside from Federation scientists and researchers using it to observe past events—and those even rarer occasions when someone had actually stepped through it to take advantage of its staggering abilities—it stood here, silent.

As it had for most of its entire existence, the Guardian of Forever awaited a question.

"Guardian," said Wesley, his eyes narrowing as he regarded the time portal. "Can you hear me?"

In response to his simple query, the ellipsoid began to glow and pulse from within, the effect generated by minerals or other materials that defied all attempts to scan or classify them. Its aperture became blurred and indistinct, awash in a tumult of swirling colors. Now that it was active, Wesley sensed the distress that had drawn him here in the first place, along with an increase in the waves of temporal-displacement energy that accompanied the time portal's activation.

"I am the Guardian," said a deep, baritone voice that seemed to echo off the nearby ruins and rock formations. *"I hear you, as I hear all."*

Wesley felt a new instability in the energy the artifact now generated. These were far more powerful than had been recorded by scientists studying its operation, and instinct told him they were in response to something it perceived as a threat. Outside stimuli, assaulting the Guardian from . . . elsewhere.

"You're under attack." It was a statement, rather than a question. Wesley could feel surges of power escalating as they pushed against the portal. "Do you know by whom? Or what?"

The Guardian replied, *"By all that was. By all that will be."*

"Yeah, that's helpful."

Though drawn here by the immense energies generated by the ageless time portal, Wesley had come seeking answers of his own. He guessed the portal, being one of but a handful of known temporal-based phenomena scattered across the galaxy, might attract his still-unidentified pursuers. Would it provide protection from his mysterious enemy? There was no way to be certain, given that the limits of the Guardian's powers remained a mystery even to him. At the very least he thought the temporal distortions caused by the artifact's obvious distress might shield him from detection and give him time to figure out the nature of his adversary.

You can run, he reminded himself, *but you can't hide.*

"Do you know how long you've been under attack?" he asked.

Its internal mechanisms still pulsing with power, the Guardian replied, *"The assault has not yet begun. The assault has continued since time immemorial. The assault will never begin, and yet will continue for eternity."*

Gritting his teeth, Wesley shook his head in frustration. "What the hell does that mean? How am I supposed to understand you?" The Guardian's penchant for speaking in conundrums was legendary, a practice that only lessened when asked direct questions about specific abilities it possessed. Why, then, did it persist with such obfuscation now? What was he missing? Perhaps the ancient portal simply did not know what menaced it. Considering this, Wesley groped for some query he could pose that might elicit more useful answers.

Wait, he thought. *What is . . . No!*

Something was different now. He sensed the sudden spike in energy cascading outward from the Guardian mere heartbeats before the colors swirling within the portal intensified in brightness, becoming a frenzy. This was far more extreme even than the outpouring of disruptions, as though the portal was now marshaling all of its power to fend off a new, even more vicious attack than it had ever experienced. The sheer force of the escalation washed over Wesley, as though he were caught in rushing floodwaters surging from different directions to converge on the Guardian. And him.

Not water! His mind screamed the realization. *Time!*

That was it. Relentless, unyielding streams of time, all massing here and driven by forces still unknown. Until now, Wesley had not faced his pursuers. They had offered no hint as to their identity or reasons for hounding him. Instead, they simply attacked as though driven by unfocused rage, but he knew better. He sensed the purpose as well as the determination, particularly now as battering rams of time itself charged toward him.

There was something more here. Wesley could feel it, coursing over and even through him as the torrential outpouring continued to increase. He understood a purpose, an *intent* in motion. Whatever it was did not simply want him. Wesley could not shake the perception—the absolute certainty—that his still unseen enemy wanted *everything*.

Wesley felt the first hints of fear lurking around the edges of his consciousness. At this point of his remarkable life, after everything he had experienced, it was almost an alien sensation, and yet he could not deny it. What if he was unable to stop or even fight whatever was coming for him? What about . . .

For the first time in longer than he could remember, Wesley Crusher forgot everything about the tremendous being he had become as mind and emotions contracted on a single thought, a single person for whom he cared above all others, and whom he might be powerless to protect.

Mom.

2

"Wesley?"

The image of her son, or at least what she was certain had to be her son, flashed in Beverly Crusher's vision. Then everything disappeared in a rush of dizziness and she felt her balance giving way. She reached out for something to steady herself, falling against the nearby patient bed.

"Doctor? Are you okay?"

The voice sounded faint and distant, unable to overcome the sudden ringing in her ears. Now leaning against the bed, Crusher felt a hand touching her forearm, and she realized it had to be her patient. Her vision was already starting to clear, and the vertigo was fading. Colorful blobs took on more distinct shapes, including the large one right in front of her. Seconds later it coalesced into a human male with blond hair, Lieutenant Bryan Regnis. The security officer, who until a moment ago had been undergoing her physical examination, stared at her with an expression of open concern.

"Doctor Crusher," said another voice, and Crusher turned to see Tamala Harstad crossing the *Enterprise*'s sickbay toward her. She was wearing civilian attire and for an odd moment Crusher found herself wondering why the young doctor was even in sickbay during her off-duty hours. Behind her, Doctor Tropp emerged from the suite of offices designated for the ship's medical staff. The Denobulan physician, who served as her assistant chief medical officer, caught up with Harstad just as both doctors reached Crusher.

As was his habit, he wore over his Starfleet uniform a blue lab coat used by the sickbay team.

"What happened?" asked Harstad, speaking to Lieutenant Regnis, who now was sitting up and in the process of swinging his legs over the side of the patient bed.

Regnis cast a wary look to Crusher before replying, "I'm not sure. She was just running her scan over me and asking how I'd been feeling." He tapped the bed next to his right leg. "The next thing I know she looks like she might faint." His worried expression deepened as he regarded her. "Sure you're all right, Doctor?"

Forcing a smile, Crusher nodded. "I think so, Lieutenant. Thank you."

"Let me be the judge of that," said Tropp.

Instructing Lieutenant Antoinette Mimouni, one of the nurses on duty in the sickbay, to see to Regnis, the Denobulan guided Crusher out of the patient area and to her office with Harstad following behind them. Once they were out of sight and earshot of subordinates and anyone else, Tropp indicated for Crusher to take a seat behind her desk, and she saw he was already pulling a medical tricorder from the pocket of his lab coat. She smiled, realizing Tropp had taken the extra step of removing her from the treatment room so as not to cause a further stir among her staff and patients in the event his scan revealed something that troubled him. As he worked, Harstad made her way around the desk, and Crusher once more took note that her clothing was very much not her regular Starfleet uniform. The brightly colored top and beige leggings played off the doctor's dark skin and harmonized with the gold band she wore to keep her black hair away from her face. The outfit was enough to remind Crusher her colleague was not even supposed to be in sickbay at this hour.

"What are you even doing here, Tamala?" asked Crusher. "You're supposed to be having an early dinner with Geordi before trying out some new holodeck program he found. *Sunrise on Zeta Minor*, or something like that?"

Harstad leaned against the desk. "So he said, but he's still down in engineering tinkering with some regulator or flow sensor or whatever. I decided to wait for him while catching up on some reports I still need to finish." Leaning closer, she added with an almost conspiratorial tone, "Word of advice: never get involved with a starship's chief engineer."

"And whatever you do," said Crusher, "definitely don't marry that ship's captain."

"We're supposed to be heading for shore leave." Harstad sighed. "I'm pretty sure I'm going to have to kidnap him to get him off the ship once we get there."

Crusher replied, "Starbase 11 has some of the nicest beaches I've ever seen. One of the perks of being on a planet rather than a space station. They have these bungalows that sit on stilts out on the water. You can dive into the ocean right from your bedroom. There's nothing like a moonlight swim, and your closest neighbors are a hundred meters away."

"What are you saying, Doctor?" Harstad's right eyebrow arched.

"I'm saying if you sell it right, you won't need to kidnap him."

Their moment of levity was enough to make Crusher feel better. Whatever had happened seemed to be over, leaving only the sorts of questions she knew her fellow doctors would now ask.

As Tropp waved his tricorder's compact diagnostic scanner over Crusher's head, Harstad asked, "Have you experienced anything like this before? Recently?"

Crusher shook her head. "No. Nothing." She leaned back in her chair, her lingering feelings of unease now faded and leaving her with questions about what the image of Wesley might mean. "I wasn't even thinking about him just then. At least, not consciously." When the comment elicited looks from both her companions, she realized they likely had not heard her in the treatment area. "I'm sorry. For a brief moment, I was—" She paused, considering her word choice. "I was consumed by a vision of my son Wesley."

"You think of him often, I assume?" asked Tropp. He deactivated the scanner, his right hand forming a fist around the device as he studied his tricorder readings. Crusher noted his features; like most Denobulans he was usually easy to read.

Crusher replied, "Of course I do." She waved one hand as though to dismiss her answer. "I mean, I don't think about him every waking moment, but he's my son. I think about him all the time. You're a parent, Doctor. You know how it is."

When he smiled, Tropp's face seemed to stretch with no effort made to conceal his obvious pride. "Indeed I am. Eight children, thirty-four grandchildren, and three great-grandchildren." He stopped himself, directing his gaze to a point somewhere behind Crusher before holding up a finger. "Thirty-five grandchildren. The newest one I've not yet met, and the older I get, it's sometimes difficult to keep track of everyone."

"Listening to all of that just makes me tired," said Harstad.

The comment elicited smiles and laughter from all three doctors before Tropp closed his tricorder and returned it to the pocket of his lab coat. He kept his hand there, mimicking the action with his other hand in the garment's other pocket. His smile was gone, replaced once more by an expression of professional concern.

"When was the last time you saw your son?" he asked.

Crusher replied, "Not since that business with Data and the Machine planet at the center of the galaxy."

Wesley and his mentor, the Traveler, had sought help from the *Enterprise* after observing the mammoth construct annihilating entire star systems. Other Travelers, fearing the Machine's power, had withdrawn, leaving Wesley to summon aid from the people he trusted most. Working together, he and Data along with Picard had persuaded the Machine to give up its goal of destroying subspace along with faster-than-light travel and communications, setting the stage for it to eliminate all living beings in the galaxy. Following the conclusion of that crisis, Wesley had returned to traveling the cosmos that now were his home. Without a means to communicate with him, Crusher had no way of knowing what he was doing or how he might be feeling; she could only hope one day he might return.

"Been having any dreams where he pops up?" asked Harstad.

Releasing a small sigh, Crusher shook her head. "Not that I recall. Whatever it was, I've never felt anything like it. I don't even know how to describe it except to say it was very intense. Like a momentary lapse into daydreaming but much stronger, while at the same time vague and undefined." She closed her eyes, reaching up to rub the bridge of her nose. "Maybe I'm just tired. It's been . . . well, it's been a long year. Hasn't it?"

Harstad tapped the desk. "Well, she's back to asking rhetorical questions. That has to be a good sign. Right?"

"My scans did not detect any abnormalities," said Tropp before pursing his lips. After a moment, he added, "I would like to run a full exam, just to be on the safe side." As though anticipating her protest, he pulled his right hand from his pocket and held it up. "We can do it after we've discharged the patients we have. There's no one who's here for anything serious and sickbay will be empty within thirty minutes. It might even boost the crew's morale. Let them see the chief medical officer being subjected to the same medical tortures we inflict upon them." His broad grin returned, reassuring Crusher he was being facetious.

"They get enough of that when I make the captain undergo his physicals."

Crusher knew there was no point arguing against Tropp, who was just as formidable a physician as she was and would not take no for an answer when it came to something like this. Tempted as she was to simply let the matter drop, common sense insisted she allow the doctor to conduct the examination. If nothing else, it would rule out any obvious physiological or neurological possibilities.

"You win," she said, holding up her hands in mock surrender. "I submit myself to your tender mercies, Doctor."

Appearing satisfied with this response, Tropp nodded. "Very

well. I will see to our remaining patients. I would prefer you pass that time here in your office. Just in case there's another . . . occurrence?"

"I can help with that," said Harstad. "I've still got a bit of time to kill, and if Geordi comes looking for me, he can park it while we finish up." She exchanged knowing glances with Crusher. "Serves him right for keeping a lady waiting."

Crusher replied, "Absolutely." She rose from her chair, reaching for a padd on the corner of her desk. There were records of her own she could see to updating while waiting for Tropp. "Please apologize to Lieutenant Regnis for me."

"I certainly will," replied Tropp. "Though, I suspect he won't—"

The sound of the ship's intercom interrupted the doctor, followed by the voice of Hailan Casmir, the *Enterprise*'s lead civilian educator and supervisor for the ship's childcare center.

"Education center to Doctor Crusher."

Crusher's first instinct was to glance at the chronometer display on her desktop computer interface. Had she lost track of time and forgotten to pick up her son René from school? The chronometer assured her this was not the case, which only served to ignite an all-new anxiety. She tapped the communicator badge affixed to her uniform tunic.

"This is Doctor Crusher. What is it, Mister Casmir?"

The Argelian's tone was one of worry as he replied, *"I'm terribly sorry to bother you, Doctor, but it's René. He started crying a moment ago and we've tried to calm him, but he seems quite inconsolable. Would you mind—"*

"On my way."

3

Another wave of temporal distortions spat forth from the Guardian's central opening, which was now a vortex of pulsing, iridescent light. The sound of the barely restrained frenzy was loud enough that Wesley winced in mounting discomfort. Was it his imagination, or was the ancient time portal actually trembling from the force of the onslaught?

"Guardian!" he shouted, barely able to hear his own voice over the growing din. "What's happening?"

"A battle begins," replied the artifact. *"A battle ends. A battle is averted. A battle begins yet again."*

Wesley shook his head at the Guardian's formidable ability to remain enigmatic. It was particularly vexing at this precise moment. How was he to understand what the portal was enduring, let alone help it fight whatever attacked it, if the ageless construct could only spout riddles?

Maybe that's the key.

Could the Guardian be trying to offer him some kind of clue or information in the hopes of eliciting his help? Perhaps the attack to which it was being subjected prevented it from answering in a more comprehensive manner. Was it possible the portal was directing all of its resources to defend against the assault, leaving little with which to communicate or even ask for assistance? That, at least, made sense on some level, Wesley decided. But what could he do?

Focus, he told himself. *Focus on the Guardian.*

Directing his consciousness inward, Wesley gathered his thoughts and forged them into a single, simple line of interaction he could direct toward what he recognized as the Guardian, a lone point of stability within an ever-increasing storm of chaos and fury. He pushed forward, reaching deeper into the tempest and extending himself to where he was sure he could almost touch whatever it was that passed for the island of awareness that was the time portal's own sense of self.

I am the Guardian of Forever.

The statement thundered in Wesley's mind, pushing aside all other thoughts and perceptions. He was there. He had made it. Contact, and perhaps understanding, was in his grasp.

I am Wesley Crusher.

You are a Traveler.

And I have traveled here because I sensed you are in distress. I feel the assault you're experiencing. Who's responsible?

I do not know.

How can I help? Tell me what to do.

There is nothing for you to do, Wesley Crusher. At least, not for me. I am but a tool. Some see me as a weapon. Others see me as salvation. Many such journeys are possible, but it is not for me to decide which are worthy. I can only serve—

Wesley flinched as the Guardian's central opening flashed brilliant white light, pulling him back to the here and now before . . . *something* exploded from the portal. A blurred mass, dark and rippling, followed by three more ominous silhouettes, emerging with such power that he saw the Guardian tremble as if struck by a physical blow. Feeling himself lose his balance, Wesley raised his arms, flailing to keep his feet.

Guardian!

Once more he reached out with his thoughts, but now he neither heard nor felt anything. It was as if the Guardian had gone dormant. There was no time to ascertain what if any damage the portal may have sustained, as Wesley's attention focused on the new arrivals.

After sailing clear of the Guardian, each of the blurred masses, easily four meters in length, solidified into large, writhing snake-like creatures. Their pale bodies, sinewy and muscled and tapering to lithe tails as they hung in the air, possessed the faintest hint of green coloring. Each serpent's head was large, with a pair of symmetrical bone spikes beginning at the crown of its skull and proceeding down its back. It was the first time his adversaries had chosen to manifest themselves as physical beings, but even now he sensed how they seemed to phase in and out of existence. They occupied space on this plane, but also somewhere else. A place Wesley had never seen and could not know.

Not really all that important right now, he reminded himself.

There was something else he was coming to understand. With each moment, the Guardian was putting out ever increasing levels of temporal disruption; doing its damnedest with whatever bizarre abilities it harbored to mount a resistance against the new arrivals. The ground trembled beneath his feet, the reverberations pushing deep beneath the surface into the bedrock. To Wesley it felt as though the Guardian might be calling upon the very planet itself to augment its defenses.

Rather than being intimidated by this, it appeared as though the serpents were feeding on this new, increasing outpouring of energy. He sensed the creatures drawing strength from it even as the Guardian seemed to pull back in on itself as if fighting to keep the serpents from exploiting it. The artifact's struggle was palpable, and Wesley recognized the shift in energy as it turned inward, feeding a barrier he now understood to be forming around the Guardian.

Then the creatures turned their attentions to him.

At first their attack resembled little more than a pack of wild animals driven by simple bloodlust as they launched themselves at him, swimming through the air as eels might navigate water. It took Wesley an instant to comprehend this was something more. The serpents separated, coming at him from different directions and forcing him to continue moving in order to keep track of their individual lines of advance. Spreading out as they crossed the desolate ground, they were attempting to hem him in, driving him toward one of the nearby rock formations so that he'd be trapped and vulnerable.

"Nice try." Glaring at his assailants, Wesley spread his fingers as he raised his hands. "But I don't think so."

Summoning the abilities he had honed during many years spent wandering—no, *traveling*—the universe, Wesley directed that power at his attackers. The response was immediate, with each of the four serpents halting in midair, frozen as though stuck in time. It was an ability Wesley had refined in the decades since discovering his true place in the universe and his capacity to move through it unlike any mere human or other mortal. His first experience with the power had come by accident, fueled by fear and anguish and resulting in the pausing of everything and everyone around him. Only then had he begun to truly comprehend his place in the universe, thanks to the mysterious alien he had only known as "the Traveler." With his unlikely mentor's help, Wesley had seen his life as a normal human end that day, only to begin an all-new journey toward higher planes of existence and understanding.

The powers he had not even known he possessed during that moment of transition had been nurtured to the point that they acted at will. The strain he once felt as he struggled for control was long gone, replaced with the easy confidence of one at total peace with their own existence, abilities, and limits. The serpents, locked in stasis as they hung in the air before him, were his to control.

Wesley's first thought was that he should destroy them, for they would surely kill him given the chance. The better option would be to attempt sending them back from whence they had come. Maybe he could track them to their point of origin and learn who had dispatched them and for what purpose. Surely there was more to this than him? In the vast reality that was the cosmos, he had to believe he was insignificant. Without realizing it, did he pose a threat to someone or something? Why? There were too many questions, and he now held before him the clues to finding answers.

You have nothing.

The words hammered Wesley's ears, echoed in his mind, and resonated across the forsaken landscape around him. At the same time, he saw another figure emerging from the Guardian. The new arrival was a humanoid, cloaked in dark, flowing robes that concealed most of its body. Wesley was still able to make out an oversized head that was partially covered by a hood pulled low across the figure's brow. Standing on the ground near the Guardian, the humanoid placed one hand on the portal's stone edifice and Wesley winced at the abrupt increase in the waves of temporal energy being generated by the artifact.

"What are you doing?" Wesley took a step toward the stranger only to realize the serpents were beginning to overcome the hold he had on them. He felt them shifting in and out of phase. They were manipulating their bodies in and around spacetime like someone attempting to dodge raindrops at the beginning of a storm, only the creatures were having greater success. Within seconds they extracted themselves from the makeshift prison in which he had trapped them and once more set their sights on him.

"Whoever you are," Wesley said, "you're not giving me much choice here."

Turning his attention to the nearest serpent, Wesley clenched his fists and punched the air. Bursts of crimson energy spat forth from his hands, crossing the space between him and the creature and striking it head-on. The serpent released a pain-racked shriek as its body disintegrated from the force of the dual blast. Its three companions halted their advance, at least for the moment wary of this new threat. Taking advantage of their hesitation, Wesley pivoted to face another of the creatures, drawing strength for another strike. He stopped as the humanoid raised a hand, and the remaining serpents broke off their attack. Retreating, they moved past their apparent master, who still stood with one hand resting on the

Guardian, disappearing into the vortex of energy emanating from the portal. Once they were gone, the lone figure turned as though staring at Wesley, its features cloaked in the shadow of its robes.

"What the hell is this?" Pointing to the stranger, Wesley started walking toward it. "Who are you? What do you want?"

You know nothing. Even as the words seemed to pummel Wesley's very consciousness, the humanoid raised a hand to point at him.

You are . . . nothing.

Turning to the Guardian, the figure disappeared through the portal. In the same instant, Wesley shivered as new waves of energy burst forth, flowing without restraint from the very core of the ancient construct.

"I am my own beginning." The words roared from the artifact. *"I am my own ending."*

Then the Guardian came apart, its stone halo disappearing in a fresh onslaught of unhindered temporal distortions. Wesley gasped at the raw power announcing the ageless portal's demise. All of its secrets and knowledge, the questions it harbored and the answers it defended, lost forever as it crumbled to dust before his eyes. The resulting shockwave spread outward from where the portal had stood, gaining strength and speed as it washed across the ground and through the air.

Wesley held up his hands, able to slow the advance but not stop it. Sheer will met sheer force and the force was winning. He felt it already starting to overtake him. There were only seconds remaining in which to act, and but a single thing he could do. He fled.

Wesley threw himself into the void between moments, separating himself from this point in spacetime. From his detached point of view, he observed monstrous fissures crisscrossing across the Guardian planet's surface. Mountain ranges and other terrain features disappeared into widening chasms as the planet collapsed in on itself. It disappeared in a torrent of light and energy that surged outward, radiating away from what had been the world's core. Wesley felt the waves of temporal distortions rushing across and between points in time, fractures and splinters erupting all around him not just in this reality, but in so many others he sensed at the edges of his consciousness. He allowed himself to be pushed along with them, seizing the opportunity to regain some of his own depleted strength.

Where the hell did you go?

The question echoed in his mind as he absorbed the magnitude of what had just happened. The Guardian was gone. Also lost was the promise—and the threat—to anyone willing to undertake the journeys it offered, journeys that were no longer possible. While there were those who might breathe easier knowing it could no longer be exploited for nefarious reasons, Wesley could not help thinking it was a line of defense now forever beyond reach.

There's no time for this, he chastised himself, recognizing the irony even in that simple thought. Forcing his mind to focus on the matter at hand, Wesley extended his senses. He almost missed it amid the chaos, but there it was: a faint trail, left behind by the mysterious humanoid as it disappeared through the Guardian. Who was the stranger, and where was it going? What did all of this mean?

As he reached across time and space, searching for this enigmatic adversary, he was all but overcome by the sensation that had earlier taunted him: *fear.* It was so palpable it was as though Wesley could sense someone—no, some *thing*—dying. The dread extended far beyond the confines of any individual, stretching to the ends of his perceptions and perhaps even reality itself. Faces, billions of them and all lacking discernible features, flashed in his consciousness, then faded just as quickly. Stars born, burned, and died in the blink of his eye. Was he feeling the death throes of . . . everything?

No, he decided. It was more targeted than that, but he could not define or describe it even to himself, or see a way toward an explanation. Driven by sudden apprehension, Wesley pushed himself from this plane of existence. He sailed through the folds between realities, dodging the visions of death and destruction as his senses hunted for those who held the answers to his questions. As he traveled, two faces emerged from the indistinct blur of everything and nothing, staring at him from the edges of oblivion. These he recognized: his mother and a young boy he barely knew and yet had known forever; a tangible, precious link to a life he had left behind and still treasured.

He did not understand how or why, but with every atom of his being Wesley Crusher knew that everyone and everything stood on the precipice of annihilation.

It was, he realized, simply a matter of *time*.

4

Leaving Tropp and Harstad to mind sickbay in her absence, Beverly Crusher was almost at a full run by the time she reached the entrance to the ship's education center. No sooner did she enter the room than her eyes were searching for René, but he was nowhere to be seen. It was the time of day when the few preschool-aged children were gone, having been picked up by a parent. The handful of older students also were gone, their lessons for the day imparted along with homework from their teacher. Indeed, a glance to the doorway leading to a classroom just off this foyer told her the room beyond was dark, its lights and desktop computer interfaces deactivated for the day.

So, where was her son?

"René?" she called out, moving away from the entrance and deeper into the facility. She knew that the short passage just outside the classroom led to the offices used by Hailan Casmir and Hegol Den, the ship's counselor. Additional workspace was assigned to two young civilians, a human male and a Vulcan female whose names Crusher could not remember. The pair worked as assistants to both Casmir and Hegol as well as the *Enterprise*'s library and archive section, which was co-located with the education center.

Casmir emerged from the office corridor, wearing a loose-fitting brilliant-jade tunic with a high collar over black trousers. His long blond hair was worn in a ponytail not all that different from Commander Worf's, while his beard was trimmed to an exacting precision even William Riker could appreciate. To Crusher's relief, Casmir did not seem agitated as he had over the intercom, and even extended his hands in greeting as he approached her with a warm smile.

"Doctor, thank you for coming so quickly. I regret alarming you. You know I would only reach out to you in case of a true emergency, and René has never engaged in such alarming behavior. I decided prudence was best."

Not sure how to react to the teacher's comments, Crusher looked past him in search of René. "No, I'm glad you called. Where is he?"

Gesturing for her to follow him, Casmir turned and headed back the way he had come. Though she listened for crying or other signs of distress, she heard nothing. They continued down the short passage to Casmir's office. On the sofa positioned just inside the door and opposite the Argelian's curved desk was her son René Jacques Robert François Picard.

With a head of thick auburn hair that landed somewhere on the color spectrum between her own locks and those the boy's father had sported a lifetime earlier, he sat quietly with his attention focused on the book in his lap. Rather than employing a padd, René had established a preference for reading physical books, a habit he came by in an honest fashion thanks to his father's own predilection. He read at a level well above what might be expected from even a precocious six-year-old child. She did not recognize the book that so engrossed the boy just now, guessing it was an adventure story of the sort he loved listening to her husband read to him at bedtime. Hearing her arrive in the doorway, René looked up from the tome and his face stretched into a wide, toothy grin.

"Mommy!"

He set the book beside him on the sofa, and she almost laughed as she watched him taking care not to crease the volume's spine or any of the pages before pushing himself to his feet and crossing the room to her. Well on his way to seven Standard years, René was already taller than her waist, which he embraced as he came within reach. Though she noticed the redness of his eyes indicating he had been crying, there seemed to be no other sign of the earlier episode. Unprepared for this reaction, Crusher looked with uncertainty to Casmir, who responded by shrugging and holding out his hands in supplication.

"When I called you he was very upset," explained the teacher. "One moment, he's engrossed in his history lesson, the next he started whimpering and looking around as though something was frightening him." He gestured to the sofa. "I took him out of the classroom and brought him here, hoping I might help him calm down. Once we were away from the other children, he started muttering things I couldn't understand, except for a single word."

Her attention divided as she knelt in front of René and let him hug her, Crusher took an extra moment before realizing Casmir had hesitated. Looking over her son's head at the teacher, she regarded him with narrowing eyes.

"Hailan," she prompted. "What is it?"

His expression softening, Casmir replied, "He said, 'Wesley.' So far as I know, it's the first time he's referred to his brother by name, at least here at school. I know René hasn't seen very much of him, and I have no idea what sort of bond they share. Without more information, it does seem a bit unusual for him to call out for Wesley as opposed to you or Captain Picard."

It was true René knew very little of his older brother. Wesley's last visit, driven as it was by the nature of the emergency that had prompted him to seek out her husband and the *Enterprise* for assistance, had left little time for a personal moment. His meeting with his younger sibling had been short yet emotional, all too brief due to Wesley needing to see to the aftermath of the Machine planet crisis and make sure the agreement they had reached with it was upheld. The magnitude of Wesley's life as a Traveler were as significant as they were astounding. His journey from innocent child to precocious teenager to disillusioned Starfleet Academy cadet to a being with almost limitless potential passed seemingly in the blink of an eye.

Where had all that time gone? For Wesley, time had little meaning, at least in the way a normal human might perceive it, but to Crusher it felt as though a part of her life had swept by in a blur, come and gone before she even had time to register its passing. Thanks to his abilities, Wesley could even—if he chose to do so—travel back to some point before today and visit her as though none of that time were lost. Did the fact that she had no memories of such a visit mean it had never occurred, or that Wesley had done something to negate introducing some anomaly into time itself, of the sort her temporal mechanics instructors had bemoaned during one lecture or another during her time at Starfleet Academy? Her mind boggled at the notion, much as it had during many of those same classes.

Crusher became aware of a new presence at the entrance to Casmir's office and looked up to see her husband, Jean-Luc Picard, standing in the doorway. Dressed in his normal duty uniform, he was as always the very epitome of a Starfleet officer. She doubted Casmir could even tell the captain was only slightly flustered from what she guessed was a hurried transit from the bridge.

"I'm sorry, Hailan," said Hegol Den as he moved from the corridor to stand beside Picard. "I contacted the captain before realizing the situation was already under control."

"Quite all right, Doctor Hegol," said Picard, holding up a hand. "I appreciate your diligence." He spoke with his usual composed demeanor and level tone, though Crusher noted the faintest hint of concern as his gaze fell to René. Despite this, she was glad to see him. Though he was and would forever remain a creature of duty, there was precious little in this universe that could keep him from his son if he sensed danger or distress.

"How is he?" he asked, stepping into the office and dropping to one knee as René extricated himself from his mother's arms and moved to him.

Crusher replied, "Apparently, he's fine. Whatever upset him seems to be over." This was neither the time nor the place, she decided, for her to tell him about her own incident in sickbay.

After offering René a loving embrace, Picard held his son at arm's length and gave him a quick appraisal. "René, is something the matter? Something you want to talk about?"

"No," the boy replied, shrugging his right shoulder.

"What," said Crusher, "my medical opinion not good enough for you?" She smiled to take some of the sting out of her gentle ribbing.

Picard smiled. "I never doubted you." His attention still on René, he asked, "Can you tell us what made you upset?"

For his part, René seemed to consider the question for a moment before answering, "I was scared, but I don't remember why."

"But you're not scared now?"

René shook his head. "Not anymore. He helped me to stop feeling scared."

Her eyes narrowing as she took this in, Crusher asked, "Who helped you?"

"Wesley." There was no hesitation, and no uncertainty in the boy's answer, and it was sufficient to draw skeptical looks from Crusher and Picard as well as Casmir and Hegol. All four adults looked at one another, each doubtless wondering what the others were thinking.

"René," Picard said, his voice gentle, "are you saying you saw Wesley?"

The boy nodded, his eyes widening. "He told me I didn't have to be afraid. He told me he'd come to see me again soon."

Picard looked to Crusher. Though he said nothing she saw the question in his face, and she shook her head.

"I haven't seen or heard from him." Once more she considered telling him about the sensations she had experienced in sickbay, but opted against it. She would wait until they were alone.

Releasing René and allowing his son to return to Crusher, Picard turned to Hegol and Casmir. "Has he said or done anything else either of you would consider out of character for him?"

Casmir replied, "No, Captain. I've never had any issue with him so far as personal behavior. He's a model student."

"I agree," added Hegol. "René has always acted very mature for his age and has never mentioned feeling out of sorts about anything."

Now holding René's hand, Crusher said, "I'd like to take him to sickbay. Just to make sure everything's all right."

Nodding in agreement, Picard said, "Of course." He then smiled at René. "You go with your mother. I'll be along shortly."

As she exited the education center with René in hand, Crusher's mind raced. This could not be coincidental, could it? There had to be a connection between what René described and her own experience in sickbay. Nothing else made sense, but what did it mean?

And what did Wesley have to do with *any* of this?

5

———

Leaning with crossed arms against the threshold leading into René's room, Jean-Luc Picard watched and listened to his sleeping son. So far as he could tell, the boy was deep in slumber's embrace, the events of the day forgotten. For that, Picard was thankful despite the questions he harbored.

Throughout his young life, René had never been a fussy child. As a baby he had rarely cried, and had begun sleeping through the night within the first month after his birth. He had never required a pacifier or some other distraction to keep him from becoming upset. Progress reports from Hailan Casmir, first from the *Enterprise*'s childcare facility and later the education center once he was old enough to attend school, described a student with unlimited potential coupled with an innate ability and desire to embrace new knowledge. To Picard's continual gratification, René's love of reading was an extension of his own passion for the written word in all its forms. He eagerly anticipated the days ahead when they might discuss at length some shared favorite book. Those and so many other things done together awaited him.

Look at you, Picard chided himself. *Remember when you feared the very idea of being around any child, let alone one of your own? If only Robert could see you now.*

There was a time when such an errant thought might have made him feel despondent for his brother, killed long ago along with his own son for whom René was named. A fire at the Picard family vineyard on Earth had taken them, leaving Picard stricken upon hearing the news. After decades of being at odds, the two brothers had finally reconciled their differences and established a bond that had been far greater than the one that linked them during childhood. As for his nephew, Picard had mourned the loss not only of such a precious, innocent life, but one ended far too early. While their deaths had not consciously pushed Picard toward the idea of parenthood, he could not deny their influence. Robert and René had shown him how such a role, though he had never considered it necessary or a requirement in order to live a full life, could add a rewarding dimension. Such thoughts had begun during his time as captain of the *Enterprise*'s predecessor starship, which carried far more civilians and families than his current command.

He had resisted the pull of such feelings for several years, his awkwardness—he knew—making him appear surly and unapproachable to some of the ship's children. Smiling to himself, Picard was reminded of his first meeting with Will Riker upon the younger man's reporting for duty as the *Enterprise*-D's first officer.

I don't feel comfortable with children, he recalled telling the commander. *But, since a captain needs an image of geniality, you're to see that's what I project.*

"You were oh so right, Robert," he murmured, almost laughing at himself. "What a humorless, insufferable ass I was."

"Was?"

Turning from René's room, Picard saw Beverly Crusher standing in the main room of their shared living quarters, her hands resting in the pockets of her lab coat. He realized he had been so engrossed in his own thoughts that he failed to hear the doors to their suite open.

"Just remembering my earlier days as a reluctant role model." He stepped away from the bedroom, allowing its door to slide closed behind him. "Did I ever tell you how my brother reacted when I first told him I was taking command of the *Enterprise*?"

"I don't think so." Crusher removed her coat, tossing it over the back of a chair positioned before the room's angled viewing ports. Moving to a nearby cabinet, she retrieved a bottle of wine and two glasses before returning to the table.

Picard smiled at the memory. "Though he liked to pretend he couldn't care less, Robert always followed my career. It's entirely possible he knew about the assignment before I did." Pulling another of the chairs out from the table, he held it for Crusher before taking the seat next to her. "When the subject of families with children being aboard came up, he laughed so hard he nearly choked on his wine."

"Not this wine, I hope." Crusher held up the bottle and Picard recognized the familiar Château Picard label, smiling at the vintage as she poured for them.

"Twenty-three sixty-four." Picard could not help another small, wistful smile. "Beneath that gruff exterior, Robert was a man of deep sentimentality about a great many things. Family was very important to him. When our father died, he saw himself as the caretaker of the Picard legacy. Even though it took him many years to understand why I chose a life away from the family vineyards, he still kept tabs on me."

He gestured for the bottle and she handed it to him, the fingers of his free hand caressing the label. It was a rare vintners' reserve, consisting of just fifty bottles from a yield Robert had overseen personally from vine to bottle in commemoration of his brother taking command of the Federation flagship. Picard had not known about the special bottling before receiving the consignment from Robert's wife, Marie, months after the fire that had taken her husband and son from her. It had been Robert's intention to present the batch to him as a surprise gift on the tenth anniversary of the assignment. While Picard had expected to still be commanding the *Enterprise*-D at that time, fate and circumstances ended up having other plans, both for the ship and Picard along with his brother and nephew.

After he was cleared by a Starfleet board of inquiry following the ship's destruction and assigned command of its successor, Marie had sent the shipment, a congratulatory gift for the new posting. Her handwritten note, included with the shipment and containing these revelations, had brought Picard to tears. Over the ensuing years, he had been frugal with the wine, but a recent conversation with Marie reminded him that it was meant to be enjoyed, not hoarded. To that end, he allowed himself a glass, usually with his wife but also with close friends. He would enjoy Château Picard 2364 to all but the last bottle. The lone holdout remained tucked safely away in quantum storage until just the right occasion presented itself.

They sat in silence for a moment, enjoying the wine, before he said, "I take it by your demeanor you found nothing wrong with René."

Holding her glass by its stem while slowly swirling its contents, Crusher frowned. "Not a thing. Physically and neurologically, he's perfectly healthy. I asked Doctor Tropp to conduct the exam, just to make sure I wasn't seeing what I wanted to see. Or, not seeing, as the case may be." She contemplated her wine for another moment before adding, "Even if I could be convinced to chalk it up to him daydreaming, or even making up a story for attention despite his never having done anything like that before, that doesn't explain everything."

Picard sat in silence, his confusion and concern increasing as Crusher recounted her own experience in sickbay. His first impulse was to demand why she chose not to contact him as soon as it had happened, but he quelled that notion. On its own, it could have been explained by simple exhaustion or a mental trick played upon her by her own subconscious mind. Only after being called about René did she begin to put together pieces of this odd puzzle. Like his wife, Picard did not for a moment believe this was coincidence, and likewise he was at a loss to even speculate what it all might mean.

"Is it possible Wesley is trying to contact you?" asked Picard. "Or René?"

Crusher took a sip of her wine before replying, "I wish I knew. Don't think I haven't tried contacting him. I feel silly standing around calling his name, but I don't know what else to do. If he could hear me, I'm sure he'd come, but that's not the way it works, is it?"

Picard replied, "It would seem not." He had never tried to comprehend the nature of Wesley Crusher's evolution from human to Traveler, though he had secretly wondered what such a life might be like. There even were times he felt envious of the man who had entered his life as a gifted teenager and departed as something far beyond mortal understanding. Where had he gone? What wonders had he beheld? These were questions Picard wanted to ask Wesley, but there had been no opportunity to do so. He hoped that chance might one day come.

"What if he's in trouble?" asked Crusher. "What if he's reaching out for help?"

Picard could not keep himself from considering such possibilities. How might a Traveler call for assistance? If Wesley was doing this, what could he, Picard—a mere human—even do?

Recognizing the first hints of anguish beginning to darken his wife's features, he reached for her hand. "Beverly, Wesley's been doing this for many years now. He would call on another Traveler like his mentor." The thought made him realize he did not even know how many such beings existed. What if they were unable to respond to Wesley's call, leaving him to seek support from wherever he could find it?

You're getting ahead of yourself, Jean-Luc, he cautioned himself.

Attempting to reassure her, Picard patted Crusher's hand. "If he is trying to contact us, we have to trust he'll do so for the right reasons, and at the proper time."

Though she smiled, he could tell it was an effort. "I'm sure you're right."

Picard continued holding her hand, feeling her squeeze his even as he struggled with his own words of encouragement.

I only hope I am.

6

———

Alert lights flashed, illuminating the otherwise darkened corridor. Ahead of him, Worf saw shadows sliding across the walls, indicating movement from people just out of sight beyond the curve of the passageway. Bodies seemed to be everywhere, some slumped against bulkheads while others lay strewn across the deck. A pair of legs extended from an open doorway. Smoke or something like it hung in the air before him, but he smelled nothing burning or scorched.

Why were there no audible alarms? For that matter, why was main power out? Where were the backups? Worf had no answers. His muscles tensing, he moved at a slow, deliberate pace up the corridor, choosing each step with care as he maneuvered over and around the bodies of fellow crewmembers. Only then did Worf realize he wielded a phaser rifle. Short and lightweight, it barely felt like a weapon in his hands. Its dual handgrips were positioned almost too close together for him to maintain a comfortable hold on the rifle. Like the corridor around him, there was something familiar and yet out of place about the phaser. How long had it been since he last held one? He could not remember, nor could he explain to himself why that mattered just now. An extra second passed before he noticed another detail. His uniform, maroon and black like the one he had not worn for many years, or had he? Somehow, it felt correct, and at the same time out of place.

He dismissed the thought as calls for help echoed in the corridor, coming from both behind and ahead of him. Something buzzed in the air like energy but Worf thought he sensed an actual *presence*. Intruders, that had to be it. The ship was being boarded by unidentified assailants. That was why he was here. His crew-mates were in distress. There were enemies to fight, invaders to repel. He needed to act.

Shouts for assistance to his front seemed closer. Worf hastened his pace around the curve in the passageway. All he saw were more bodies. How many people had already fallen to this unknown foe? What number of intruders was the remaining crew facing?

Maneuvering around one final bend brought him to a junction, with a new corridor heading off to his right. A glance at signage told him he was on deck twelve near the biohazard ward of the medical section's intensive care unit. He did not remember taking the turbolift to this part of the ship from the bridge, but given his proximity to the primary medical facility, he had to wonder why no one from that section had yet been deployed in response to the obvious emergency now confronting the crew. Where was everyone?

He tapped his combadge. "Worf to sickbay. Medical emergency. Deck twelve, section forty-three alpha. Respond."

There was no reply, even after he repeated the call.

A new sound, what might have been hushed whispers, seemed very close. He sensed movement to his right, and swung the phaser toward the corridor junction to see . . . *something*. It was a fig-ure, cloaked in shadows that seemed to swell and envelop it. Worf pressed the weapon's firing stud and a beam of intense orange en-ergy burst forth. Darkness retreated for the briefest of moments, giving him a chance to see the beam strike the bulkhead. The fig-ure was gone.

More motion from his left made him pivot in that direction to see a crewmember falling to the deck, while beyond her an-other shadowy figure was retreating up the corridor. Again Worf heard the odd whispering as he fired at the assailant but once more missed his mark. Before he could try again the thing was gone, swallowed by blackness and leaving only the stricken crewmember lying on the deck. The woman, with auburn hair and wearing the gold of the operations division, was in obvious pain. When she saw Worf, she reached out for him.

"Lieutenant Worf!"

Then the whispers were back, drowning out the crewmember's pleas and filling Worf's ears as the shadows seemed to peel away from the bulkheads, curling toward him.

Jerking upright, Worf pushed himself from his bed. His bare feet hit the carpet of his quarters as he assumed a defensive posture, arms out and hands up. He swung at the darkness, trying to force its retreat.

"Computer, lights!"

Standard illumination flooded the room. Maintaining his stance, ready to strike, Worf scrutinized his surroundings. Nothing hid in a corner or crouched beneath or behind any furniture. Turning in place, he inspected the entire room. Satisfied nothing lay in wait, he moved to the front room and repeated the process, completing his assessment with the lavatory.

Still alert for possible threats, Worf stood in the middle of his main living area, taking stock of every item and detail. Nothing was missing or out of place. His penchant for neatness offered no quarter for anyone or anything hoping to blend in without notice. There were no dangers here. Casting a glance toward the row of viewing ports that highlighted the room's sloping rear bulkhead, he observed the multicolored streaking effect of stars as the *Enterprise* passed them at warp. There were no whispers, but instead only the steady, ubiquitous drone of the ship's engines.

He was alone.

"A dream."

He grunted in frustration and no small amount of embarrassment despite there being no one else to witness what had occurred. If it was a dream, then it had been among the more intense ones Worf had ever experienced. Before he could give this further thought, the silence of his quarters was interrupted by the ship's intercom.

"*Sickbay to Commander Worf,*" said Doctor Tropp.

"Worf here."

The Denobulan physician replied, "*Is everything all right?*"

"Everything is fine, Doctor." Worf frowned, confused. "Why do you ask?"

"*You contacted sickbay. I'm on duty so I answered the call, but then you severed the connection. Are you in need of assistance?*"

He had called sickbay? There was a faint recollection of doing that in his apparent dream. Like everything else, that also had seemed so real. Had he truly acted out in his sleep?

"I'm sorry, Doctor. I was asleep and have no memory of contacting you. Please accept my apologies for disturbing you."

"*It isn't as though you woke me up, Commander.*" Worf heard the gentle humor in Tropp's voice. "*I don't think I've ever heard of a sleepwalking Klingon before. Are you sure you're all right?*"

"I'm fine. Good night, Doctor."

Worf severed the connection before Tropp could say anything further, leaving him alone with his own thoughts. That he had experienced a powerful dream did not bother him. Of more pressing concern was that he would act out while in the grips of such delirium. That warranted further reflection and perhaps more tangible steps.

Pacing his quarters, Worf glanced through the doorway to his bedroom, knowing slumber would elude him for some time. Unable to relax, there was no way he could attempt returning to sleep. Thankfully, he had a dependable means of releasing some of this energy.

The creature lunged, swinging a double-bladed battle-axe ahead of it as it closed the distance. Worf sidestepped the attack, causing his opponent to overextend and take an extra step forward in a bid to regain its balance. The error presented a vulnerability and an opportunity Worf wasted no time exploiting, thrusting up and outward with his *bat'leth*. Polished steel reflected the light of nearby fires as the weapon's blade sliced up and into the creature's jaw. Such was the force of the attack that the strike continued through, carving open his opponent's head with no resistance. The top portion of the creature's skull came away, disappearing along with the rest of its body in a shower of energy.

"Seven of seven opponents dispatched," said the voice of the *Enterprise*'s main computer. *"Simulation complete. Duration of exercise—"*

"Disregard." Worf blew out his breath, calming himself in the wake of the lengthy exertion. He did not need the computer to tell him that his time to run through the training scenario was more than his normal or even his average score. "Reset simulation and stand by to begin on my command."

The computer replied, *"Program complete. You may begin when ready."*

"Impressive."

Spinning around at the unexpected voice, Worf held the *bat'leth* across his chest in a ready position as his eyes found Doctor Tropp. The Denobulan stood amid the ruins of the ancient, burning temple that was the setting for this training scenario. Behind him was the entrance to the holodeck, the arch with its direct interface to the ship's computer visible along with the open doorway and the *Enterprise* corridor beyond. Unlike Worf, who had dressed in a Klingon warrior's traditional battle garb, Tropp wore a blue medical lab coat over his normal Starfleet uniform. His hands rested in the coat's pockets.

Annoyed at the interruption and the breach of holodeck etiquette, Worf lowered the *bat'leth* while fixing Tropp with a stern glare. "Doctor."

The physician nodded in greeting. "I apologize for intruding, Commander, but I admit to being troubled by our earlier conversation. I don't wish to pry, but it is my job to safeguard the crew's well-being, and that's particularly true of the ship's senior officers.

On the other hand, I can also appreciate a desire for discretion when it comes to matters of this sort. I assure you this is an informal visit on my part. Off the record, as the saying goes."

Sensing Tropp's genuine concern, Worf relaxed. "Very well." He shifted the *bat'leth* so that it rested in the crook of his right elbow, blades facing downward as the pair began walking through the holodeck's computer-generated jungle setting. "I appreciate your candor, Doctor, and the care you're exercising. As you have likely guessed, I apparently contacted sickbay while I was asleep and dreaming. I admit this troubles me."

"Understandable," replied Tropp. "Is it common for you to experience such vivid dreams?"

Worf shook his head. "No. I do dream, but I do not recall anything of this nature, and certainly nothing that made me act out in my sleep." Having given the matter more thought while conducting his calisthenics simulation, he added, "The closest I've ever come to such a sensation occurred during my childhood, when I traveled to Qo'noS to undertake the Rite of MajQa."

"I'm familiar with this ritual," said Tropp. "As I recall, it involves fasting for several days and extended meditation. If I correctly understand the intentions, it is a time of deep reflection and contemplation about the life one chooses to lead."

Impressed with the doctor's knowledge, Worf replied, "One undertakes the rite in hopes of receiving a revelation about one's past or future. I fasted for three days while meditating within the volcanic Caves of No'Mat, at which time I was visited by a vision of our greatest warrior, Kahless. He told me I would one day do something no other Klingon had done."

Stopping before the temple's entrance, Tropp turned to Worf. "Fasting under such conditions is known to produce powerful hallucinations. I'm certainly not dismissing what you saw, Commander, and I also know how highly you regard Klingon tradition and Kahless the Unforgettable in particular. Did it feel real to you, being visited in this manner by one you hold in such esteem?"

"As real as anything I've experienced. I've thought of it many times in the years since then, and it continues to inspire me." Worf paused, considering the past hours as he moved his free hand to rest on one of the *bat'leth*'s handgrips. "While my dream was not as strong, it possessed a quality that made it seem far more real than previous dreams. There was something else; something I can't explain."

He was startled by the abrupt activation of a tricorder. Turning back to Tropp, he saw the doctor holding the device in his left hand while waving a smaller scanner in Worf's direction. The tricorder warbled its familiar rhythmic tones as Tropp worked.

"I'm not detecting any neurological irregularities or anything that might explain experiencing a hallucination." The doctor closed the tricorder and returned it to the pocket of his smock. "Physically, you're in excellent health. You could benefit from getting some more sleep, but I think you know that. I could conduct a much more comprehensive examination, but that would require your coming to sickbay."

Worf considered the suggestion. Should he subject himself to such measures? He did not feel ill, and Tropp's impromptu scan of him only bolstered his confidence. On the other hand, if he was in the grip of some as yet undetected impairment, was it not prudent to allow Tropp to examine him, for the good of the *Enterprise* and its crew?

"I imagine you're weighing personal preferences against duty," said the physician. "That you confided in me at all tells me where your priorities lie, Commander. Your word that you'll come to me if you experience anything like this again is sufficient for me to keep this conversation confidential, at least until such time as I'm made aware of justification to do otherwise. Like you, I also have an obligation to the ship."

Worf nodded. "I appreciate your trust, Doctor. You have my word I will tell you if I have a similar experience."

"Good enough for me." Tropp smiled. "And with respect to

your encounter with Kahless, no one can argue that you've already done several things no other Klingon has accomplished. The first Klingon in Starfleet. First Klingon to refuse an appointment as chancellor of the High Council in order to transfer it to another you thought more deserving and better suited for the role. Federation ambassador to *Qo'noS*. First officer of the Federation flagship, serving under one of the most respected captains in Starfleet history. If anything, I think Kahless underestimated your potential. You are a credit to the Klingon people, Commander, as well as to your uniform."

Pride swelling within him, Worf drew himself up. "Thank you, Doctor." He glanced around the holographic simulation. "I have taken up much of your time." Moving the *bat'leth* from its resting position along his shoulder, he held the blade at his side. "I thought I would complete one more training exercise before returning to my quarters."

"May I join you?" asked Tropp.

The question took Worf by surprise. "I wasn't aware you had any combat training."

His smile widening, the Denobulan replied, "I've been in Starfleet for quite a long time, Mister Worf, and I haven't always been confined to sickbay." He removed his lab coat and folded it with care. "Computer, please provide me a *bat'leth* matching the same specifications as the one currently being employed by Commander Worf." Within seconds, a *bat'leth* identical to Worf's materialized on the ground at Tropp's feet, and the doctor retrieved it. He held it for a moment as though studying its weight and balance before offering a nod of approval.

"Excellent," said Worf. Nodding with respect to Tropp, at the same time Worf made a mental note to review the doctor's service record at his first opportunity. He suspected some interesting reading awaited him.

7

U.S.S. *Relativity* NCV-474439-G
13th Century, Exact Temporal Coordinates *Classified*

Sitting alone in the ship's observation lounge, Juel Ducane sipped *katheka*, an Andorian beverage for which he had acquired a taste in recent years, while studying the enhanced viewing port forming the room's rear wall. A single, curved piece manufactured from a blend of duranium and transparasteel, the port also served as a viewscreen and computer interface. Those features now supplied Ducane with the latest information from *Relativity*'s vast array of sensors, streamed as a series of augmented-reality overlays directly to this display.

With his free hand he waved away various readouts and status reports while highlighting the latest telemetry from the scans directed at the area of space under current scrutiny. According to the information before him, nothing had changed in the immediate vicinity in the last eleven hours, thirty-six minutes, and nineteen seconds.

Twenty seconds, he thought, watching a chronometer on one of the displays. *Twenty-one. Twenty-two. Twenty . . . all right. Enough of that.*

Another annoying feature of the viewing port was its effectiveness in capturing his reflection, leaving Ducane to regard his own features. Where had all the lines come from that now etched his face? His forehead in particular had borne the brunt of these changes, though of course none of them were new. Like his once brown hair, which had gone gray while also receding from his temples, none of these signs were mysterious. His was a profession that tended to prematurely age those who undertook its challenges. At least, that was the consensus among his comrades, even if their observations held no basis in scientific fact or logic.

Still, there was no denying the effects of his extended service, which Ducane accepted as ironic given the casual frequency with which he and others in this branch of Starfleet tended to move back and forth across time.

Tempus fugit, and all that, he mused.

Behind him, he heard the sound of doors parting, and he swiveled his chair to see Commander Ailur, *Relativity*'s second-in-command and senior science officer, standing in the doorway, hands clasped behind her back.

"Captain," she said, pausing at the threshold, "am I intruding?"

"Not at all." Ducane gestured to the chair nearest him. "I was just about to call you to ask about the anomaly you promised me."

Ailur made her way around the conference table. As always, her dark hair was pulled back from her face and secured at the base of her neck, leaving a long ponytail draped over her right shoulder and revealing the points of her ears. Her uniform was a match for his, consisting of a black jumpsuit with a high collar trimmed in white and a Starfleet insignia over the left breast. While his right shoulder and sleeve were swathed in command blue, Ailur's own uniform was highlighted in gray to denote the sciences division.

"We are still well within the window of occurrence," she said. "According to our estimates, the anomaly should manifest itself at some point within the next three hours."

"When you told me you'd plotted temporal coordinates to get us within twenty-four hours, I was hoping you meant somewhere toward the leading edge of that estimate."

Unperturbed by her captain's remark, the Romulan replied, "Despite the resources at our disposal, time travel remains a largely inexact science. This is particularly true when charting the life cycle of a temporal phenomenon such as the one we are attempting to study."

Ducane smiled. "Is that your way of telling me you think your calculations are off and you're not sure why, so you've just been making it all up as you go this whole time? There's no shame in that, Ailur. I admire anyone who can adapt to evolving situations while keeping their wits about them."

"A sentiment I hope you keep in mind the next time we spar on the holomatrix, Captain." It was a challenge, though one tempered with good-natured teasing of the sort in which the two officers routinely engaged. "As I was the victor in our last contest, the choice of training environment, weapons, and difficulty is mine. I look forward to observing *your* ability to maintain your composure while adapting to evolving situations."

"You're on," he said. "Loser buys dinner our first night on shore leave."

An alert indicator caused Ailur to turn so she could study the array of displays projected on the viewing port. She waved her hand across one of the readouts to produce a new image, and Ducane recognized it as a star map of the region in which *Relativity* now found itself. He noted the small, arrowhead-shaped icon designating the ship's current position relative to the nearest star. He also eyed a timer in the display's upper left corner, counting down seconds toward zero. It was already inside of ten seconds when Ailur turned to him.

"Your patience is about to be rewarded, Captain."

No sooner did she make the comment than Ducane's attention was drawn to the viewing port just as an area of space fluctuated. A hole appeared, as though something had pierced the very fabric of reality itself, and for a moment a storm of energy was visible, seeming to push and pry its way from one plane of existence into another. Then the light faded, and the rupture seemed to repair itself, leaving Ducane to once more gaze upon a normal and—dare he say it—boring starfield.

"That's it?" he asked, unable to suppress a small grin.

Ailur turned from the viewing port. "We've known for two centuries the temporal distortion within the Typhon Expanse was an example of a spatial anomaly effecting an inverse trajectory backward through time." She looked back at the sensor displays projected on the window. "Although it is microscopic at the moment, we know the distortion will continue to grow from this point forward. It's a paradox for which we have no explanation." She stopped, raising her left eyebrow. "You know all of this, Captain."

"I do. I just like hearing you explain it." Rising from his chair, Ducane gestured with his mug toward the viewing port. "It's microscopic now, but in a thousand years or so, it'll gobble up a Federation starship and hold it for ninety years, at which time another Federation ship will happen across it. A thousand years after that, it'll finally push its way into our universe and be a visible phenomenon too dangerous for any ship to approach." He shrugged. "And then the whole thing will start all over again. At least, that's what the projections tell us."

"Even though we are able to scan the continuum to that point in the future," replied Ailur, "no expeditions have been authorized by Starfleet. However, given the abrupt nature of our current assignment, one might logically conclude such a mission is forthcoming."

"I'm sure the commission will tell us what this is all about in their own good time." Rolling his eyes at his own weak time travel–inspired joke, Ducane drank the last of his *katheka* before placing the mug on the conference table and waving his hand over it. Sensors in the table dematerialized the cup, initiating the process of transforming it back into raw materials for reuse by the ship's replicator systems.

At the viewing port, Ailur waved a hand over one of her sensor displays. "I have initiated a full-spectrum scan of the anomaly from end to end. Now that we've established its approximate span across time, we may be able to discern how it was created in the first place."

"Or why," said Ducane. "Or by what. Or whom."

Ailur turned to regard him with skepticism. "All indications are it is a naturally occurring phenomenon, Captain."

"But that's just so—"

The rest of Ducane's comment was cut off by the abrupt blaring of the red alert klaxon followed by a voice over the ship's intercom.

"Attention, all personnel. Sensors detecting a Class-B temporal incursion. All hands to action stations. Captain Ducane and Commander Ailur, please report to the bridge."

Ducane tapped his communicator badge, which was a stylized representation of the Starfleet insignia pointing to his left. "On our way."

A short turbolift ride from the observation lounge brought Ducane and Ailur to the upper level of *Relativity*'s two-tiered main bridge, which was already abuzz with activity. Wider from port to starboard than it was fore to aft, the command center was oriented before a large multipurpose viewscreen filling the room's curved forward bulkhead. It was more expansive than its predecessor, installed less than a month ago as one of the many upgrades the ship had received during its recent overhaul. Before the screen on the bridge's lower level was a dual console with workstations for a flight controller and an operations officer. Four additional stations occupied space on the upper tier, set into the room's aft bulkhead. The starboard half of the top level was given over to a transporter platform.

Officers worked at each of the bridge stations, including Ducane's command console, which was positioned at the edge of the upper tier so that it overlooked the lower level and the viewscreen. Noting the captain's arrival, the Bolian crewmember on duty there, Lieutenant Faroti, nodded in recognition and vacated the chair.

"What've we got, Mister Faroti?" asked Ducane, settling in at his station as Ailur moved toward the four consoles at the rear of the bridge's upper deck.

The operations officer replied, "Three minutes after Commander Ailur initiated the full-spectrum scan of the anomaly, we began receiving feedback. We're trying to pinpoint the origin of the reaction, but it appears to be coming from somewhere in proximity to our own time, sir."

Frowning at the report while Faroti returned to his own station, Ducane moved his hands across his console's sleek surface. The command-level interface boasted a number of features including interactive holographic controls as well as an array of touch-sensitive keypads. Despite the innovations in holotechnology that had continued unabated for centuries, Ducane preferred controls he could feel beneath his fingers. He dismissed the holo-interfaces with a wave of his hand and tapped a command sequence into the console's primary input pad. The instructions routed telemetry from the sensor station to him.

"It can't be something we caused," he said, studying the scan data. "That wouldn't make any sense. All we've done is sit back and watch the thing. None of our probes should've had any sort of effect on the anomaly." Sensor systems installed aboard all *Wells*-class starships were modulated for a level of passive scanning that provided status information about the target of such scrutiny across time without risking any sort of disruption or other interference that might result in an inadvertent temporal incursion. The slightest misstep, even while simply observing events in another time period, could have ramifications that might affect past and future history. For this reason, strict protocols were in place to prevent such mishaps.

Despite all of this, Ducane had to wonder if his ship or his crew had somehow made a terrible error.

Behind him, Ailur said, "Captain, we're receiving an emergency signal on a secure temporal displacement frequency. It's from the *U.S.S. Tempus*."

Ducane joined his first officer at the aft stations. As she normally did while on duty, Ailur had configured the console nearest the transporter pad to serve as a master systems interface, giving her access to every shipboard system. One of the station's displays now projected a holographic, three-dimensional wireframe diagram of *Relativity*, highlighting more than a dozen points across the ship in bright red. It took him only an instant to understand that the icons represented the vessel's complement of personnel and cargo transporter bays.

"It's Admiral zh'Crivash, sir," said Ailur. "She's on the *Tempus* and has transmitted an emergency retrieval signal. Our systems are already locking on to the crew's temporal transporter beacons. I'm also receiving sensor data from the *Tempus*, along with an incoming transmission. Trying to lock into the latter signal now."

She entered another rapid series of commands, and a moment later a column of energy appeared in the space between the aft stations and the temporal transporter pad. It coalesced into the somewhat disheveled figure of Admiral Jenishan zh'Crivash. Varying between shades of red and blue, the hologram suffered a constant flicker indicating a problem either on the admiral's end or with *Relativity*'s difficulties in receiving the signal across time. The Andorian's white hair was mussed, and the rightmost of the two antennae extending from the top of her skull was bent at an unnatural angle. The left sleeve of her uniform was blackened and tattered, exposing blue skin that Ducane could see had suffered some kind of burn. She seemed a bit unsteady on her feet.

"Admiral?" He had no idea why the head of Starfleet's Temporal Activities Division would be on the *Tempus* or any other ship rather than in her office on Earth. "What's going on?" Given the complexities of transporting from one timeframe to another, even with the technology at the disposal of Starfleet and the Temporal Integrity Commission, a direct transport from ship to ship was an unusual request. It only served to reinforce the seriousness of whatever situation in which zh'Crivash and the *Tempus* now found themselves, but it still did not explain why the admiral was caught up in the middle of whatever was happening.

"Captain Ducane, I'm sending this distress call to the rest of the time fleet before we have to abandon ship. We're under attack from something originating inside the Typhon Expanse. Their identity remains unknown, but they've already crippled my ship. You should have already received sensor telemetry from our scans of the anomaly and what little we know about our attackers. Together, we need to analyze that information and determine a course of action. Stand by to receive the Tempus *crew."*

From the operations station at the front of the bridge, Lieutenant Faroti called out, "Captain, I am scanning the *Tempus*. Spatial coordinates indicate their position as . . ." His voice trailed off and Ducane watched the Bolian's hands swipe and wave through a rapid string of commands using the console's holographic interface. "Sir, their coordinates confirm they're *here*, in the Typhon Expanse, but in our own time. Stardate—"

"Temporal transport beacons from the *Tempus* are locked in," reported Ailur.

Ducane said, "Bring the admiral directly to the bridge."

"Acknowledged." Ailur entered another command series. "Emergency transporter protocols activating now."

Turning to the transporter station, Ducane saw a single form materializing on the rear pad. He counted off the seconds he knew were required to complete the byzantine process of beaming a living being across centuries of time, feeling his pulse beginning to accelerate when that interval elapsed and the form of Admiral zh'Crivash was still trying to solidify before she vanished altogether.

"Captain," said Faroti from the ops console. "We've lost all sensor contact with the *Tempus*." He turned in his seat, his expression one of shock. "I think it's gone, sir. Destroyed."

Ducane began, "What about—" but he stopped when he saw Ailur shaking her head.

"We had 218 transporter beacons," she said. "We lost them."

Feeling his jaw tighten, Ducane could not force his eyes from the very empty transporter pad. "Ailur, start going through the *Tempus* sensor logs. Set a course to those same spatial coordinates and prepare for immediate jump to that location."

8

"If you keep tapping it like that, you're going to leave a dent in it."

Lost in thought as he gazed through the nearby viewing port from his table in the *Enterprise*'s crew lounge while the ship traveled at warp, Geordi La Forge realized he was no longer alone, and he sensed someone sliding into the chair on the table's opposite side. Turning from the window, he smiled in recognition as Tamala Harstad settled into her seat. Only when his finger came to rest atop the padd lying on the table did he catch the meaning of her words.

"I'm sorry." La Forge rested his hand on the padd. "I guess I'm just a little preoccupied." Looking around, he noted the lounge had attracted far more visitors than were present when he arrived. How long had he been staring out into space? Nearly every table was occupied, and at least twenty crewmembers stood at the bar positioned near the front of the room. Some, like La Forge, wore their Starfleet uniforms while others, like Harstad, had opted for more comfortable civilian attire.

"Still focused on work, I see." Harstad patted the table before pointing to the padd under La Forge's hand. When he looked down at it, he noticed the file he had been reading was still displayed on its screen. Now feeling self-conscious, he tapped the control to deactivate the device. It was an action that did not go unnoticed by Harstad, who acknowledged it by cocking her right eyebrow in that manner La Forge knew she employed when her curiosity was piqued.

"Everything all right?" she asked.

La Forge forced a smile. "I'm fine, and I'm sorry about having to reschedule dinner. It's just been . . . one of those days."

"I knew what I was getting into when I fell in love with you, Mister Chief Engineer of the Federation flagship." Harstad's smile was brighter than his, but La Forge could still see it was not entirely genuine. She turned it up a notch as Jordan, the lounge's civilian host, stopped at their table to take their orders for dinner and drinks, but as soon as the man was gone, her expression shifted just enough for him to notice.

"I know that look," he said. Just as he was occupied with his own thoughts, it was easy to discern she was distracted. "Something you want to talk about?"

Making an obvious effort to shake off whatever was bothering her, Harstad replied, "Sorry. It was a bit of an odd day in sickbay too." La Forge knew better than to push that particular line of discussion any further, always careful to respect her need to maintain confidentiality with respect to the crew and whomever she might see as a patient. As though sensing his apprehension, she held up a hand. "Don't worry. Nothing too serious or anything like that." She shrugged. "Besides, it kept me busy while I was waiting for you."

"Ouch." La Forge chuckled, holding up his hands in mock surrender. "I deserved that. I *really* am sorry for making you wait." He sighed. "There's always something on this ship that needs a little extra attention."

Reaching across the table, Harstad took his hand in her own. "And right now, that something is me." She squeezed his hand and when she smiled this time, La Forge knew it was real. "So, unless we run into a strange space anomaly or get attacked by an alien armada, you're mine for the rest of the evening."

"Deal." La Forge glanced down at the padd before tapping it with his free hand. "Since we're on the subject, there's something I wanted to talk to you about. To be honest, it's something I've wanted to talk about for a couple of days, but there just didn't seem to be a good time."

Harstad leaned across the table, her eyes narrowing as she studied him with an expression of mischief. "You've found someone else."

"Nope, but I may have found some *thing* else. I was contacted by Doctor Cygmunt at the Starfleet Research Division."

"I know that name." Harstad paused, as though searching her memory. "You had a meeting with her before we left Earth."

La Forge nodded. "That's her." From his point of view, the encounter had been a pleasant happenstance while he had been visiting colleagues at Starfleet Headquarters and the Earth-based office of the Utopia Planitia Shipyards on Mars. He made it a point to remain up to date with the latest developments in Starfleet ship design, and that meant keeping abreast of the newest theories pushing technology forward in any number of areas. It was its own full-time job, on top of his responsibilities as chief engineer, but La Forge had never considered the effort as work. Opportunities to visit with the leading minds in his field were rare, given *Enterprise*'s infrequent visits to Earth, but he had crossed paths with Zhoreń Cygmunt, one of the Starfleet Research Division's leading civilian starship designers. Their meeting, brief yet cordial, had not seemed important at the time.

I guess I was wrong, La Forge mused.

Harstad asked, "What did she want?"

"She offered me a job."

That was enough to make Harstad sit up in her seat and pull her hand back, and La Forge reactivated the padd before spinning it so she could read the file displayed upon it. He waited while she reviewed the transcript of the message sent from Cygmunt, watching her brow furrow as she took in the words. When she looked up, her eyes were wide with surprise.

"Is this for real?"

La Forge smiled. "As real as it gets."

"What would you be doing?" asked Harstad.

Unable to keep the excitement from his voice, La Forge replied, "Doctor Cygmunt wants me to lead one of the teams she's putting together to design the next generation of deep-space, extended-mission exploration vessels." He waved his hand in the air before him. "Bigger than the *Enterprise*, even grander than the *Galaxy* class. They're talking about sending these new starships out on missions that could last decades or longer, without returning home. Barring anything unforeseen or bizarre, they'd cycle back to a starbase maybe once every five or six years at most." The very idea was enough to fill him with exhilaration at the possibilities such a vessel offered, let alone the challenge of actually designing the craft and helping to shepherd it from imagination to reality.

"Unforeseen or bizarre," said Harstad. "You just described daily life on this ship."

They paused again as one of the lounge's other servers brought them their drinks. While he took a sip from his cocktail, Harstad ignored her own beverage as she read the message transcript for a second time. "Are you thinking about it?"

"A little." As he replied, La Forge realized that for the first time, the thought of accepting the position had not been real until he spoke the words aloud. It was also the first time in a long time he found himself thinking of leaving the *Enterprise*.

Harstad eyed him. "No, not a little."

After a moment spent just looking at her—appreciating everything about her as she sat across from him—La Forge nodded. "More than a little." It was his turn to reach for her hand. "I mean, from time to time I've thought about doing something else, but I always come back to deciding I like it here. I *do* like it here. I *love* it here, Tamala. Most days, I can't imagine doing anything else or being anywhere else."

"So, what's different this time?"

"I've never gotten an offer like this before." He sighed. "I don't know if it's up there with being promoted to chief engineer, but it's damned close."

The memory of that momentous occasion was as fresh as the day it happened. Standing in Captain Picard's ready room on the *Enterprise*-D after being summoned by the ship's first officer, Commander Riker. The list of possible replacements for the ship's retiring chief engineer was long, filled with the names of some of the most accomplished engineers in the service, assigned either to other starships or some of the Federation's foremost design facilities. Picard, at Riker's urging, had bypassed all of them in favor of La Forge. According to the first officer, La Forge had consistently demonstrated tremendous aptitude in all areas of engineering as part of the cross-functional training the captain demanded of all junior officers. It was a long-standing practice, as Picard believed the most effective officers were those who possessed expertise in diverse skill areas rather than focusing on a single area of specialization. This was, he judged, particularly important for those wishing to pursue a career track toward starship command. At one point that had been La Forge's goal, until he discovered his love for starships and everything that made them the wondrous fusions of form and function.

"I've been a chief engineer for more than twenty years. Until I got Doctor Cygmunt's message, I was sure I would be happy doing it until I retired, but now?" La Forge blew out his breath. "It's a lot to think about, and one of the most important questions I'd like to ask is if you'd want to come with me. I'd never ask you to do anything you didn't want to do, and if that means you want to stay on the *Enterprise*, then I absolutely respect that." As he spoke, his ocular implants picked up the changes in her heart rate and the flush in her cheeks, but he could tell from her body language it was not anger.

"Would my wanting to stay make you turn them down?" she asked.

"It makes me want to talk about it until you and I are both

happy with whatever the decision is. I don't want to do anything that might jeopardize what we have, Tamala. Whatever might happen next, I don't want to do it unless it's with you."

Harstad placed her other hand over his. "You know I love you, Geordi, and I want you to do what's best for you. If that means heading back to Earth to lead a design team, then so be it. Do I think you'd be happy if you stayed here? I do, but I know why you're hesitating. You don't want to leave the *Enterprise*, and you don't want to leave Captain Picard."

"I'd be lying if I said that wasn't a part of it. The *Enterprise* is my home. It's *our* home, Tamala. Still, being on the leading edge of the next phase of starship design? I don't know if I can pass up, but part of me feels like leaving before the *Enterprise* heads out for who knows how long is just . . . I don't know . . . *wrong*, somehow." La Forge's loyalty to the *Enterprise* and Picard were absolute, but what Cygmunt offered was a literal opportunity of a lifetime.

"Captain Picard would be the first to tell you to go," said Harstad.

La Forge knew she was right. The captain had always been one to champion his officers advancing their careers. He would never stand in the way of anyone pursuing the next chapter of their lives. This left La Forge with one burning question to answer.

Was he ready to turn the page?

Drink in hand and leading the way to one of the Happy Bottom Riding Club's few remaining open tables, T'Ryssa Chen cast a look over her shoulder at Taurik, continuing the discussion they had begun at the bar.

"Hey. You know second contact is pretty important too."

The *Enterprise*'s assistant chief engineer said nothing in response to her comment, itself an unusual reaction from the Vulcan.

"Did you hear what I said?" asked Chen as they settled into seats at a small table in the middle of the room.

Taurik set his own drink on the table. "I did indeed hear you. I have heard everything you have said to me since our arrival."

"Then why didn't you say anything?"

"I find no fault with your statement, and I have no reason to dispute it."

Casting a wary eye at Taurik, Chen said, "You're being very Vulcan today."

"I endeavor to be Vulcan every day."

Chen rolled her eyes and sipped her drink before replying, "Well, I walked into that one." Setting down her glass, she rested her forearms on the table, and leaned toward her friend. "Come on, Taurik. This is a big deal. At least, it could be. I'm seeking actual advice here."

"What advice do you believe you require?" Taurik clasped his hands before him and steepled his two forefingers in that manner Chen recognized as the Vulcan entering a contemplative state. She knew she finally had his full attention.

"Should I stay? Should I go?" Chen began running her hand along the table's smooth surface. "This is new to me, Taurik. I've never been specifically requested for a duty assignment before. It's a weird feeling."

Taurik's right eyebrow arched. "Admiral Nechayev selected you to join the *Enterprise* when she tasked Captain Picard to investigate Borg activity near planet NGC 6281."

"That was different." Her introduction to Captain Picard and the *Enterprise* came seven years ago after her previous ship, the *U.S.S. Rhea*, was attacked by Borg forces. The *Rhea* had been investigating a newly discovered life-form, the "Noh Angels," later discovered to be responsible for attempting to protect the ship's crew during the Borg attack. At the request of Admiral Alynna Nechayev, Chen accompanied the *Enterprise* back to NGC 6281, lending her knowledge as a contact specialist to further investigate the new life-form while rescuing the *Rhea* and its crew. Following their recovery and after the life-form helped Picard and his crew to defeat a Borg vessel, Chen remained aboard the *Enterprise*.

"You were chosen for that task because of your specific expertise," said Taurik. "Not simply your familiarity with the *Rhea* and its crew, but also the life-form you encountered. Your particular qualifications were key to the success of that mission."

Chen reached for her drink. "Sure, and after that there was a pretty long period where I did everything but be a contact specialist."

"In other words, you adapted to your situation," Taurik replied. "You cross-trained in several other technical disciplines. You contributed time and effort to assisting your crewmates in tasks wholly unrelated to your own area of specialization. You developed a diverse and highly versatile skill set, in keeping with Captain Picard's long-standing directives for junior officers. Rather than simply succeeding in this endeavor, you excelled at it." His expression, as always, was unreadable, and his tone was its usual neutral self. Chen knew he was not contradicting her but stating simple facts as he understood them, enhancing the statements with what she figured he might call "professional observations."

"Damn, Taurik," she said, forcing herself not to pat his arm or show some other emotional reaction that might draw attention. "That might be one of the nicest things you've ever said about me."

The engineer said, "I am merely pointing out what I know to be true. Your assignment to the *Enterprise* was not a random occurrence; it was done with a purpose in mind. I believe the opportunity you've been offered is for similar reasons."

The invitation was as intriguing to Chen as it was unexpected. During the months spent charting the Odyssean Pass, the *Enterprise* had encountered several advanced civilizations. Not all of those meetings had been without incident, but most had resulted in communications with those societies in order to foster relations. Finding potential allies was one of the major goals motivating the exploration of that largely unfamiliar area. Expanding the Federation's sphere of influence in that direction could only be done with the cooperation of those calling that region home. Solidifying the tentative bonds already forged by the *Enterprise*'s initial contact with these newly discovered worlds required an ongoing effort. To that end, Starfleet was assembling a task force devoted to conducting "second contact" with those planets where the *Enterprise* had broken the proverbial ice.

What Chen had not anticipated was Starfleet wanting her to contribute to that mission.

"I'm a contact specialist, Taurik," she said. "It's what I'm good at."

"You possess an impressive range of knowledge and skills," replied the engineer.

"But you have to admit, being the first to encounter newly discovered civilizations is like nothing else. It's why there's a Starfleet. We're out here, doing the things they tell us about at the Academy, what other ships have been doing for two centuries." When Taurik offered no comment, Chen continued, "That said, the idea of helping to make something more permanent out of whatever we manage to do during a first-contact scenario? Helping solidify new alliances, sharing knowledge? We've only scratched the surface so far as the potential we have with the people we've met in the Pass. You can't tell me you wouldn't want to go back and study some of the technology we've encountered."

Taurik replied, "Some, yes. Others are best left forgotten."

"Maybe you should come with me," said Chen. Although she blurted the suggestion without considering how it might be received, the more she thought about it, the more she warmed to the idea. "It'd be fun."

"It is an interesting notion." The engineer seemed to be giving actual consideration to the idea, before adding, "However, I am content with my duties aboard the *Enterprise*, and it is where I feel

I am the most useful. You should choose a path that offers you the same sense of satisfaction."

Chen smiled. "That sounds like you're telling me to follow my heart, Taurik."

Once more, the Vulcan cocked his eyebrow. "Perhaps I am."

9

Framed by the bridge's main viewscreen, chaos ran amok.

"What the hell is that?" asked Juel Ducane. Standing at the bridge's upper tier railing, he was getting his first look at the sea of fury, which had all but consumed the region of space once called the Typhon Expanse. No sooner had *Relativity* arrived at this point in spacetime and activated its sensors than hell seemed to unleash as if from nowhere. Something was obviously affecting the ship's scanning capabilities, as the resulting image translated to the viewscreen was a jumbled, distorted mess.

Behind him at the aft workstations, Commander Ailur turned from her console. "Sensors confirm that is the Typhon Expanse temporal anomaly. It's generating a distortion field that is interfering with our scans and other shipboard systems, including communications as well as navigational and deflector shields."

"How is that possible?" asked Ducane. "It's not supposed to reach this level of intensity for centuries."

In the twenty-ninth century, *Relativity*'s home location in spacetime as well as its present position, the anomaly was a routine target of observation and study by Starfleet as well as the Temporal Integrity Commission and the Department of Temporal Investigations. The last two ships to experience its time-shifting effects were enough for Starfleet in the mid-twenty-fourth century to declare the Expanse a hazard to navigation. Despite such warnings, rumors about ships reportedly operating in the area before being listed as missing had persisted for centuries. These and other cautionary tales—real or fabricated—had not stopped vessels from traversing the area for any number of reasons, many of them less than legal.

Starfleet continued to monitor the region in the event any ships did emerge. Ongoing attempts to understand its properties had so far brought little in the way of new information. Automated probes had been sent in and returned after months and even years, their internal systems registering the passage of mere minutes. Other sensor readings were muddled and useless, making it impossible to determine whether anything might still be ensnared within the region. What little data Starfleet had managed to gather showed the anomaly was growing larger with the passage of time, but Ducane knew from reports, gathered by observation teams sent into the future, that it was not supposed to be exhibiting any of the characteristics he now saw displayed before him.

Ailur said, "As Admiral zh'Crivash indicated, something appears to have affected the anomaly in a way that's forcing it to deviate from its expected rate of growth. According to the data the admiral sent us, indications are this interference is deliberate, not a natural phenomenon."

"How could she be sure?" asked Ducane.

"The *Tempus* dispatched an automated survey probe to the farthest point in the future where we know the Typhon anomaly exists. They lost contact with that probe, but not before receiving some telemetry. It was sufficient to conclude the disruptions were not an artifact of the anomaly itself, but rather something happening inside it and radiating backward through time. Other probes sent to different points in time gauged the progress of these distortions, and in each case the effects decreased the farther back in time the anomaly was studied."

"So zh'Crivash sent us all the way back to its beginning." Catching himself, Ducane raised a hand. "Sorry, what *should* have been its beginning, but everything's backward."

"Precisely," said Ailur. "We've always known the Typhon anomaly represents something of a paradox, created in the future and affecting an inverted pathway back through spacetime, but we've never been able to figure out why. All evidence showed it had to be a naturally occurring phenomenon, albeit one we didn't understand. This new activity indicates it is not at all natural."

Blowing out his breath, Ducane rubbed the bridge of his nose. "And we have no idea who or what might be responsible for it, or why. It's already cost us one ship, and now it seems to be responding to our efforts at engaging it. I'm not inclined at this point to think whoever's behind this has peaceful intentions." He moved to the stairs leading down to the lower tier. "What about the other ships?"

At the operations station near the front of the bridge, Lieutenant Faroti turned in his seat. "Captain, sensors are picking up the *Haddix*, the *Mobius*, and the *Crichton* all on approach vectors toward the anomaly." He gestured to the viewscreen. "It's emitting waves of temporal distortion that's affecting our scans, sir. I'm having trouble pinpointing the others ships' exact locations. I've already requested a power boost from engineering."

Ducane asked, "What did the *Tempus* sensors record about these temporal distortions?"

"According to their logs, they first detected abnormal readings a week ago, indicating a temporal fluctuation from within the Expanse that appeared to be manifesting at different points in time. Though Admiral zh'Crivash kept the reasons classified, she dispatched *Relativity* and other ships to different temporal coordinates to verify the readings. Based on her own observations as well as those of members of the *Tempus* science team, the distortions apparently became more pronounced as our ships arrived at the various coordinates and began subjecting the anomaly to sensor scans. Admiral zh'Crivash believed whatever is behind the distortions reacted to the proximity of the ships. I recommend we maintain a minimum distance of twenty thousand kilometers from the anomaly's outer boundary."

Stepping toward the ops station, Ducane pointed to Faroti. "Lieutenant, open a channel to the other ships and give them that information."

"Hailing on all frequencies, Captain," replied Faroti. "No response."

The whistle of *Relativity*'s internal communications system wailed across the bridge, followed by the voice of the ship's chief medical officer, Doctor Jeva Myras.

"Sickbay to bridge. Medical priority."

Tapping his combadge, Ducane replied, "This is the captain. What's wrong, Doctor?"

"Captain, the computer's health monitoring system is recording elevated neural activity in nearly every member of the crew. It started almost at the same time we dropped out of warp, so I'm presuming it has something to do with the anomaly."

Calm and reserved in nearly every situation, the Bajoran only rarely raised his voice above a conversational tone and his inflections were almost Vulcan in their delivery. Now, however, Ducane heard the obvious concern.

"Any idea what the larger effects might be?"

Jeva replied, *"I'm only just now trying to figure this out, but based on the readings I've received, along with corresponding increases in pulse rate and respiration, the most immediately noticeable effects are liable to be an increase in anxiety and uncertainty. If the effects continue to increase, it might start to impair judgment and even escalate to panic."*

"What can we do?"

"Getting away from here is probably the easiest thing to do, but I'm guessing you're about to tell me that's not an option."

Pressing his lips together, Ducane opted to avoid any flippant responses. Instead, he said, "I'm hoping you might have another option."

"I'm continuing to monitor the readings," said the doctor. *"I'll let you know if I come up with anything. Jeva out."*

No sooner did the communication end than the deck trembled beneath Ducane's feet. At the same time, an alert tone sounded from the flight controller's station. The officer crewing that console, Lieutenant Rabal, cast a look over her shoulder.

"Another distortion wave, Captain." The Saurian's gray, scaled hands moved across her console's touch-sensitive and holographic controls. "They are increasing in intensity. I am having to increase power to maneuvering systems to maintain our position. Primary propulsion systems are also being affected. We still have main power, but engineering reports they need to take warp drive and the temporal impeller offline."

Ducane processed the news. The lack of warp drive or the ability to jump out of this time period meant no quick escapes if they encountered a serious threat. Moving closer to the forward bridge stations, he said to Faroti, "Increase power to forward deflectors. Any luck raising the other ships?"

The Bolian shook his head. "No, sir. I am also unable to maintain a solid sensor lock on them. The stronger these distortion waves grow, the more they're impeding our scans."

"I believe I know why," said Ailur. "Our sensors are detecting several fractures in spacetime. The distortions emanating from the anomaly are creating new and divergent temporal pathways." Having returned to the bridge's aft stations, she gestured to one of the console's sensor displays. "We're registering multiple localized fluctuations in the spacetime continuum. If these readings are correct, time itself is shifting around us. The *Tempus* recorded similar readings, but the effect now is much more pronounced."

"New timelines," said Ducane, feeling a knot forming in his stomach.

Ailur added, "There are eleven different time streams emanating from the anomaly, and indications are those could begin splitting off into their own branches."

Faroti added, "She's correct, sir. Scans show the variations are affecting the other ships, as well. I've lost contact with the *Crichton* and readings for the *Mobius* are unstable, but I still have a fix on the *Haddix*."

"According to her logs," said Ailur, "Admiral zh'Crivash detected the same phenomenon during her own encounter with the anomaly. The Temporal Integrity Commission suggested an attempt to reintegrate the diverging time streams by identifying points of origin and preempting the eruption of temporal distortions at those locations with chroniton-based weapons. This is what the *Tempus* was trying to do."

Ducane replied, "Every time she thought they were making progress, another fracture appeared. It was like trying to suture an open wound while someone's still slashing at you with a knife. But, if we concentrate our firepower at a single point where the time fractures are occurring, we may be able to disrupt it."

"We have no way to predict the effects on the anomaly at different points in spacetime," said Ailur.

"I don't think we have a choice." Ducane turned toward the front of the bridge. "Mister Faroti, target those coordinates with a full spread of chroniton torpedoes, and have a second spread on standby. We're going to punch this thing in the mouth."

Ducane felt the minor tremor in the deck plating beneath his feet as power was routed to *Relativity*'s weapons systems and the ship launched a group of eight chroniton torpedoes. The weapons, four pairs moving along their programmed course, arced away from the ship and adjusted their approach vectors as they drew closer to their target. They vanished into the multicolored frenzy at the heart of the anomaly, and an instant later Ducane lifted a hand to shield his eyes from the sequence of explosions as each torpedo detonated.

"Scans detecting fluctuations within the anomaly," reported Ailur.

"Fire second spread." When the next set of torpedoes hit their target, Ducane turned away from the viewscreen as the new round of explosions erupted. On the screen, the anomaly appeared unchanged, at least to the naked eye.

Ailur said, "I'm registering a shift in energy output, and the waves of temporal distortion are decreasing in intensity."

"Stand by with another torpedo spread," said Ducane. "We'll—"

"Captain," said Faroti, cutting him off. "There's a new reading from inside the anomaly."

On the viewscreen, Ducane could see a small, indistinct dark shape pushing its way out from the center of the maelstrom the Typhon anomaly had become. From this distance it was impossible to identify, but even before he could order image enhancement Ducane glimpsed more shapes of varying sizes appearing from within the vortex.

"What the hell are those?" he asked, casting a look over his shoulder to Ailur.

The Romulan shook her head. "Unable to determine precise readings, Captain, but—" She turned, casting her gaze toward the main screen. "They appear to be life-forms, ranging in size from five to fifty meters in length. Their biological readings are in flux, so I am unable to attempt a positive identification."

At ops, Faroti called out, "Captain, there are dozens of them emerging from the anomaly. They're dividing into groups and . . . and they're moving to intercept our other ships. The *Crichton*'s under attack."

The lieutenant was already swiping and punching at controls, and the viewscreen shifted to display *Relativity*'s sister ship. Ducane almost flinched as the other vessel's deflector shields flared under what had to be a tremendous assault of directed energy, and he felt his pulse quickening as he watched more than a dozen dark, heaving silhouettes slamming into the shields at different points around the *Crichton*.

"Scans show the life-forms are phasing in and out of spacetime," reported Ailur. "We're unable to establish a firm sensor lock. The *Crichton*'s shields are already stressing to the point of overload."

On the screen, Ducane watched numerous flares of energy as the unidentified life-forms drove themselves at the other ship's shields. The tactical display Faroti had cast to the screen now showed more of the creatures moving to intercept the *Mobius* and the *Haddix*, and a moment later a proximity alarm began echoing across *Relativity*'s bridge.

"Incoming!" warned Faroti.

Before Ducane could even give the order, Lieutenant Rabal was entering commands to guide *Relativity* into the first of whatever evasive maneuvers she had at the ready. Status displays on both her and Faroti's consoles indicated the automatic diverting of power from nonessential systems to the ship's defenses and weapons. On the viewscreen, the image of the anomaly shifted up and to the left as the ship responded to Rabal's instructions. At the same time, the tactical readout showed more than a dozen red dots moving toward *Relativity*.

"Stand by, all weapons," said Ducane. "Target all incoming signatures, and tell engineering we may need to get out of here in a hurry. We need warp drive."

He barely spoke the order before energy flared across the viewscreen in response to direct impacts against *Relativity*'s deflectors, and Ducane noted the status indicator reporting the strain already registering against the ship's shield generators. As the effects of the first barrage faded, he got his first real look at the life-forms responsible for the attack.

"What in the name of—" The rest of Ducane's obvious question faded as one of the creatures appeared to charge toward the screen.

Though it was only a computer-generated image, he still flinched as the life-form smashed once more into the shields and evoked yet another energy discharge. For the most fleeting of moments, the nearly shapeless mass solidified into . . . something. Ducane had the impression of an immense, sinewy shape covered with grayish-white scales all but filling the viewscreen image. Its body led up to a flared head peppered with dark pits that might be eyes, and a wide mouth filled with rows of sharp, gleaming teeth. Protrusions along its skull suggested vertebrae, and its skin colors seemed to change as the creature came into contact with the shields. Ducane wondered if it might actually be feeding on the energy evoked by each of its strikes. Then it withdrew and its form was lost, blurring again as its body shifted in and out of phase.

"Multiple attacks to our deflectors," said Ailur. "Shield strength has dropped below eighty percent and the rate of decline is accelerating."

Ducane waved to the screen. "Phasers. Fire at will. All available targ—"

Another strike, this one far more concentrated and powerful, raked across *Relativity*'s shields, washing out the viewscreen's image and making every bridge light and console flicker and sputter. Holographic displays generated by the various stations disappeared. The drain on the ship's systems was evident in the way primary illumination failed to return, replaced instead by emergency lighting. The main screen framed nothing but static, and Ducane realized the ops and conn stations had gone dark.

"No helm control," called Rabal. The Saurian exchanged worried looks with Faroti, who shook his head.

"Main flight and navigation systems are offline," said Faroti. "Backup systems are engaging, but they're slow."

"What about the shields?" asked Ducane.

The Bolian ops officer replied, "Forty-six percent and dropping, sir."

Static on the main screen faded, offering a view of the immediate vicinity. Ducane saw one of *Relativity*'s companion vessels, surrounded by dozens of the creatures, and noticed there were no telltale flashes of energy from the other ship's shields.

"It's the *Mobius*, sir," said Ailur, and Ducane looked behind him to see his first officer standing at the upper tier railing. "Its shields have failed, and I'm picking up signs of direct hull penetration. The smaller life-forms appear to be burrowing into the ship."

"Weapons," said Ducane, but before Faroti could respond, a blinding white light erupted onto the viewscreen, momentarily obstructing the anomaly from view. The flash disappeared as quickly as it occurred, leaving behind the distortion field as though nothing had happened.

Ducane looked to Ailur, who offered a somber nod. "The *Mobius*. Our sensors detected a warp-core breach, just before detonation. The *Haddix* has initiated evasive maneuvers, but the *Crichton* is already crippled. I'm picking up power signatures in numerous escape pods. Indications are at least some of the crew are attempting to abandon ship."

Still processing the end of the *Mobius* that he had just witnessed, Ducane turned to Faroti. "Try to contact the *Haddix* and see if they can retrieve any escape pods that make it away from the *Crichton*. We'll assist as soon as we regain helm control."

Another series of impacts against the shields rocked *Relativity*, their effects flaring across the viewscreen before a new alarm sounded on the bridge.

"Our shields have failed," said Faroti. "Shield generators are offline, but engineering's already working to cycle them and route power from nonessential systems." He looked up from his station, and Ducane saw in the Bolian's expression the answer to his own unasked question.

We don't have that kind of time.

"Captain." It was Ailur, who had moved back to her own station on the bridge's upper tier. "We have hull breaches on decks eight, four, and three. The creatures are . . . they're phase-shifting through the hull."

The fate of the *Mobius* still fresh in his mind, Ducane ordered, "Intruder alert, all decks. All hands, prepare to repel boarders."

In response to his command, Faroti and Rabal moved from their stations to a recessed weapons locker along the bridge's starboard bulkhead. Selecting a sleek, compact phaser rifle for herself, Rabal then handed an identical weapon to Ducane, who looked up to see Ailur and the remaining bridge officers also arming themselves. The first officer brandished a phaser rifle while her two companions held hand phasers and tricorders.

"More hull breaches, Captain," called out Ailur. "Decks nine and five. Force fields are in place, but they are showing no effect. If those creatures make it to engineering . . ."

Her report was punctuated by a dull thump from somewhere above their heads. It reverberated through the overhead, followed by two more, similar impacts. Another warning wailed for attention.

We have to get out of here.

The odd thought sprang from the depths of Ducane's mind, suddenly demanding his full attention. He felt a wave of disquiet beginning to wash over him, and for a moment he was all but consumed with the desire to run and hide. Doctor Jeva's warning about such feelings manifesting themselves was still fresh in his mind, and he did his best to push away the errant thoughts.

Focus, he chastised himself.

"Outer hull breach directly above the bridge!" said Ailur, her normally cool demeanor appearing to falter. Pushing herself away from her station, the Romulan brandished her phaser rifle as though searching for targets.

Above them, Ducane heard the unmistakable sounds of something large and powerful doing its level best to tear its way through bulkheads, growing louder with every passing second. Every dull thud against the plating seemed to make his heart race that much faster. Swallowing, he tried to get his escalating sense of dread under control, cursing himself for these strange feelings that had come from nowhere and now seemed hell-bent on paralyzing him.

"Lock out all stations and transfer all command functions to engineering," he snapped. A moment of clarity amid the rising chaos had shown him a path. "Clear the bridge."

10

It required significant effort for Picard to maintain his composure, refusing to allow emotion to betray his true feelings as Worf stepped onto the bridge. Despite his own formidable self-control, he knew he could not maintain this façade much longer. The matter before him required immediate action.

"Commander Worf," he said, his tone sharp as his first officer exited the turbolift and stepped onto the bridge. "How good of you to join us."

The imposing Klingon stepped toward the command well, the silver baldric draped over his right shoulder and across his Starfleet uniform tunic reflecting the bridge's lighting. As always, his features were fixed in a flat, neutral expression belying the strength and ferocity he could bring to bear should circumstances warrant. Now, however, there was an air of uncertainty as he stood before Picard. Ever the vigilant warrior, Worf studied his surroundings. In rapid fashion he scrutinized the faces of the entire bridge crew, all of whom had turned from their stations and whose collective gaze now focused on him. The entire action took just a second before he returned his attention to Picard.

"You wished to see me, Captain."

"Indeed I did. I've just received a communique from Admiral Akaar at Starfleet Command. You were the subject of that message, regarding a matter of most pressing concern. It seems a command billet has become available, and it is the admiral's intention to submit your name to fill that posting."

Worf's eyes widened, though only slightly. To most people the break from his normal unyielding bearing would be all but imperceptible, but Picard noticed it. Years of working alongside his first officer had attuned him to the Klingon's moods and mannerisms, and even the most subtle shift was obvious. In this case, Picard noted the surprise Worf tried to hide.

"A command?" His response was so genuine it made several of the bridge officers smile and even elicited a giggle from Lieutenant Dina Elfiki at the science station.

"The *Prometheus*. Captain Adams has been selected for promotion to admiral and an assignment to oversee Starfleet sector operations at Starbase 173. His first officer, Commander Roaas, is being promoted to captain and she'll command one of the ships detailed to the starbase. Not only is the *Prometheus*'s center seat available, but you'll also get to pick your number one. I trust you'll do me the courtesy of informing me if you intend to make off with a member of my crew." Pausing to glance around the bridge, Picard added, "There is no one more deserving of this promotion, Commander. It is long overdue. I hope I'm not being premature, but I'd like to be the first to offer you my congratulations, *Captain*."

He extended his hand and Worf shook it to enthusiastic applause from the bridge crew. For his part, Worf took the attention in his usual composed manner, but Picard saw the satisfaction in the Klingon's eyes.

"Thank you, sir."

Once the ovation faded, Picard looked to his senior flight control officer, Joanna Faur. "Lieutenant, you have the bridge." With a gesture, he indicated for Worf to follow him to his ready room.

Once inside his dedicated workspace just off the bridge, Picard moved to his desk. He made a point to ignore the status and personnel reports and the alerts on his desktop terminal's display screen reminding him of meetings and other commitments on his daily schedule. All of that could wait.

"Please have a seat, Number One." As he stepped toward the replicator, he glanced over his shoulder. "Can I get you anything?" It was an offer made out of habit and one Picard knew Worf would decline, but civility required such gestures.

"No. Thank you, sir," replied the commander before moving toward one of the seats positioned before the captain's desk. Picard ordered and retrieved a cup of Earl Grey tea from the replicator before moving to the chair behind his desk. Setting the cup and its accompanying saucer atop the table's polished surface, he reached for the lone padd he had left next to the desktop terminal.

"The *Prometheus*." Worf seemed to savor the name. "A most impressive vessel."

Picard relaxed into his seat. "As is the mission it will be given. Starfleet has decided the *Enterprise*'s exploration of the Odyssean Pass warrants greater attention than can be provided by a single vessel. Not just for the region itself, but also for whatever might lie beyond it."

Though the *Enterprise* had charted several star systems and made first contact with a handful of newly discovered species, much of the Odyssean Pass—which Federation cartographers had named on star charts more than a century earlier—was unexplored. Initially charted by automated survey probes and a small number of civilian ships, most of the area remained a mystery even now. The *Enterprise* was Starfleet's first comprehensive attempt to explore the region.

"The Romulans have also begun making their own forays into the Pass," said Picard. "Reports indicate they may soon accelerate their efforts to explore the area, which makes sense, given it's one of the few directions they can expand their territory. Why they haven't done so before now is a mystery, but that's par for the course when we're talking about Romulans."

In truth, the Romulan Empire had kept to itself in recent years, retreating behind its borders and all but disappearing from the interstellar stage. An attempt to entice the Ferengi to withdraw from the Khitomer Accords and ally themselves with the Empire and the other members of the Typhon Pact had met with failure. This did not seem to Picard like the sort of event to derail the rival coalition and its plans to "compete" with the Federation to win the hearts and minds of various non-aligned powers in the Alpha and Beta Quadrants. However, the inability to secure the alliance of even a relatively innocuous party like the Ferengi did not speak well for the Pact's recruiting acumen.

What began with great fanfare several years earlier had sputtered in response to recent events. The Romulans along with the Tholian, Breen, Kinshaya, Gorn, and Tzenkethi all seemed content to go to their respective corners, at least for the time being. Starfleet Intelligence reports indicated little in the way of cooperative activity among the six powers, and Picard knew the Romulans were key to any major activity the Pact might put into motion. This made their recent forays toward the Odyssean Pass of great interest to Starfleet Command. In theory, the region was large enough for both the Federation and the Romulan Empire to give each other a wide berth. History and experience told Picard such an arrangement was unlikely to remain peaceful.

"There are already long-term plans afoot, Number One," he said. "In addition to expanding its exploration efforts, Starfleet wants to establish a permanent presence in the Pass. They're looking at two starbases to provide security for civilian traffic and an infrastructure to support colonization. Several of the uninhabited star systems we've surveyed are attractive candidates, and the inroads we've made with those civilizations we've encountered should prove mutually beneficial. We can only hope the trust we've cultivated with those societies will make us more attractive allies than the Romulans."

Things were moving rapidly, if Picard was to believe the latest reports coming from Starfleet Command. The *Enterprise*'s successes in the Odyssean Pass fueled much of this activity. For the first time in many years, he felt as though the Federation had finally, truly managed to put behind it the succession of crises that had all but consumed it. War with the Dominion followed by an attempted coup of the Romulan government and a thwarted attack on Earth by the renegade Shinzon had been enough to rattle Starfleet and the Federation. The final Borg Invasion just two years later had nearly brought the Alpha Quadrant to its knees, and the effects of that brutal assault were still being felt today. In the midst of that recovery had come the rise of the Typhon Pact and Andor's brief yet tumultuous secession from the Federation. The loss of a founding member—one of humanity's earliest and steadfast allies—had tested relationships dating back more than two centuries. Add to that scandals which had brought about the removal of two Federation presidents and the assassination of a third, and it would be easy for any reasonable person to be lost in a pit of despair. The optimism that had driven Federation ideals and Starfleet's ambitions to continue pushing ever outward the boundaries of knowledge and understanding of the universe had seemed on the brink of being lost forever.

Thankfully, and as Picard always believed it would, that positivity emerged once more into the light. Federation President Kellessar zh'Tarash, the true successor to the late Nanietta Bacco, had made reform a top priority. After years of being on a war footing or simply dealing with the aftermath of conflict, Starfleet had returned to its primary mission of exploration, with the *Enterprise* at the forefront of this renewed undertaking. More than a year after accepting zh'Tarash's offer to conduct the first comprehensive exploration of the Odyssean Pass, the *Enterprise* had barely scratched the surface with respect to the region's potential. After the unpleasantness of the past few months, he was more than eager to return to doing what had drawn him to Starfleet service so many years ago: going where no one had ever gone before. If other ships were to follow the *Enterprise* into that vast unknown, it would comfort him to know at least one of those vessels was commanded by someone he trusted with his life.

"So," Picard said after a moment. "What do you say, Mister Worf? Ready to take the reins of your own steed? I know you've had some experience commanding the *Defiant* during your tour with Deep Space 9." Leaning forward, he rested his forearms on his desk. He could not resist a knowing smile as he regarded his first officer. "But, with all due respect to that vessel and its capabilities and accomplishments, there really is no comparison to a capital ship."

Worf nodded. "I understand this posting is one of great prestige. Surely, there are other officers with greater seniority and experience, and more deserving."

"Your modesty is commendable, Number One." Picard rose from his chair, indicating with a gesture for Worf to remain seated. Moving around the desk, he leaned against one corner and folded his arms as he regarded the Klingon. "Your service record as my first officer is unimpeachable, Mister Worf. That is not a matter of opinion. It is irrefutable fact. Even if you didn't already have the support of several admirals at Starfleet Command who share his view, Akaar is the one putting forth the recommendation. It goes without saying he has my full endorsement, as do you."

Worf sat up a bit straighter in his chair. "Thank you, sir." He turned his gaze to the padd in his hand and the message from Admiral Leonard James Akaar it displayed. "The honor of standing by your side has never faltered. After everything that has happened, and with your personal situation now finally settled, it somehow feels wrong to leave. It would be presumptuous of me to speak for the crew, but I am confident most if not all of them feel the same as I do."

Never comfortable with praise, especially when he felt it to be effusive, Picard felt an abrupt rush of self-conscious uncertainty. The strain of the past months and the board of inquiry he had endured, prompted as it was by the revelations of Section 31's long history of unsanctioned operations from the fringes of Federation and Starfleet authority and accountability, had weighed on him. Most of all, his unwitting role in one of that corrupt organization's more recent and heinous acts had made him question not just past choices but also the reasons and motivations that had driven those decisions. Despite the best of intentions and a firm belief that the ends had justified very questionable means, Picard remained convinced that forcing Federation President Min Zife from office, however repugnant the idea may have been, had been necessary. His role in the president's forced resignation had troubled him every day since making that decision, all while being unaware of Section 31's subsequent actions. Learning Admiral Ross and the other high-ranking officers participating in the coup had seen to the assassination of Zife appalled and sickened him.

In the aftermath of Section 31's centuries of crimes coming to light, there were those within the halls of Starfleet leadership who believed Picard knew the full truth all along and had sanctioned the president's murder. Friendships cultivated over many years were tested. A few did not survive the harsh challenge. Through it all, Worf and nearly every member of his crew had stood by him, certain the faith they placed in their captain was justified.

Clearing his throat, he pushed himself from the desk and began pacing the length of the ready room.

"Mister Worf, your allegiance to this ship and to me has never been in question. Given how the Klingon people and you in particular value personal honor, you humble me with the unwavering loyalty you've always shown. It's in the spirit of such devotion that I believe you're ready for a command of your own, and it's my duty to encourage you to seize this opportunity. It isn't a reward for a job well done. You've earned it along with the respect and esteem that comes with that post. I have absolutely no doubt you'll make a fine captain."

He extended his hand, and Worf rose before taking it.

"There is a great deal to consider, sir," said the Klingon.

"Agreed." Picard appraised his first officer. "We're not scheduled to depart Yko until the end of the week. Take as much time as you need between now and then to make your decision." He paused, considering the ramifications of Worf's choice. "I'd also like a recommendation for your potential successor. I have my own thoughts, but I'd like to hear yours." Eyeing Worf with amusement, he added, "Besides, I'd like some warning if we're going to end up fighting over the same person to be our new Number One."

11

U.S.S. Relativity NCV-474439-G
29th Century, Exact Temporal Coordinates *Classified*

Juel Ducane recoiled at the sudden, intense gust of cold, putrid air that seemed to waft into the engineering section. The reinforced security hatch separating the compartment from the adjacent passageway parted, revealing an indistinct humanoid life-form. Dark, flowing robes concealed it from head to foot. Ducane leveled his phaser rifle at the intruder and fired. The humanoid seemed to flinch as the phaser beam struck its chest, halting its entry into the room.

When the intruder did not fall, Commander Ailur and Lieutenant Faroti added their own weapons to the effort. Having adjusted their rifles' frequency modulation to adaptive mode in an attempt to counteract the creature's apparent state of temporal flux, Ducane kept his finger on the phaser's firing stud until the combined force of the three energy beams began to take effect. The intruder's body began to come apart, clothes tearing and skin and muscle peeling back to reveal the stark white bone of its skeletal structure before the creature succumbed to the onslaught and it disintegrated. Only the open hatch remained as evidence of its attempted entry.

"Secure that hatch," snapped Ducane, gesturing with the muzzle of his rifle. In response to his order, two of *Relativity*'s engineering staff turned their attention to the compromised door.

Faroti, examining his own phaser, said, "It won't hold for long." There was obvious fear in the lieutenant's voice, mirroring

Ducane's own growing feelings of anxiety, which he was finding increasingly difficult to hold at bay while focusing on their deteriorating situation.

"It won't have to." After verifying his phaser rifle's power cell was already down to half its original charge, Ducane looked around the room. "All we're doing is buying time anyway." Making his way to where Ailur now stood before one of the engineering workstations, he asked, "Any idea who or what we're dealing with?"

"Internal sensor scans are inconclusive." Ailur, with the assistance of *Relativity*'s central computer, had reconfigured the console to oversee various station functions from the main bridge. She allowed her phaser rifle to hang from its tactical sling across her chest while she worked the console. "I'm detecting seven such lifeforms. They register as humanoid, but appear to be shifting in and out of temporal phase in a manner similar to the larger creatures that attacked the ship. So far as I can tell, they boarded the ship through the resulting hull breaches. Beyond that, I am at a loss to explain their presence."

"Can you identify them?"

Ailur shook her head. "I can't get any sort of definitive reading."

"Sickbay to Captain," came a new voice over the intercom. *"Emergency!"*

Stepping closer to Ailur's console, Ducane tapped a control to enable the intraship communications frequency. One of the station's smaller display monitors flared to life, revealing the disheveled form of Jeva Myras. He could see the doctor was under obvious stress as he stared out from the screen. His thin gray hair, usually brushed back from his face, was askew, and Ducane noticed the ornate earring he almost always wore as a symbol of his faith was missing and his right earlobe was bleeding.

"Myras?" prompted Ducane. "Are you all right?"

Instead of answering, Jeva replied, *"Captain, the computer's reporting elevated neural activity in every member of the crew. The readings spiked as soon as those things started punching their way into the ship, and they're continuing to rise. My medics are treating people in the hallways who are paralyzed with fear."*

"I'm sending security teams to protect sickbay," said Ailur. "They should be there momentarily."

"I'm worried about the crew becoming incapacitated," warned Jeva. *"How's the evacuation coming?"*

Glancing at a status monitor on Ailur's workstation, Ducane frowned. "Slowly. Half the crew should've been in escape pods by now." Were his people becoming compromised to the point of being unable even to run for their very lives?

"At this rate, we don't have much time, Captain."

"Understood, Doctor. Keep me informed. Ducane out."

The connection severed, and he turned his attention to the massive hatch that was the main component of their paltry and dwindling defensive options. The door, like the bulkheads encompassing *Relativity's* engineering section, was constructed from a composite of duranium and rodinium. Starfleet engineers touted the combined material as being among the strongest, most durable substances in the known galaxy, capable of absorbing the direct assault of even ship-based weaponry. Its use in *Wells*-class starships in this and other key areas was intended to isolate the ship's temporal warp core and other equipment necessary for maneuvering through time from interfering with other vital onboard systems. That just one of the alien creatures had managed to break through the hatch—albeit after several minutes of focused attention on its goal—was disconcerting. Ducane watched as a pair of engineers had forced it closed and were now applying an emergency seal around its edges to keep it in place. He knew it was at best a temporary measure.

More of those things are coming, he reminded himself, and the very thought seemed to conjure another bout of anxiety and near panic. It required increasing effort on his part to keep his emotions at bay so he could concentrate on the matters at hand. What bothered him more than his own mounting dread was the knowledge he was not alone. Everyone in the engineering section appeared to be suffering from similar distress. It was playing out just as Doctor Jeva had warned. Ducane had already observed Commander David Cambria, *Relativity*'s chief engineer, scolding two members of his team who appeared to be losing their bearing and allowing their emotions to run unchecked. The situation was deteriorating, and they were running out of time to take any decisive action.

Still working at her console, Ailur said, "Internal sensors show the creatures are converging on those areas where power output is at its highest. Shielding around the warp core and temporal systems is holding, but if we lose primary power—"

Ducane cut her off. "Then we blow up and die." There was no mistaking that this was a coordinated attack. The larger creatures had pummeled the shields of *Relativity* and the other ships, weakening them to the point that smaller ones could penetrate the hulls. For what purpose, he did not know. Despite his people's valiant attempts to repel the intruders, he knew it was a lost cause, which is why he had wasted no time with his order to abandon ship. All he could do now—with the aid of Ailur and his senior staff—was try to hold things together long enough for the crew to reach the ship's shuttlecraft and escape pods. With luck, there would even be time for him and his remaining officers to reach their own shuttle.

"Do the sensors show them giving off or emitting some kind of energy?" he asked. "If we had some idea how they're affecting the crew, maybe we could counteract it." Even as he spoke the words he knew it was a futile gesture. There simply would be no time to create a defense.

Ailur confirmed his fear by shaking her head. "Scans have detected no such emissions, but most of our scans are being scattered. I am unable to ascertain if they are wholly living organisms, artificial constructs, or some combination."

"They know to focus on key areas of our ships," said Faroti. "Destroying the *Mobius* and the *Crichton* was no accident or stroke of luck. They knew where to go."

Ducane pressed his lips together upon hearing the names of *Relativity*'s sister ships. Only after fleeing the bridge and transporting to engineering had he and the others learned of the *Crichton*'s fate, destroyed just moments earlier from an attack similar to that which had taken the *Mobius*. As for the *Haddix*, its condition remained unknown, though it had managed to move far enough from the Typhon anomaly to hopefully buy time for its crew to launch a counterattack or at least abandon ship. If nothing else, the loss of the other ships had given Ducane's crew valuable information, as Ailur and the engineering team routed power to the ship's internal defensive systems and modulated the shielding around the warp core and temporal impeller.

"What's the status of the warp drive?" he asked.

"Not a chance," replied a new voice, and Ducane turned to see David Cambria. Human and even older than the captain, he glistened with perspiration. Thanks to the unforgiving harshness of the emergency lighting, his normally pale complexion looked even more pallid than normal. The chief engineer looked exhausted, and Ducane thought he saw a hint of defeat in the man's eyes.

Waving a hand toward Ailur's console, Cambria blew out his breath. "We've modulated the temporal shielding to block the worst of the anomaly's effects, but if we can't get some distance from it, then we can't generate a warp field."

"Impulse engines are at less than half power," said Lieutenant Rabal from where she stood at another reconfigured workstation across from Ailur. "Helm controls are sluggish, but I've got us moving again."

Though he said nothing, Cambria shook his head and Ducane knew what it meant.

Engineering was where they would make their last stand, but there was still one thing they needed to do. "We can't get away, but we can at least try to finish what we started."

Ailur cast a quizzical glance at him. "Captain?"

"Whatever's in there reacted to our previous attack. We might be able to knock them out of commission permanently, but even if we threw every torpedo we have, it probably wouldn't be enough power. We need something bigger." Ducane knew it was a long shot and time was running out, but he also was aware *Relativity* was destined to share the fate of its sister ships. All that was left was to try getting his people to safety, but that did not preclude flinging one last gesture of defiance toward their attackers.

"You are suggesting using the ship as a weapon," said Ailur. Despite her composed demeanor, Ducane still heard the skepticism in her voice.

Having overheard the conversation, Commander Cambria said, "We can set the warp core to detonate and trigger it remotely once we're on a shuttle." The engineer shrugged. "It's the only real play we have left. May as well go down swinging."

"Get it ready, and plot a course back to the anomaly," ordered Ducane. "We'll beam to the shuttle as soon as it's set up and guide the ship from—"

He was interrupted by the sound of something slamming against the nearby bulkhead. Another strike followed, this time at the reinforced entry hatch, after which came another pair of similar impacts along another wall. At the same time, an alert tone from her console made Ailur turn to consult the new readings.

"Three of the life-forms are converging on engineering," she reported.

Ducane was already aiming his phaser rifle at the pressure door and the hasty repair work put in place by the engineers. Was it his imagination or had it already buckled from the force of a strike?

"We have to get out of here," said Rabal, her head turning from side to side as though trying to keep watch on the entire engineering compartment.

"Stand fast, Lieutenant," snapped Ducane, hoping the sharp command would help the Saurian focus her attention. Instead of holding her position, she was starting to step back as though she might bolt and run at any moment.

Another solid hit against the door broke through the hull patch. It fell to the floor and Ducane caught a glimpse of movement through the renewed opening. He leveled his phaser rifle at the hole and fired.

"Over there!"

It was Cambria, pointing toward the bulkhead on the room's far side, and Ducane risked looking in that direction long enough to see part of the wall giving way. Beyond the gap, something dark and hazy moved with incredible speed, pushing its way into the opening and forcing it wider as it burrowed deeper into the room.

"Fire!" Ducane shouted, pivoting toward the danger and shifting his aim. To his left, he glimpsed Ailur pointing her own phaser rifle at the main door just before he heard the sound of her weapon discharging.

Then he was firing at his own target, which now was in the room. As with its companion, the humanoid figure was swathed in robes that concealed its true form. It moved with astounding speed, lunging toward Lieutenant Faroti. Scrambling backward, the Bolian tried to avoid the attack while leveling his phaser at the intruder, but it was already too late. The creature placed a hand on Faroti's chest, and the lieutenant froze. As Ducane watched in horror, Faroti's body was enveloped in a flash of silver energy. Skin paled, wrinkled, and cracked as he crumpled before dissolving into a thin cloud of particles that fell slowly to the floor.

"Captain!"

There was a hand on Ducane's back before he felt himself pushed to his right. It was Ailur, moving him out of danger an instant before another of the creatures whipped past him, missing him but reaching out to touch her. He could do nothing but watch her body absorb the full brunt of the attack, shriveling and falling in on itself before dissipating into another cloud of . . . *ash?* Ailur was still fading away as the humanoid turned as though collecting itself before springing toward Cambria and wrapping him within its long arms. The chief engineer barely had time to scream before he was gone, the echo of his final utterance fading as quickly as his body.

Before his mind could even process what was happening, Ducane was backpedaling, putting distance between himself and the creature while lifting his phaser rifle. Another phaser beam lanced across the space, fired by Rabal and striking the humanoid as it lunged toward Ducane. The attack caught the thing full in the face, halting its advance and buying Ducane precious heartbeats to move farther out of the way. He aimed and fired his own weapon in one fluid motion, and the combined power of the two rifles kept the intruder in place long enough for the sustained fire to bring it down. Its robes disintegrated first before the rest of its body followed suit, skin rippling and peeling away before the creature vanished without a trace.

"Stay alert!" he shouted. "More are coming!" Moving back to the console, Ducane gave it a hurried look. He could see that Cambria had managed to input the navigational settings to the ship's computer. All that was needed to execute the final commands to put *Relativity* on its final course back to the Typhon anomaly. He entered a hurried string of instructions and the computer acknowledged him. A moment later he heard the telltale thrum of the ship's engines as it began maneuvering into position.

Looking first to Rabal, then to those members of the engineering team he could still see, Ducane called out, "That's it! All hands to the escape pods. Abandon ship!"

He tapped his combadge, activating its preprogrammed emergency transporter sequence just as another of the creatures rested the flattened palm of its hand on his chest.

12

Having shifted himself just far enough out of phase from this dimension to render himself invisible to those around him, Wesley Crusher arrived at engineering in time to see Juel Ducane die. The human captain's body and the uniform he wore aged and decayed within a fraction of a second, helpless against the effects of the energy wielded by the alien interloper. Other members of the engineering staff fell victim in identical fashion, unable to bring their weapons to bear fast enough to mount any kind of defense.

It was not the first time Wesley had witnessed such a horrific scene. Decades spent vainly pursuing these adversaries and others like them—long bouts with no appreciable progress peppered with rare moments in which his efforts occasioned results—were marred by visions such as what he now witnessed. These creatures, who continued to defy identification and capture let alone direct confrontation except in the most extreme circumstances, seemed to delight in frustrating him at every turn. Previous encounters with them had shown him their capabilities and their cold, efficient ruthlessness. He knew they fed on the energy of other living beings, reducing their quarry to dust with little apparent effort or thought. Though Wesley had witnessed the effect during other meetings, this was only the second time he had been close enough to feel the victim falling prey to the assault—neural energy spikes, the loss of mental faculties and physical control—as though the person's literal life force was being seized in violent fashion. Each time it happened, he sensed the assailant gaining strength from the obscene appropriation, and he experienced revulsion and fury at the casual malice of it all.

Unlike those earlier meetings, this time Wesley was ready for a fight.

The strain of maintaining his state of existence already beginning to wear on him, Wesley ignored the growing discomfort while brandishing the transphasic disruptor he carried slung across his chest. It was a weapon of his own devising, and today would be the first time he utilized it against the enemy despite creating it for this singular purpose. Prior meetings with these beings had provided Wesley that most precious of commodities: information. Since his first encounter with them on the Guardian planet, he had spent the intervening years learning about them, bit by excruciating bit. His previous attempts to track their movements had proven futile, but every infrequent and seemingly random engagement offered him an additional sliver of insight. Only recently, after decades of futility, had he begun to make any real progress, which only served to heighten his concerns. What were these creatures doing now, after being seemingly dormant for so long?

There's only one way to find out. His observation taunted him as he checked the disruptor's power cell. He had created the weapon following earlier encounters with the creatures that had forced him to draw and focus power from within himself. Such action tended to weaken him, and he did not want to risk becoming incapacitated at a critical juncture. Previous attempts with the disruptor had fallen short, forcing him to analyze those failures and apply lessons learned while preparing for future encounters. Those were few and far between and though he could not be certain, Wesley seemed to recall this same sequence of events playing out in somewhat similar fashion. He could not recall any direct memories of that encounter, how it may have deviated from what was now happening, or even if it had occurred more than once. Such was the nature of moving through endless divergent temporal realities.

The "ghost," as he had taken to calling these humanoids who acted as masters of the larger serpentlike creatures that had attacked *Relativity* and the other ships, returned to the center of the engineering section, black robes flowing behind it despite the lack of any appreciable airflow within the compartment. It appeared like an apparition, moving unconstrained by the physical laws of this universe, at least until it phased completely into this reality and its feet touched the deck. The ability of this entity and others like it to accomplish such a feat was not all that dissimilar from the gift he had been given. More accurately, it was the innate talent with which he had been born and later taught by his mentors to control that allowed him to traverse different realities just as normal beings might step between rooms.

Tensing, Wesley felt his slide between planes of existence slipping and his body emerging into this reality. His attempts to remain out of phase and therefore hidden faltered and the ghost reacted by pivoting to face him. The intruder's features remained cloaked in shadow while it raised both hands in Wesley's direction.

Wesley was faster, leveling the disruptor's muzzle at his opponent and firing. The weapon hurled an intense, roiling orb of harsh violet-white energy that struck the ghost's chest before expanding to cloak its body. The figure jerked backward, spasming in response to the attack while at the same time shifting and wavering as if the ghost was attempting to shift itself out of this reality. Another bolt from the disruptor slammed into the ghost's torso and this time Wesley caught a glimpse of facial features from beneath the hood of the intruder's robes. A large mouth opened as though releasing a cry of pain, but whatever sound it may have made was lost as transphasic energy washed across the ghost's body. Only as the figure dissipated did Wesley hear one final shriek of agony before his adversary faded to nothingness.

"I guess it worked."

It was a shock to hear his own voice, which to his ears sounded old and worn. How long since he had spoken aloud? He could not remember. Looking down at his disruptor, he noted the weathered, wrinkled skin of his hands protruding from the frayed sleeves of his jacket. A new rush of fatigue and dizziness gripped him, and he sagged against a bulkhead for support. The energy and concentration required to cross the different states of existence, or to hold himself between realms as a defensive mechanism, had long since begun to wear on him. Despite his abilities, decades of pursuing an adversary that thwarted his every effort to identify it while simultaneously hunting him had taken their toll. Complicating matters was the fact that he was not and never would be immortal. He had managed to slow the normal human aging process, but stopping it was not within his power. Even Travelers had limits.

You don't have time for this, he reminded himself while reaching into one of his jacket pockets to retrieve another piece of equipment. A slender, rectangular box somewhat larger than the Starfleet tricorders he used in another life, it consisted of a drab neutronium shell encasing and protecting its far more sensitive internal components. Wesley flipped open its lid and the device activated, projecting a compact holographic display with strings of vertically scrolling data. Information was color coded to distinguish scan readings about his immediate environment—atmosphere, temperature, gravity, and so on—from information regarding energy sources both natural and artificial, and it also detected the presence of life-forms within a prescribed scan radius. Swiping at one of the data streams tightened that focus to *Relativity's* interior, showing Wesley the location of the ship's remaining crewmembers. There were far fewer than the 250 people this vessel was supposed to carry. Many had already made it off the ship via escape pods and shuttlecraft, while others had fallen prey to the intruders. Wesley knew more would be added to that latter group in the few minutes of life this ship possessed, but there was little he could do about that now.

"Where are you bastards?" he said, eyeing the "Omnichron," as he had taken to calling the device. Like the disruptor, it was a recent creation based on knowledge gathered about his adversaries while incorporating what he had learned after many years spent traveling the universe. Even the expertise developed in a life all but forgotten—technology mastered while living aboard a starship—came into play. It was not a substitute for his own abilities but rather a means to help him focus his powers in service to the specific task of hunting his quarry while collecting information he might find useful. Capable of scanning across time as well as dimensional planes, it could detect points of intersection between such temporal divides and branching realities. It was this feature that allowed him to pinpoint the presence of the six intruders who were still on-board. They were scattered throughout the ship but converging on its most sensitive areas. The temporal-impeller and field-stabilizer systems located in the vessel's aft section, the components most vital to *Relativity*'s ability to navigate through time, seemed to be drawing the most interest, but Wesley knew the temporal warp core located in this compartment was another obvious target.

Setting the Omnichron to active scan before pocketing the device, he moved to the workstation configured for the chief engineer and verified the course for the Typhon anomaly was locked in. *Relativity*'s crew had no way to know the disruptions coming from this region were little more than a means to an end. The anomaly was just a single piece of the larger game the aliens were playing, waging war against time itself. Even if Wesley succeeded in destroying the thing, it was just one of the many resources his enemy could use or discard, it seemed, with casual ease. That they used it now offered no real insight into their true motivations, which remained unknown despite his ceaseless efforts. What he did know was that temporal oddities of this sort, even if barely understood by the sentient beings of this time period, still presented potential avenues of exploitation against whoever or whatever had set these events in motion. Wesley suspected his adversaries knew that, which is why they likely had used it here and now to assess Starfleet's threat potential, only to find it lacking.

All the while, they carried on with the larger scheme known only to them.

Time to shut this thing down for good, Wesley decided.

The ship was only capable of impulse speeds, but he calculated it would take less than five minutes at maximum power for *Relativity* to arrive at the selected coordinates within the Typhon anomaly. It was an eternity given the nature of the attack the ship faced, but there was nothing to be done about that. Detonating its warp core should be sufficient to collapse the temporal disruption here in this present and release a cascading effect across the time stream to its respective endpoints in this reality. There was no way to predict the effects, if any, on other branches of time. All he could hope for was that this most drastic of measures would put his adversaries back on their heels. Denying them this means of launching attacks across time would impede them, if only for a short while.

It took him a moment to understand the console's array of touch-sensitive and holographic displays, after which Wesley entered the command to set *Relativity* on its final course. That the ship might not reach its destination before the ghosts found their way to one of its sensitive systems remained an issue, but he had a plan for that. Putting it in motion required him to do the one thing he had consciously prevented from happening since his arrival.

"Warning," intoned the voice of *Relativity*'s central computer. *"Vessel self-destruct has been activated. All personnel report to evacuation stations immediately. Four minutes, forty seconds to detonation."*

Leaving engineering and stepping into the corridor, he allowed his physical form to complete its shift into this reality. No longer a simple observer to the events transpiring here or invisible to the denizens of this realm, he knew his hunters would also have no difficulty detecting him. Perhaps he could interest them in him and possibly hold their attention for just a few moments.

"Come and get me, boys."

Flashing alert indicators bathed the passageway in harsh crimson light, though the alarm klaxons remained silent. Members of *Relativity*'s crew scrambled ahead and behind him, heading away from the center of the ship toward escape pods or the shuttlebay. Some were armed with hand phasers or the larger rifle versions slung over shoulders or across chests. The ship's small size and utilitarian design, constructed as it was around the temporal warp core and other systems necessary for normal beings to travel through time, offered few options for evasion or protection in the event of a hostile boarding. Its crew, despite Starfleet training, was simply not equipped or prepared for repelling such an attack, in particular an incursion from the enemy it now faced.

From the ship's intercom, *Relativity*'s computer droned, *"Warning. Vessel self-destruct in three minutes, thirty seconds. All personnel report to evacuation stations immediately."*

Wesley heard the sounds of fighting and terror as he approached a four-way junction in the passageway. He halted his advance as he saw a trio of *Relativity* crewmembers, two humans and an Andorian, back-stepping into the junction from another corridor to his left. One of the group wielded a hand phaser and fired at an enemy Wesley could not yet see, the beam streaking away out of sight. A familiar rush of air and a whine of energy he knew all too well filled the air just as the trio scrambled around a corner. They continued moving backward up the passage, but now they were vulnerable, caught in a straight stretch of corridor.

A moment later another of the ghosts moved into view.

Like the other intruders, it was dressed in the same style of dark robes. It did not continue its pursuit of the *Relativity* crewmembers, for now it had a new target: Wesley. No sooner did the intruder see him than it raised its right hand in his direction. The hand was already beginning to glow with energy the ghost commanded.

"Get down!"

Wesley's shouted warning toward the *Relativity* officers came at the same time the computer offered another of its monotone updates. Lifting the disruptor, he fired in a single smooth motion. Once more the weapon spat forth a churning ball of violet fury that struck the intruder's hand. The effect coursed up the ghost's arm to envelop the rest of its body. It wavered, buckling in the face of the assault when Wesley fired a second charge. This time the strike was sufficient to shred the ghost's entire form. He heard not a sound from the creature before it disintegrated.

"Who are you?" asked one of the humans, a woman with disheveled hair and uniform. Wesley sympathized with her shocked expression, knowing what he must look like to them. Long hair, almost white, fell below his shoulders, accompanied by a thick, unkempt mustache and full beard. What skin was visible on his face was beset with deep lines, each one harboring a story he had no time to tell.

"*Warning,*" said the computer. "*Vessel self-destruct in one minute, thirty seconds.*"

"You have to leave." Wesley gestured with his disruptor down the corridor behind them. "Get off the ship while you still can."

The woman's Andorian companion eyed him with disbelief. "But what about—"

"*There's no time for anything!*" Wesley's fervent command echoed in the passageway. "You can't save the ship. Grab whoever you can on the way but get to an escape pod. *Now!*"

He could see by their expressions the officers were in the grip of the crippling fear evoked by the intruders and permeating whatever remained of *Relativity*'s crew. It was interfering with their ability to reason and triggering fight-or-flight responses that only hindered their ability to react to the threats confronting them. His barked instructions had penetrated that veil of anxiety and uncertainty, but Wesley knew it would not last.

Movement beyond the beleaguered crewmembers caught his attention, and he looked past them to see another of the ghosts gliding up the passageway. Its arms already extended, it was on the officers before any of them had a chance to react. The Andorian officer was the first one touched, and Wesley could do nothing but watch him cry out in pain as his body convulsed before crumbling in on itself. Wesley sensed the transfer of energy from prey to predator, and he had to fight back a wave of queasiness at the helplessness of it all.

The Andorian's two companions tried to move out of the way even as Wesley raised his disruptor, but they were much too slow. The ghost already had them in its grip and their bodies began putrefying before Wesley howled in rage and fired his disruptor. Without waiting, he followed with a second shot and both salvos drilled into the intruder with sufficient force to knock it back from its victims. The *Relativity* crewmembers were already lost, as Wesley felt their neural energy siphoned away while their decaying corpses dropped to the deck, so he fired again. This third strike was enough to rip through the ghost's body before it disappeared altogether.

Only then did Wesley realize he had walked into a trap.

In his pocket, the Omnichron beeped its warning just before he sensed the dimensional shift an instant before a quartet of the intruders—what should be the final four of the group that had attacked the ship—appeared in the passageway. Two emerged from bulkheads, one appeared from the corridor junction that was now behind him, while the last one rose from the deck plating. Only after moving into view did their bodies solidify as they completed their transition to this plane of existence. How had he not sensed them maneuvering on him? It was now obvious to him that the other two intruders, with no other real reason to be in this part of the ship, along with their victims, had been a diversion, buying time for their companions. So caught up had Wesley been in the plight of the hapless crewmembers that he had lowered his guard.

"Well played."

If the intruders heard him, they offered no indications of understanding or caring. The pair who had come out of the walls moved together, advancing on him before halting in place as the ship shuddered around them. Wesley knew what it meant. *Relativity* was entering the Typhon anomaly's outer boundary. Less than a minute remained before it reached its destination. There would now be no stopping the vessel's final act, so why were the intruders still here?

In that moment, realization struck.

They're here for me.

The thought screamed in his mind just as the first attack came from behind him. He sensed it in time to begin shifting out of this reality, which was the only reason the ghost's arm passed through him rather than touching him. Stepping clear of his assailant, Wesley brought the disruptor around and leveled it at the intruder's back. The first round fired as he shifted back, the weapon's energy discharge catching the ghost just below its neck and sending it sailing down the corridor toward two of its companions.

He could not sustain this action. Not here, not now. From his pocket he heard the Omnichron emit a string of alert tones, telling Wesley the device was picking up temporal variations. A possible link to these creatures' origin point? A trail he might follow?

"Warning. Vessel self-destruct in thirty seconds."

He felt the remaining ghosts moving in. Beyond the ship's bulkheads, he also sensed *Relativity* arcing toward its final fate. His opponents reached for him.

"Warning. Vessel self-destruct in ten seconds."

As he had done uncounted times before, Wesley hurled himself from this moment in time and space and plunged headlong into the void.

13

Lifting his head toward the rich blue-green sky, Picard closed his
eyes and relished the warmth of the sun on his face. He listened
to the sounds of gentle surf washing over his feet along with the
rest of the fine white sand covering this stretch of beach. A light
breeze played across his skin, and he allowed himself a sigh of con-
tentment. For the first time in longer than he could remember, a
genuine sense of serenity seemed to embrace him. He had not felt
this way even during the *Enterprise*'s most recent visit to Earth.

"Your smile is even brighter than your legs," said Beverly
Crusher, from somewhere behind him. Though Picard chuckled at
her observation, he remained where he was, relishing the moment.

"If I didn't know better," she continued, now drawing close
enough he could hear her footsteps in the shallow water around
them, "I'd think you were genuinely happy. I'd almost forgotten
what that might look like."

"You're not alone."

Although the captain had taken advantage of downtime to enjoy the fresh air both in San Francisco as well as the home at his
family vineyard in France, chasing relaxation proved an exercise in
futility. The specter of the board of inquiry hanging over his head
was more than sufficient to dampen any enthusiasm, but all of that
was now behind him. Earth, as it had been for the majority of his
adult life, was once again a distant planet, separated from him by
an ocean of stars within which he had always felt more at home.

"I was surprised to learn how many people we know who've retired here," said Crusher after a moment. "I'd never considered that before now, but I have to say it's pretty tempting."

That was enough to make Picard open his eyes and turn to regard his wife. Like him, she had eschewed her Starfleet uniform in favor of a much more comfortable ensemble. In her case, that meant a dark blue single-piece bathing suit with a silk sarong featuring a vinca pattern wrapped around her waist, and bare feet. Rather than looking at him, Crusher's gaze was focused on the ocean and the dazzling blue water stretching away from them toward the horizon. The breeze played with her bright red hair, and her mouth was set in a small, wistful smile. When her eyes moved to look at him, the smile widened.

"I'm just saying there are worse places to settle down."

Although retirement was something he had considered on occasion—and with more frequency in recent years—he had never given much thought as to where he might find himself at the end of his Starfleet career. There was the château on Earth, but his sister-in-law, Marie, still lived there, overseeing the Picard family vineyards. Overcoming the loss of Robert, her husband, and her son, René, Marie had turned her attention to reinvigorating the Château Picard property and label. The vineyards now were more active and productive than they had been in over a century, owing to her seemingly tireless energy along with steadfast devotion and focus. Picard had no wish to encroach upon her accomplishments or space, assuring Marie during his last visit that the château belonged more to her than it ever had to him. Without question, it was her home.

"Career Starfleet officers retiring and relocating to a starbase?" asked Picard, offering a wry grin. "That's more than a little clichéd, isn't it?"

Crusher's right eyebrow cocked. "Clichés are clichés for a reason, my dear." She gestured toward the ocean. "Besides, this is a view I could get used to waking up to every morning."

Yko, an Earth-like planet in many respects, had served as the home for Starbase 11 since the late twenty-second century. Even with the encroachment of Starfleet ground installations and orbital docking facilities, the world retained its natural splendor. A constant tropical climate, brilliant blue oceans, and lush green forests made it an ideal world on which to establish a planet-based installation. Its location made it a hub for several patrol routes as well as merchant and passenger traffic, and the establishment of the starbase had attracted numerous civilian interests.

While a fair number of people had relocated to Yko as an escape from the bustle of more densely populated Federation worlds, there were those who saw the mercantile advantage of catering to such a large, permanent Starfleet presence. The small town originally founded at the outskirts of Starbase 11's terrestrial footprint had grown over the past century to become its own vibrant community. Picard knew many of the Starfleet personnel assigned to duty here opted to live in apartments and other housing located off base. In addition to being a popular shore leave destination for many a starship crew, Yko was a favored permanent relocation choice for those leaving or retiring from active Starfleet duty.

"As long as I don't end up playing shuffleboard," he said, "we can settle anywhere you like. However, I have no intention of retiring anytime soon." While he enjoyed respites such as this, to him it was nothing more than a brief hiatus. Soon, Picard would be back among the stars, bound for whatever discovery and fate awaited him.

"No shuffleboard." Crusher nodded. "I'll see what I can do."

The sounds of splashing made them turn to see René running in the surf toward them, dressed in a red sleeveless shirt and tan bathing shorts that fell to his knees. As instructed by his mother, he ventured just far enough into the water for it to cover his feet, which did little to prevent him from kicking up spray with every lunging step toward them. A broad smile lit up his face, and Picard noted flecks of fine sand on his skin and his hair.

"Is it time to eat yet?" asked René, arriving with one final leap and a splash that sent water upward in all directions. Picard forced himself not to retreat as water pelted his dark shorts and jade-green shirt.

"What about your construction project?" asked Picard. Gesturing behind the boy, he indicated the beginnings of a modest sandcastle taking shape in front of the pair of outdoor recliners and the large umbrella shading them from the sun.

René shrugged. "I can finish it later. Can we go to the place where they cook the food while you watch?"

Among the first to disembark the *Enterprise* following its arrival at Starbase 11, Crusher and René wasted no time exploring the small cluster of seaside villas she had chosen for their shore leave stay. By her estimation, they had been on the planet surface for less than an hour before finding the beachfront restaurant. Picard could not remember the name or even the cuisine the establishment offered and neither did he care. What he did recall was his son's excitement upon learning cooks prepared the meal right at their table. The ingredients were replicated, but the cooking was conducted by chefs employing a mix of presentation and performance. For Picard, the boy's enthusiasm was enough to seal the deal.

"I think we need to investigate this for ourselves," he said, gesturing down the beach. "Do you remember where it is?"

Jogging past him and Crusher, René looked over his shoulder toward them. "I know the way. Follow me!"

Crusher eyed Picard. "A natural-born explorer. Wonder where he gets that?"

Holding hands, they set off after their son, but at a more leisurely pace as they continued to walk on the wet sand that was occasionally visited by a gentle ocean surge. There was nothing ahead of them but open beach for at least a quarter of a kilometer, populated by a few dozen people scattered across the sand either individually or in groups of two or three.

"He seems to have shaken off whatever it was that bothered him before," said Picard. "Has he said anything to you?"

"Not a word." Crusher brushed locks of windblown hair from her face. "It's like it never happened. I asked Doctor Tropp to give him a full neurological scan and he didn't find anything wrong. René is a perfectly healthy six-year-old boy."

"He'll be seven before we know it," replied Picard. "And in the wink of an eye, he'll be off to university or the Academy. Or maybe he'll do neither of those things." While Picard the Starfleet officer might be pleased to see his son follow in his parents' footsteps, Picard the father—and the dreamer—hoped René might defy all expectations and forge his own path.

Another family tradition, Picard reminded himself.

Squeezing Crusher's hand, he asked, "And how are *you* feeling?"

"Fine." To Picard's ears the reply seemed to come just a hair too fast, but he remained silent as she continued, "I had Tropp do the same scans on me, and again there was nothing. I've had odd moments where I thought about Wesley before, but never anything like this. It was much more powerful, almost focused. Normally I'd chalk it up to being tired or just missing him, but with what René experienced, I have to wonder."

The captain long ago learned not to chalk up such things to happenstance without further information or evidence. For now, he would trust the judgment of both *Enterprise* physicians, who had pledged to keep him updated about any changes no matter how minor.

"Do you think Wesley was trying to communicate with you?" he asked. "Or René?"

Crusher shrugged. "Maybe. He's done it a few times before, but it never felt like this." She blew out her breath before straightening her shoulders and reaching over to pat his arm. "Kids. Once they're grown and they leave home, they never call or come home often enough. Something else you have to look forward to, *Dad*." When she smiled, Picard could tell it was forced, but he opted not to comment before she changed the subject. "I suppose you're getting a little taste of that now, aren't you? How are *you* doing?"

"I don't understand." The question caught Picard by surprise. "What do you mean?"

"It's not that big a ship, Jean-Luc. News and gossip travel fast. The word's out about Worf, and Geordi, and Chen, along with a few other people."

"If only starships could travel as fast as any rumor." Picard regarded her with a knowing look. "So far as I know, no one's made any decision yet." Following his meeting with Worf, while the ship was still en route to Starbase 11, he indeed had been visited in separate meetings by Geordi La Forge and T'Ryssa Chen, both of whom had felt compelled to discuss with him the offers of new assignments and opportunities they each were considering. He knew about them, just as he did any potential departure by a member of his crew. La Forge and Chen wanting to discuss their situations prior to making any decision was a testament to their loyalty not only to the *Enterprise* but to him.

"I got the sense they wanted me to talk them out of leaving." He cast his gaze to the beach's exquisite white sand. "Or perhaps that was wishful thinking on my part. Regardless, I encouraged them to consider the decision objectively, not just for their career but also their personal lives. I know they would stay if I asked, and I'll be damned if I didn't actually consider doing just that. There was a time in my life where I would never have entertained such an idea; not for a moment."

Crusher replied, "There was a time when you'd never even consider having a family."

Despite forging several lifelong friendships with other officers and civilian professionals with whom he had served over the years, Picard had for most of his career taken comfort in maintaining a strict separation between his professional and personal relationships. The death of his best friend and Crusher's former husband, Jack, nearly thirty-five years earlier had played a large role in Picard reinforcing the barrier between those aspects of his life. Even though he had captained the *Stargazer* for twenty-two years, changes in the makeup of that crew over time saw to it he maintained a discreet professional distance even from those aboard that ship with whom he closely worked. It was not until taking command of the *Enterprise*—its predecessor, in fact—that he had begun to soften his stance, and only then after serving for several years with the cadre of officers comprising the ship's senior staff. He had now commanded two vessels with that storied name, and his combined tenure as the *Enterprise*'s captain exceeded his tour of duty aboard the *Stargazer*. Part of him wished he had learned to "lower his shields" many years earlier.

On the other hand, Picard considered that such a period of extended personal detachment had served a greater purpose. It allowed him to fully appreciate and even lament what he had sacrificed in service to his career. In turn, he now possessed the wherewithal to understand and treasure such bonds and the value and balance they brought to his life.

"We've spent so many years with these people," he said as they passed another couple on the beach. "They are as much family as anyone who shares our bloodlines. In some ways, even more so. It's taken me far too long to arrive at a point where I'm completely comfortable embracing that notion. I should have said or done something for them far sooner."

A fool, I was, he conceded. *At least there's still time to correct such pointless oversights.*

"And now some of them are thinking of leaving the nest." Crusher nudged him with her shoulder. "Welcome to parenthood, Jean-Luc. This started with you when Will and Deanna left for the *Titan*. Will was on the fast track to his own command even before you met him. Could've had his pick of nearly any ship in the fleet, and yet he stayed on the *Enterprise* for fifteen years because of you. Other people thought he was hurting his career. Even you thought that, but he didn't care because he wanted to learn from the one person he thought could best teach him about being the right kind of starship captain, and now look at him. You don't think you had anything to do with that?"

Picard grimaced. "Will forged his own path. I won't detract from his accomplishments by claiming I had anything to do with them."

"You did have something to do with them. You entrusted him with the job and provided the environment for him to learn and grow, just like you've done with all your officers. The rest was up to him, and he took the opportunity you gave him and ran with it. He's not the only one."

Never at ease with praise of this sort, Picard shook his head. "I did what a good leader is supposed to do."

Crusher replied, "Exactly. You gave them the opportunity to find their place and improve themselves. *That's* what good leaders do. Look at Geordi. He was a junior officer with an interest in engineering on a different career track when he got to the *Enterprise.* Now he's one of Starfleet's leading engineering minds. And Worf. Even with the reprimands in his record, there's no denying he's one of the best officers in the fleet. It took the admirals a while, but they're finally seeing it your way. Even T'Ryssa Chen's getting new assignment offers. There's practically an entire generation of Starfleet officers out there who owe their success to the example you provided and which they sought to emulate. You need to remember all of this when you finally get around to writing your memoirs."

Despite himself, Picard could not help a small laugh. "Now you're making me feel old."

"Age is a number, my dear," replied Crusher. "What do people say? 'Eighty-two is the new fifty-two'?"

"That's not what people say. I know no people who say that."

Tugging his arm, Crusher stopped walking and turned to face him. Her hand still grasping his, she raised it and gently pushed it against his chest.

"*I'm* saying it. I'm also saying you've done your job properly, *Captain*. The people you trained to be the leaders who will stand in your stead whenever you decide it's time to enjoy your well-earned retirement are more than ready to answer the call. They're not leaving you; they're carrying your legacy into the future." Now she pressed her other hand to his chest. "Meanwhile, you have another family who loves you, and another future for which to nurture and prepare someone."

She looked away from him and Picard followed her gaze to where René, who had run perhaps thirty meters ahead of them, was now standing on the beach looking at them. His smile was unabated, but it was obvious the boy was growing impatient waiting on his parents to catch up. For a brief moment Picard envied him: his innocence and the rich, full life he hoped awaited René in the years ahead.

That time will come all too soon.

Only when Crusher asked, "What?" did Picard realize he had said the words aloud. Blinking away the momentary reverie, he looked to his wife and smiled.

"Sorry. I was just thinking about—"

The rest of his explanation was lost amid a sudden rush of displaced air from above. Picard looked up and saw what appeared to be a hole in the sky, perhaps fifteen meters overhead, discharging a column of pale white energy down toward the beach. Sand and water erupted from the point of impact, forming a depression in the ground at least three meters wide. Beyond the disturbance, Picard saw René and other beachgoers retreating from the immediate area even as Crusher yelled for their son to stay clear.

"Jean-Luc," she began, then stopped as a dark object appeared from the aperture in the sky. Cloaked within a haze of energy, it did not descend as though in freefall and neither did it move as though under its own power. Picard's first thought was that it moved as if maneuvered by a tractor beam, controlled and directed with purpose. As the object slowed on its way to the newly created depression, the energy surrounding it began to fade, allowing Picard to make out what could only be a humanoid figure. It came to rest within the shallow basin, the column of energy dissipating as it withdrew back into the sky, taking the opening with it as though neither had ever existed. All that remained was the prone form lying on the sand.

"Beverly!" Picard snapped as Crusher rushed toward the unmoving figure, but he knew it was a futile warning. He sensed his wife was reacting as demanded by years of training and experience, to say nothing of her inherent desire to help anyone in distress.

By the time he caught up to her, Crusher was already kneeling next to the new arrival, whom Picard now could see appeared to be an elderly humanoid male. He was dressed in worn clothing, including a shabby brown leather jacket, clutching in his right hand a weapon of unfamiliar design. Long gray hair and a matching beard obscured his face and Beverly reached to brush aside some of the unkempt locks, only to freeze as she revealed the unconscious man's features. A gasp of recognition escaped her lips, and Picard's eyes widened in disbelieving comprehension as he regarded the man lying before them.

It was Wesley Crusher.

14

———

Falling.

Not falling, Wesley corrected himself. In point of fact, and at least so far as his abilities allowed him to navigate space and time, he knew on some level his movements were more akin to sailing, or perhaps gliding through the cosmos and its unending permutations of differing realities. For the first time in more decades than he could remember, he perceived the beat of his heart and the rush of blood through his veins. It was as if his humanity, that part of him that remained following his transformation into an altogether different and superior being, was attempting in these last moments to reassert itself. His strength ebbing, Wesley was only vaguely aware of universes emerging, expanding, living, and dying all around him.

Choosing one of these pathways and traversing it to a specific point was a gift without peer, and one he had never taken for granted. The Traveler who had served as his mentor taught him in those first years the unequaled measure of powers he had not granted Wesley but instead had seen within him. Coaxing those latent abilities, calling them forth and teaching his young protégé how to master and respect them, had been the Traveler's sole purpose, until such time as Wesley was ready to journey on his own.

Only then had Wesley been able to truly revel in being able to wander the stars, bearing witness to sights and events fated to remain unseen by others of his kind for millennia, if not forever. He had traveled to the limits of the universe, beholding the wondrous boundaries as defined by chaos and entropy before returning to favorite worlds to sit at the base of a tree and watch the gentle flow of an ocean's tides washing ashore at sunset. His perception of time, long ago unshackled from the conventions of linear thinking, allowed him to travel anywhere with but a thought provided his body could summon the power required to focus such notions and call upon the energy they demanded.

He felt his command of that energy slipping away.

Sensing the severity of his wounds, Wesley struggled to maintain focus. It was increasingly difficult to hold his destination in his thoughts as he slid across different realities. The lure of succumbing to his injuries and allowing himself to be swept away into some cosmic interstice grew with every passing moment.

Wait.

His goal was within reach. How long had he been traveling? An instant, and yet forever. What distance had he crossed? Nothing, and everything. Wesley felt at ease, but then his calm was shattered as pain threatened to overwhelm him. His body, at first evanescent, re-formed around him as every atom screamed in agony.

There was darkness ahead of him, broken only by a single point of light. Then the darkness was gone, and the light was all. Wesley saw nothing, his eyes useless in the void, but then sight returned and he beheld the one vision he hoped awaited him at the end of this, his final journey.

"Mom."

The word was a whisper, barely audible to Picard's ears as he moved closer to the impossibly aged man that could only be Wesley Crusher. Still kneeling beside him, Beverly was already at work inspecting him from head to toe in a frantic attempt to assess his condition. Her internal struggle was palpable, a tug-of-war between the physician and the mother whose firstborn son lay broken before her. There were obvious bruises and lacerations on the exposed skin of his face, neck, and hands, along with scars and discolorations indicating wounds sustained long ago. The man,

Wesley, attempted to raise one feeble hand but instead it fell to the sand beside him.

"Wesley," Picard began, but whatever else he might have said died in his throat. Feeling helpless, he could only study the older man's face, the matured yet still recognizable features of the young Wesley Crusher. Aside from that first hint of acknowledgment to his mother, he seemed to lack awareness of his surroundings. He muttered a litany of words and phrases that seemed to make no sense, in languages Picard did not understand.

"I need a tricorder," said Crusher, her tone professional though still laced with very human concern. "He may have internal injuries."

Still attempting to process, let alone believe, what was happening, Picard became aware of other beach visitors now coming closer. At least one was moving with greater purpose and determination, perhaps a doctor himself, jogging toward them from where he and a companion had been sitting in nearby beach chairs. Among these onlookers was René, the boy's gaze fixed on Wesley. Along with the shock evoked by the man's sudden appearance, Picard also noted the comprehension in René's face.

"Wesley?"

Picard reached for his son as he drew closer. "Wait. He needs our help." Reaching into his pocket, he retrieved his communicator badge and tapped it. "Picard to Starba—"

"Not . . . here."

The weak, almost inaudible plea came from Wesley, who had lifted his head and whose eyes now possessed a disquieting clarity. Despite his pain from whatever injuries he had suffered, he had forced himself to focus enough to utter those two words. Then the moment was gone. Wesley went limp, his head falling back to the sand as he resumed his incoherent mumbling.

"Beam us to the *Enterprise*," snapped Crusher, her hands and attention still on him.

There was no questioning her decision. While Starbase 11's

medical facilities might be superior to those onboard the *Enterprise*, Crusher's familiarity with the latter might decide the course of the next few minutes.

"Picard to *Enterprise*. Four for emergency transport directly to sickbay."

Over the open link, Commander Worf replied, *"Acknowledged. Stand by for transport."*

Within seconds, the beach disappeared in a flash of transporter energy and Picard along with René, Crusher, and Wesley materialized in the middle of the ship's sickbay. The room was already a flurry of activity with Doctors Tropp and Tamala Harstad directing a team of nurses and assistants in anticipation of an incoming emergency.

"Get him on the table," said Tropp, and Picard looked up to see the Denobulan pointing to the patient treatment table near the oversized diagnostic monitor dominating the room's rear bulkhead. Tropp along with Crusher and a pair of nurses worked together, lifting Wesley onto the table. Built-in scanners rose from its frame, arcing over the patient's implausibly aged body and connecting above his chest. This activated a restraining field around him, immobilizing him from the shoulders down and securing him for treatment.

"Initiating full-spectrum trauma scan," said the voice of the ship's computer.

With a gentle touch to René's shoulder, Picard guided his son away from the group gathering around Wesley, allowing his wife and her team to work. For her part, Crusher spared a quick glance over her shoulder, and when her eyes fell on René, her expression softened for a beat before returning her attention to her patient.

"It's all right, sweetheart," she said, and Picard heard the lie in her voice.

To his great relief, one of the nurses, a male Bolian whose name escaped him just now, approached him and offered to take René into Crusher's office. Grateful for the offer, Picard knelt so that he was eye level with the boy.

"Go with him, René. Your mother needs to work. I'll be along shortly."

Distressed yet understanding this was not the place for him, René responded with a small, uncertain nod. "Yes, Papa." The nurse led René into the office, leaving Picard to return his attention to where Crusher and her team continued working. Despite the overpowering urge to step closer, he forced himself to remain well out of their way so as not to impede their work.

"His internal organs look like they're in a state of flux," reported Doctor Harstad, who stood between the treatment table and the diagnostic monitor that now depicted a computer-generated representation of a humanoid male. Icons, pointers, and blocks of text scrolled across the display, highlighting the various bio-functions it now oversaw. Even without specialized medical knowledge, the monitor left Picard little doubt that the patient's condition was serious. Too many indicators flashed in bright crimson.

"His neural network is suffering from a similar effect." Harstad frowned at the information before her. "I can't get a solid lock on anything, but . . . can these readings be right? The scans say he's over three hundred years old."

If that fazed Crusher at all, she offered no hint of it. Instead, her attention remained on her patient and the scanners working to treat him. "It's some kind of cellular degradation, like nothing I've ever seen before. Almost as if—" Instead of continuing, she tapped additional instructions into the scanner's interface.

On the other side of the table, Tropp said, "An interphasic scan?"

"I think he's shifting in and out of phase." Crusher entered the commands necessary to initiate the scan. "We can't properly diagnose him so long as this keeps up. Get a cortical regulator on him. That might help stabilize his neural activity."

Brushing locks of long gray hair away from Wesley's forehead to apply the compact device, Tropp glanced to the diagnostic monitor. "Interphasic scans don't seem to be working. We could try a biospectral phase discriminator. Maybe that can isolate any quantum irregularities and stop him from shifting?"

"Good idea." Crusher entered the instructions. "I feel more like an engineer than a doctor, but right now I'll try anything." Looking up from the scanner, she turned to Picard. "We can't get a clear reading of his physiology. Whatever happened to him has thrown his entire molecular structure out of balance. His quantum signature keeps fluctuating as though he's caught between two different phases of reality."

Picard nodded. "Like the Traveler, when he was injured and trying to help us?"

He recalled how the mysterious being, a native of Tau Alpha C, had visited the *Enterprise*-D many years earlier, while ostensibly helping a supposed Starfleet propulsion expert, Kosinski, to improve the starship's warp-engine efficiency. That experiment had taken a startling turn when the Traveler, pretending to be Kosinski's assistant, inadvertently sent the *Enterprise* plunging at impossible speeds out of the galaxy and millions of light-years across the universe. With the aid of Wesley Crusher, then just a teenager, the Traveler was able to reverse the process and return the ship home. The experience served to underscore the vastness of space and time but also how intrinsically linked both were to the power of thought, especially in Wesley. It was to be the beginning of a journey that would transform one young boy's life.

And bring us to where we are. Picard could not help the bleak thought.

"Do you have any idea what caused his injuries?" he asked.

Her attention once more on Wesley, Crusher shook her head. "Not a damned clue. Whatever it was has affected him at a cellular level." She paused, studying the persistent stream of readings being fed to her via the table scanner. "Hang on. The degree of cellular disruption seems most concentrated in his upper right torso, near the shoulder." She tapped another key on the scanner's control pad. "Similar to a particle-based weapon, but I'm not picking up any kind of residual energy signature."

Picard considered the ramifications of what he was hearing. "Could he have been attacked by someone, or some *thing*?"

"I don't know that we can rule out anything at this point, Captain," replied Tropp.

The question seemed to catch even Wesley's attention, as the man's head jerked from side to side before his eyes opened. As he had on the beach, he began mumbling a string of incoherent syllables. Then he went limp and his eyes closed once more.

Is he trying to warn us? Wesley's reaction was enough for Picard. "Sickbay to bridge," he said, raising his voice for the benefit of the internal communications system. "Commander Worf, initiate a security scan of the entire ship. It's possible we may be facing an intruder situation."

"Aye, sir," replied the *Enterprise*'s first officer. *"Lieutenant Šmrhová is conducting the scan now. Do you have any further information, Captain?"*

"I wish I did, Number One." Picard spent the next moments updating Worf on the situation with Wesley and how he came to be in the ship's sickbay. "It's possible he's been attacked, and given the method of his arrival, I'm not ruling out someone or something following him in similar fashion."

Worf replied, *"Understood. I will apprise you of any updates, sir. Bridge out."*

No sooner did the channel close than Picard noted Crusher moving to the table's other side, her gaze now fixed on the interface set into that half of the scanner.

"The phase discriminator's having an effect, but it's marginal," she said. "His pulse is racing out of control. We need to get him stabilized before we do anything else."

"Improvoline," suggested Harstad. "Five milliliters, at least to start. It's a general sedative and should have some effect at lowering his pulse rate."

"If we can slow things down enough, maybe the shifting will subside," added Tropp. "We can try something more targeted once we get a handle on his condition."

"Agreed." Crusher entered the necessary command to administer the sedative before looking back to Harstad. "Any change?"

"No, Doctor." Harstad grimaced. "The improvoline metabolized almost as soon as it was introduced. I've never seen anything like it, but the readings are all over the place."

Tropp said, "What about increasing power to the phase discriminator?"

"That might push him too far the other way." Crusher was leaning against the patient table as she worked, propping herself on the scanner with her left arm. Picard saw that hand clenching to the point her knuckles were almost white, the only outward indication she was fighting to keep her emotions at bay. "Increase the improvoline dosage to fifteen milliliters."

When Tropp replied, his voice was quiet yet firm. "Doctor, that's approaching the safe limit without something else to mitigate its effects."

"His own body is mitigating the effects." Frustration laced her every word as Crusher split her attention between the table scanner and the wall monitor just as the latter flashed a new alarm at the same time Wesley began convulsing despite the table's restraining field.

"He's going into cardiac arrest," reported Tropp, gesturing to one of the nurses. "Cardiostimulator, now." Reaching for the scanner, he punched a control and the hum of the restraining field increased, forcing Wesley's spasms to subside.

Crusher added, "And increase improvoline to thirty milliliters." When Tropp began to protest, she said, "He'll likely metabolize it, but if I can get an idea of how fast that's happening, I may be able to figure out a correct dosage."

"We've never tried anything like it before," said Harstad, turning from the wall monitor.

It was Tropp who provided the unwanted voice of reason and finality. "We can't stabilize him, and his organs are shutting down. Anything we try at this point will take too much time."

"*Time.*"

The single word was weak and almost lost among the rush of Crusher and her team, but Picard heard it escape Wesley's lips. Moving toward the table, he extended a hand. "Wesley?"

His eyes open once again, Wesley seemed almost lucid as he raised his head from the table, apparently oblivious to whatever was happening to his body. He looked around the room as though unfamiliar with his surroundings, until his gaze fell upon Crusher.

"Mom?" His voice was weak and raspy, as if he were parched from extreme thirst, but it was enough to break through his mother's professional façade. She leaned close, resting her hand on his aged, lined face.

"Wesley. Is it really you?"

He managed a nod. "Been . . . away . . . a bit. Time . . . can't stop . . . Tried . . . fight . . . Can't . . . anymore . . . No future . . . *try again* . . ." Then, his eyes seemed to come into sharp focus as he stared at her. "I love you, Mom."

A chorus of alarms, beeps, and other brash tones erupted from all of the equipment monitoring Wesley as his head dropped back to the table and his eyes closed. His body jerked again as if from some new invisible attack, but the response this time was far more subdued. One of the beeping sounds, until now a steady beep that had increased in frequency as Wesley's readings changed, became a solid tone Picard had heard far too many times, often while standing in this room or one very much like it.

"No!" Pushing herself back to the scanner, Crusher slammed her hand against the unit's control pad. "Cardiostimulator, sixty microvolts." Her finger stabbed the control to initiate the procedure, and Wesley's body twitched in response to the direct stimulation to his heart.

Tropp, his voice level, reported, "No change."

"Doctor," Harstad began.

Ignoring them both, Crusher said, "Seventy-five microvolts." Wesley appeared not to react to the increased stimulus, his body absolutely still on the table.

Picard stepped closer. "Beverly."

"Doctor," said Tropp. "It's over."

Though her hand ceased its movements across the scanner, Crusher left it resting against the unit's polished black surface. She remained there, frozen, as Tropp, Harstad, and the nurses deactivated the monitoring equipment. Within seconds, the room was silent except for the low, omnipresent hum of the *Enterprise*'s engines and the soft, forcibly controlled yet anguished breathing of a grief-stricken mother standing over the body of her child.

Wesley Crusher was dead.

PART II

CROSSED WITH ADVERSITY

15

U.S.S. *Enterprise* NCC-1701-D
2373

His grip on the command chair's armrests tight enough he could feel his fingers beginning to tingle, Captain William Riker forced himself to relax. There was no way to be completely at ease just now, but the least he could do was avoid damaging the chair's compact control pads before his ship entered battle.

"Forty-five seconds to target," reported Lieutenant Sariel Rager from the flight controller's station. Glancing over her shoulder, she added, "Sensors show it's pretty crowded, sir. I'm adjusting our course to give us some breathing room."

Riker nodded in understanding before shifting in his seat to look up and over his shoulder. "Tasha, put Starfleet frequency one-four-eight-six on audio."

Standing above and behind him at the tactical station built into the large, curved railing separating the bridge's upper stations from the command area, Lieutenant Commander Natasha Yar replied, "Aye, sir. On audio."

The bridge was flooded by a string of conversations, orders, and status updates originating from multiple sources, to the point that Yar quickly adjusted the volume to make it tolerable, allowing Riker to sort out some of the more prominent reports.

"We have visual confirmation. Its course is zero point two-one-five. Speed warp nine point six. We're matching speed and trajectory but—"

"Stand by to engage at grid alpha fifteen—"

"They've broken through the defense perimeter. We need reinforcements—"

Rager reported, "Dropping out of warp in ten seconds."

"Route power from nonessential systems to deflector shields," ordered Commander Data, the *Enterprise*'s first officer, from his customary place in the seat next to Riker's right side.

"Acknowledged," replied Lieutenant Worf from the forward operations station next to Rager. "Shield generators at maximum."

"Weapons on standby," added Yar. *"All* of them, sir."

Riker sensed the shift as the ship's warp engines reduced power. On the viewscreen, the kaleidoscope of streaking stars shrank back to distant points of light as the *Enterprise* emerged from subspace. Utter chaos obscured them, filling the screen in the form of dozens of starships buzzing about a single, much larger craft: a Borg cube. A knot formed in Riker's gut as he beheld the massive construct. It was not his first time seeing one, but the fear he now felt brought to the forefront memories that already had been churning from the moment the *Enterprise* received word from Starfleet about this latest incursion.

Beyond the menacing vessel, Riker could not keep his gaze from lingering on Earth. Though still millions of miles away, it was entirely too close, with only these handful of starships attempting to mount a defense. As with the cube, the sight of his home planet served only to hammer home the reminder that he and his crew had been here before. In the wake of the disastrous battle at Wolf 359 seven years earlier and the huge toll it had taken on Starfleet— including the personal tragedy visited upon the *Enterprise* and its crew—preparations for another engagement proceeded apace. Repairing or replacing the thirty-nine ships lost that day naturally presented its own challenges, but the more than ten thousand lives taken were gone forever. Starfleet had come within a hairsbreadth of losing not only Earth but perhaps the entire Federation, and though they had won the day, the victory had come at tremendous cost. Despite himself, Riker could not help thinking of the one life whose absence aboard this ship was keenly felt every day, even more so right now as he studied the Borg cube dominating the viewscreen.

He almost flinched as a hand came to rest atop his, and looked to his left to see Commander Deanna Troi, ship's counselor and his wife, studying him with obvious concern. Under normal circumstances, Riker would discourage such an overt display of personal affection on the bridge, but just as she could read his emotional state, he also sensed her worry for him.

"I'm all right," he said, keeping his voice low. "It's just . . . been a while, is all."

And yet, not nearly long enough. It never will be.

"We knew this could happen someday," replied Troi. "That doesn't make it any easier."

Feeling his jaw tighten, Riker drew a deep breath. "Actually, it makes it a lot easier." Rather than allow his churning emotions to get the best of him, he would redirect that energy where it was needed: on the enemy who had taken from them a beloved leader and friend.

"Captain," said Yar from behind him. "The ionizing effects of the Borg weapons are creating localized distortions that are affecting communications. I'm picking up what appears to be a targeted disruption of the Starfleet comm frequency. I think the Borg are trying to break in."

No sooner did the security chief make her report than the background chatter from the other starships faded, replaced by an ominous tone and a voice that was at once new and yet grimly familiar.

"We are the Borg. Lower your shields and surrender your ships. We will add your biological and technological distinctiveness to our own. Your culture will adapt to service us. Resistance is futile."

"They're using Captain Picard's voice," said Worf, and Riker saw the Klingon's hand clenching as it rested atop the ops console.

Data said, "Although it is an intriguing psychological strategy, it seems unusual for the Borg to employ it. However, we know from our previous encounters with them that the Collective's adaptive ability goes beyond mere technological assimilation. Captain Picard was an excellent tactician, possessing a capacity to place his opponents at a psychological disadvantage."

"You're saying they learned how to mess with people's heads? They're doing it because they know we'll react emotionally." Riker knew it was true, because he also had felt that brief glimmer of despair, but he refused to let it distract him. Instead, it only hardened him for the coming battle. Riker looked around the bridge, making eye contact with each of his officers, including an extended moment shared with Troi.

Rising from his chair, he moved to stand behind Worf and placed a reassuring hand on the lieutenant's shoulder. "They want us angry or afraid because they've studied us. They know how we feel about Captain Picard, and they think they know how we'll react. It's okay to be mad, people. Just be sure to channel that anger where it belongs. The Borg took Captain Picard from us, and we're long overdue for some payback." He turned back to facing the viewscreen and the Borg cube displayed upon it. "Conn, take us in."

The image on the screen shifted as the *Enterprise* altered its trajectory to maneuver it deeper into the fray. All around the cube, smaller starships made strafing runs as they fired phasers and quantum torpedoes at the immense vessel. Riker could see the attacks were having negligible effect. Even with the new model of torpedo, designed specifically to fight the Borg, along with the phasers' ability to automatically and randomly alternate resonance frequencies, it was only a matter of time before the Borg defenses adapted.

This is what you've been waiting for, Riker reminded himself. *This is what Picard—the other Picard—prepared you for.*

"Captain," said Yar, "we're being hailed by the *Endeavour*, sir. It's Admiral Hayes."

"On-screen."

The image on the main viewscreen shifted away from the battle to show the weathered, anxious face of Jeremiah Hayes. Static filled the screen, a consequence of the interference with communications, and the scene behind Hayes was one of near bedlam. Various consoles offered an array of warning indicators. Crewmembers were moving about, doing their best to maintain control of a deteriorating situation, and then the *Endeavour*'s bridge shook as the starship absorbed what had to be only the latest of brutal strikes from the Borg cube. Hayes gripped the arms of his command chair as the image rocked and blinked, and sparks exploded from a console over his left shoulder.

"Enterprise! *We're down to minimal power and I've ordered all hands to abandon ship.*"

"Scan for escape pods," ordered Data.

On the viewscreen, Hayes said, *"We've got enough power for one more run. Captain Riker, take command of the fleet and provide cover for us. I'm setting controls for a collision course before we aban—"*

The admiral's visage along with the *Endeavour*'s bridge disappeared in a flash of intense white light before the viewscreen image shifted to show the beleaguered vessel. It vanished in an abrupt release of unrestrained fury, beginning with a pinpoint of hellish white-blue erupting from its engineering section and engulfing the starship within seconds. What little debris remained was flung away from the center of the explosion, but even that was already dissipating, leaving behind no evidence the *Endeavour* had ever existed.

"Their warp core breached," reported Yar, her voice low and somber. "Scans show about seventy percent of the *Endeavour*'s escape pods were able to launch. Other ships are maneuvering to pick them up, but most of them are still taking heavy fire from the Borg cube."

Riker choked down bitterness and growing anger. "How much damage are they inflicting on that thing?"

Studying the status monitor situated next to his chair, Data replied, "Sensors show it has sustained heavy damage to its outer hull, and I am reading fluctuations in their power grid. Most of that occurred during the battle's opening moments, but it appears the Borg are already adapting to our quantum torpedoes. More recent strikes show decreasing levels of damage. This is also true with the new modulating phasers. I estimate our conventional weapons will be useless within the next two to three exchanges of fire."

It's time, Riker decided. *We've got one more card to play.*

"Set a course for the cube," he ordered. "Route power from aft deflectors forward. I'm not counting on getting more than one shot at this." Turning to Yar at the tactical station, he drew a deep breath. "Tasha, bring the new torpedoes online. Two full spreads."

This was it, Riker knew. No matter what happened in the next few minutes, there was no turning back from the decision he had made, which was but the last in a long string of actions he had taken over the past several years to reach this point. It began with a chance encounter with Jean-Luc Picard, not the captain he once had known but instead another version of the man who in a different reality survived his abduction and assimilation by the Borg. In that parallel plane of existence, Picard commanded the successor to the *Enterprise*-D from a point several years in the future, a new and more powerful class of starship that benefited from a number of technological advancements as well as lessons learned fighting the Borg. The two ships and their crews—each with members both familiar and not to the other—along with a Romulan warship from still another reality and more than a century in the past, had been brought together by a freak series of events involving alien scientists and their experiments to travel between dimensions.

During their unlikely time together, Captain Picard and the crew of the other *Enterprise* did their best to observe the Temporal Prime Directive. The regulation forbidding Starfleet officers caught up in time travel incidents, particularly to any point in "the past," was supposed to help prevent one from doing anything that might affect the natural progression of the timeline. As his counterpart had been in this universe, the other Picard was a staunch protector of such principles. However, also in a manner befitting the captain Riker had known, he was not afraid to look past those rules and guidelines if it meant serving the greater good. Without divulging much in the way of details or reasons, let alone how such technology had come to be in his universe, Picard gave Riker specifications for a new form of weapon, a transphasic torpedo. He also offered that it had proven most effective against the Borg during a time of great crisis. Suspecting the Federation of this reality might one day face a similar challenge, Picard suggested this information be kept secret, with Riker trusting only those among his crew who could create the weapon from the schematics, until or unless circumstances allowed for no other option.

"Captain," said Troi, her dark eyes fixing him with a stare Riker knew too well. "Are you sure about this?"

"If we can't stop them here and now, Earth's a sitting duck." To Riker, there was no other option. "It's now or never."

"Transphasic torpedoes ready," reported Yar.

Riker nodded. "Send a message to the rest of the fleet. Tell them to break off their attacks, and retrieve as many escape pods as they can." To Rager, he said, "Conn, take us in."

Entering the necessary commands to her console, the lieutenant replied, "Aye, sir. Optimum firing point in fifteen seconds."

"Tasha, target the following coordinates and prepare to fire on my command." Riker recited a string of numbers committed to memory years ago, beginning with the first time he had read the information provided by the other Captain Picard.

Worf looked up from the ops console. "Captain, those coordinates do not appear linked to any vital system."

"Trust me, Mister Worf."

Just as the other Picard had not explained why he shared the transphasic torpedo schematics, he also did not enlighten Riker as to the nature of the specific location within the Borg cube. What he had said was that all such vessels were laid out in nearly identical fashion, and when the time came to deploy the new torpedoes, those coordinates should prove a most desirable target.

Assuming this even works, Riker reminded himself. His chief engineer, Geordi La Forge, had taken the information provided by the other Picard and adapted it for use with the weapons systems of the *Enterprise*-D's *Galaxy*-class specifications, but there had been no practical test of a working torpedo. For better or worse, *this* was the test.

His position behind both Rager and Worf gave Riker a full report of all ship systems. Dividing his attention between their consoles and the viewscreen, he noted how the other eleven starships were moving away from the cube, each describing different trajectories as they evacuated the areas in anticipation of whatever the *Enterprise* was doing. For its part, the Borg cube broke off firing at the retreating ships and refocused its defenses on the new threat. Energy flashed as the starship's deflectors absorbed the brunt of a new assault. Despite all of this, Riker counted down the seconds as the *Enterprise* closed the distance.

"Optimum firing range, Captain," said Rager.

"Fire torpedoes. Full spread."

Riker watched a quartet of bright red orbs launch away from the *Enterprise*, appearing from the bottom of the main viewscreen as they surged toward the Borg cube. Within seconds they converged on the chosen target and slammed into the side of the massive vessel. A hell storm of energy tore through hull plating and continued drilling into the ship, and a huge section of the cube's hull obliterated, spewing forth debris and vented atmosphere. Not waiting, Yar launched the second spread, and four more torpedoes bored their way through the fracture and unleashed still more destruction.

Examining his status monitor, Data reported, "Reading numerous secondary explosions, expanding from the point of impact. They appear to be having a cascading effect. I am detecting power fluctuations across the ship, including their main engines."

"Containment systems are failing," added Worf. "They're on a buildup to detonation."

"Conn," said Riker. "Back us out of here."

Rager began maneuvering the ship away from immediate danger, while the main viewscreen maintained its image of the Borg ship. Riker could see greenish energy appearing from numerous fissures in the cube's hull as the effects of the transphasic torpedoes continued to escalate. This was followed by more than a dozen eruptions across the vessel's surface, all of which were only the cube's death throes before the entire construct came apart, disappearing in a cloud of debris and violently released energy.

"Sensors are detecting another ship," said Yar. "Smaller, and spherical in shape, but it's definitely Borg. It has to be their version of a lifeboat, sir, and it's on a direct course for Earth."

Riker scowled as the viewscreen shifted to show the smaller vessel, its orblike shape simple yet as ominous as its larger, cube-shaped cousin. "Conn," he said. "Pursuit course. Tasha, prep another spread of torpedoes."

"Captain," said Data. "Our sensors are detecting chronometric particles emanating from the sphere. I believe the Borg are attempting to create a temporal vortex."

On the screen, Riker watched as a circle of roiling energy appeared, partially blocking Earth from view. To him it looked like a hole ripped through the fabric of space itself. The sphere's trajectory left no doubt it was heading directly for the new rift.

"Time travel?" asked Troi. "They can do that?"

His attention still on his monitor, Data said, "The vortex is stabilizing, and . . ." He looked up from his instruments. "I am detecting something coming *out of the vortex.*"

Before Riker could respond to the new information, his eyes fixed on a large, dark object emerging from the rift. Only when it cleared the tear's boundary did he realize it was not a single entity but instead several, each dozens of meters in length and moving together in tight formation. Their combined mass was still smaller than the Borg sphere but that seemed not to matter. Circling one another as they pressed forward, the new arrivals took aim at the sphere before striking it head-on. There were no explosions and no signs of impact. Instead, the things seemed to just lance through the Borg ship as though it was not there. As they exited its opposite side, the sphere fractured, splintering into countless shards of debris that continued on the craft's original course before disappearing into the temporal vortex.

"What the hell are those?" asked Riker, staring transfixed at the viewscreen's horrific image until he realized the things now appeared to be heading directly toward him. "Conn, evasive! Get us out of here!"

The order came too late as something—or several somethings—smashed into the *Enterprise*'s deflector shields. Despite the layers of protection, the force of the attack was enough to make the deck shift beneath him, and Riker grabbed onto the back of Lieutenant Rager's chair to avoid being thrown off balance. Lights flickered and he heard the sound of the ship's main engines warble in response to the assault. Then the bright illumination shifted to harsh crimson and a new alarm began wailing.

"*Warning,*" said the *Enterprise*'s main computer. "*Intruder alert, decks nine, twelve, twenty-one, twenty-four, and thirty.*"

16

―◆―

"Intruder alert. Deck twelve, section forty-three alpha."

Holding his phaser rifle across his chest, Worf charged toward the commotion as the *Enterprise* computer relayed its newest warning. It was difficult not to be distracted by the bodies of fallen shipmates all around him, but he pressed on. Whatever boarded the ship had moved through this section with ease, rebuffing whatever hasty attempts at resistance personnel here could mount with little or no warning.

A surprising aura of uncertainty gripped him, halting his advance. He searched for an enemy but found none. Then why did he feel . . . fear? There was a palpable energy in the air along with a fetid odor that reminded him of death, but Worf also sensed something else. A presence? It came upon him without warning, but he knew on some level this was not a natural reaction. It was too sudden, and without immediate justification. Intellectually, he knew it had to be the intruders, whatever they were, attempting to manipulate his emotions and provoke a response, perhaps even to somehow incapacitate him. Worf could not deny the impression was profound, despite a life spent learning to control such feelings in battle. Other members of the crew would almost certainly be affected to a greater degree. This seemed borne out by the increasingly erratic phaser fire coming from around the turn at the far end of the corridor.

Shadows danced in erratic fashion across the bulkheads as he drew closer, and he approached a final curve almost at a full run. Catching sight of the first salvos of phaser fire, he raised his rifle and sidestepped around the corner as the *Enterprise*'s assistant security chief, Lieutenant Christine Vale, and a male Tellarite, Ensign Ronlav, fired their weapons toward a figure in black, flowing robes farther down the corridor. The phaser beams passed through the intruder without inflicting any noticeable damage, and only then did Worf see that the figure seemed to be shimmering as though enveloped in a column of transporter energy or perhaps shifting in and out of phase. Its face shrouded by a large hood, black robes and shadows obscured the figure as it began moving forward.

Worf aimed his own phaser rifle at the intruder and fired. Once more, the energy beam passed through the figure, doing nothing to halt its advance.

"Pull back!" shouted Vale, slapping Ronlav on his shoulder before backpedaling up the corridor toward Worf, who stepped up in a bid to provide covering fire. Vale joined him, and Worf realized she had set her weapon's power level to maximum. It cut through the wall just ahead of the intruder and she guided it toward her target, but, as before, the attacker's form seemed to shift so that the beam passed through, chewing into the bulkhead behind it.

"Watch out!"

It was Ensign Ronlav, moving to put himself between Vale and the intruder just as it seemed to lunge forward. Moving with incredible speed, it reached out to touch the security officer. The Tellarite attempted to duck out of the way but his attacker was faster, appearing to solidify as arms clothed in thick, dark robes embraced him. Silver energy flashed from the point of impact, and Ronlav cried out as it expanded to sheathe him. Worf watched the ensign withering as if all the fluids in his body evaporated in an instant. Skin shriveled, cracked, and fell apart, revealing crumbling bones before he was gone, disappearing in an expanding cloud of particles that rained to the deck.

"No!" Vale fired her phaser again, though Worf knew it was a futile gesture. The weapons were useless against this adversary. He was certain Vale understood the situation, but he recognized she was lost in the heat of battle.

The intruder paid no heed to the weapon, continuing its advance until it was almost on top of her. Worf moved to pull her out of the way before she ducked to avoid the attack, pivoting toward him and extending her arm for him to grab. He could not get there before the figure's shadowy embrace swallowed her. Vale shrieked in pain, her body vanishing in a flash of energy. The echoes of her final screams were all that remained, filling Worf's ears as the intruder turned its attention to him.

From where he sat in his command chair, Riker studied the hellish vision on the bridge's main viewscreen. The vortex created by the Borg sphere seemed to turn back on itself and now was projecting energy in all directions.

"Data, what the hell is this thing?"

Having moved from his seat in the command well to one of the science stations at the back of the bridge's upper deck, the ship's first officer replied, "I cannot identify it, Captain, except that it is a temporal anomaly unlike anything previously recorded. Its chroniton readings exceed our ability to measure, but I am detecting waves of temporal distortions impacting the fleet's remaining ships and continuing to spread outward. Earth and the Moon are in the immediate path, and the waves show no sign of dissipation."

Mulling this as he rose from his chair, Riker asked, "Are you telling me this thing is sending out temporal distortion waves that can cross the entire solar system?"

"It would seem so, sir." Data turned from the workstation. "What I cannot explain is why none of the distortion waves seem to be targeting the *Enterprise*. I have examined the dispersal pattern as each new wave exits the vortex, and we are being avoided, sir. Deliberately."

Riker ascended the ramp to the bridge's upper level, moving to stand next to Data. "Why can't we track whatever these things are once they've boarded the ship?"

"The internal sensors are registering energy disruptions at the point of entry through the main hull," replied the android. "However, the life-forms themselves are somehow able to evade our scans. I suspect it is a form of temporal phasing. Our deflector shields have only limited effectiveness, and I suspect our internal force fields will not be any better."

"I can feel them," said Deanna Troi, rising from her seat next to Riker's chair. "But I'm not sensing any emotion like rage or a desire to kill. Whatever they are, it's like they're driven by simple determination. Pure focus. A will to accomplish some goal."

"Goal?" Riker frowned. "Killing all of us seems like the goal, but why? Are they just more Borg, or something else?"

Troi shook her head. "Definitely not the Borg. There's nothing like that here, except perhaps their desire to complete their objective is almost machine-like. Even with Borg drones, I can sense something, but there's nothing like that here. The only emotions I'm sensing are in our own people reacting to the intruders." She paused, wincing as if in pain. "Fear, panic, pain. Emotional reactions are spiking across the ship. People are terrified."

"Captain!"

It was Lieutenant Rager, looking up from her flight controller's station and pointing toward the viewscreen. On the display, Riker and everyone watched as one of the other Starfleet ships, a *Galaxy*-class vessel like the *Enterprise*, seemed to fall in on itself as a wave of energy distortion washed over it. Within seconds, two smaller vessels—from the few that remained of the fleet assembled to defend against the Borg cube—followed suit.

"The *Excalibur*, sir," reported Yar. "Along with the *Sao Paulo* and the *da Vinci*. The rest of the fleet is breaking off its attack and taking evasive action."

"Conn," said Riker, still reeling from what he had just witnessed. "Pull us back. I want some maneuvering room. Lay in a course for Jupiter Station and stand by for full impulse." Thinking about Data's earlier report, he added, "Just in case, have a fallback course for Starbase 7 and be ready to go to warp." Located in the Andor sector, the installation was one of several designated rally points in the event of an emergency requiring evacuation of the Sol system. Prior to today, it had been seven years since the option had even been contemplated during the Borg's previous attack on Earth. Before that, more than a century had passed since such a relocation was put into motion.

At least then we knew what we were facing. Riker chewed on that thought as he returned his gaze to the bizarre vortex on the viewscreen. Seven years earlier, a single Borg vessel had stood poised ready to inflict an all but mortal wound into the heart of the Federation. Now, in this moment, that enemy had been vanquished by something perhaps more powerful. Their attacks made those by the Borg pale in comparison.

"Data, is there any way we can close that vortex? Collapse it somehow?"

His fingers moving across the science station's console almost too fast for Riker to follow, the first officer replied, "Given the variables relating to its creation and whatever is powering it now that the Borg sphere has been destroyed, I am not certain conventional weapons or other resources at our disposal are sufficient to close or collapse it. However, we may be able to inflict sufficient damage to mitigate its effects. I recommend using our remaining transphasic torpedoes, detonated at equidistant positions around the vortex's event horizon. That placement would provide a consistent disruption across the fissure itself."

"Prep the torpedoes and program the firing pattern," ordered Riker. On the viewscreen, the vortex continued to spew forth its waves of temporal distortion. He couldn't help his mounting frustration at not knowing who was behind this apparent attack. What were their intentions? Whoever they were, how did they define victory? They were destroying ships, and now they were inside his own vessel. What could—

"Tasha," he said, struggling to order the frenzy of his thoughts colliding with one another. "Are any of the other ships reporting boarding attempts?"

Studying the information relayed to her station, the security chief shook her head. "I'm not seeing anything, sir. So far as I can tell, we're the only ship being attacked directly."

Before Riker could even try to ponder what this might mean, the ship's computer reported, *"Warning. Intruder alert, deck thirty-six. Emergency force fields activated."*

"Main engineering," said Yar, her attention focused on her console. "I'm routing security teams there now."

No sooner did she make her report than the ship's intercom blared to life. *"La Forge to bridge. We've got intruders down here! Protective force fields aren't stopping them!"*

The *Enterprise*'s chief engineer started to say something else before the sounds of phaser fire erupted from the speakers, followed by shouts of alarm along with alert tones emanating from the ship's engineering section. Panicked voices in the background were unintelligible, but there was no mistaking the fear behind the words Riker could not decipher.

"Warning. Coolant leak in main engineering. Magnetic locks ruptured. Antimatter containment field disruption."

"Geordi," called Riker. "Geordi, are you there?"

"They've disrupted the coolant system," shouted La Forge. *"I'm trying to get it back online but the bypasses are fused. If I can't stop the leak, we're looking at a warp-core breach inside of three min—"*

Static drowned out the rest of the engineer's report as the frequency went dead. Still working at the science console, Data turned to face Riker.

"Captain, I am detecting no life-form readings in main engineering."

Geordi? The question felt to Riker like a gut punch. *Everyone down there? Gone?*

"Warning," said the computer. *"Warp-core breach imminent. Estimated time to detonation two minutes, forty seconds."*

Troi said, "That's not enough time to evacuate the entire ship."

There was no need for such a declaration. Riker, along with everyone else on the bridge, had already reached the same conclusion, but hearing it somehow made it real. The harsh, brutal truth of the report served to underscore what was about to happen and how helpless any of them were to stop it.

On the other hand, they were not powerless to act with what little time remained to them.

"We're not going out without a fight," said Riker, moving from the upper deck to the command well to stand before the captain's chair. "Data, are the torpedoes ready?"

"Affirmative. Six torpedoes programmed and ready to fire at your command, sir."

From Yar's security console came a new tone, and the commander's expression darkened as she checked it. "Captain, new energy distortion waves coming from the vortex. They're heading for us."

"Conn, evasive maneuvers!"

Even as Lieutenant Rager began attempting to maneuver the *Enterprise* away from incoming danger, Riker cursed under his breath. Had their adversary somehow divined what he and his crew were planning? Could they stop it?

Don't give them a chance, he commanded himself.

"Antimatter containment field is at twelve percent," said Data. "Failure is imminent."

The entire ship shuddered around them. It was as though the *Enterprise* knew its own death was at hand. Only then did the finality of what was about to happen settle upon Riker. This was it, the end. Nothing could save them, but perhaps their final act might serve some purpose and save someone else from a similar fate.

He sensed Troi moving to stand beside him, felt her take his hand in hers as she gripped his arm. Pressing against him, she squeezed his hand, and her voice was in his head, soft and serene as she reached out to comfort him.

It's all right, Imzadi. *We're together. That's all that matters to me now.*

He shared a final, longing look with her, each comforting the other in these last moments before he redirected his gaze to the vortex roiling on the viewscreen. Bracing himself, Will Riker drew one last deep breath.

"Fire torpedoes."

17

U.S.S. Titan NCC-80102
2387

It was not her own dream that pulled Deanna Troi from sleep. Instead, it was her husband's.

She awoke, lifting her head from her pillow, perplexed in that first moment as her conscious mind reasserted itself and reoriented her to her surroundings. Despite the near darkness, it took her only an instant to recognize the comfortable environs of the bedroom in their family quarters. One of the *Titan*'s running lights was close enough it offered feeble illumination through the trio of viewing ports set into the room's sloping rear bulkhead, just enough light by which to see.

Beside her in their shared bed, Will Riker slept. She turned on her side to face him, resting her hand atop the sheets covering his chest. Although his body seemed relaxed, Troi felt the turmoil raging within the depths of his subconscious. Whatever he was feeling—or at least what he might be experiencing within the realm of his dream state—ran the gamut from fear to resolve and, ultimately, sadness. A grim determination seemed to grip that latter sensation, one Troi knew all too well thanks to their bond, forged nearly two decades earlier. Then she felt a surge of emotion an instant before Riker's eyes snapped open and he sat upright in the bed, releasing a gasp loud enough to echo within the room. Sheets fell to his lap and he was swinging one leg to the floor before Troi gripped his arm.

"Will."

Her voice was soft yet still carried enough force to halt Riker before he could push himself out of the bed. Returning to a sitting position beside her, he blinked several times in rapid succession, one hand reaching up to wipe his face. Troi repeated his name, at which point he finally seemed to snap out of whatever gripped him. He turned to look at her, his expression one of confusion.

"Deanna."

"You were dreaming." She squeezed his arm before pushing herself to a sitting position. Keeping quiet, she listened for signs that her husband's outburst might have awakened their daughter. Fast approaching seven years of age, precocious Natasha Miana Troi-Riker valued her sleep, and it would not do for her to come storming in here to investigate who or what had disturbed her slumber. Satisfied the young girl remained asleep, Troi began re-arranging the pillows behind her to act as a backrest.

Riker looked around their room. At first Troi thought he was doing what she had done upon awakening, reacquainting himself with his surroundings while pushing away any residual vestiges of sleep. This felt like something more. She sensed genuine confusion from him, as though questioning whether he should be here or somewhere else. After a moment, she felt him start to relax, though there remained a lingering hint of uncertainty. Pushing himself back so he could sit next to her, he reached for a glass of water on the table next to his side of the bed. After taking a long drink, he sighed.

"Some dream. I don't even know where to start." He cast another look around the room, and despite his attempt to hide it, Troi still sensed his uneasiness. "It was so real, so vivid, but at the same time it still had that odd, detached quality you normally get."

Troi shifted so she could lean toward him, pushing aside the sheets. "What do you remember?"

"We were on the old *Enterprise*. I think I was the captain. You were there, and so was Worf, and Data." Riker's brow furrowed. "And Tasha. We'd run into something that started attacking the ship. Wait, before that. We were fighting the Borg." He sat up straighter in the bed. "We were fighting the Borg cube at Earth, like we did . . . what? Fourteen years ago? But, Captain Picard wasn't there."

Troi watched him react as more of the dream came back to him. "We destroyed the cube, pretty much the same way we actually did it. The Borg Queen's sphere made a run for it and opened the temporal vortex, but something came out of it. Something came from the other side, destroyed the sphere, and kept coming until it hit us. It was like . . ." His voice drifted away as if losing track of the dream's remaining thread. "There's a lot that's blank after that, along with a sensation of falling. And shadows. I remember shadows of something. They were everywhere. And I feel like I was overcome with this sense of *defeat*. We were beaten, but I don't remember the end. I don't remember what happens after." He shook his head. "It's there, but I can't pull it in. Whatever it was, it's gone."

"Have you had this dream before?" asked Troi. "Or anything like it?"

Draining his glass, Riker shrugged. "No, I don't think so." Then, as if recalling some detail he had overlooked, he added, "Transphasic torpedoes."

"What?" Now it was Troi's turn to look confused.

"Transphasic torpedoes. I ordered them fired. From the *Enterprise*-D."

"But we didn't have those back then." As she spoke the words, realization struck. "Wait. You said Data, Worf, and Tasha were there, but it was years after her death."

Riker was nodding. "No, but Captain Picard gave them to us," he said, following her train of thought. "Well, a version of us."

"The alternate universe he told us about." It had been part of a larger, wide-ranging conversation during the *Enterprise*-E's most recent visit to Earth. Despite his returning home under less than auspicious circumstances, a board of inquiry held for his role in

President Min Zife's removal from office eight years earlier, Picard and Beverly Crusher had entertained Troi and Riker in their former captain's ancestral home in France. Over the course of that rather fine meal and even better wine from the Picard vineyards, Picard and Crusher recounted their bizarre encounter with an *Enterprise*-D from another reality; one in which Picard had not survived his assimilation by the Borg, leaving Riker to take over as captain of the ship. Prior to taking on the complicated task of returning the other *Enterprise* to its own dimension, Picard did something completely out of character for him. He had given that Riker schematics to manufacture transphasic torpedoes, a technology not yet developed in that other reality, as a future defense against a devastating Borg invasion that had not yet happened in that universe. Picard had done so, despite its being what could only be described as an egregious violation of the Temporal Prime Directive, because he had felt so strongly about possibly preventing what had happened in this reality from occurring anywhere else. Starfleet Command and the Department of Temporal Investigations had taken him to task for that breach of regulations, but ultimately had not seen fit to charge him. The sentiment on which he had acted was shared by many a senior flag officer within the upper echelons of Starfleet Command.

"That's an odd thing to dream about," Riker said. "Don't you think?"

Troi was not so sure. "Our dinner with the captain and Beverly was only a few weeks ago. Have you given much thought to it since then?"

"Maybe?" Frowning, Riker reached up to scratch his beard. "I know I thought about it a lot that night after we went to bed, but then things got busy and I can't honestly say if I gave it more than a passing thought since."

It was a reasonable reaction, Troi decided. As an admiral, Riker was a key advisor to Starfleet's commander-in-chief, Admiral Leonard James Akaar. In that capacity, he served as an amalgam of consultant, strategist, and troubleshooter, depending on the situation. As formidable as that role's demands were, they supplemented his primary duties as the sector commander for Starfleet's presence in the Alpha Quadrant frontier zone, a course the *Titan* was currently navigating. All of that was more than enough to occupy his waking hours along with an unhealthy portion of time that should be devoted to rest. There was no telling how the formidable amounts of information he was required to process might infiltrate his dreams.

Pushing himself out of bed, Riker retrieved his empty glass and returned it to the replicator set into the bedroom's far wall before ordering more water. He retrieved the new glass and downed its contents, then drew a deep breath.

"The whole thing just seemed so . . . *visceral*," he said, abandoning the glass to the replicator. "It's like I was really there. All the familiar sounds, everything. I can't remember having a dream that was so intense." He reached up to rub the bridge of his nose. "I don't know. Maybe I'm just tired, or working too hard, or all of the above."

Seeing an opening, Troi smiled. "Admiral Riker, working too hard? Is such a thing even possible? What will they say back at Starfleet Command?"

"That's privileged information, Counselor." With a grin of his own, Riker returned to the bed. "Counselor-patient confidentiality, and all that."

"Point taken." Her tone turning serious, Troi said, "On that subject, maybe you should talk to Doctor Ree. He could prescribe something to help you sleep. You know he's probably still up and in his office." The *Titan's* chief medical officer tended to keep late hours, using the quiet time late in the evening to ensure crew medical records along with other files and reports were up to date.

Riker rubbed her bare arm. "I don't need anything from Doctor Ree to help me sleep."

Ignoring the unsubtle suggestion, she persisted. "If not him, then maybe you could discuss your dream with Lieutenant Haaj or Doctor Hulian. Haaj is probably better suited to talking about dream interpretation than I am." Given what her husband had described, she suspected a conversation with Pral glasch Haaj, the burly Tellarite who served as one of the *Titan*'s two other counselors, would be an animated one.

"I'll think about it," said Riker, doing her the favor of not outright rejecting her idea. "It's just one dream, but if it happens again I'll let you know."

Troi eyed him. "Chances are good you won't have to tell me."

They adjusted the sheets and resumed their places in the bed, with Troi resting her head on his chest. Despite his earlier playful comment, Riker relaxed with his arm around her, and within a few minutes she heard his breathing change, indicating he had once more fallen asleep. Even in that brief interval as he crossed from wakefulness, she sensed his fading uncertainty, but after another moment even that was gone.

However, she was wide-awake and considering not just what her husband had said, but what he had felt. No, she decided. What he had *experienced*, at least so far as he was concerned.

What did it mean?

U.S.S. *Enterprise* NCC-1701-D
2373

From where he stood near the door leading to the observation lounge behind the bridge, Wesley Crusher shrouded himself from Captain Riker and his officers by shifting just far enough out of this dimension to render him invisible to them as well as the ship's internal sensors. He could not prevent the *Enterprise*'s destruction. He could only hope it would not be for nothing.

Though he did not know this version of the people he had come to love like family, that lack of personal connection would do nothing to lessen the impact of their looming deaths. The pain would be no different from the other occasions he had beheld similar scenes. How many was this? Five? Fifty? The number had long ago ceased to matter, even those occasions where he had watched another Will Riker, Deanna Troi, Geordi, Captain Picard, or even his own mother meet similarly violent ends. Forced to accept the brutal, unrelenting truth of what he had seen in those other realities, he also had no choice but to concede he had no power to prevent what was going to happen.

At least, not yet.

Each instance he endured—every tragic end, whether to strangers representing a previously unknown race or members of his own species and even now with yet another iteration of people he knew and loved—brought with it the opportunity to learn more about whatever was responsible for such wanton destruction on an unparalleled scale. Every encounter carried with it the potential he might discover how to defeat this adversary. Wesley could only hope the deaths he witnessed along the way, far more than he could easily count, ultimately would not be wasted. This included all those aboard the *Enterprise* facing its demise.

Wesley had sensed the Borg's creation of the temporal vortex at this position in time, and the maelstrom's subsequent hijacking by the unknown entities that had haunted him all these years. After the Guardian planet encounter with the strange humanoid and the creatures it commanded, he had begun formulating theories about how these beings moved. Temporal portals, naturally occurring as well as those created by artificial means, seemed to attract them. His initial encounter with the mysterious humanoid just five years earlier—objectively speaking, but decades ago from his own unique perceptions of time's passage across multiple realities and permutations—indicated to him these creatures were not dependent upon existing phenomena of this sort. Even during that initial encounter, he figured they must employ their own means of traversing time. This latest appearance only cemented his belief, but what drew them to other temporal anomalies, like the Guardian or the Borg-created vortex?

Standing mere meters from her, though she was totally oblivious to his presence, Wesley watched as Tasha Yar—only slightly older but still the striking blond woman he remembered from so long ago when he was an awkward teenager during that first year aboard the *Enterprise*—carried out Captain Riker's orders.

"Firing torpedoes." On the main viewscreen, five pulsing orbs of hellish energy made their way toward the yawning vortex.

At the same time, Commander Data, an odd sight in his maroon command division uniform, studied information at the rear science stations. "Captain, incoming temporal distortion waves. They will most certain—"

The entire ship rocked as the energy field struck, overcoming the *Enterprise*'s deflector shields and slamming into the hull. Wesley watched as the bridge started crumbling at the exact moment the barrage of transphasic torpedoes detonated as they reached their targeted positions along the vortex's event horizon. He was able to glimpse the utter futility of the attack as the weapons' effects were neutralized by still more surges of temporal displacement. Riker and the others did not even have time to register their failure before the viewscreen cracked and went dark. All of the workstations blacked out just before the bridge's transparent dome shattered, exposing the crew to vacuum. Then the *Enterprise* was collapsing on itself, crushed by unrelenting surges of time that snuffed it out in an instant before continuing to expand away from the vortex.

Wesley did not need to see what he knew would happen next, as he had already observed scenes like this far too many times. Earth was already coming apart with the Moon close behind. The rest of the Sol system would be next, the effects of destruction escalating and accelerating with every passing moment. This reality was doomed. A splinter, a permutation veering away from another, far more stable timeline, its demise was all but preordained. There was nothing more for him here.

Marshaling his abilities, Wesley prepared himself to move to another reality when he sensed . . . something? It was unknown and yet familiar. Was it calling to him? He reached out with all the awareness he could muster, probing the cosmos. There, he felt it growing in intensity as if responding to his attempts to find it. Sudden clarity gripped him and Wesley now sensed where he needed to go.

Home, he realized. *After a fashion.*

18

———◆———

From his seat at the head of the conference table, Picard listened to the ever-present drone of the ship's engines, made all the more noticeable thanks to the otherwise heavy silence engulfing the observation lounge. He had interrupted no conversation when he entered the room to find Worf, Geordi La Forge, and Beverly Crusher waiting for him. Aside from the usual courtesies extended his way upon his arrival, no one had said anything. The obvious cause for the somber quiet currently gripping his senior staff was no different from his own swirling emotions. Crusher, who had barely acknowledged him as he took his seat at the table, offered a furtive glance in his direction before returning her gaze to where her hands lay clasped in her lap.

"I empathize with what you're feeling," he said, after allowing the silence to continue uninterrupted for an additional moment. He let his gaze linger on his wife. "I would be lying if I said I wasn't wrestling with this myself." It demanded at least some consideration, and Picard had no greater wish than to afford his officers—his friends, and indeed his family—the time and space for such reflection.

Allowing a small interval after Picard's statement, Worf said, "Admiral T'Raan has contacted us again, requesting a follow-up report from you about what has transpired." He seemed uneasy as he added, "It is her third request, sir."

Picard almost grimaced at his first officer's report but managed to hold his bearing; the reminder made him cast his gaze to the lounge's observation ports, where the planet Yko still spun as the *Enterprise* maintained its orbit. He had made a report to Starbase 11's commanding officer in the immediate aftermath of Wesley Crusher's sudden arrival and subsequent death. The hours since then had been spent simply coming to terms with what had happened and awaiting any sort of useful information that might shed light on the otherwise inexplicable events. It was not his intention to keep T'Raan waiting any longer than necessary, but at the moment there was nothing more to tell her.

Except that there's nothing more to tell her. Picard was certain the admiral, a Vulcan, would find as little humor in such a report as he would attempting to make it. Better to use the time and energy searching for something worth reporting.

"I will advise Admiral T'Raan following our meeting," he said. "But first, there are a great many questions before us, and I hope our attempt to find answers will help us process what we've experienced."

Clearing her throat, Crusher shifted in her chair, moving to rest her forearms on the conference table. "Doctors Harstad and Tropp have completed an examination of . . . the body. According to their findings, he's at least four centuries old. There were also residual chroniton- and quantum-fluctuation readings indicating he had undertaken extensive temporal displacement over an extended period of time. Years, perhaps even decades." She paused, as though pondering what she had just said. "That seemed to introduce its own set of abnormalities."

Picard frowned. "Abnormalities?"

"At Doctor Crusher's request, I examined the scan records, sir," said La Forge. "We know from past experience with alternate realities and time streams that all matter within a given reality resonates at a consistent quantum signature unique to that universe. Based on the readings Tropp and Tamala—I mean, Doctor Harstad— recorded during their examination, Wesley's quantum signature appeared to be in a state of flux. This indicates prolonged exposure not just to other quantum realities but also time travel and perhaps even temporal weapons."

Worf turned to face the chief engineer. "Temporal weapons?"

"It's a guess, but I don't know what else to call it." La Forge leaned forward in his chair. "Wesley's injuries included temporal disruption at the atomic level. Rapid aging, offset to varying degrees by what I can only guess are attempts to heal older wounds. I can't even tell if some wounds actually were older, or affected somehow by his moving through different time streams. It could be a consequence of technology he had at his disposal, or something used against him by someone else, or even some natural ability he possessed as a Traveler."

Picard asked, "Do we have any idea where he came from? Or when?"

Shaking his head, La Forge sighed. "I'm afraid we don't, sir."

"He didn't have a chance to say anything," said Crusher. "It all happened so fast, and he was incoherent most of the time." She raised her gaze to meet Picard's once again. "Except for that moment at the end."

There had not yet been any real opportunity for Picard to talk in private with her following what had happened in sickbay. Following Wesley's death, she had remained in her office, studying the scans and test results gathered by Tropp and Harstad as they conducted their autopsy. Picard's initial attempts to engage her were met with gentle refusals as she cited the importance of understanding the information provided by the examination.

Only able to imagine what she must be feeling, Picard considered postponing the briefing until she had more time to process what had happened, but he stopped himself. Crusher would resent being perceived as unable to carry out her responsibilities despite her personal grief. Further, he knew her well enough to be certain she would push through this. Compartmentalizing her feelings, Beverly would devote her energy to doing what she could to help answer the myriad questions raised by Wesley's appearance. Despite this, Picard had to believe she shared his own bewilderment at the loss of her son, someone she had last seen as a man barely approaching middle age, while trying to cope with the knowledge that he had lived for centuries.

And what of Wesley? What had he been doing all that time? Where had he gone, and what had he seen? Picard marveled at the possibilities of the incredible life he must have led and the sights and wonders he likely had beheld. As he lamented Wesley Crusher's death, so too did Picard regret the opportunities lost to simply sit and talk with the astonishing man he once had known as a wide-eyed, curious teenager. He recalled their first meeting that fateful day aboard the previous *Enterprise*—little did Picard know what a profound impact that boy would have not just on his life but uncounted other lives.

"He must have come to us for a reason," said Worf. With a glance to Crusher, he added, "He *is* a Traveler, and could have gone anywhere in the universe. If the scans of his quantum signature are correct, he apparently could have gone anywhere in any *other* universe. It stands to reason he came here, to us, for a specific purpose."

Picard considered his first officer's point. "The abrupt nature of his arrival obviously suggests something extraordinary." He turned to Crusher. "Doctor, forgive me for asking yet again, but you're certain you've had no recent contact with him?"

"No." She paused, looking around the room as though searching for something. "There have been times when I thought he might be nearby, or maybe it was just a feeling that he might be . . . I don't know . . . checking up on me or even looking in on René, but of course I can't be sure." When she smiled, Picard could tell it was forced. "Or maybe that was just a mother's wishful thinking."

There had to be something, Picard decided. Too many questions lingered for which Wesley—his body, at least—along with his clothing and personal belongings, might provide answers. Picard knew Crusher was aware of this, and to that end, the autopsy had been noninvasive, utilizing medical scanners and other equipment to record every possible detail. With the exam completed, Wesley's body was now being held in a medical stasis chamber in sickbay until the next step could be decided. Doctor Harstad had discreetly informed Picard that Crusher had spent some time in the morgue following the autopsy. He had kept this information to himself, respecting his wife's privacy as she struggled with what must be enormous shock while laboring to understand the circumstances that had brought her son to her in such grim fashion.

The ship's intercom beeped, followed by the voice of Lieutenant Commander Taurik. *"Engineering to Commander La Forge."*

"La Forge here. What is it, Taurik?"

The assistant chief engineer replied, *"My apologies for interrupting you, sir. One of the objects that belonged to Mister Crusher has . . . activated."*

Picard led his officers from the observation lounge to main engineering. Whenever he entered the busy section, he took a moment to glance about the multilevel compartment, noting members of the engineering staff immersed in their various duties. The pulse of the warp core at the center of the room was even more evident here, the heart that gave the *Enterprise* its power and speed, but also saw to the protection of the fragile beings who called the vessel home.

Now back in his domain, La Forge moved to where Taurik, along with Lieutenant T'Ryssa Chen, stood inside an alcove set into the room's starboard bulkhead. Ever the stoic Vulcan, Taurik stood with hands clasped behind his back as he awaited questions or instructions. Chen, her dark hair pulled back from her face and held in a tight ponytail, stood next to him, also affecting a cool and professional bearing. Nevertheless, Picard could tell from her expression that the current situation bothered her.

The engineering nook contained consoles as well as a small worktable, upon which lay the few personal items Wesley Crusher carried with him. One was obviously a weapon, a version of a short-barreled rifle with a compact stock and what was likely a rectangular power cell protruding from the weapon's underside just behind its forward handgrip. To Picard it looked custom made, like a blend of components from different styles of armaments. What he surmised to be a replacement power cell lay next to the weapon. The other prominent item on the table, though slightly larger than an older-model tricorder, bore at least a superficial resemblance to one. Its dull casing at first appeared to be a single piece, but closer examination revealed almost invisible seams that looked capable of opening in different ways and perhaps even assuming different configurations. Also apparent was the subtle, almost recessed indicator light that now blinked a soft, steady blue. Beneath it, that section of the table glowed pale yellow, indicating a scan was in progress.

"Captain," said Taurik, offering a subtle nod of greeting to Picard before acknowledging the other senior officers. He gestured to the unfamiliar device. "We have been maintaining a constant scan of the item since Commander La Forge retrieved it from Doctor Crusher. The activity started approximately sixty-three seconds before I contacted you. So far as we know, it is the first sign of internal operation it has revealed since Mister Crusher's arrival."

Unable to keep himself from glancing to Crusher, who revealed no outward reaction to the engineer's comment, Picard asked, "Do we know what it's doing?"

"Not yet," replied Chen before looking to Taurik. "Sorry, sir."

Taurik said, "The lieutenant is correct. Despite this development, we remain unable to conduct a comprehensive scan on the item's internal components. We can confirm it is emitting signals that resonate across multiple quantum resonance frequencies, indicating an ability to either scan or communicate with other realities and dimensional planes."

"We have seen Wesley demonstrate his Traveler abilities before," said Worf. "But I do not recall him carrying equipment of this sort."

Crusher replied, "I don't remember him having anything like this either." She stepped closer to the table, leaning in so she could get a better look at the item. "Maybe he built it himself." She reached out to run her fingers along its smooth surface. "He was always good at that sort of thing."

As if in response to her voice or perhaps her touch, the blue light on the device began blinking at a more rapid pace, and Picard now was sure he heard a low hum emanating from it.

"Hello." Reaching for the device, La Forge held it closer to his face, and Picard could see the chief engineer's ocular implants subjecting it to every manner of inspection the visual prostheses could bring to bear. After a moment, he placed it back on the table and pressed a series of controls on an interface built into the table's surface. The intensity of the illuminated area beneath the device shifted to a bright orange glow at the same time several displays set into the table activated. Moving closer, Picard noted the scroll of schematics and other information as scanning resumed.

"Whatever it is," said La Forge after a moment, "I think it's awake now."

Chen moved to the table's opposite corner and another set of controls and displays. "It's still blocking a lot of our scans, but I'm definitely picking up increased activity." She tapped a few more controls. "I'm applying a dampening field to try and screen out some of the quantum flux activity."

"Good idea," said La Forge. "Screening out some of the interference might finally let us have a look inside."

Picard blinked when the hum coming from the device increased in pitch and volume, sharing glances of concern with the rest of the group. "Mister La Forge?"

"Lieutenant Chen's action seems to be working," said Taurik, who had moved to stand next to her. "At least some of the quantum resonance frequencies appear to be mitigated if not nullified."

"We're down to one signal." La Forge leaned over the table, dividing his attention between his controls and the device. "But now I'm picking up something else. Much lower power. I'm not sure what—"

The item's top panel opened, splitting along a recessed seam as both halves separated, flipping over to reveal the device's innards. Picard moved closer, studying what appeared to be a translucent crystal sphere gyrating within a bronze cradle and surrounded by other modules that bore no resemblance to any sort of circuit or component with which he was familiar. The opening was accompanied by an increase in volume from the mechanism's interior.

"This is incredible," said La Forge. "According to our scans, most of this thing's internal components exist within numerous quantum realities simultaneously. The center crystal is acting like an aperture from this reality into dozens of others. I can't get an accurate count, but I can confirm it's trying to send multiple signals. Our quantum dampening field is inhibiting most of that." He looked up from the table to Crusher. "Doctor, if I'm reading this right, the signal it's emitting activated within seconds of you touching it. I think it's keyed to you somehow."

"A message from Wesley?" asked Picard.

Before anyone could answer, the device's internal components seemed to stop all of their activity. The tone it emitted faded and the crystal stopped its rotations before radiating a warm cobalt blue.

"It just locked in on something," said La Forge, his attention once more on the table's array of controls. "Don't ask me where. Or when, for that matter."

Then, two more of the device's outer panels flared open before it lifted itself from the table, rotating as though searching for something. Picard tensed when the device seemed to pause, its center crystal regarding him like a single, unblinking eye. It moved slowly toward him, but something about its hum and almost hesitant movements told Picard not to be afraid.

"It's scanning you," reported La Forge. "A passive scan; nothing dangerous."

The device hovered before Picard, making no other moves. The sounds it emitted had lowered almost to a quiet purr. On instinct, he cupped his hands and held them out to the device.

"Captain," said Worf, a warning note in his voice.

Picard said nothing as the item lowered itself into his hands before going inert.

"I'll be damned," said La Forge.

"I guess it likes you," added Crusher.

Regarding the device in his hands, Picard grunted. "Indeed." It was cool to the touch, and he sensed no internal mechanisms at work within its casing. Was it broken, or depleted of whatever energy source sustained it? What could even power a device with the capabilities La Forge and his engineers had described?

A bright light erupted just outside the nook, accompanied by a sound not unlike a rush of air. Gasps and other reactions of surprise came from crewmembers in the larger engineering space. Still carrying the device, Picard exited the smaller room with his officers behind him. There, a sphere of light was fading to reveal a humanoid figure. Worf stepped in front of Picard, getting between the captain and this potential intruder, but Picard touched his first officer's arm as he stepped forward.

"It's all right, Number One."

He recognized the new arrival. The light faded, coalescing into the form of Wesley Crusher.

19

Not nearly so old as the individual who had come to them in far more dramatic fashion, this version of Wesley was much closer to what Picard would expect to see from a human male of forty to fifty Earth years of age. His hair was still longer, unkempt, and much grayer, as was the matching beard. Deep lines creased his face, but an intensity burned in the man's brown eyes. He wore a dark shirt and matching pants, thick-soled boots, and a weathered leather field jacket. A drab canvas satchel hung from his left shoulder, slung across his chest and resting against his right hip. He turned to look at Picard and the others, offering a weary yet sincere smile.

"I should have known."

Pushing her way past Picard, Crusher stopped just short of racing to embrace her son before relenting and throwing her arms around him. She buried her face in his neck, leaving him to face the others over her shoulder.

"Hi, Mom."

Lifting her head, her voice trembling with emotion, Crusher said, "You really need to call your mother."

"I know."

After disengaging himself from her while still holding her hand, Wesley regarded Picard and the others. "Hello, Captain. It's good to see you again."

"The feeling's very mutual, Mister Crusher. I only wish it could be under something resembling normal circumstances." He held up his hands, which still cradled the strange device. "I believe this may belong to you."

Allowing Worf to return to the bridge and Taurik and Chen

to resume their normal duties, Picard along with Crusher and La Forge gathered with Wesley in the engineering nook. Crusher explained what they had experienced with his older self's arrival and subsequent death in sickbay, and the investigation of the items he carried. Wesley, having already given the device a visual inspection, placed it on the table. The crystal sphere at the item's center once again emitted a soft blue glow, while the rest of its visible internal components appeared to remain inactive, or at least operating in a passive state that offered no outward signs of activity.

"I've never seen anything like it," said Wesley after several moments of silent contemplation, during which he examined it from all sides of the worktable while also perusing the scan data collected by La Forge and his team. "But I can't shake an odd feeling of familiarity. Like I should know what it is and how it works."

As if on impulse, he reached across the table and placed his hand on the crystal. The response from the device was immediate, with the crystal's glow changing from blue to green as it began a rhythmic pulsing. Picard noticed Wesley's eyes had closed.

"There's a massive amount of information stored here," he said. "Years' worth. Decades, I'm guessing. It's staggering." His eyes opened. "Apparently, I collected all of it. Or will collect all of it. By the looks of things, I've been pretty busy." After a moment, he added, "There's some kind of encryption protecting the data. I can't seem to bypass it." With a look of irritation, he removed his hand from the crystal, at which point the device once again became inert. "There's also damage to some of the internal components. I think it may have taken a glancing blow from a type of temporal weapon. Most of the data's protected, and once I figure out how to get in, I may be able to reconstruct what's compromised. As far as I can tell, my older self brought it back here to give to . . . me."

"To you?" asked Crusher. "I don't understand. How would . . . I thought when I touched it, that meant . . ." The rest of her sentence trailed off, and she cast looks at Wesley as well as Picard and La Forge. "I'm sorry. I guess I just don't understand."

"Neither do I," added Picard, describing to Wesley how the device seemed to pick him out from the group and—for lack of a better description—entrust itself to him.

Wesley offered a small smile. "The O.C. reacting to both of you was a feature he programmed into it." Now it was his turn to regard the others. "I guess I mean I programmed it. From what I can tell, my future self intended to travel to this point in space-time, but he wasn't sure if he'd be able to explain himself to any of you when he got here." His expression fell. "Looks like he was right."

"O.C.?" asked La Forge.

Gesturing to the device, Wesley said, "Sorry. It's short for 'Omnichron,' the name I gave it. Or, will give it. You could say it's a combination of quantum receiver and a very powerful tricorder, obviously with far more storage, and capable of scanning across time and space using techniques that simulate how we—other Travelers and I—see them. At least, I think that's the case."

"In sickbay," said Crusher after another moment, "you—he—said something about trying to stop *something*. That he'd been trying to *fight* something but couldn't do it anymore."

Picard remembered those last agonizing moments. "Yes. He also mentioned time. Trying to fight something, but he'd run out of time?"

"Yeah." Wesley's expression fell as though he were lost in thought.

"Residual chroniton particles indicate he was likely traveling *through* time, though there's no way to know if he came from the past or the future, or even from this reality."

His attention still elsewhere, Wesley blinked away his apparent reverie and regarded the engineer. "I've been doing a lot of that myself lately. If what he was doing is related to that, then we might have a bigger problem than I thought."

"Might?" Crusher's eyes narrowed. "Aren't you him? Wasn't he you?"

"Not necessarily. Multiple timelines and realities mean multiple versions of individuals. That would include me. For all I know, my older self is from a different quantum reality."

La Forge said, "There were enough fluctuations in his quantum signature that it was impossible to lock down to just one resonance frequency. I'm guessing the same would be true for you."

"Maybe." Wesley held up his right hand as though studying it. "Travel between dimensions can definitely screw with your internal makeup, and that's before you add in anything artificial like being hit with a temporal weapon."

"There was something else," said Picard, recalling the older Wesley's last few words. "No future, he said. Something about there being no future and having to try again. Is it possible he deliberately came back to this point in time, knowing you—or a version of you—would find us?" He pointed to the Omnichron. "And this?"

"It makes a certain sense, doesn't it?" Wesley eyed the device on the table. "If I were going to give something to my younger self, you'd think I would make it easier to use. It's almost as if . . ." His voice trailed off and he said nothing for several seconds, his attention focused on the Omnichron. "The encryption. I just realized it had its own temporal fluctuation."

"We caught that with our scans," said La Forge. "The crystal and other components are in a state of flux."

Wesley nodded. "I've seen that before, but this is something different." Once more, he reached to the device, his hand settling over the pulsing crystal. This time, Picard watched as his hand seemed to blur and dematerialize, and he recognized it as the beginning of a quantum shift.

Crusher moved toward him. "Wesley?"

"It's all right, Mom." He held up a hand. "I'm just . . . getting a feel for it." After a moment, he said, "Hang on. I think I'm finding a way in. The encryption is there, but it's fluid, almost like it's reacting to the passage of time while I'm connected to it. I don't—"

He gasped. Instead of pulling his hand from the Omnichron, the shifting effect obscuring his hand now moved up his arm.

"What's happening?" Crusher asked.

"Something's reaching out." Wesley grimaced. "No. It's more than that."

His other hand darted from his side, grabbing on to Picard's right arm with such speed and force that the captain started to pull back. Wesley's hand clamped around his wrist as the quantum shift expanded across his body. Then Picard felt a tingling along his arm, and he realized the effect was moving to include him.

"Captain!"

It was La Forge, along with Crusher, reaching across the table toward them before they, along with everything else, disappeared from Picard's vision in a vivid white light.

The *Enterprise* was gone, replaced by a foreboding landscape filled with rock formations, ravines, and little to nothing in the way of vegetation as far as Picard could see. Instead of the drone of the ship's engines, he heard the soft moan of wind passing between gaps in the broken terrain. The scene stretched away from him toward a range of mountains looming on a horizon beneath a blanket of dark, ominous clouds swirling overhead. Lightning crisscrossed the sky, and at first Picard thought he might be observing the simple fury of a natural weather event. That notion fell apart as he watched all of the clouds being drawn toward something in the distance. He realized he felt a pull on him, compelling him in that same direction while at the same time he sensed something else pressing inward on his body. No. On his . . . *consciousness*?

It took him an extra second to notice he still felt Wesley's grip on his arm, and he looked to see the younger man standing beside him.

"What happened to the *Enterprise*?" asked Picard.

Taking in their surroundings, Wesley replied, "We're here, but we're also there." He released the captain's arm. "I see Mom and

Geordi. He's scanning us with a tricorder. To them, we probably look like we're stuck in some kind of transporter beam, which isn't completely wrong."

Eyeing the dismal valley around them, Picard asked, "Did your device bring us here?"

"After a fashion. This is the O.C.'s doing. Apparently something my future self left for me to find. I'm sorry for grabbing you like that. It told me to bring you along." He gestured toward the mountains and the clouds above them. "Can you feel it? The pull?"

Picard nodded. "Like a magnetic attraction. You say your older self left you a message. To come here? Have you been here before?"

After taking another look at the bleak scene around them, Wesley replied, "I don't think so." He regarded Picard. "At least, not *yet*. Maybe I come here at some point in my future. I'm guessing the O.C. will be able to tell me for sure, but I realized in those last seconds before we came here that the encryption isn't like a security code. It's linked to a sequence of events. It wouldn't let me access all of the data until I first navigated a particular segment."

"A test?" asked Picard.

"Not so much a test as an . . . *overture?*" Wesley shrugged. "I sensed it as some kind of obstacle it wanted me to negotiate before it would allow me full access."

"This is the encryption?" Once more, Picard considered their dismal environs.

Wesley nodded. "From the O.C.'s point of view, I guess it is." Closing his eyes, he held up his right hand, palm facing away from him and toward the mountains. "The pull's growing stronger, but now there's something else."

Though he did not understand at first, it took Picard only a moment to comprehend what his companion meant. His attention was drawn to a pinpoint of light appearing ahead of them. Floating above the broken, desolate soil, it stretched and expanded, growing outward in all directions while blocking from view the terrain behind it. There were no defined edges, but within the field's perimeter he now saw a rush of intense colors swirling about one another. He started to step backward as it continued expanding toward them, but Wesley once more grabbed his arm.

"No, Captain." His voice was calm. "It's all right."

Within seconds the wash of colors surrounded him, blotting from view everything else. For a brief moment Picard fancied himself standing in the middle of a holodeck simulation run amok, but despite the visual frenzy he felt no vertigo or other unease. As the scene seemed to settle around them, from out of the colors emerged a series of moving images. Blurry and indistinct, they reminded Picard of dream fragments that he might recall but struggled to decipher. The images began coalescing, moving about while staying within the limits of the orb's boundary even as the sphere itself began to spin, affording Picard a view of still more imagery.

"What are we seeing?" he asked.

"I'm not sure. They're almost like . . . memories?" His eyes still closed, Wesley turned in place. To a casual observer, he might appear to be straining to listen, trying to pick out a single voice or sound from out of a crowd. "No, that's not right. Some of these images are familiar. I've observed some of these events firsthand, but the point of view isn't mine."

Watching the procession of scenes before him, Picard tried to make sense of what at first was little more than an unrestrained torrent of information. As he focused, some images seemed to emerge from the chaos. Living beings representing species he did not recognize. An indistinct crystalline lattice sitting atop a towering mountain. Vessels of unusual configuration in space. Entire worlds, subjected to some sort of destructive energy washing across their surfaces. The rush of imagery was slowing, becoming less frenetic and allowing him to study it all with greater clarity. Some scenes remained unidentifiable, but others bore hints of familiarity. Picard gasped when he beheld a depiction of his former starship, the previous *Enterprise*, only to watch it destroyed under the onslaught of some form of distorted energy wave engulfing it and ripping it apart.

Then he was on the bridge, standing mere steps from Will Riker, older than he had been when serving on that starship and bearing a captain's rank. His and other faces—close friends and family, some of them long dead—careened past him, dissolving as if to dust.

Another image surged toward him, this one of a desolate landscape not unlike the one in which he and Wesley had found themselves. At the center of the vision was an odd ellipsoid; a stone edifice situated among the ruins of a long-dead city. Picard recognized it immediately.

"The Guardian."

His eyes still closed, Wesley nodded. "Yes."

Picard watched a humanoid figure place hands upon the Guardian before stepping through it. Seconds later the ancient time portal crumbled, unleashing into the sky the merest hint of the staggering energy it once commanded.

"I watched it destroyed," said Wesley. "Twice."

"What about the *Enterprise*-D?" Picard gestured at the image of that ship, once more playing out its scene of destruction as if trapped in a vicious, cruel loop. "That's not our ship."

"No, it wasn't." Wesley raised both hands, extending them toward the sea of colliding visions. "It was from another reality. You encountered them last year. Captain Riker and his crew continued their mission for several more years before meeting their fate. I tried to stop that from happening too. Three times, and every time I failed."

Still more appalling visions spilled forth. Ships, space stations, entire worlds laid waste. People, entire crews and whole civilizations, washed away in what Picard could only describe as tempests of unrelenting fury generated by forces unseen. That he did not know these victims did nothing to diminish the magnitude of their deaths, which to him seemed like nothing less than wanton genocide.

"What is behind all of this?" he asked, his voice little more than a horrified whisper.

Wesley said nothing as another series of images took form

around them. These depicted what Picard surmised to be a Starfleet crew. Although they wore uniforms of a type he did not recognize, the insignia on their tunics was that of the familiar delta, albeit turned ninety degrees to the wearer's left. The technology they utilized featured echoes of the systems with which he was versed, while also showcasing capabilities that to him seemed incredibly advanced.

"The twenty-ninth century," said Wesley, his tone somber while still effecting his trancelike state. "The less you know about it, the better." He said nothing else, leaving Picard to watch the people in this series of images subjected to more of the odd energy distortion waves pushing through the future ship's interior. Moments later, the vessel collapsed in on itself before withering and disintegrating into a plume of ashes.

Wesley moved his hands in slow circles as if trying to cycle through the cascade of visions. "I've been there, but I don't recall meeting those people in that manner. The record's in the O.C. In fact, there are multiple iterations of this encounter. My future self must have returned there in a bid to fix whatever he failed at during earlier attempts."

"Fix what?" asked Picard.

Around them, the swirl of visions had begun pulling back in on itself. Everything stretched and shrank, the scene withdrawing to the original, lone point of light that had set off the entire sequence. Then it blinked out of existence, leaving Picard standing with Wesley on the same desolate plain that had greeted their arrival. One mountain remained in the distance, awash in a haze or fog that seemed to cloak it from prying eyes and topped with the odd structure he had glimpsed earlier. Then, like everything else, the mountain vanished from existence.

Lowering his arms, Wesley opened his eyes. Picard saw the weariness there, as if he had aged decades—perhaps even centuries—in a matter of moments. The captain realized he had seen that look before, in Wesley's older self.

"Wesley," prompted Picard, "what was he—*what are you*—trying to fix?"

His shoulders slumping as though cowed beneath some invisible, oppressive burden, the other man regarded him with an expression of disillusionment and submission.

"Time, Captain. Time itself is what I'm trying to fix."

20

Sounds of surprise and relief greeted Picard and Wesley as the *Enterprise*'s engineering section materialized around them. No sooner did the effect fade than Picard felt Beverly Crusher's arms around him. The hug lasted a brief moment before she disengaged and repeated the action with her son.

"Captain," said Geordi La Forge. "Are you all right?" He moved his gaze between Picard and Wesley. "You seemed to blink out there for a minute."

Frowning, Picard regarded the chief engineer. "A minute? That's all?"

La Forge shrugged. "Okay, it was more like two minutes."

"How are you feeling?" asked Crusher. Even without a tricorder or other medical equipment, she still appraised Picard and Wesley with a doctor's shrewd eyes.

Picard patted her arm. "We're fine." He looked to Wesley, who nodded in agreement before responding to the captain's prompt to explain their experience. Listening in silence, Picard replayed the scenes he had viewed as Wesley recounted them while attempting to explain what they might mean.

"It started as an isolated incident," he said to the three of them. Still ensconced in the nook just off the main engineering floor, Wesley placed his left hand on the worktable, supporting himself with that arm while he reached for the Omnichron, which remained at the table's center. He placed his free hand on the device's center crystal. The translucent orb glowed blue, and a moment later a spherical holographic projection appeared in the space over the table. Picard recognized it as the representation of a star map depicting an area of the Alpha Quadrant near the Federation-Romulan border.

"I was . . . traveling," said Wesley. "And I sensed a temporal disturbance in Romulan space. It was a wormhole connecting to a point in the Delta Quadrant, and while it was far too small for a ship, signals could still be transmitted through it. A Romulan science vessel had discovered the wormhole and established communications with a ship on the other end. The catch was that the two ends of the wormhole were separated by time as well as space. Twenty years' difference."

"I know this story," said La Forge. "*Voyager*, while it was stranded in the Delta Quadrant, found a wormhole and made contact with a Romulan scientist from twenty years in their past. This was at a point before Starfleet knew *Voyager* hadn't been destroyed in the Badlands. Captain Janeway and her crew sent messages to him to deliver to their families, to let them know they were all right but on the other side of the galaxy. The scientist promised to keep the messages and his contact with *Voyager* a secret for twenty years to avoid possible disruptions to the timeline, but he died a few years before their original mission even started."

Crusher also knew the story. "Telek R'Mor. He died of a rare Romulan blood disease, T'Shevat's Syndrome, as I recall."

"Yeah, well, in the version I saw, something came through the wormhole, pushing out from both ends to destroy *Voyager* and R'Mor's ship." Wesley grimaced as the projection shifted to show a rush of energy consuming an older model of Romulan civilian vessel. Next to it, a Federation *Intrepid*-class starship met a similar fate.

"A different timeline, obviously," he continued. "The nature of the attack was like nothing I'd ever seen before. Literal waves of temporal distortion pushed through the wormhole, overtaking both ships within seconds. The energy waves subjected the ships to rapid aging and degeneration to the point they simply fell apart. Disintegrated."

"Those events are like the ones you showed me," said Picard. "You're certain these are deliberate attacks?"

Wesley replied, "At first I thought it could be a tear in spacetime, or some other natural phenomenon. We've encountered those before, but the directed nature of the attacks convinced me this had to be artificial. Someone is generating these distortion waves, but I'll be damned if I know how they're doing it, and they don't stop with whatever ships or people happen to be near the point of attack. Planets, solar systems, galaxies. Everything. Entire time streams, entire *realities*, are being ripped apart."

"Entire realities?" Picard could barely even begin to envision destruction on such a scale. "Each of those incidents represents a different branch of time?"

Wesley touched the Omnichron's crystal again, and this time the projection changed to portray what looked like a curving line arcing through a starfield. A flash at its forward end caused another line to begin arcing away from that point while the original line continued weaving its own trajectory. The new strand emitted its own flash, creating a new fork, and several more followed in rapid succession. Within seconds a tangled mass of branches and other divides filled the space above the worktable. The original strand was continuing to create divergent threads and splits, adding to the chaos developing before the group's eyes.

"From what I can tell," he said, "they use different temporal phenomena as starting points for introducing branching points within an established timeline. The newer an alternate strand is, the more fragile it is, and this appeals to them for some reason. It's like they're introducing deliberate instabilities into different points in the spacetime continuum for the express purpose of collapsing the resulting timelines. I have no idea how, let alone why."

"What about who?" asked La Forge. "Any clue as to who or what's behind it all?"

Shaking his head, Wesley blew out his breath. "No. After this initial incident, I tried tracking the origin point of the time distortions. Utilizing existing temporal phenomena helps mask a lot of their movements. There's not much evidence of their passing, and most of our meetings have been the kind where I haven't had the time to stand around and watch what happens." He cast a guilty look at his companions. "Let's just say they always seem to find ways to keep me busy."

Picard asked, "Wesley, how long have you been tracking this?"

"Years. Different points in time and space. Only recently have I had contact with the actual beings I think are behind it all." Wesley moved his hand over the Omnichron's crystal and the projection began displaying a series of images depicting shadowy, robed humanoid figures. "Most of the time, it's someone or something like this. I say 'something' because despite their appearance, I've never gotten the sense they're actual living things. They're not holograms, because I've fought them both before and apparently in the future."

"Fought them," said Crusher, her voice soft. Picard looked across to her and saw her casting her gaze down toward the worktable. He suspected she was thinking of the older Wesley, whose body remained in stasis, and the circumstances that had brought him to them.

Pulling away from the Omnichron, Wesley placed his hand on her shoulder. "Sorry, Mom. I didn't mean—"

"It's all right." Crusher cleared her throat. "I was just . . . never mind." Picard watched the way her mouth set, the familiar sign of her pushing aside her personal feelings and focusing her attention on the work before her. "These . . . people. Were you able to scan them? Get any sort of physiological data on them?"

Wesley gestured to the Omnichron. "If I did, it was the future me, and it's in there somewhere. Whatever they are and whatever they're doing, they're persistent, across multiple points in space and time, and they're not alone. These humanoids, or whatever they are, also control other creatures. Larger, space-going life-forms that are able to generate and absorb tremendous amounts of energy. I've watched them attack ships and burrow through their deflector shields before punching right into the hulls. Once they get inside a ship, they wreak total havoc. I haven't figured out how to fight them. Not yet, anyway."

Pointing to the Omnichron, La Forge said, "Maybe your future self has something about that in there too. We just need to dig it out."

"Even with its internal damage, we should still be able to retrieve something." Wesley lifted the device from the table and held it up. "I've been thinking how we might interface this with the ship's computer."

La Forge nodded. "Yeah, me too."

Despite himself, Picard could not help feeling a sense of *déjà vu*.

All around him was a scene not unlike what he had experienced earlier with Wesley, standing in the midst of a desolate landscape on some unfamiliar world. Standing on dry, broken soil next to Crusher and La Forge, he looked up to see a large moon dominating a deep violet sky. Rather than a typical sphere, Picard instead saw at least a third of the natural satellite appeared to have been obliterated. Beneath that startling image, mountains loomed in the distance, while various rock formations and other features of broken terrain marked the ground around them. Craters pockmarked the plain, bearing mute testimony to the cataclysm that must have resulted following whatever event had shattered the nearby moon. In and around this devastation lay the ruins of an ancient, long-forgotten city. It was not the same vista he recalled from the visions he and Wesley had shared, and yet it carried a hint of what Picard might describe as connective tissue. Subtle features of design and architecture were apparent to him.

"All right," said La Forge, holding a padd as he stepped away from Picard and Crusher. "Thanks to Wesley guiding the way, I managed to create a connection between the Omnichron and the main computer." He tapped the padd's interface. "Using the holodeck matrix, we should be able to access the Omnichron's central memory core directly, generating representations based on its recorded data. The processor had several familiar pathways and algorithms built into it. Made the interface a whole lot easier." He smiled. "Nice to see you didn't forget everything we taught you, Wes."

"Where are we?" asked Crusher. Although the temperature here was not cold, the doctor still stood with arms folded tightly across her chest.

Standing some meters away from them, eyes closed as he faced them, Wesley answered, "As far as I know, this planet doesn't even have a name." Just over his right shoulder, the Omnichron hovered in the space behind him.

"I'm pretty sure it's not on any Federation star charts," he continued. "It's in a system at the farthest edge of the Beta Quadrant, well beyond where even automated survey probes have explored at this point in time. I haven't traveled far enough into the future to see how long it takes anyone or anything from the Federation to get there. Suffice it to say it'll be a while, but someone else definitely makes their way there."

Opening his eyes, Wesley waved his hand and the scene before them shifted. The effect was as though Picard and the others were moving forward, over the bleak terrain toward the mountains at a pace far greater than could be achieved on foot. The mountains grew larger while still remaining out of reach, as the clouds moved across the sky, continuing to churn as if ready to unleash total fury. At the same time, Picard's attention was drawn to another set of ruins that appeared to have escaped the worst of whatever disaster had visited this world. Massive octagonal columns rose from the soil, interspersed at irregular intervals in and around what remained of collapsed walls, stairs, and other structures of varying size. Everything appeared to be carved from what Picard guessed was a kind of polished limestone. Severe angles dominated the design of the columns along with most of the buildings, at least those portions that had survived, and etched into their sides were glyphs and other indecipherable script that Picard nevertheless recognized.

"Iconian." The *Enterprise* had encountered the advanced—and very dangerous—technology from the ancient, long-dead civilization on more than one occasion over the years. "We know they used their gateway technology to extend their empire to different points across the galaxy, but that was two hundred thousand years ago. Are you saying they're somehow behind everything you've been tracking? Traveling through time for some unknown purpose?" The very thought made Picard uneasy.

Wesley shook his head. "On the one hand, you're right. But, based on everything I could find here, the Iconians aren't our problem." As the sensation of accelerated advancement faded, the Omnichron, which had been trailing them, resumed a position ahead of him, and Wesley turned to face his companions. "I couldn't find a single trace of them. It's almost as though no one ever lived here." He gestured to the stone columns. "Those descend deep underground, with conduits that channel geothermal energy from the planet's core to generate power. They're all part of an immense antenna array, apparently for focusing massive amounts of energy toward different points in spacetime both in this universe and others. They're grouped like this in different locations all around this world."

"What about the towers?" asked La Forge. "They look newer than everything else, and that doesn't look like stone to me."

Picard studied the edifices rising over the wreckage around them, which looked very much out of place with their surroundings. Beginning with wide, flat bases, they narrowed in sweeping curves as they rose toward the sky. Unlike the adjacent ruins, the towers seemed to be formed from a metallic alloy that displayed no seams or any clue to their construction. They also appeared to be in better shape than the collapsed structures.

"You're right," said Wesley. "We're talking tens of thousands of years. I'm also pretty sure they're consistent with what little technology I've been able to link to whoever is actually behind the incidents." He gestured to the ruins. "From what I could tell, they act as a sort of frequency modulation system, strengthening and focusing whatever energy was being transmitted via the columns. Someone or something piggybacked onto Iconian technology to utilize that energy projection, but with the modulation the energy they were pushing was—"

"A temporal distortion," said Picard.

"Right." Wesley gestured across the ruins. "But based on what I learned during my future visits here, it wasn't meant to be long-term or even something done multiple times. The scans I took indicated it was activated once, maybe twice, thousands of years ago. I traveled back in search of clues as to where in spacetime the energy was directed, but I didn't find anything. I think this was all some kind of experiment, a test to see if their technology could be merged with the Iconians'."

La Forge said, "If they only used it once or twice, maybe the test failed and they abandoned it."

"Or they accomplished their goals," replied Picard. "But we don't know where or when that goal was sought or may have been achieved."

"Exactly." Wesley frowned. "Whoever it was, they covered their tracks."

"If all of this is in your Omnichron," said Crusher, "that means you've been here more than once."

Wesley nodded. "I visited this place for the first time around two years ago, but I didn't have anything like the O.C. My future self must have come back here and used it to scan everything, and most of that data is in its memory."

"I just wish we could access all of that data," said La Forge, once more tapping his padd. "Even with you helping guide me through these pathways, I'm still blocked from getting to a lot of the information stored in that thing."

"You can't decrypt it?" asked Picard.

Wesley raised his right hand in the Omnichron's direction, which had the effect of calling the device. It moved toward him, dutifully lowering itself into his hand.

"I can't seem to decrypt everything. At least, not all at once. If I didn't know any better, I'd think it was forcing me to complete specific tasks in a predetermined order."

Crusher said, "We are talking about time travel, both you and your future self. If we're to believe he built the Omnichron and was using it to gather information and eventually give it to you, it makes sense he'd want you to avoid the mistakes he made." Her brow furrowed. "Aren't you altering the timeline by trying to change what happens in the future?"

"If only it were that simple." Wesley smiled.

Having resumed studying and tapping his padd, La Forge held up his free hand. "Hold on a second. I'm looking at the scans you made—or will make—of this area. According to the Omnichron, it picked up traces of tachyon and chroniton particles, which are consistent with temporal-displacement technology or phenomena. There's also something else, so faint your scans barely detected it." He looked up from his padd. "It's a triolic energy signature."

It took Picard a moment to recall why that term was familiar, and when realization struck, he felt a definite chill down his spine. He glanced first to La Forge and Crusher, who would also remember, before shifting his gaze to Wesley.

"Devidians."

21

"Devidians?"

His holographically generated presence occupying a spot to the left of the viewscreen in the *Enterprise*'s observation lounge, Admiral William Riker scowled in recognition as he uttered the single word. *"That's a name I haven't heard in a hell of a long time. Are you sure?"*

"As sure as we can be with the information we currently have," replied Picard.

Standing opposite Riker near the viewscreen's right edge, a holoprojection of Meyo Ranjea from the Federation's Department of Temporal Investigations added, *"We've kept our eye on the Devidians. After Captain Picard and his crew disrupted the one group's activities and destroyed their means of creating the temporal vortex to nineteenth-century Earth, we put the entire planet under surveillance. Since your initial encounter, they have carried out other instances of time travel, but their activities have been so limited and contained to their own world that they've resulted in only negligible disruption to the timeline. Indeed, they take exceptional care to prevent such disturbances. So far, we've only been required to take minimal action on isolated occasions, as they've chosen to keep to themselves."*

"That may not be the case anymore, Agent Ranjea," said Wesley. "Even though they've obviously taken steps to mask their movements and reduce their chances of being discovered, my future self still found traces of triolic energy. They weren't as prevalent as what the *Enterprise* crew found when they confronted the Devidians, but I can't believe it's coincidence."

Silently, Picard stood next to Wesley as he brought Riker and Ranjea up to speed on his experiences and the reasons that had brought him here. When prompted, Picard offered information about Wesley's older and equally time-displaced *doppelgänger* and how he came to be in their midst along with his Omnichron and the information it contained. Riker listened with great intent, his expression running the spectrum as he listened, shifting from professional interest to skepticism to unguarded concern. Meanwhile, Ranjea betrayed nothing. A Deltan male with smooth, bronze skin that only accentuated his bald head, he appeared fit and trim, as was the norm for his species. Picard noted the waistcoat and high-collared shirt worn beneath his jacket and made from the same material. "Nondescript" was the adjective that came to mind whenever he encountered any agent from the Federation's Department of Temporal Investigations.

"I'll admit it's suggestive," said Ranjea. *"But not conclusive. That said, there's still a lot we don't know about the Devidians. Their existence outside of phase with this universe makes them notoriously hard to track. The only time we're able to monitor them is if we detect a temporal incursion we can trace back to them, but as I said before, those are rare. Because of this, the Devidians remain very much a mystery."*

Riker asked, *"Wes, what about those other creatures you mentioned? They sound similar to the ophidians used by the Devidians to create the temporal vortex that took them to Earth."*

Wesley replied, "I'd never seen anything like them before that first meeting. These were much bigger than the ophidian you described, and a lot more dangerous. Some were so big they were able to directly attack starships, while others were small enough to penetrate hulls and attack the interior spaces. I call them Nagas, after the *Nāga* from Hindu mythology. Those were serpentlike deities that could take on human form, or even something that was a mix of human and serpent." He shrugged. "It's not a perfect comparison, but it worked for me."

"Still, between these creatures—Nagas, as you call them—and the triolic energy readings," said Picard, "our list of suspects would seem to be narrowing. I've had our people pull everything we know about the Devidians based on our previous mission, but that was nearly twenty years ago."

He had tasked T'Ryssa Chen to comb the library computer for any mention of the mysterious and elusive race, members of which were first encountered by the *Enterprise*-D upon discovering they had inserted themselves into the events of nineteenth-century Earth. Traveling from their homeworld to 1893 San Francisco, they used a cholera plague already ravaging the city as cover for their activities, which involved draining sick and dying humans of their neural energy as a form of nourishment. The human version of this energy apparently held particular sustaining properties for the Devidians, and the disease afforded them a veritable buffet of victims on which to prey. Because they lived out of phase with most other life-forms in this universe, they were all but invisible to the humans of that time period. They also possessed the ability to shapeshift, making themselves appear as ordinary humans for brief periods. Learning of the aliens' actions, Picard and his senior officers were able to follow them back to the past and defeat them, after which the *Enterprise* destroyed the area on their home planet that allowed for the temporal incursions to Earth.

Moving away from Picard and the holographic representations of their audience, Wesley began pacing the length of the conference table. "Based on the *Enterprise*'s previous meeting, it certainly seems like it could be the same species. I've never come across them, at least not knowingly. I don't know anything about them beyond what the *Enterprise* learned when you dealt with them." He reached the table's far end and turned around, rubbing his hands together. "One thing, though: the humanoid I encountered on the Guardian planet didn't resemble the Devidians you described."

"We know they have shapeshifting abilities," said Riker.

Wesley absentmindedly spun the closest chair before turning back to face Picard and the holograms. "There was something else. I didn't get the sense the humanoid was . . . alive? To me, it felt like a shell of a living being, or maybe a living being within a nonliving host." He scowled. "I really don't know. There was never time to learn more about them. When they attacked ships or planets and I was near other living beings, there were indications something was affecting them physiologically and neurologically. Victims became disoriented, even panicked. Survival instinct sometimes kicked in, but just as often someone might be paralyzed by fear."

Ranjea said, *"We know the Devidians themselves aren't capable of time travel; they used the ophidian creatures, but it was a two-part process. They genetically engineered the original ophidians to create spacetime distortions, then employed triolic energy waves to focus those distortions into temporal rifts or vortices. After the* Enterprise *destroyed that cavern on their homeworld, they had no immediate way to re-create the vortex. It stood to reason they'd try again, if not with humans, then other species that could provide similar forms of neural energy, which is why DTI continues to monitor them."*

Picard said, "We were lucky to find them the first time and figure out what they were doing. Even though it was affecting Earth, it was but a single planet. Based on what Wesley's described, they may be up to something much bigger."

"If it's the Devidians," countered Ranjea. Picard heard the skepticism in his voice, but also a hint of calculation. The agent likely was not dismissing anything to chance or coincidence.

Neither was Riker. *"There are too many similarities we shouldn't overlook. If they've found a way to mask their activities from detection—even from DTI or anyone else similarly equipped to monitor changes in time—then for all we know, we may already be too late to stop them."* Picard knew that tone and the look on his friend's face all too well. Riker was considering the situation from all possible angles—scientific and strategic along with the potential threat level, and not just from a direct or localized perspective. His duties now required him to examine things from a much larger perspective as it related to Federation security rather than the safety of a single vessel, be it the *Titan* or the *Enterprise*.

"Whoever it is," said Wesley, "whatever they're doing crosses multiple timelines. They're deliberately effecting divergences in spacetime, only to collapse them. The question is why?"

Riker replied, *"If it is the Devidians, they feed on neural energy generated by some humanoids, and we know that energy is heightened during periods of high stress or fear. Could they be doing all of this because they've somehow figured out it's an easy way to get the energy that sustains them? Could it really be that simple?"*

"The humans on Earth who they preyed on," said Picard, "were people dying of disease, with no hope of recovery. It could be argued their actions, aside from being parasitic, did no real damage to the timeline. If the Devidians are behind this, could it be a variant of that original approach, albeit on a far greater scale? Creating timelines for the express purpose of destroying them, just to harness the neural energy of untold millions or even billions of life-forms?" The very idea was almost too much for Picard to comprehend.

"Mister Crusher," said Ranjea, *"given my organization's job is to monitor time while keeping our interference in temporal affairs to a minimum if at all possible, I know my next question is going to sound unusual. I have to ask it: Does your future knowledge, or that collected by your future self in the device you described, offer any hint about how we should proceed?"*

As if embarrassed, Wesley cast a glance to the lounge's carpeted floor. "Not so far. There's a lot I don't know or understand, and I haven't yet been able to access all of the information my future self collected. A lot of it's still locked within the O.C. At this point, I'm convinced it's guiding me to undertake specific tasks in a pre-scribed order. I think this is so I'll avoid at least some of the errors my future self made. That seems to be how it's gone so far. I think the triolic energy scans Geordi found in the O.C. are a clue, directing us to Devidia II to investigate."

"I was afraid you'd say that," said Ranjea.

Looking to Riker, Picard said, "Will, I want to take the *Enterprise* to the Devidian system." To Ranjea, he offered, "It's not our intention to bring about another temporal event, but we have to know, one way or the other."

For the first time since the meeting began, Ranjea showed actual emotion by releasing a sigh of resignation. *"I agree,"* said the Deltan. *"This needs to be investigated. At the same time, I'll order a recheck of everything we've been doing to monitor them from here."* He held up a hand. *"As for you and your crew, Captain: Investigate. If at all possible, avoid any direct action against the Devidians. The last thing I want to do is add yet another temporal violation to your file. Any more of those and you'll end up in our Hall of Infamy along with Archer, Kirk, and Janeway."* Ranjea offered that last comment with a knowing smirk, but there could be no mistaking the agent's larger point.

Picard grunted in amusement. "Fine company to be in."

"Not in my line of work." Ranjea looked away from Picard for a moment as if considering his next words. When he looked back to Picard, it was only to say, *"Keep me informed, Captain. Good luck. Ranjea out."*

He severed the link, his holographic representation fading to nothingness and leaving Riker standing alone at the viewscreen. The admiral's grin had returned and was now even broader. *"And you thought you didn't have any pull anymore."*

"Indeed," said Picard.

"I'll brief Admiral Akaar." To Wesley, Riker said, *"Wes, just once, I wish when you show up, it's because you want to spend your vacation with us, or you're inviting us all to your place for a barbecue or a baseball game. You know, something boring."* He offered a small smile to soften the remark.

"Sorry, Admiral." Wesley returned the grin. There had been precious little time for pleasantries after Picard made the decision to contact Riker and explain what they had learned from the

Omnichron. Serious matters remained at hand, but there was no denying the *Enterprise* crew, past and present, remained a family. The brief diversion was enough to remind the three of them of this.

"It's still good to see you. Thanks for helping us. Good luck to you all, Riker out."

After the admiral's holo-projection disappeared, Picard turned to Wesley. "Are you sure about this?"

"As sure as I can be, Captain." Wesley shook his head. "I guess there's only one way to find out."

22

Leonard James Akaar waited until the viewscreen in his office went dark and William Riker's visage disappeared from the display before releasing a heavy, exasperated sigh.

"Time travel. I know I've been in Starfleet long enough that nothing should surprise me, but something like this always does." Turning from the viewscreen, Akaar regarded Laarin Andos, director of the Federation's Department of Temporal Investigations. "I'm guessing you already have more information about this than even Riker and your agent did a few hours ago."

Seated in one of a cluster of chairs situated near the bay windows of his expansive office, Andos regarded him with pale gold eyes and an otherwise unreadable expression. "I wish I could provide a more comprehensive report, Admiral. I've only just issued instructions for reviewing all information we have on the Devidians and their activities. A complete evaluation will take some time, but at the moment it's our top priority."

"If Captain Picard's right, we may not have a lot of time," said Commander Tom Paris from where he sat by his wife, Commander B'Elanna Torres. Then, casting a sheepish look in Andos's direction, he added, "Sorry, Director. I didn't mean that as a joke." In his early forties, Paris along with Torres were among the few veteran Starfleet officers who also possessed extensive experience with temporal and other spatial anomalies along with the species and others that might create them. Given the evolving situation, that made them practical assets to Akaar just now.

Andos shook her head. "No apology needed, Commander. Even if it were meant as such, I long ago became anesthetized to such things."

The reply was offered in her usual matter-of-fact style that Akaar had come to respect in short order. A Rhaandarite—tall and lean with thin pale hair and a pronounced frontal lobe—there was no outward evidence that Andos, at 260 Standard years, was well over a century older than Akaar himself. Born before there was a Federation, Andos had spent the majority of those years in its service, including being on hand when the DTI was founded. Only near the beginning of the current century had Andos reached maturity by her species' standards, graduating to one of the department's field agents after beginning her career working in an administrative capacity. Now, nearly eighty years later, she sat before Akaar as the leader of that agency, a position she had held for almost two decades while serving at the pleasure of five different Federation presidents and three presidents pro tempore. Her reputation as a calm, thoughtful voice of reason—a precious commodity given the organization she supervised—preceded her. Though Akaar had no direct experience with time travel, he was informed about such incidents enough to know they were not to be taken lightly. Hence, his immediate request for Andos to join him as he processed Will Riker's report.

Crossing from the viewscreen, Akaar seated himself in the remaining empty chair, across from Andos. "I know your department's been monitoring the Devidians. You're sure they've not done anything that might have warranted closer attention?"

Rather than take umbrage at the subtle accusation, Andos replied, "As Agent Ranjea indicated, the Devidians have remained a species of interest since Captain Picard's initial encounter nineteen years ago. We haven't been compelled to respond to anything they may or may not have done except in isolated and very limited circumstances."

Turning in her seat to face Andos, Torres asked, "What kind of circumstances are we talking about?"

Andos replied, "We know they've attempted to replicate the temporal phenomenon that allowed them to travel to nineteenth-century San Francisco. The original effort required them to subject that underground cavern on their home planet to a form of molecular polarization that made it suitable for focusing the ophidian creatures' ability to generate a temporal rift. They've tried re-creating another space that can provide the same function, but we have prevented that." She paused. "At least, in the present. We have no way of knowing what progress they might make in the future, unless they elect to travel to a point in the past as they did before. However, so far we've detected no such indications."

"Would we even know?" asked Paris. "If they had changed something in the past, affected the timeline in some manner, how would we detect something like that?"

"Our sensor and information archives utilize a series of redundant temporal phase discriminators designed specifically to insulate them from changes in the timeline." Andos held her hands before her, the right one higher than the left. She then gestured to Paris with her left hand. "This gives us—for lack of a better term—a 'baseline' with which to compare past sensor data with whatever we might collect in the future." Her right hand motioned toward him, punctuating the brief explanation.

"I wish we'd had something like that on *Voyager*," said Torres. "Dealing with the Krenim would've been a hell of a lot easier, and maybe we would have known about it."

Akaar was familiar enough with the Krenim, having reviewed the revised mission logs from *Voyager*'s original seven-year journey through the Delta Quadrant. The logs were updated after its crew's subsequent learning of the year they spent in an alternate timeline, locked in battle against members of the Krenim Imperium who commanded a formidable temporal weapon capable of altering history. The Krenim's brazen tactic of using the weapon to write their enemies out of existence had numerous detrimental effects on the timeline, but daring action taken by *Voyager*'s captain, Kathryn Janeway, saw to it the weapon ship was destroyed and the timeline restored. That action resulted in the crew harboring no memories of that encounter; not until *Voyager*'s eventual return to the Delta Quadrant as part of Project Full Circle, Starfleet's extended exploration initiative of that distant region.

"Could the Krenim be somehow involved in this?" Looking to Andos, Akaar asked, "Would your protected sensors and data archives be able to track that?"

"The only information about the Krenim we have is that supplied by Admiral Janeway and the rest of the Full Circle fleet based on their encounters." She nodded toward Paris and Torres. "And that was only due to a sequence of improbable events that are unlikely to be repeated. If not for Full Circle's return mission to the Delta Quadrant, we might never have known the true extent of Krenim activities."

Akaar said, "My understanding after Full Circle's last contact with them was the Krenim knew we'd leave them alone so long as we didn't detect any sort of timeline alterations. That was five years ago, before Admiral Janeway and *Voyager* left the galaxy."

"And in those five years we've detected *no* alterations." Andos paused before adding, "At least, of the sort that leads us to believe the Imperium are taking action against Federation interests. So far as we can tell, they appear to be behaving. It's worth noting that what Captain Picard and Mister Crusher reported doesn't seem at all consistent with what we know of Krenim methods. There's also the distance involved between Imperium space and the Alpha Quadrant. They would have had to develop or obtain some form of transwarp or similar technology to get here so quickly. As a consequence, any temporal alterations they might make would be localized to their own space."

Paris said, "And that still presupposes a reality where Annorax or another Krenim is employing a time weapon. Based on what we know, that never happened in the timeline Admiral Janeway restored." He eyed Andos. "Unless you've heard something we haven't?"

"So, we're back to looking at the Devidians," said Akaar. "Or some other as-yet-unidentified party." Remembering something from Riker's briefing, he asked, "Director, have you looked into some of the other claims Mister Crusher made about his previous contacts with his unknown assailants?"

Akaar noted Andos shifting in her chair, for the first time exhibiting apparent discomfort with the topics of discussion. She adjusted her hands in her lap before replying. "The team I sent to the Guardian planet confirmed the time portal is destroyed. According to their scans, the attack occurred approximately fourteen years ago. We are examining all relevant data from our protected archive, but so far we have yet to identify any measurable changes in our timeline."

"The Guardian," Torres whispered, making no effort to hide her concern. "That's incredible."

"But didn't you say your protected archives would pick up on changes like this?" asked Paris.

Andos said, "You've just identified our chief concern, Commander. Whatever is happening, we don't seem to be able to track its effects. At least, not so far. There's also the Typhon Expanse. We've recorded unexplained energy emissions from the temporal anomaly, and the ship I dispatched to the region has launched survey probes into it. Thus far, no useful information has been returned by those probes."

"What about other known temporal anomalies?" asked Paris. When Akaar directed a questioning look his way, the younger man added, "I'm just wondering about whoever this is, Devidians or someone else, and their connections to the Guardian and the Expanse. Aside from being known time portals, what's attracting their attention?"

"Commander Paris is quite astute," said Andos. "We've posed

similar questions, and I've directed field teams to investigate other known temporal phenomena."

Torres asked, "Do I want to know just how many of those there are?"

"No," replied Andos. "And even if you did, I wouldn't tell you."

"Fair enough."

Rising from his chair, Akaar moved to where his desk was positioned along the office's far wall, arranged perpendicular to the windows and affording him a view of them as well as the room's entrance. He paused, staring out at San Francisco Bay while weighing what he had learned over the last few hours against his own instincts.

"Picard and Crusher seem pretty confident in their theory," he said after a moment. Looking away from the windows, he returned his attention to his guests. "What do you think?"

Paris was the first to speak up. "I don't know anything about Wesley Crusher except what I've read, but if anyone can get to the bottom of this, it's Captain Picard and the *Enterprise*."

"I agree," said Torres. "He's got what sounds like a solid lead, and if there is something brewing, this may be our only chance to get out ahead of it."

Sitting quietly while the commanders made their case, Andos added, "Despite whatever issues we may have with his propensity for temporal violations, I agree, Admiral. The *Enterprise* should conduct its investigation as Agent Ranjea has already directed. We will, of course, be monitoring their activities to the maximum extent possible."

"In case Mister Crusher is wrong, or Picard makes a mistake?" asked Akaar.

Andos shook her head. "No, Admiral. In case they're right."

23

Ezri Dax felt the shift as the controlled chaos of the slipstream corridor evaporated and the *Aventine* emerged in normal space. Within heartbeats of the transition, alarms began wailing across the bridge. The image on the main viewscreen shifted, bringing into focus a modular, utilitarian space station that at the moment appeared perched at the edge of oblivion.

"What the hell is that?"

The question came from the ship's first officer, Commander Samaritan Bowers, seated to Ezri's right. Like him, everyone on the bridge could not help but be transfixed by the sight on the viewscreen. A storm of color filled the screen, spiraling outward from a single point to form a violent backdrop for the station, bathing it in waves of cascading energy.

"Deflectors at full power," reported Lieutenant Lonnoc Kedair from the tactical console to Ezri's left. "Sensors are detecting temporal distortion emanating from the object. Bezorek Station is taking the full brunt of it." The Takaran looked up from her console, her pale green features communicating her concern. "It's deployed temporal shielding, but they're fluctuating, and shield strength is down to forty-nine percent and dropping. At their present rate of deterioration, their generators will fail within three minutes."

"Maintain this distance," said Ezri, shifting in her command chair. "Hail the station."

After a moment, Kedair shook her head. "No response, Captain. Sensors also detect no life readings anywhere on the station."

"None?" asked Bowers. "According to the briefing info we received, there should be over a hundred people there. Mostly Vomnin, but also a few Federation representatives including a detachment from Temporal Investigations."

Kedair replied, "I am continuing to conduct scans, Commander, but the results are the same. No life signs anywhere aboard." She gestured toward the viewscreen. "It is possible the disturbance is interfering with our scans, but I am finding no such disruption."

The ship shuddered around them, making Ezri grip the arms of her chair. "Speaking of disruptions. We've all had the briefing about the station and why it's here. Helkara, what can you tell us that's new?"

From where she sat at the science station positioned along the bridge's starboard bulkhead, Lieutenant Commander Gruhn Helkara turned in his seat. "The artifact the Vomnin safeguard here is emitting levels of temporal distortion far above anything previously recorded." With an air of cold detachment for which the Zakdorn people were well known, he added, "Our sensors are unable to penetrate the artifact's outer shielding, so I cannot determine whether any life-forms remain aboard. I have been evaluating the readings from our sensors, and if I interpret the data correctly, the artifact is in danger of self-destructing."

The artifact.

Ezri rolled the term around in her mind. Helkara, like everyone else among the *Aventine*'s senior staff, had been fully briefed by a representative from the Department of Temporal Investigations while en route to Bezorek Station. The device in question was a piece of ancient technology discovered by the Vomnin, a spacefaring race that only recently began interstellar exploration after discovering faster-than-light travel. They discovered its ability to invert both temporal and spatial axes, which created a pocket dimension allowing travel between moments in time as easily as one might travel through space. Communication, travel, and interaction between civilizations separated by thousands and even millions of years was possible. The risk to past and future events was incalculable.

The occupants of the construct called their creation the Axis of Time, and operated the device according to a strict code of conduct that prohibited casual or grievous use in order to avoid contaminating this or any other timeline. Despite such assurances, Starfleet, and in particular the DTI, viewed the device as an existential threat not just to Federation security but the entire universe.

And now it's acting up, thought Ezri. *Or, acting out.*

"Kedair," she said. "Let's see it."

The security chief tapped a control on her console and the viewscreen image shifted away from Bezorek Station to the object it guarded. An incandescent sphere, the Axis of Time held position at the center of the fury it generated. Ezri studied the storm emanating from the artifact, noting how the waves of energy distorted her view of distant stars.

Bowers asked, "Any idea if this is a natural occurrence, or a deliberate action on someone's part?"

"Without more information or contact with anyone overseeing the artifact," said Helkara, "we have no means of making such a determination."

Another alert sounded from Kedair's station at the same time all lights and consoles around the bridge flickered, accompanied by an audible shift in the omnipresent background drone of the *Aventine*'s warp engines.

Helkara said, "Distortion waves are increasing in strength and frequency, and it's beginning to affect our deflectors."

Ezri tapped the communications control on the arm of her chair. "Bridge to engineering."

Without the faintest hint of preamble, the *Aventine*'s chief engineer, Lieutenant Mikaela Leishman, replied, *"I know about the shields, Captain. We're routing additional power from the warp engines, but we're already seeing strain on the shield generators down here."*

"It is most likely the temporal distortions," offered Helkara. Was it Ezri's imagination, or had the science officer's already high-pitched, nasally voice risen an octave? "They are producing a transphasic effect that our shields are ill-equipped to block. I would advise increasing our distance from the artifact to reduce the strain on our shields."

"That may be harder than it sounds," said Lieutenant Oliana Mirren, the senior operations officer. Looking up from her console, she shot a look of concern toward Ezri. "The artifact is beginning to emit some form of magnetic field. It's acting like a tractor beam."

Seated next to her at the flight controller's station, Lieutenant Tharp replied, "The effect is increasing. I'm compensating with our impulse engines, but I'm already up to one-quarter power just to hold us in place."

"Do what you have to," ordered Bowers, "but hold this position." Turning to Ezri, he added in a softer voice, "We may need to retreat, Captain."

Ezri shook her head. "Not until we're sure there's nobody to evacuate." Looking to the science station, she said, "Helkara, increase power to the sensors, and sweep Bezorek Station one last time."

"Captain," said Kedair. "I have attempted contact with the station on every frequency, including a private encoded link established by the DTI for direct communication with the facility's director, Vennor Sikran. There has been no response on any channel."

At the ops station, Lieutenant Mirren said, "The station's shields are down. The distortion waves are hammering it."

"Look!"

It was Lieutenant Tharp at conn, and Ezri turned to see the Bolian pointing toward the viewscreen, which now depicted Bezorek Station collapsing as it began sliding away from its stationary position and toward the artifact. Various modules and structural extensions collapsed as the facility folded in on itself, crushing down to what should have been an impossible degree before it faded from view altogether. The progression from shields failing to utter annihilation lasted less than ten seconds by Ezri's count.

"Damn." Her gaze lingered on the artifact and its vivid display of energy distorting everything in proximity to it. The effect was becoming more distinct with each passing moment. "What happened?"

Helkara replied, "Our scans registered signs of extreme metallurgical fatigue throughout the station, as if the entire construct aged centuries just within the last few minutes. The further the station's shields deteriorated, the more pronounced the effect." Turning away from his instruments, the Zakdorn added, "Captain, I believe the temporal distortions directed at the station phaseshifted it out of our spacetime continuum."

Bowers eyed the science officer with unchecked skepticism. "Are you saying the station just grew older right in front of us? It literally withered and died before our eyes?"

"I believe that to be the case, Commander. Someone or something has found a way to divert the artifact's inversion of temporal and spatial axes outward from the pocket dimension in which this event normally takes place. If my analysis is correct, the effect would have been much more devastating and far quicker to any life-forms aboard the station."

Ezri said, "Which means if our shields start to give in, the same thing will happen to us." She tapped the intercom control again. "Bridge to engineering. Whatever you have to do, you keep our shields up."

"We're working on it, Captain," replied Leishman. *"But the generators are already showing strain. I'm working on a formula to channel power from the slipstream drive."*

Helkara said, "If done properly, the new configuration would act as something of a transphasic shield, offering us far better protection than standard deflectors, but the risk of losing the drive system is not insignificant."

"Do what you can to help, Gruhn."

More alarms, now from the tactical station as well as Helkara's science console, while at the same time the ship shuddered around them. The lighting blinked again, and one of the environmental control stations along the bridge's port bulkhead went dark.

"Life-forms," reported Kedair. "They came out of nowhere. Eight readings, scattered around the ship and probing our shields. I don't recognize them."

Ezri pushed herself from her chair. "Show me."

The viewscreen changed images and she saw a massive mouth with jagged teeth run face-first into one of the *Aventine*'s deflector shields. Green-white energy crackled at the point of impact. On the bridge, the effect resonated in the form of dimming lights and blinking stations along with a commensurate vibration running across every surface. The creature withdrew in response to the shock, giving Ezri a better look at its overall form, including the dual rows of intimidating bone spikes sprouting from its dark hide, starting at the crown of its large head and continuing down its back.

"I've never seen anything like it," said Bowers, who had risen from his seat and moved to stand next to Ezri. "It's like a serpent that dwarfs even the biggest blue whales on Earth, but how does it survive in space?"

Kedair replied, "Scans show they're phase-shifting in and out of spacetime, so we're unable to get conclusive readings. I cannot tell if they're organic or artificial. Most are huge, thirty to fifty meters in length, but a couple are much smaller, between four and five meters. They all move very quickly, and they're also too close to engage with our weapons. I can't get any sort of lock on them."

"Their ability to shift represents a danger to the ship, Captain," said Helkara. "They may be able to penetrate our shields, then pass through the hull simply by altering their position in spacetime to pass through normal matter."

A succession of impacts against the shields made themselves known, with the ship's power systems registering the strain, including another deep drag on the engines themselves. The deck heaved just enough to make Ezri reach for Lieutenant Tharp's chair to steady herself.

"Shields at seventy-three percent," reported Kedair. "It's like they're probing for a weakness to exploit."

"Engineering to bridge," said Chief Engineer Leishman over the intercom. *"We're ready to route power from the slipstream drive to the shields. We can't hold it for very long, or else we risk overloading the shield generators."*

Ezri sighed in frustration. "Give me a number, Mikaela."

"Three, maybe four minutes. Assuming that thing doesn't throw us another curveball."

"Do it. Hopefully, it's enough to irk our friends out there."

Everyone on the bridge knew when Leishman made the change. The entire ship seemed to shake in protest as its quantum slipstream drive came back online but not for its intended purpose. All of that was suppressed by a new low hum coursing through everything, and even the deflector shields themselves reacted, energy arcing and popping across the main viewscreen as the shields received additional power.

"Deflectors at seventy-five percent and rising," said Kedair. "The new transphasic configuration seems to be working. The life-forms are reacting to the change and are halting their probing action."

"Look," said Bowers. "They're heading for the artifact."

On the viewscreen, Ezri watched as eight dark, coiling masses moved away from the *Aventine*, heading for the Axis at the heart of the temporal maelstrom. Was that their point of origin? Did they exist within the artifact's pocket dimension, or had they arrived from some other point in spacetime? That presupposed a deliberate act rather than chance. Who could be responsible?

Kedair said, "Sensors are detecting a rise in energy readings from the artifact. The intensity of the temporal distortions is increasing."

"Of course it is." Bowers punctuated his comment with an exasperated grunt.

"Captain," said Tharp. "I'm having to increase impulse power to keep this position. We're at one-half now."

With Bezorek Station and its team of caretakers lost, Ezri reasoned, there was only one thing left to do here. "Back us out of here, Conn. Full impulse." She looked to Bowers. "We can't leave that thing to keep throwing out temporal energy like this. Who knows what it can do if these distortions keep intensifying."

"It's a hazard to navigation," said Bowers. "If we can't contact its occupants, then so far as we know, there's no one controlling it. To me, there's only one choice."

"Agreed." Ezri pointed to Kedair. "Ready a full spread of transphasic torpedoes, and target the artifact."

"Wait!" It was Helkara, intent on his controls. "It's too late. Energy distortions are spiking, and I don't believe our shields can handle them. We need to withdraw, now!"

Ezri turned to Tharp. "Conn, hit it."

"We're at full impulse already," replied the Bolian as he stabbed at the controls on his console. "And I can't take us to warp. The distortions are blocking the engines from forming a subspace field."

"What about slipstream?" asked Bowers.

Tharp shook his head. "We'd have to stop transferring power from the drive to the shields. If we do that—"

"Something's happening inside the artifact," Kedair called out as she pointed to the viewscreen. "I think it's an overload!"

"Route all power to forward shields," said Ezri. "All hands brace for impact!"

Her warning came an instant before a bloom of intense white light erupted from the center of the artifact. The sphere that was the Axis of Time crumpled in on itself, disappearing in seconds, the tempest of energy swirling around it dissipating into nothingness. Seconds later the resulting shockwave slammed into the *Aventine*'s shields. The deck heaved beneath Ezri's feet, throwing her and Bowers off balance. She dropped to the deck as a chorus of alarms rang out across the bridge.

"We're being pushed away," reported Kedair, who was holding on to her console to avoid being thrown. "Scans show the temporal distortions are fading."

Standing up, and holding out a hand for Bowers, Ezri assisted her first officer to his feet. "What about those creatures?"

"No sign of them," reported the security chief. "It's possible they disappeared into the artifact's temporal field before it collapsed."

Bowers said, "They deliberately turned and headed into that thing. Why? Were they sentient, or did someone else send them, and for what purpose?"

"I have no idea," said Ezri before blowing out her breath. "Wow. Temporal Investigations isn't going to be happy when they hear about this."

"Assuming they don't already know." Bowers shrugged. "They're insane about this stuff." He nodded toward the viewscreen. "Maybe they can even tell us what those things were."

Ezri considered that notion. "It'll be a question worth asking."

"Captain," said Kedair. "There is something else. Another energy reading, just before the artifact's destruction. Sensors registered it as a signal of some kind."

"Any idea who they were signaling?" asked Bowers.

Helkara rose from his science station and clasped his hands behind his back. "It was a tight-beam transmission sent through subspace, Commander. According to my calculations, it was directed at the Devidian system."

24

It was odd, Wesley Crusher decided, to gaze upon one's older self, and even more so while that other representation was dead.

"I've seen a lot of strange things," he said to no one in particular even though he was not alone in the room. "Some truly bizarre things, including a few I still can't explain. With everywhere I've gone and everything I've done, you'd think something like this wouldn't shock me, but it sure as hell does."

Standing in the morgue, a quiet area tucked into an unobtrusive section of the *Enterprise*'s sprawling medical facilities, Wesley stared at the body of his future self. In accordance with Starfleet regulations, the remains were to be preserved until funeral arrangements could be made. Further, there also lingered a possibility the body might yet hold some unrevealed clue about the circumstances that had brought the older Wesley Crusher here. Encased in a transparent pod that emerged from the storage unit tucked into the room's rear bulkhead and enveloped by the warm blue glow of a stasis field, the unmoving form was—Wesley guessed—exactly as it had been following the postmortem activities. Clothing and personal items had been removed, allowing Wesley to see not just the recent fatal wounds but also numerous other scars and blemishes of varying age and severity mapped across the pale, aged skin. One prominent knot of puckered, discolored flesh at the junction of the left arm and shoulder made Wesley reach for the corresponding area of his own body. He had not yet sustained such a wound, let alone the majority of other injuries his older self had endured. Deep lines creased the dead man's face, at least those areas not covered by thick white beard or scraggly hair. It was difficult to recognize the visage as one day belonging to him, but at the same time Wesley felt the connection on something other than a simple visual level.

"If it helps," said his mother from where she stood behind him, "this is a first for me too."

Despite the room's solemn atmosphere and purpose, to say nothing of his reasons for being here, Wesley could not help smiling at her remark. Turning from the stasis pod, he looked to where she had remained these past few moments. Leaning against the open doorway with arms folded across her chest, she had said nothing after accompanying him to the morgue. He could tell from his mother's face that she was compartmentalizing what she was feeling.

Rather than make his mother step farther into the room to talk with him, Wesley instead touched a control to return the stasis pod into its storage compartment. He watched his body slide into the wall until the cabinet's door closed before turning to exit the morgue.

"I can only imagine what this must be like for you," he said, taking the hand she extended toward him. They left the morgue, navigating the maze of short corridors linking offices, laboratories, and other workspaces on their way back to the main sickbay. "I'm sorry. Hopefully at least some of it will make sense soon."

Her grip tightening on his hand, she said, "I haven't really had a chance to ask this since you got here, but how are *you*? How are you feeling? Are you . . . hurt? Is there something we can—"

"Mom, I'm okay." Even as he attempted to provide reassurance, Wesley released a heavy sigh. "More than anything, I'm just tired. I've been tired for a while. I feel like I've been trying to get to the bottom of this forever." He shrugged. "In some ways, it feels like years are passing in the blink of an eye."

"Congratulations, my son. You just described parenthood." Crusher offered a halfhearted smile, another sign she continued to struggle with her emotions while processing the events of the day. "You'd do well to get some sleep, and maybe a decent meal. Do Travelers even eat?"

Wesley could not help chuckling at his mother *being* his mother, fretting that he was not taking proper care of himself. "When we're hungry, Mom. Still, I like the sound of all that. Right now I feel like I could sleep for a hundred years." He had gone through periods of extreme inactivity, almost always as a means of conserving energy or as part of a healing process taught to him by his mentor. The thing about being a Traveler was that one could engage such measures while existing outside normal spacetime in a way that to outside observers appeared as though no time had passed. It was, he mused on occasion, the closest thing to true immortality he likely would ever know.

They entered the sickbay's primary workspace, consisting of its patient treatment and care areas, surgical wards, and offices for the staff. There was more activity here, in the form of Doctor Tropp and several nurses and orderlies either working with members of the *Enterprise* crew or else tucked away behind desks or at workstations. Wesley was not surprised to see that he recognized almost none of them. The lone exceptions were Tamala Harstad and Tropp, whom he remembered from his previous visit. Both doctors greeted him with warm smiles; however, he sensed their unease as they beheld a younger version of the man who had died despite their best efforts to save him. Their nervousness was echoed in the faces of the other staff members, at least some of whom he guessed had assisted the doctors during that futile endeavor.

"It's good to see you again, Wesley," offered Harstad.

Tropp added, "Indeed. Welcome home, Mister Crusher."

When she gestured in the direction of Crusher's office, Harstad's smile widened and this time Wesley saw it was genuine. "You have a visitor. He's been waiting very patiently to this point, but I don't know how much longer we can keep him at bay."

Turning toward his mother's private workspace, Wesley was pleasantly surprised to see René bounding through the doorway. The boy dropped the padd he carried in his left hand, letting the device fall to the carpeted floor as he ran to meet his older brother. He did not hesitate at the sight of Wesley's craggy appearance, seemingly recognizing him despite the longer, grayer hair and worn clothing.

"Wesley!" With unwavering trust, René launched himself toward his brother, who caught him and hauled him in for a firm embrace.

"Hey, buddy. How've you been?" He exchanged surprised looks with Crusher, who despite her self-control was wiping a tear from her right eye.

Pulling his head back so he could see Wesley, René replied, "I've missed you."

"I've missed you too. How old are you now?"

"Six. I'll be seven soon!"

Smiling, Wesley lowered him back to the floor. "That's old."

Harstad and the others left them to their reunion, and Crusher led the way back to her office. Once they were out of the patient ward, Crusher said, "He called out for you the other day, you know. Out of the blue." Wesley listened as his mother explained the odd experiences she and René shared, thinking he must have been trying to contact them through the visions they had seen. It took him only a moment to realize the connection.

"I was thinking about you both," he said, taking a seat on the couch opposite her desk and allowing René to sit beside him. "I was . . . worried." He recalled the feelings of dread gripping him on the Guardian planet, a sensation of powerlessness in the face of the emerging threat he still did not understand. "There's so much we don't know about what's going on. So much *I just don't know.* Even if it is the Devidians, I have no idea what it means, or what's at stake, or how it affects me or you or everyone else." He rubbed his face. "It's a lot to think about."

"I can imagine." Propping herself against her desk, Crusher crossed her arms. "Wesley, there's something I've been thinking about since you arrived. You, and . . . and your older self and how his quantum signature was fluctuating. I suspect yours is, as well. Are you—" She stopped herself, considering her words. "Are you from this time, or some other reality?"

"Yes." Wesley offered a small shrug. "And no. It's hard to explain."

This seemed to do little to satisfy his mother's concerns. "I guess the easy way to ask this is: Are you my Wesley? How can I be sure?"

With as much self-assurance as he could muster, Wesley replied, "I'm sure."

Although he moved at a brisk pace, Taurik could not evade his pursuer.

"Hey, where are you going in such a rush?"

Mindful of what still awaited him, Taurik turned at the sound of T'Ryssa Chen's question to see her jogging up the corridor to meet him. Behind her, the doors to the Riding Club closed, blocking off the sounds of fellow crewmembers enjoying their off-duty hours. He also had been off-duty, but that did not prevent the summons he had received that now demanded his attention. He did not stop in response to Chen's call, but he slowed his pace so she could catch up to him.

"I have a task I must complete," he said. It was not a lie, but neither was it a reply he knew would satisfy Chen. She was nothing if not inquisitive, a trait that served her well but on occasion could also be problematic. Now, for instance.

They approached a turbolift and its doors parted, allowing Taurik to enter. Chen followed.

"In engineering?" she asked. "Something I can help with?"

Instructing the lift to take him to deck thirteen, Taurik raised an eyebrow. "Are you not currently on a 'date' with Lieutenant Konya?"

"Someone sounds jealous."

"Not at all." Despite his comment, he did not allow his eyebrow to climb any higher. "I simply meant it would be unfair to him for you to accompany me when you were already engaged in activities with him."

Chen eyed him. "You're being very Vulcan again." As the lift slowed and the doors opened, she said, "You have something to do in your quarters?" Then, as Taurik knew she would, she grinned. "You sure you don't need hel—"

"I have been contacted via subspace," he said, forestalling her inevitable yet innocuous flirtation. "They are waiting for me, and it is to be a . . . private conversation." Exiting the turbolift, he proceeded along the corridor toward his quarters.

Her expression turning from playful to serious, Chen said, "Sorry, Taurik. I'm not trying to pry, but is everything okay?"

Realizing his truthful yet evasive answers were only prompting more questions, he stopped in the passageway. "T'Ryssa, I apologize for not being forthcoming. I am not in any personal distress, but the conversation in which I am about to participate is important, and sensitive."

"It's DTI, isn't it?" Chen gently slapped his arm. "It has to be. I wondered when they'd be calling you."

Giving his eyebrow free rein, Taurik asked, "On what do you base this conclusion?"

Chen offered a mock scowl. "Really? Two different Wesley Crushers show up from two different points in spacetime, including one from the far future, and I'm not supposed to remember you've got a head full of future knowledge you're not allowed to share and, for all I know, is related to all of this? Did you just forget I'm also half Vulcan, so my deductive reasoning skills are at least half as good as yours?"

In truth, Taurik was certain her command of logic and reason equaled if not surpassed his own even if she chose to embrace her human heritage to what many Vulcans might consider an alarming degree. "Your analysis is sound."

"So that's a yes?"

"I am unable to engage in falsehoods, and any failure to answer would fuel further speculation on your part. Therefore, I am left with only one alternative." He resumed walking toward his quarters.

"I knew it!" Chen ran to catch up. "Can I watch?"

"Given the probable topic of discussion, that would not be appropriate."

"Will you tell me about it later?"

"That also would likely be ill-advised." They approached his door, and Taurik turned to her. "However, it is possible there may be a time when it will be prudent to discuss this with Captain Picard and other members of the crew."

"Tease." Chen smiled again, before resuming a more professional bearing. "Look, seriously. If there's something I can do to help, you know you can count on me."

"Indeed I do. Thank you, T'Ryssa. Enjoy your evening with Mister Konya."

Chen touched Taurik's arm. "I will. Thanks."

The contact was minimal, but Taurik still felt the flickering presence of her mind reaching out to touch his own. Was she attempting a meld? No, of course not, judging by the way she withdrew her hand with a shocked expression.

"I'm sorry," she said. "I didn't mean. It just hap—"

Taurik held up a hand. "T'Ryssa. It is . . . fine." Had his thoughts, focused as they were on his upcoming conversation, revealed to her anything he preferred to keep to himself? Without thinking, he pushed those images aside, but was he too late? He did not believe so, and he was confident she would ask if something gave her cause for concern. "While your apology is unnecessary,

I nevertheless appreciate it." He paused, studying her expression. "Perhaps we might talk again, later."

She said nothing for a brief moment and Taurik sensed an unspoken question, but then she blinked as if dismissing an errant thought before offering a small smile. "I'd like that, Taurik."

They exchanged a look of the sort shared by close, trusted friends, each of whom knew without hesitation the other would always be a source of support no matter the circumstances. Chen then headed back to the turbolift, leaving Taurik alone as he entered his quarters. The first thing he noticed was the icon flashing on the computer interface on his desk and its accompanying message: "Incoming Subspace Transmission." Taking a seat at the desk, he tapped the interface's control to open the communication link, and the desktop screen shifted to an image of Agent Meyo Ranjea of the Federation's Department of Temporal Investigations, who nodded in greeting.

"Commander Taurik. I trust you're well."

"Agent Ranjea, thank you for agreeing to talk with me. I apologize for the delay in responding to your incoming transmission, I was . . . unavoidably detained."

The Deltan nodded in understanding. *"Life aboard a starship is often fraught with unexpected developments and demands on one's time. Given the current situation and the report I received from Captain Picard, I suspect I know the nature of your request to speak with me."*

"If you have anticipated my questions, then I hope you are able to provide answers. Does the information provided to us by Mister Crusher have anything to do with what I learned from the Raqilan weapon ship we encountered in the Odyssean Pass?"

When the agent said nothing, Taurik found himself unsure how to proceed. An enormous vessel that had traveled back through time from late in the twenty-fifth century had turned into the *Enterprise* crew's first contact with a species hailing from the previously unexplored region. The Raqilan, the alien race responsible for its construction, had surrounded an enormous particle weapon with just enough infrastructure to support the crew tasked with its deployment. It was their solution to a conflict that had waged for generations. By sending the weapon ship back to a point before the war began, the Raqilan hoped to destroy their enemies, a civilization called the Golvonek, living on an adjacent planet. Although the ship made a successful jump from its own time to the mid-twenty-third century, damaged systems overseeing its crew failed to revive them from a state of suspended animation. The ship drifted, inert, for more than a century before the *Enterprise* crew discovered it and determined it to be a product of Raqilan scientists who reverse-engineered technology they found within the hulk of another immense vessel, a planet-killer device similar to those previously encountered by Starfleet on multiple occasions.

Although the ship, as well as its destructive potential, was impressive, it was its onboard computer systems and data storage facilities that had been the target of Taurik's investigation during an away mission to investigate the alien craft. Upon accessing the voluminous data banks, which contained information about future events pertaining to the Raqilan and the Golvonek, Taurik made an inadvertent discovery that compelled him to quarantine the weapon ship's computer data in a secure sector of the *Enterprise*'s own main computer before reporting about his discovery to Starfleet Command. With the assistance of another DTI agent, Teresa Garcia, Ranjea debriefed him, and Taurik was ordered not to divulge anything he had learned while interacting with the Raqilan information.

On the screen, Ranjea cleared his throat. *"At this time, we're unable to ascertain whether there is a connection. We simply don't yet know enough about this unidentified aggressor Mister Crusher has encountered. Without more to go on, it'd be premature to speculate about anything we've found in the Raqilan data cache."*

Taurik understood Ranjea's position. Without more information, there was no way to ascertain if what he had seen bore any relevance to the situation described by Wesley Crusher. However, given the nature of the future events to which he had gained insight, to Taurik there remained questions demanding answers which were independent of the current circumstances.

"Be that as it may, and giving due consideration to the nature of what I observed, it stands to reason Captain Picard will eventually approach me about this topic." Following his debriefing, Taurik was sworn to secrecy, with no allowances made for his own commanding officer. Since then, he had carried with him the burden of future knowledge, but without proper context and nuance. Acting on what he had seen without that supporting data was just as much a threat to possible future history as taking deliberate action to sabotage such events. Further, doing so would be seen as a violation of the Temporal Prime Directive, a regulation enacted more than a century ago. In truth, he had infringed upon the rule simply by accessing the data from the weapon ship's computer. Since the directive's activation, enforcing it and investigating such breaches was one of DTI's primary responsibilities.

"*We anticipated this even before Captain Picard contacted me,*" said Ranjea. "*Of immediate concern is Mister Crusher's contention that this situation may be affecting multiple timelines. It's this theory that's driving much of our current investigations and research. I have teams scouring the protected archives, hunting for anything that might be a clue that changes are affecting the past or present, but there's only so much we can do without more information.*" The Deltan leaned forward in his chair and closer to the comm link's visual pickup. "*I'll soon be sending a status update to Picard. I intend to suggest he include you in the planning of any next steps. You may be able to spot connections of the sort we're looking for before anyone else, including Mister Crusher.*"

Taurik nodded. "I will assist in any way that I am able."

"*I know you will.*" Ranjea sighed. "*This is a very tricky business, Commander, but I know you appreciate the gravity of what we're doing. It's our best shot at finally getting something resembling the whole picture about this thing. The only way we're going to get any answers is to keep pushing forward and see how things work out, and be ready to adapt at a moment's notice."*

"You are suggesting we expect the unexpected." Taurik considered his own comment. "That does seem an odd outlook for someone whose duties require understanding how and when events are supposed to unfold in a prescribed manner."

"I'm a DTI agent, Commander, not a fortune teller. Protecting the timeline is all about expecting the unexpected."

25

U.S.S. Enterprise NCC-1701-E
2387

Those portions of the planet not cast in shadow were pale, yellow, and uninviting. In that sense, they were precisely as Picard remembered them from the *Enterprise*'s last visit here, and also how the world was depicted in the sensor data he had reviewed from that mission nearly two decades earlier. Though he knew there were other planets in this star system, for some reason the world now growing larger on the bridge's main viewscreen seemed small and forlorn, as though it were all alone and long forgotten within the vast cosmos.

"Approaching Devidia II, sir," reported Lieutenant Joanna Faur, the ship's senior flight control officer. "We're at one-half impulse. Estimated time to orbit, ninety seconds."

Rising from his command chair, Picard moved to stand just behind her and Glinn Ravel Dygan, the Cardassian exchange officer occupying the bridge's forward operations station to Faur's left. "Continue on course. Standard orbit, Conn."

From one of the science stations along the bridge's starboard bulkhead, Lieutenant Dina Elfiki called out, "Conventional sensors detect no life signs anywhere on the planet, Captain. The atmosphere contains heavy dust and other contaminants, and scans show a massive crater on the southern hemisphere's largest landmass. It's more than twelve kilometers across, and there are indications of mineral substances not native to the planet and which weren't registered by the *Enterprise*-D's previous visit here." She turned in her seat. "I think an asteroid hit the planet, sir. Ten years ago, fifteen at the outside, judging by the spread of atmospheric contaminants."

"Is it safe to beam down?" asked Worf.

The young Egyptian woman nodded. "You don't necessarily need environmental suits, sir, but I wouldn't recommend staying too long."

Having taken over the station next to hers, Geordi La Forge said, "I'm not picking up any life signs with the transphasic sensor I've set up, either." He shook his head. "I had to come up with it in a hurry and from memory, so I'm not sure I got everything right." Glancing over his shoulder to Picard, La Forge added, "Sorry, Captain. I'm still working out the kinks."

Picard nodded at the report. "Understandable, Commander. I appreciate what you managed to accomplish so quickly."

He knew La Forge faced a challenge reconstructing technology he created nearly twenty years earlier, the first time the *Enterprise* encountered the Devidians. After following a group of the aliens to nineteenth-century Earth as part of an away team commanded by Will Riker, the engineer had figured out a means of alerting them to the presence of any Devidian life-forms via the traces of triolic energy they left behind. It had been, as Riker later reported, an unconventional yet impressive feat, modifying a tricorder using whatever tools La Forge had available to him nearly five hundred years in the past. Following that mission, he logged what he had done into his official report, which was subsequently confiscated by Starfleet Command at the request of the Department of Temporal Investigations along with everything else the *Enterprise* crew had discovered about the Devidians and their time-travel capabilities. The debriefing Picard and his senior staff received from DTI agents made it clear this was information best forgotten.

If only wishing made it so.

"Lieutenant Elfiki," said Worf, directing his attention to the science station. "Any signs of temporal disturbances?"

"No, Commander. Scans aren't picking up any traces of chronitons or triolic energy. What I am detecting is evidence of orbital bombardment in the planet's northern hemisphere. I'm guessing this is the mountain cavern you targeted the last time you were here."

Still studying the planet that had grown to fill the bridge's viewscreen, Picard said, "Mister La Forge, that cavern had been modified by the Devidians to help them focus their temporal-distortion abilities into the vortex they used to travel to Earth. Are our sensors detecting anything like that?"

It was Elfiki who replied, "No, sir." She turned in her seat. "Commander La Forge, I reviewed what little information we have in the computer about this planet, and I've attempted to configure our sensors accordingly, but I'm not sure I know what I'm looking for, sir."

La Forge shrugged. "It's okay. We weren't sure the first time either. It took a while to home in on exactly how far they existed out of phase with the rest of us. That was the trick, because it really wasn't all that much. Point zero-zero-four percent displacement was the original discrepancy, but it's entirely possible they can increase that gap. I'm hoping the adjustments I've made to this transphasic sensor setup can detect that variance."

"That's it." Pushing herself from her chair, Elfiki moved to stand next to La Forge. "I have an idea." She reached for the console, then hesitated. "Sorry, sir. May I?"

Giving her room to work, La Forge gestured to the controls. "Be my guest. What are you thinking?"

"You're mostly there, sir." She reached for the console and began tapping instructions in rapid, one-handed fashion. "You said it yourself. They may be able to increase the degree to which they exist out of phase, but what if the degree of that phase-shifting isn't constant? They could be fluctuating all the time, making it harder to detect them. So, we need to scan the same way, and we already have a way to do that."

La Forge smiled. "The targeting sensors in a transphasic torpedo. They're designed to adapt to fluctuations in spacetime when locking onto a target in temporal flux. Good thinking, Lieutenant."

"It's only good if it works, sir." She entered one final string of instructions before stepping back from the station, and within seconds a tone sounded just as one of the console's display screens began scrolling a new procession of information.

"Bingo," said La Forge.

Watching the two officers work, Picard said, "You found something?"

"Something," replied the chief engineer. "It's faint, but definitely something artificial, located deep underground on a sizable landmass near the planet's southern pole. I'm not picking up any energy readings."

Worf asked, "Is this something new? Was it not here during our previous visit?"

"There's no way to be sure from up here, sir," replied Elfiki. "An on-site scan might be able to make that determination."

"A regular tricorder won't do it, Captain," added La Forge. "But I can probably rig up a portable scanner we could connect to the ship's sensor array."

"I can help with that."

Picard turned at the new voice to see Wesley Crusher, who had arrived via the port-side turbolift at the rear of the bridge. A few hours' rest and a shower had done wonders for his appearance. His hair and beard looked trimmed, and he had acquired fresh clothes, although Picard noted they otherwise appeared identical to the bedraggled ensemble in which he had arrived. Despite this effort, he still looked very much out of place as he took in the bridge and the officers manning the various stations. Was there a hint of melancholy in his eyes?

Nodding to Picard as he stepped farther onto the bridge, Wesley said, "I've modified about a dozen hand phasers and almost that many rifles based on the technology my older self used to create his transphasic disruptor. They'll operate on the same principle as your torpedoes and even Geordi's scanner. Their power cells will drain faster, but the difference is negligible."

"Meaning?" asked Worf.

Wesley replied, "Meaning if these things show up and we get into a firefight, I give us less than two minutes before we're all screwed."

"Perhaps we should simply destroy the site from orbit," offered the first officer. Looking to Picard, he added, "Engineering reports that in less than two hours, they will have completed fabricating six transphasic torpedoes from the specifications in the main computer."

Picard shook his head. "Not until we investigate this firsthand, Number One. That said, complete the torpedo assembly and have them on standby."

As if regretting his earlier comments, Wesley said, "Maybe I should go alone. There's no telling what I might run into down there."

"That's precisely why you need someone to go with you," countered Picard. "There's no need to do this by yourself." He could not help the sudden vision of the older Wesley, dying in sickbay with his mother and the other doctors unable to help him. "Besides, Starfleet sent me here to investigate. I need to see this for myself."

He cast a final look at the dull, uninviting planet on the viewscreen. What awaited them down there?

Enduring Worf's citing regulations, and his protests at being left behind, Picard exercised a captain's prerogative to lead the away team that included Wesley, La Forge, Dina Elfiki, and Lieutenant Aneta Šmrhová. As he solidified and the transporter beam released him, he saw six more columns of energy forming to his right. They coalesced into the forms of Lieutenant Rennan Konya along with five other members of the *Enterprise*'s security detail. Within seconds, the party of eleven found itself standing in a subterranean cavern. Without question, it was far larger than the chamber he recalled from his previous visit, and according to La Forge's pre-transport briefing it was located thousands of kilometers away from that original location. High, sloping walls curved upward to form a domed ceiling. Dark apertures decorated the walls near ground level at more than a dozen points around the cave, each leading to winding, narrow tunnels. To Picard's eyes, the cave did not seem to be the result of underground erosion or other natural forces. The symmetry of something fashioned via artificial means seemed obvious to him.

"Konya, deploy a defensive perimeter," said Šmrhová, and he acknowledged the order with a nod before using hand signals to direct his security detail to fan out. Without speaking, the team moved toward the walls of the cavern, leaving Šmrhová to watch over the captain. The security chief positioned herself less than an arm's length from him, to which he responded with a questioning stare.

"Commander Worf's orders, sir." She hefted her phaser rifle, which along with those carried by the rest of the security detail had been modified by Wesley to replicate the transphasic disruptor functionality of the weapon carried by his older self. "He told me if anything happened to you, I should just look for a nice place to live here."

Picard grunted in mild amusement. "Mister Worf *is* something of a mother hen, isn't he?"

"I'll leave that for you to tell him, sir."

Stepping away from the group, the strange weapon crafted by his older self slung across his back, Wesley walked toward the middle of the chamber. Picard followed him past several rock formations until he saw the depression at the cavern's center. He guessed it to be perhaps ten meters in diameter, carved out of the cavern floor. Smooth sides descended at most two meters at a gradual angle to reach the basin's bottom, on which sat the ruins of . . .

something. At first, Picard thought it might be the remnants of a building or other structure, perhaps a dwelling, but the nature and amount of the debris suggested something not meant to be occupied.

"A statue of some sort?" the captain asked. "A marker or monument?" He gestured to some of the larger pieces, covered in layers of dust or dirt which did not hide sharp angles and straight lines that could not be natural occurrences. "It's all rather elaborate."

Lieutenant Elfiki, tricorder in hand, replied, "Stone exterior, covering some kind of metallic composite, sir. The pieces are mostly solid except for narrow conduits running through some of them. I'm not picking up any signs of internal mechanisms."

"I don't think you'll find anything like that," said Wesley. "Not here, anyway." Reaching into his jacket pocket, he extracted the Omnichron and touched one of its outer panels before tossing it toward the ruins. Arcing through the air, the device began to hover over the debris.

"Captain." It was La Forge, who had moved to stand near Elfiki a few meters away and was consulting his tricorder along with a somewhat larger device, the engineer's hastily assembled phase-discriminator module, attached to it. "The walls of this cavern have been subjected to a molecular polarization effect similar to what we found in the original cave. I'm definitely picking up indications of phase displacement, but they're very faint."

Wesley had begun walking around the depression's perimeter. "Hang on." He stopped, holding out a hand toward the Omnichron that now hung above the exact center of the ruins. "It's onto something. The phase variance you reported during your last encounter put you out of temporal sync with the Devidians by less than a second, but it was still enough to render them invisible to you, and you to them. I should be able to pick up on that slight a variance even without the O.C., but this is much greater."

"How much greater?" asked Šmrhová, who was shadowing Picard as he approached the depression's edge.

"Centuries, at least." Wesley closed his eyes, his hand still extended toward the Omnichron. "And I think it's shifting, like Lieutenant Elfiki described. Sort of a moving target."

The security chief studied the ruins as if searching for threats, the muzzle of her phaser rifle pointed toward the ground while still aiming toward the debris. As they drew closer, she instructed Lieutenant Konya and the security detail to tighten their perimeter to ten meters out from the depression.

"What does that mean?" she asked. "They could be here, centuries ahead of us—or behind us—and still be occupying the same space?"

"Only if they phase-shift to match us, or we shift to catch up with them," said La Forge. He indicated his equipment. "This phase discriminator along with my tricorder don't have enough power to bridge a gap like that."

"Commander," said Elfiki. "We could do what you did last time, with a subspace force-field generator and a larger power source for the discriminator. I read about it this morning. It'll take some time to set it up, but I think—"

"I can do it," said Wesley. Opening his eyes, he regarded his companions. "Not for all of us, and not for very long."

"What are you suggesting, Wesley?" Picard gestured to the ruins. "That we time shift across centuries?"

Nodding to where Picard indicated, Wesley replied, "If we want to get to an origin point for whatever this is, then yes. We don't need to be there long. Just long enough to verify what the O.C. is telling me."

Picard tried to consider the variables of proceeding along this path, but doing so was impossible given the unknowns this situation presented. If they were going to prove the Devidians were behind what Wesley had shown them, this appeared to be their best option.

"Very well. Make it so. You, me, Mister La Forge, and Lieutenant Elfiki." When Šmrhová cleared her throat, Picard added,

"And Lieutenant Šmrhová, lest she earn Mister Worf's wrath." He waited as she updated Lieutenant Konya and told them to maintain their perimeter before nodding to Wesley to proceed. The team gathered closer, matching Šmrhová's stance with their hand phasers, and Wesley held out both arms.

"It might feel a little weird," he said, before his body began to shimmer and dissipate, fading from existence.

Then, so did everything else, at least from Picard's perspective, taking on an ethereal quality while dissolving into a sapphire haze. At first there was no indication anything in the cavern around them was changing with this apparent transition from one plane of existence to another. After a moment, what Picard expected to see began to occur, in the form of the ruins reconstructing themselves. Wesley's phase-shifting bridged however many decades or centuries separated them from their own point in spacetime as dust retreated from the pieces and they pulled back to become whole once again. The result was a stout base that tapered as it grew upward from the canyon floor.

Standing to Picard's left, La Forge held up his tricorder. "I'm picking up a triolic energy signature. Faint, but growing stronger."

Although the shape seemed rudimentary and lacked aesthetic qualities, Picard realized he had seen the basic configuration before. Now assembled, the tower began to glow with some unknown form of energy.

"The planet we re-created on the holodeck," he said. "The towers scattered among the ancient city, used to focus temporal distortions."

Wesley replied, "But not as sophisticated. It's like a rough draft of what we saw."

"There's an energy signature coming from inside it," said La Forge. "Triolic waves, and chroniton particles."

"I'm detecting life signs," added Elfiki. "Well, I think I am."

Near the base of the construct, Picard noted a series of blue-white silhouettes emerging out of emptiness. He saw a single humanoid figure, along with four other life-forms that were larger and serpentine in shape. Ophidians, he realized. Similar to the one they encountered all those years ago, but much larger. These were Wesley's "Naga" creatures. Nearly five meters in length and a meter across, they looked very much like the predators he suspected them to be.

"We've got company," said Šmrhová, who was already hefting her phaser rifle and pointing it toward the new arrivals.

"I see them." Wesley's outstretched hands turned to clenched fists and the sensation of movement stopped. The new figures around them were in motion, including the quartet of Nagas that undulated as they moved, but to Picard it seemed akin to watching a visual playback with forward progress ground almost to a halt.

La Forge said, "I guess we now know for sure the Devidians are behind all of this." He held up his tricorder. "The readings aren't clear because of the interference, but those things are similar to the smaller ophidian we encountered before."

"Similar." Picard regarded the scene before him. "Yet far more dangerous, I imagine."

As if in response to his comment and in sluggish yet deliberate fashion, all of the alien figures turned toward them.

26

Picard had no chance to shout a warning or anything else before the creatures vanished and the blue haze enveloping everything in the cavern swirled around him. Unlike the earlier transition, which by comparison felt gentle and unhurried, this time he was all but overwhelmed by the sensation of being pulled along like a swimmer caught in a powerful current. Within seconds the effect began fading and Picard saw the walls of the cavern re-forming around him. The tower, visible once again, had returned to the destroyed, abandoned pile of collapsed stone that had greeted them upon their arrival.

"What happened?" he asked, looking around to see that the rest of the team had returned with him. He locked eyes with Wesley. "Was that . . . ?"

"Yes." Fatigue showed on the other man's face, and Picard saw concern in his eyes. "I can sense them coming. I don't know if I got us out of there fast enough to keep them from tracking us. We need to leave." He extended his hand, and the Omnichron, which had been holding station over the ruins, returned to him.

"Over there!"

It was Elfiki, pointing beyond the ruins to the depression's far side. A pinpoint of light appeared in the air, rapidly stretching and widening until a dark mass appeared from its center. Picard recognized it as one of the serpent-like creatures he had seen around the construct during their aborted phase shift to centuries in the past. Long and sinewy, its body rippled and twisted as it emerged from the newly formed vortex.

Lieutenant Konya yelled, "Security team, engage target!" He moved forward, leading his security detail as the six officers converged on the Naga. Pulling his phaser rifle into his shoulder, he sighted down its length and let go the first volley. Brilliant orange energy slammed into the creature's head but did nothing to slow it down. Now free of the rift, the Naga arced its long, sinewy body toward Konya as the rest of the security team converged on him, bringing their weapons to bear. Five more phaser beams struck the creature but momentum was continuing to carry it forward. Even as Konya backpedaled to give himself maneuvering room, the thing closed the distance, its considerable bulk sideswiping the lieutenant before catching the other security officers as it glided past. Pockets of silver energy erupted from its body, enveloping all six members.

"Konya!" shouted Šmrhová, but Picard knew it was too late.

He watched in horror as the bodies of Konya and the security team shriveled and disintegrated, caving in on themselves before vanishing in clouds of ash.

Šmrhová unleashed a hoarse, anguished cry, lunging forward and firing her phaser rifle at the Naga as it twisted away from the carnage it wrought and came about as though searching for new targets. Having unlimbered his own weapon, Wesley joined her, his first salvo driving into the creature's belly. It thrashed in response and seemed to turn its attention toward him, but by then Šmrhová was firing again.

"All weapons to bear!" snapped Picard, adding his hand phaser to the effort. La Forge and Elfiki joined him and when Wesley fired again, the assault's combined force halted the Naga in midflight. It wavered, hovering in the air as if trying to summon the strength to repel the attack, but within seconds Picard watched skin and muscle peel back from the creature's head and upper body, releasing what must be its blood and exposing bone. Its immense, maw-like mouth opened but no sound emerged before the serpent's head came apart. The rest of its body slumped as it succumbed to the phaser barrage, and it fell backward before landing at the edge of the depression. Momentum carried the Naga over the edge, sending it sliding to the base of the ruins.

"Oh, my god," said Elfiki, her voice low.

His ears still ringing from the effects of the intense firefight, Picard could not keep his gaze from drifting to where Konya and his team had stood mere seconds earlier. Nothing remained, not even the dust that had punctuated their sudden, violent departure from existence. Six members of his crew, gone in an instant. Despite the shock, anger, and grief he felt welling up within him, he knew there was no time.

"Captain," said La Forge, and even with the single word Picard heard the strain in the engineer's voice. Holding his tricorder in one shaky hand, the other man looked toward the ruins. "I'm picking up increased triolic energy levels."

"And chroniton particles," added Elfiki, also sounding strained as she rallied to maintain her composure. "I think it's another temporal distortion."

Wesley said, "It's them. They've tracked us somehow."

Picard tapped his combadge. "*Enterprise*, emergency transport."

Over the open link, Worf replied, *"Acknowledged. Transporter rooms two and three locking on—"*

The rest of the first officer's response was lost in a burst of static at the same time another fissure formed in the air in front of the ruins. It was much larger this time, and Picard watched it grow to obscure the tower remnants, and inside its boundary he could make out the structure they had seen during the phase shift. New and vibrant, it pulsed with power.

"With the vortex open, I'm able to scan the other side," said La Forge. "Triolic energy levels from the tower are spiking."

"*Enterprise*," said Picard after once more tapping his combadge. "Do you read?" Static erupted from the open frequency, making him wince, but some of Worf's reply made it through.

". . . ing with comm . . . porters effect . . . attemp . . . pensate . . ."

Wesley gestured toward the cavern wall behind them. "We need to buy some time. The tunnels. Head for the tunnels!"

Šmrhová moved to stand in front of Picard, lifting her phaser rifle toward the fissure. "We'll cover you. Go. Go!"

Picard saw the other three Nagas within the vortex surging toward the opening. They moved in a formation, as though communicating with one another as they advanced. Raising his phaser, he took an involuntary step backward while gesturing for La Forge and Elfiki to stay with him as Šmrhová and Wesley moved to protect their retreat.

Šmrhová commenced her initial phaser barrage as the first creature cleared the vortex. The modified weapon caught the Naga and brought it to a lurching halt, allowing Wesley to again bring his disruptor to bear. Taking more care with his aim, he fired the weapon's first salvo at the creature's head. The effect was much more immediate, with the Naga going limp as the disruptor punched through its skull. It fell to the earth, coming to rest on the cavern's stone floor.

As if learning from their companion's misfortune, the other two Nagas broke away from each other, each launching on a different trajectory away from the rift. One continued straight toward them.

"Fall back!" yelled Picard, firing his hand phaser at the Naga rushing them. It was, he knew, a hopeless cause. Even with their modified weapons, the five of them could not hope to fend off two of these creatures in such rapid succession. He saw La Forge and Elfiki retreating toward the nearest tunnel, but already one of the Nagas was moving as if to intercept them.

Šmrhová grabbed him with her free hand, pulling him to follow her as she resumed her grip on her phaser rifle and fired toward the other creature. At the same time, Picard heard another crackle from his combadge.

"*. . . Picard . . . by for trans . . .*"

He felt the familiar tingle of a transporter beam wrapping

around his body and forced himself to stop moving long enough for the process to take hold. To his right, he saw Wesley firing his disruptor toward one of the creatures just as it approached La Forge and Elfiki. Columns of transporter energy showered down to envelop all three just as the Naga lunged ahead, passing through the space occupied by Elfiki.

"No!"

The outburst faded amid the transporter effect whining in his ears as the cavern disappeared in a flash of light, replaced a heartbeat later by the familiar interior of an *Enterprise* transporter room. Even as he finished materializing, Picard turned his head to look behind him, seeing Elfiki, La Forge, Šmrhová, and Wesley all solidifying on their respective transporter pads.

The hum of the transporter beams could not hope to drown out Dina Elfiki's wail of agony and terror.

Even as the materialization process finished, Picard stared in desperate horror as the young science officer's body fell apart. Skin, muscle, bones, and even the material of her uniform wilted and buckled, dispersing into a mist of ashes that filled the transporter chamber. As the desiccated remnants of their crewmate and friend scattered across the away team, Picard stepped back and almost tripped on the stairs leading down from the platform.

"Dina!"

La Forge held out a hand toward the now empty transporter pad. It was a futile gesture but Picard understood it. For her part, Šmrhová was looking around the room to see if one of the creatures might somehow have made the trip. No one else said anything, including the frightened young ensign standing behind the transporter console. Picard saw her pale complexion, wide eyes, and mouth open in mute shock as she attempted to process what just happened. He started to say something, but was cut off by the abrupt blaring of an alarm.

"*Red alert,*" said Worf over the ship's intercom. "*All hands to battle stations. Captain Picard to the bridge.*"

Emerging from the turbolift, Picard turned his attention to the bridge's main viewscreen. As he imagined on the ride up from the transporter room, the image depicted the pale, cloud-shrouded world of Devidia II.

"Status," he snapped.

Worf rose from the captain's chair. "We were attempting to maintain a sensor lock on the life-forms, sir, but they simply disappeared. So far, all attempts to require their biosigns have been ineffective."

"Lieutenant Šmrhová," said Picard. "What about the target site in the cavern. Are sensors still picking up any temporal distortions from that location?"

Having resumed her station at the tactical console, Šmrhová replied, "Scans show the vortex is still active, sir. Triolic energy along with residual chronitons."

"They must need that vortex to get back," said La Forge. "Which means they probably have to still be here, somewhere."

Slinging his disruptor rifle over his shoulder, Wesley said, "I can sense them. They're . . . close." He grabbed La Forge by his arm and directed the chief engineer to the science station. Ensign Oliver Trimble, the science officer crewing that console in Elfiki's stead, turned in his seat at their approach.

"Where's Lieutenant Elfiki?" he asked.

Ignoring the ensign, Wesley reached for the console and began working the controls in rapid-fire fashion. "Geordi, your shields aren't designed to protect against transphasic threats. I don't think we can keep those things from getting through, but with some modifications we might be able to slow them down and buy us time."

"Time," said Picard. "You think they mean to breach the ship?"

Wesley nodded. "I've seen it before, at least with Nagas this size. Be thankful none of their bigger brothers or sisters are around. Not yet, anyway."

"The shield generators are already set up to randomly rotate frequencies, sir," offered Ensign Trimble. "A holdover from lessons learned fighting the Borg."

Patting the younger officer on the shoulder, La Forge said, "That won't be enough, but if we bring the secondary shield generators online at the same time—"

"And augment their frequency rotation so that the primary and secondary generators cycle at random intervals, that might throw up an extra firewall of sorts. The difference wouldn't have to be much."

La Forge nodded. "Hundredths of a second is all it would take." He scowled. "Assuming it works. Only one way to find out." He joined Wesley at the science station and the two men started putting their plan into motion.

"Captain," said Worf. "We should destroy the site beneath the surface. We have four operational transphasic torpedoes. At last report, two more will be ready in less than thirty minutes, and they are preparing to fabricate more."

Picard nodded at the first officer's report. "At the very least, we could prevent more of those creatures from coming through the vortex. Conn, adjust orbit to bring us over the target site. Lieutenant Šmrhová, stand by transphasic torpedoes."

As he moved to his command chair, the deck shifted beneath his feet at the same time every light and station on the bridge blinked in protest and the ever-present hum of the ship's warp engines dropped in pitch. Turning back to the screen, Picard saw ripples of blue-white energy playing across the image, emanating from a dark mass at the display's center.

"Shields are down ten percent," reported Glinn Ravel Dygan from the bridge's forward operations console. "Three life-forms are attempting to breach the shields. The Nagas we detected on the surface. Sensor readings are indistinct. They just appeared from nowhere, and seem to be phasing in and out of our spacetime continuum."

La Forge stepped closer to the command well. "We've brought the secondary shield generators online and enabled random frequency offset from the primary generators, but I'm already seeing signs of strain. This won't hold them for long."

"Captain," said Šmrhová, looking up from her console. "Sensors are detecting a fourth life-form. It's humanoid, sir. Readings are indistinct. It's phase-shifting like the Nagas."

"They do that," said Wesley, who had again moved to stand near Šmrhová. "It's how they're able to maneuver outside an atmosphere. My older self referred to them as handlers for the larger creatures, but they're dangerous in their own right."

Glinn Dygan looked over his shoulder. "Captain, the three life-forms are maneuvering to pursue us. Every time they shift in and out of phase, they close the gap between us in quick jumps."

"It's like they're tunneling through time," said La Forge. "But they're coming right at us. How did they even sense us to begin with?"

Picard was looking at Wesley as the chief engineer asked the question, and so was able to watch the other man's expression change.

"Son of a bitch."

"What is it?" asked La Forge. "Wes, what are you—"

"It's me." Wesley turned to Picard. "I mean, it has to be me. Whenever I've come across them attacking something—another ship, a city on a planet, whatever—they almost always turn their attention to me if I've phased completely into that point along spacetime. I don't know if they just detect me as being different from everyone else, or I give off something they can pick up on because I can travel through time and shift dimensional planes, but it has to be something."

Worf turned to face him. "You are saying your presence here is a threat to the ship?"

"I think so."

Another power drain coursed across the bridge, affecting every station and system. This time, the disruption came with a new alarm klaxon.

"Warning," said the voice of the *Enterprise*'s main computer. *"Deflector shields compromised. Detecting breaches near outer hull at decks ten and sixteen. Hull breach probability ninety-seven percent."*

"Evacuate those sections," said Picard. Deck ten contained recreation facilities but also one of the ship's main phaser arrays. As for adjacent sections, the bulk of deck nine was devoted to living quarters as well as the education center.

Where were Beverly and René?

27

—◆—

"Red alert. All hands to battle stations. Security teams to decks ten and sixteen as well as sections on adjacent decks."

Listening to the computer repeat its alert notice, Taurik studied the master systems table at the center of the *Enterprise*'s main engineering space. The table displayed a schematic of the ship with its active deflector shields. Icons highlighting different areas showed how the shields were being tested by the creatures intent on breaking through those defenses. He entered instructions to the table's keypad interface, and the intensity and thickness of the line indicating the deflector shield barrier around the ship increased.

"Engineering to bridge," he said. "We are continuing to rotate deflector shield frequencies, but the effect is negligible. Sensors show breaches widening as the creatures continue their attack."

"We see that too, Taurik," replied Geordi La Forge, who at Captain Picard's behest remained at one of the bridge engineering stations. *"Wes and I are trying more modifications, but so far it's not having any effect. I'm also routing more power from the warp engines to compensate."*

Taurik noted the energy transfer from the ship's main drive systems and cocked an eyebrow. "Commander, that rate of reallocation will prevent us from going to warp speed."

"I know, but it's all we've got," said La Forge. *"The second we route that power back to the engines, that's it for the shields and those things are coming through. We can't get at them with phasers, so we're reprogramming a couple of transphasic torpedoes to take them out at close range."*

"Our proximity to those detonations puts the ship at considerable risk, sir."

"Tell me about it. I've got my hands full up here, but Wes is working on a way to reconfigure the shields to take the brunt of it. He's routing those specs to you now. We'll probably need to route more power from the warp engines, and prioritize which systems don't get interrupted. Get started on that, and we'll coordinate from the bridge." There was no mistaking the stress in the chief engineer's voice. *"We don't have a lot of time, Taurik."*

"Understood. Engineering out."

"Commander?"

Looking up from the table, Taurik saw Lieutenant Abby Balidemaj, the officer in charge of the security detail that had just swarmed into the ship's main engineering space, standing on its far side. She held a phaser rifle in her left hand, extended and proffered to him. Cradled in the crook of her right arm was another such weapon. Taurik took the rifle and with practiced ease inspected its settings, noting the modifications made to it in accordance with Wesley Crusher's specifications.

"The power cell won't last as long as it normally does," offered Balidemaj. She reached over to tap the rifle's inlaid status readout. "And it'll take at least two or three of us concentrating our fire to take out just one of those things. That's the word from Mister Crusher and Lieutenant Šmrhová, anyway."

From her voice, Taurik could tell the lieutenant was struggling to keep her emotions in check in an effort to focus on her duties. With the death of Lieutenant Rennan Konya, Balidemaj had been hastily promoted to the position of deputy chief of security under Šmrhová. There had been no time to process the loss of her colleague, let alone for any of the mourning customs humans preferred to observe at the death of a family member or close friend. Such rituals would be observed at a more appropriate time, assuming the *Enterprise* survived the coming encounter with the Nagas working to infiltrate the ship.

For his part, Taurik acknowledged the death of Lieutenant Dina Elfiki, out of respect for his own friendship with the science officer but also because he knew T'Ryssa Chen would be even more greatly affected. At last report, she was en route to the bridge, ostensibly to take on Elfiki's responsibilities. He would make a point to find her once they were past this emergency, to lend her "emotional support," as Chen might put it. In truth, he would take a measure of solace from her company, and together they would lament the loss of their friend.

Pushing aside thoughts best left for later, Taurik turned his attention to the scene around him. Several members of the *Enterprise* security team augmented the engineering staff. Areas of the deck containing sensitive systems were evacuated and sealed behind pressure doors, around which he had activated transphasic shielding as modified by himself along with Wesley Crusher and Commander La Forge. It was hoped the reconfigured defenses, along with the antimatter containment fields already in place to prevent a warp-core breach, would slow down the intruding life-forms, if not prevent them from gaining access to the critical components. According to Wesley, the Nagas were drawn to the primary energy systems aboard those starships they attacked. It was reasonable to assume they would be coming here, and the only thing standing between them and *Enterprise*'s destruction was however many phaser rifles Lieutenant Balidemaj and her people could bring to bear. With luck, the Nagas could be brought down before inflicting mortal damage to the ship.

An abrupt change in the pulsing drone of the warp core made Taurik and everyone else in the compartment look up from their various tasks to see all of the lights and each of the consoles flickering in response to an obvious power drain. An alarm indicator sounded from the master systems table and Taurik noted the line surrounding the *Enterprise*'s technical schematic had shifted from yellow to red, followed by the voice of the main computer.

"Warning. Deflector shields compromised."

Balidemaj called out, "They're punching through."

Over the intercom, Captain Picard called out, *"Attention, all* hands. *The Nagas have penetrated our shields. They have the ability to phase-shift through the hull, which means they can appear anywhere on the ship. Be on the alert for intruders."*

"There!"

It was one of the security officers, pointing toward an area near the rear of the engineering room. A rift had opened near the high ceiling of the multilevel compartment, and a dark, slithering mass was emerging from it. The first salvo from a phaser rifle came as the Naga pushed itself through the vortex, catching its solidifying body while half of it remained hidden from view. Its contortions helped it avoid that initial blast, but a second phaser shot from Balidemaj caught the creature with a glancing blow along its flank. This time, Taurik saw how the Naga phase-shifted itself to avoid the worst of the attack, and he realized the flaw in the defensive measures he and his shipmates had undertaken.

"Fall back!" he shouted. "Everyone out of this section."

Instead of heeding his instructions, three security officers advanced on the creature. Taurik understood their reasoning as they attempted to confine the intruder to one area of the larger compartment, but even as they brought their weapons to bear, it was reacting to their presence. Rather than being hemmed into a corner of the room, it twisted its body and arced up and toward its adversaries. One of the officers ducked and pivoted, trying to keep the creature in his sights, but it was faster. It glided past him and two of his companions, and an instant later their bodies disintegrated in compact bursts of silver light.

His jaw tightening at the loss of the officers even while others scrambled to engage the intruder, Taurik watched as the Naga was drawn to the warp core and began circling it. Brushing against the transphasic shielding, the creature recoiled from the impact. The shields sparked, releasing a high-pitched hum with each touch. Satisfied the shield was holding, Taurik reached for the systems table, entering commands to increase power from the warp engines to the containment shield generators.

"Taurik, watch out!"

It was Balidemaj, approaching from his left with her phaser rifle firing as she moved. Other security officers joined in but the creature bucked its body upward, avoiding most of the energy beams, while those that hit had only limited effect. Snapping its tail, it caught the lieutenant and swiped her aside, her body dissipating into a fine powder that scattered across the floor and nearby workstations. Emotions held at bay came to the fore as Taurik fired his own weapon at the Naga, its beam striking the creature but not slowing it down.

Then it coiled around toward him and surged forward.

Wesley!

René's voice echoed in Wesley's mind, and at the same time he projected to his younger brother what he hoped were feelings of comfort and calm. It was a sensation not unlike how he had previously reached out to the boy and his mother, only this time it was René inundated and all but overwhelmed by feelings of panic and worry. He knew something was wrong, even if he did not understand what was happening. Reaching out farther, Wesley sensed his mother working her way from sickbay toward the ship's learning center, but she would be swimming upstream against the current of *Enterprise* personnel in the midst of evacuation.

Wesley was closer.

I'm coming, René. Hang on.

People, crewmembers and not a few civilians, filled the corridors. Most everyone seemed to be following their training and proceeded in an orderly fashion toward the ship's interior areas. They followed the hasty evacuation plan sent from Commander Worf on the bridge, but this stretch of passageway was still crowded. Wesley Crusher knew they were in an area well away from the hull, and none of the living quarters and other rooms around him featured windows looking out at the stars. Under normal circumstances this would be a section free from immediate danger in the event of an intrusion from outside the ship, but Wesley knew they were not dealing with an ordinary enemy. Every part of the *Enterprise* was vulnerable to attack. Everyone aboard faced the same risk.

"*Warning,*" said the voice of the main computer. "*Intruder alert, deck nine, section twenty-three.*"

"This way," said Aneta Šmrhová, pointing to an upcoming junction as she jogged next to Wesley. Turning down the secondary corridor took them away from most of the personnel adhering to the evacuation instructions. From somewhere ahead of them, Wesley heard the sound of weapons fire along with shouts of alarm, and seconds later he and Šmrhová rounded a corner to see three *Enterprise* crewmembers—a human male, a Vulcan female, and a male Tellarite—standing just outside the threshold of a wider, double-door hatch, firing at something out of Wesley's line of sight.

"Recreation center," said Šmrhová. "Gym, lounges, all that. Plenty of places to hide."

Wesley frowned. "And yet no place to hide."

Farther up the passageway, a Naga was phase-shifting and passing through the bulkheads, overheads, and decks as though moving through air or water. It disappeared from view only to emerge seconds later, pushing across the corridor and through the opposite bulkhead. Each time it showed itself, the security officers fired. Those beams that struck appeared to have little or no effect.

"It's avoiding the phasers by transitioning in and out of this reality," he said. "My upgrades to the phasers weren't enough. At least, not by themselves, but this might help." Pulling his disruptor rifle to his shoulder, Wesley stared down its short barrel and waited for the creature to reappear. He fired as it emerged from the corridor's starboard bulkhead no more than five meters from the trio of *Enterprise* officers. The disruptor bolt struck the Naga's head, and it recoiled from the attack as the security team resumed firing. Despite the barrage, the creature was on them in seconds, bowling through them and curving toward the rec center's open entrance. With no time even to scream for help, each of the three officers disappeared in their respective clouds of ash while the Naga continued its advance. Then, phaser fire from inside the room added to the chaos, but the creature kept moving.

"Come on," said Wesley, running for the entrance, as it was now obvious there were people inside the large, open room. He reached the threshold to find another pair of *Enterprise* security officers with phaser rifles standing alongside Hegol Den, the ship's counselor, and the learning center's education leader, Hailan Casmir. Both civilians wielded hand phasers, and all four were firing at the Naga from somewhat covered positions behind a refreshment bar. Wesley counted six children with them including René, whose eyes widened as he caught sight of his older brother.

"Wesley!" the boy cried.

"Get back!" Wesley gestured with his free hand for the group to retreat farther into the room even as the Naga continued pushing ahead despite the torrent of phaser fire. Casmir stepped backward, indicating for the children to stay behind him while Hegol continued to target the creature. The two security officers moved forward as though attempting to draw the thing's attention, but it seemed uninterested in them.

Trying to take aim without putting the other group in danger, Wesley fired three rapid shots at the creature's head. That was enough to make it break off its attack and it turned toward him and Šmrhová. It opened its mouth and Wesley fired again. This time the energy bolt tore through the back of the creature's throat and its entire body shuddered, releasing a gurgling howl of pain. Wesley unleashed two more volleys as Šmrhová and everyone else with weapons concentrated their fire on it, and seconds later it disappeared in a flash of disruptor energy and a haze of dust.

"Over there!"

It was Šmrhová, turning to face the second Naga phase-shifting as it rose up through the deck plating in dangerous proximity to the children. So close was the creature that the two security officers could not avoid contact, their bodies crumbling and falling away to the terrified cries of René and the other kids.

Then the Naga brought itself to a halt, the forward half of its body coiling upward as it raised its head like a viper preparing to strike. Seizing the unexpected respite, Wesley stepped into the recreation center and aimed his disruptor at the creature's head. His finger tightened on the trigger when he became aware of still another presence in the room. A fetid odor assailed his nostrils just as instinct told him the new arrival was behind him to his right, and he realized he and Šmrhová had walked into the room without checking the near corners. He turned to see one of the humanoid figures he had encountered only a handful of times, but which his older self had confronted on so many more occasions. Like the others, this individual also wore flowing robes, its features remaining hidden by the shadow of its hooded cloak.

"You!" He stared down his disruptor's barrel at the intruder, but before he could fire, he heard an unfamiliar voice echoing in his mind.

The boy. He is your bloodline. We knew you would come.

Startled by the unexpected taunt, Wesley almost fired before Šmrhová shouted a warning, and he turned to see the Naga launching itself toward the children and their adult guardians. Hegol stepped forward, firing his hand phaser in a futile effort even as Casmir shoved the kids toward the room's rear corner. The Argelian got a hand on René and pushed him out of the way at the same instant the Naga coiled past him and Hegol, catching both men with a swipe of its tail. The room echoed with their screams as they died. Feeling his heart hammering in his chest, Wesley saw a thin, stray tendril of silver energy playing off Casmir's disintegrating body and only just barely catching René.

Blinded with rage, Wesley fired at the Naga, burst after burst from the disruptor rifle. Šmrhová joined him and they both kept hammering at the creature. One of Wesley's shots tore through the creature's right eye and the thing released a howl of pain that he ignored as he fired yet again, pouring it on until the Naga surrendered to the attack and collapsed in a heap to the deck.

"Wesley!"

He turned as Šmrhová fired toward the humanoid, who held up one hand toward them. A cocoon of silver energy was forming around it, and Wesley sensed the power manifesting in response to some unspoken command.

"Bridge to Wesley!" said Geordi La Forge over the ship's intercom. *"We're picking up some kind of transmission from deck nine. It's aimed right at the target site down on the planet, and we're also detecting new waves of temporal displacement."*

"Destroy it!" shouted Wesley, raising his disruptor. "Now, Geordi! Do it now!"

He adjusted the disruptor's power setting as the humanoid began to fade, doubtless caught up in whatever process it used to transport itself through time and space.

"Not this time." Having hoped a moment like this might one day present itself, he pressed the disruptor's trigger. Rather than the pulse the weapon normally released, this time the energy bolt enveloped the humanoid, whose body jerked in response to the attack. It stopped dissolving and returned to solidity, convulsing and stumbling before its knees gave way and it fell face-first to the deck. Wesley fired again and when the energy field washed over it this time, the humanoid did not move.

"What did you do?" asked Šmrhová.

His attention still on the intruder, Wesley replied, "It's sort of a phase nullifier, interrupting the shifting out of one reality and returning the transitioning object or person to their point of origin." He held up the disruptor and eyed it with an approving gaze. "First chance I had to test it. I guess it worked."

Dropping the weapon, he ran to where the children were huddling in the lounge's far corner. None of them appeared injured, but then his eyes fell on René, and he felt his jaw slacken in shock.

The boy was not dead, but neither was he a boy any longer.

His clothes shredded and aged almost to the point of total decomposition, the person lying on the deck before him was now a young man. Matted auburn hair fell past his waist, matched by a scruffy beard. Fingernails and toenails were long and discolored. He looked almost like a savage, but he was not a stranger. Wesley recognized René in the eyes of this other person, whose voice croaked with familiarity and confusion when he uttered the single word.

"Wesley?"

28

Picard forced himself not to pace. He remained rooted in the position he had taken up behind the ops and conn stations. Though every fiber of his being screamed at him to leave the bridge, he knew his place was here. Concerns for the welfare of Beverly and René ate at him, but so did the safety of the rest of his people.

Reports about the startling loss of life in engineering along with other personnel, crewmembers and civilians alike, falling victim to the Nagas and their attacks were still coming in. A glance to Geordi La Forge told him his chief engineer was struggling to keep his focus on matters at hand, and yet he still carried out his duty. Picard could do no less; not now.

"Captain," said Lieutenant T'Ryssa Chen, who had taken over the science station in the wake of Dina Elfiki's death on Devidia II. "The second Naga's life signs are gone. I think they got it, sir."

There was no mistaking the wave of relief moving across the bridge. Officers at the different stations exchanged knowing glances, and Picard did the same with Worf. Even the Klingon allowed his warrior's façade to slip just a little in acknowledgment of what the crew had just endured.

"Hang on," said La Forge, still bent over the console next to Chen's. "Something's happening down on the planet. Triolic energy readings are spiking."

Chen pointed to one of her station's displays. "Commander, there's a signal projecting from the ship to the surface. No, it's subterranean. The cavern, sir."

"It must be the other intruder," said Worf. "The humanoid."

Moving to stand behind La Forge and Chen, Picard looked over his engineer's shoulder, inspecting for himself the litany of readings and the computer's interpretation of the various pieces of information it processed from the ship's sensors. "Geordi, can you jam the signal?"

La Forge shook his head. "It's operating on some form of transphasic frequency. I'm able to detect it, but blocking it is a whole other thing. I've got the computer analyzing it, but it will take time, and I—" He stopped as an alert indicator sounded from his console, and he leaned closer to his instruments while examining the new readings. "Oh, wow. This is incredible. The temporal distortion we saw down on the planet. It's back." He pointed to one display, which depicted an increase in energy levels. "I think the intruder triggered this."

Worf said, "He is likely seeking escape, or calling for reinforcements."

"Where is the intruder?" asked Picard.

Chen replied, "The crew lounge near the learning center on deck nine, sir."

"Bridge to Wesley!" snapped La Forge, his voice activating the ship's intercom. "We're picking up some kind of transmission from deck nine. It's aimed right at the target site down on the planet, and we're also detecting new waves of temporal displacement."

The harried voice of Wesley Crusher burst from the speakers. *"Destroy it! Now, Geordi! Do it now!"* Punctuating his plea was the sound of weapons fire.

Turning from the science stations, Picard pointed across the bridge to where Lieutenant Kirsten Cruzen occupied the secondary tactical station. "Transphasic torpedoes. How many do we have?"

"Six, sir," replied the young brunette woman. "So far, that is."

Picard gestured toward the bridge's main viewscreen, where the drab, cloud-masked surface of Devidia II remained centered in the image. "All six, on that target. Fire when ready."

"Aye, sir. Firing torpedoes."

On the viewscreen, Picard watched the first four orbs of blue-white energy streak toward the planet surface. Two more followed, with all six torpedoes disappearing beneath the planet's cloud cover. Seconds later he heard an indicator tone from Cruzen's console.

"Registering six detonations, sir," she reported. "The entire cavern has been destroyed."

Chen added, "We're not picking up any signs of the ruins or the temporal distortions, Captain. No lingering triolic energy sources either. I maintained sensor lock throughout and I think at least one of the torpedoes actually made it through the vortex before it closed, but there's no way to confirm the structure you encountered was also destroyed."

"Continue scans of that area," said Picard. "Let's be sure."

Turning in his seat, La Forge motioned toward the viewscreen. "We could drop a class-one probe down there, sir. Monitor the site directly. It might pick up something more quickly than our sensors up here." His expression was strained, and Picard could tell he was struggling with his feelings. He caught the engineer's shared look with Chen. For her part, Chen was doing her best to maintain a professional bearing, but the strain was beginning to show. He felt his own normal, composed façade beginning to slip as he saw the anguish in her eyes.

"Excellent suggestion. Make it so."

"And once that's done," said La Forge, "I request permission to return to engineering, sir." He paused, clearing his throat. "I'd like to check on my people."

Picard did not hesitate. "I understand, Commander." He looked to Chen, his expression softening even further. "And you as well, Lieutenant." The pain she must be feeling over the loss of three friends—two friends and a romantic partner—must be all but overwhelming, and yet here she was, holding steady to the best of her ability. How long could that last?

"Thank you, Captain." Chen's reply was level, before she again glanced to La Forge. "I'd like to accompany the commander." She paused, as if searching for something to say. "They may need some extra help down there."

"Of course." Picard held her gaze for an additional moment, uncertain as to what further there was to say in the here and now, before returning to the center of the bridge. While Worf watched him, awaiting instructions, the rest of the officers on duty remained focused on their individual stations. Despite this, there was no denying the anguish filling the air.

"We've lost several of our shipmates. Our friends," he said, trying his best to balance the authority he knew he needed to display with an appropriate level of compassion. "It's difficult to process such tragic news while concentrating on your duties, but you've comported yourselves in the finest tradition of the values we all cherish. You've honored our colleagues' memories, and we will further honor them as best we can as soon as our mission affords us the opportunity."

Each of the bridge officers acknowledged his remarks, leaving Picard to watch as his people, well trained and experienced, went about their various assignments. As he often did during moments like these, he felt unnecessary before reminding himself that effective captains always trained their crew to carry on without them. It was a philosophy he had long embraced, and it gave him comfort to watch that playing out before him.

"*Sickbay to Captain Picard.*" It was Doctor Tamala Harstad speaking over the intercom, and Picard noted the tone of apprehension in her voice. "*Sir, your presence is requested at your earliest opportunity.*"

The words seemed forced, as if she were struggling to maintain her composure, and only then did Picard realize that in the turmoil of the past few moments, he also had succeeded in compartmentalizing his personal concerns in order to carry out the mission. With the moment over and sparked by Harstad's call, those feelings came rushing back full force, inundating him with a renewed sense of dread.

Beverly? René?

It could not be real, Picard decided, even as he beheld the young man lying before him in the sickbay bed, wrapped in blankets and what he hoped was peaceful slumber. Under the long, unkempt beard and reddish-brown hair so much like his own in his youth, the facial features were similar enough to his own that there could be no doubt. This was not a dream and neither was it an illusion. It was not even a game or some cruel joke concocted by his old adversary, Q.

Picard discounted that possibility almost without second thought. Q, whom he had not encountered in years, would not be so cruel, at least not toward someone else, for the purpose of tormenting Picard. Despite a very long list of annoying proclivities, there were rules of conduct even Q would not violate. *No*, Picard told himself. *This is real.*

The man before him was his son. This was René.

"It was the Nagas, Captain." Turning toward the voice, Picard saw Wesley Crusher accompanying his mother into the patient ward.

"Both of them converged on us," said Wesley, his eyes shifting to look at the sleeping René. "They killed several crewmembers, along with Doctor Hegol and Mister Casmir, the same way we saw . . . the same as what happened to your people on the planet."

Picard sighed, feeling the weight of tragedy pressing down on him. Hailan Casmir and Hegol Den. Although not Starfleet, they were members of the *Enterprise* crew as much as anyone wearing a uniform.

"What about the other children?" he asked. "Are they—"

"They're fine," said Crusher. "Traumatized by what they saw, certainly, but no injuries." Her gaze was fixed on her son. "Only René."

"Mister Casmir and Doctor Hegol gave their lives to protect them," said Wesley. "Casmir pushed him out of the way. If not for him, René would've been . . ." He caught himself, then drew a deep breath. "Damn."

Stepping closer to the bed's left side, Picard reached out to take René's hand in his own. The boy—the young man—did not stir.

"He's sedated." Crusher moved to the bed's opposite side. "When Wesley brought him here, he was panicked, which is understandable. The shock of what happened before—seeing what happened to Doctor Hegol and Hailan. I mean, René knew him as well as he knew anyone on the ship. He's seen him nearly every day since he was born."

Picard squeezed his son's hand. "This change. How did it happen?"

"Based on the scans recorded in the O.C.," said Wesley, "the Nagas are in a constant state of transphasic flux. This explains why conventional weapons and even the modifications I developed for your phaser rifles weren't effective. It also allows them to move through normal matter, like decks and bulkheads."

"Or the outer hull," replied Picard.

"Exactly. It also explains why sensors have a hard time consistently tracking them. As far as I can tell, they're able to control the degree to which they're phasing. So, instead of punching a hole through a wall, they simply shift out of phase just enough to pass through it. However, it looks like they also can weaponize it, after a fashion. They shift enough that when they come into contact with matter that's not phasing, they essentially push that target out of our spacetime even though it remains anchored here." He gestured to René. "We've seen what happens when someone is struck directly by this effect, but René wasn't hit like that. He was mostly out of the way, but still caught a glancing blow. It was so fast and so slight a contact that it . . . I guess you could say 'accelerated' his cells just the merest fraction of what other victims experienced."

"According to the scans we ran, he's approximately nineteen Standard years old," said Crusher. "Physically, at least. Mentally, he's still a six-year-old boy."

It took Picard a moment to process this. Despite his practiced self-control, he could not help his mouth falling open and his eyes widening in shock. Looking down at his sleeping son, he tried to imagine what such a transformation must have been like from his point of view. Having experienced an abrupt reversal of his own physical age following a transporter accident, he at least understood the sensation of being removed from the comfort of one's own body. However, being transformed into a twelve-year-old boy during that incident had left him with his adult intellect intact. He was able to reason, to deal with his situation as someone with a lifetime's worth of training and experiences. René possessed none of that on which to rely. Still an innocent if precocious child, he had been thrust into a situation he was unprepared to handle. He would need all manner of love and support, and Picard was more than ready to supply that, but what did the future hold?

"Is his condition reversible?" he asked.

Crusher shook her head. "I don't know. I know transporters have been used to reverse instances of genetic damage or other accidents, like what happened to you."

"We also used it to restore Doctor Pulaski when she was subjected to the rapid aging disease that affected the *Lantree* all those years ago," added Wesley. "But, those were both very risky procedures."

"And we don't know the extent of René's condition," said Crusher. "This transformation may not be the end of it. We need to run more tests."

Picard grimaced. "I understand, and you should get some rest, Doctor."

"So should you, Captain." The reply was not meant as a jab. Crusher offered a small smile to remove some of the remark's sting.

"We could all use a break," said Wesley. "But right now I want to find a way to talk to our guest. It's got to have at least some answers for all of this."

Placing René's hand back on the bed and releasing his hold on it, Picard straightened his posture and adjusted the bottom of his uniform jacket. "Have you identified its species?"

"No." Wesley frowned. "According to the O.C., my older self

never did, either, but based on its logs, he never got a chance to talk to one."

"But, he *was* you," said Crusher. "You'll *be* him. Doesn't that mean he did things you just haven't done yet?"

Wesley replied, "Not necessarily. Different time streams, different quantum realities. Anything is possible. Everything I've been able to unlock from the O.C. indicates it's a repository of all things my older self did right and *wrong*. I'm convinced he deliberately set this up so it could help me avoid the mistakes he made, but doing so in a way that keeps me from overtly jeopardizing future events. Is that in one reality or all of them? I have no idea." He shrugged. "It's as if he's helping me cheat on a test, but giving me one answer at a time."

"Let's hope our guest can provide us with additional insight," said Picard as he cast another look toward René. "I'm worried even more difficult tests are coming, and quite soon."

PART III

OUR REVELS
NOW ARE ENDED

29

———

The tears would not stop coming.

Lying on the bed in her quarters, T'Ryssa Chen gave up attempting to dry her eyes. The blue sleeve of her uniform tunic was damp from her repeated attempts to wipe her eyes and nose. For the first time in she could not remember how long, she wished for the capacity to employ the mental exercises she had tried to learn in her youth but never mastered. If ever there was a time to possess the renowned Vulcan discipline and emotional control, this was it. That training failed her now.

Dina. Taurik. Rennan.

Over and over, their names and faces filled her mind. Colleagues, friends, and so much more. How could Dina be gone? A science officer, whose world involved laboratories and computer simulations and research. She had participated in away missions, even dangerous ones, but . . . Dina. She was supposed to be here. They should be able to talk to each other at any time of the day or night, about work or anything else demanding the sort of immediate attention only friends can give.

And when Dina could not help, there was Taurik. Chen knew she could always count on him to be there for her, and she liked to think he knew the same was true for her. When it became obvious her role aboard the *Enterprise* would leave her with a great deal of time between those occasions when her expertise as a contact specialist was called into service, Taurik was among those most receptive to her undertaking training across multiple shipboard disciplines. He encouraged her to employ her already formidable science and technical skills wherever they might be useful, which resulted in her spending a great many hours in engineering. That program of study and self-improvement had paid off in numerous ways. On a personal level, Taurik more than any other Vulcan she had known accepted her with no reservations or judgment. He had influenced her in so many ways, helping her to be at ease with herself and her dual birthright. Despite electing not to pursue their romantic relationship, they had remained steadfast friends. She treasured him more than he likely ever knew, and now would never know.

Rennan.

Chen absently laid a hand on the side of the bed where she might find him. They had not committed to each other, though both admitted theirs was more than a casual relationship. Discussions about the future were informal, both secure in the knowledge that each wanted the other in their life. There had been no talks about "next steps" or anything "serious" so far as long-term plans. For her, it was a simple matter of not being ready to make that leap. There would be time for such pursuits later, she had rationalized. Now, there was her career and the lure of exploration, and it was her good fortune that Rennan had been here with her.

For Rennan Konya, it was a practical matter. His duties as a member of the ship's security detachment, and the risks he undertook far more often than most of his shipmates, had given him an outlook on life that some might consider cold, even callous. Every away mission carried elements of uncertainty and even danger; for Konya and those like him, theirs was a different attitude. Finding a mental place where they could undertake with great frequency missions that might result in their death was a learned discipline. It was a skill that Chen often struggled with, but duty aboard the *Enterprise* had given her ample opportunity to develop such objectivity. In his own way, Konya's approach to compartmentalizing such feelings was more effective than even the inherent mental and emotional discipline of Vulcan behavior. It was just one of the many things she loved about him, and a future without him seemed impossible to imagine.

"A future."

Chen sat up in her bed, blinking away tears as the thought emerged from the emotional chaos gripping her. Something, lurking at the edges of her subconscious. A long-buried memory resurfacing? No, she decided. This was something else.

"The future," she repeated, pushing herself from her bed. She felt the warmth of the carpet beneath her bare feet as she began pacing. Moving from her bedroom to the main sitting area of her quarters, she turned the word over in her mind. She was only vaguely aware she was conducting a circuit of the room—weaving around furniture, circling behind her desk, changing direction only when she threatened to walk into a bulkhead. Only the quiet hiss of her door jolted her out of her musing, but not until she found herself standing in the corridor outside her quarters. Chen looked down at herself, realizing she still wore rumpled sleepwear. Reaching up to touch her hair, she confirmed that was similarly disheveled.

"Okay, then," she said, to no one in the thankfully empty passageway, before returning to her quarters. Even given her current situation, it would not do for word to get around the ship that a Vulcan, even a half-Vulcan, was walking about in her underwear. Somewhere, she was sure she could hear Rennan Konya laughing. She would give anything for a last chance to punch him in the arm. And what about Taurik? If he were here, he might even be compelled to . . .

"Taurik."

That had to be it, Chen decided. An image of her friend formed in her mind, and for a brief moment she registered the sensation of standing with him. Standing with Taurik in the corridor outside the crew lounge. He had left and she had run after him, only to learn he was on his way to his quarters for a subspace conversation with agents from the Department of Temporal Investigations. The knowledge of future events to which he was privy thanks to the Raqilan weapon ship might well be connected to everything that had transpired since Wesley Crusher's arrival, but she could not be sure. She harbored no doubt Taurik had considered the possibility on his own, even before his conversation with DTI. Had he even had a chance to speak with Captain Picard prior to that?

"Picard. Damn it, of course." Annoyed with herself, Chen blew out her breath. "I'm such an idiot. Think, T'Ryssa. *Think.*"

Closing her eyes, she focused on that image of Taurik in the corridor, outside his quarters. He had been as circumspect as possible given her pestering him about the meeting, offering no clues even though she had correctly deduced the topic of discussion. Chen knew it had to have been foremost on his mind at that moment, because . . .

"Because I touched him."

It had not been a full meld. Their minds had not merged in that much more immersive and intimate manner, but even that brief flash—her hand on his arm as a simple gesture of support, friendship, and even love—had given her a passing insight into his thoughts. In that instant, she saw images Taurik had immediately attempted to guard from her: Wesley Crusher, and Captain Picard.

What did they mean? Had his conversation with DTI brought new information and clarity? She would never know, as she never had the chance to speak with him prior to the *Enterprise*'s visit to Devidia II. Whatever Taurik knew died with him.

Or had it?

"Computer," she said. "Access personal logs and messages. Has Lieutenant Commander Taurik recently transmitted any correspondence or record files for me?"

"Negative. I find no record of such a communication."

"Check Taurik's personal logs and records. Is there any mention of anything he wished to have transmitted to me in the event of . . . in the event of his death?"

"*Negative. No such record is present in any of Lieutenant Commander Taurik's logs or records.*"

Feeling the first tinges of frustration, Chen asked, "What about protected or encrypted files. Did he leave behind anything like that?"

"*Negative. No encrypted or protected records are present in any data bank.*"

"Which means anything he may have recorded for transmission to DTI was wiped." Chen began pacing again. "Computer, are there mentions in any file of the Raqilan weapon ship?"

It took the computer a moment to process the query before replying, "*One entry: Captain Picard's official report to Starfleet Command, stardate 63—*"

"Never mind."

She had not really expected her impromptu questions to yield tangible results. Taurik would never violate the pledge he had taken to keep to himself the knowledge he possessed. Not because doing so might endanger future events, but simply because that was what duty required of him. He had even kept that information from Captain Picard, and Chen believed his mandate had troubled Taurik prior to his conversation with the DTI agents. Something about what he knew, coupled with Wesley Crusher's presence and the experiences that brought him here, had weighed on Taurik. The image of Picard that Chen had gleaned from his mind had not been isolated or ephemeral. It was at the forefront of his consciousness, but why? Did Picard somehow play a role in the future events Taurik had seen? She had no context, nothing to support her suspicion, but somehow the idea felt *right*. Chen wished he had left behind some clue, some final message with instructions to be carried out in the event of his death. Even his *katra*, the very essence of a Vulcan's consciousness, was gone. He had not been given a chance to deliver his *katra* to a willing recipient so that it might be taken back to his homeworld for proper interment. If there was anything to be done on his behalf with respect to the foreknowledge he carried, Chen would have to figure it out on her own.

"What were you thinking, Taurik?" she asked the question of her empty quarters before resuming her pacing. "What were you going to do?"

She was certain his need to keep the truth from Picard had troubled him, at least inasmuch as a Vulcan could be troubled. What she also believed—what she felt with unfailing conviction—was that Taurik would act in whatever manner he deemed necessary to protect the *Enterprise* and its crew even if he could not reveal his reasons. What she did not know is how he might have acted with the integrity of future history at stake. Would simple, straightforward logic have guided him, or would loyalty to his shipmates have prevailed? Taurik could not have known, and if she were being honest, Chen knew she likewise had no answer. As for Taurik, she reasoned that even from within the parameters set for him by DTI, if he believed Picard was somehow central to their current situation, then he would have endeavored to remain close to the captain. Perhaps with the intention of serving as an information source, but also in the event he felt compelled to act in defense of whatever future events lay ahead. He could not do that now.

"But I can."

The statement sounded odd, spoken aloud in the privacy of her quarters. There was no one to hear her declaration, but that made it no less heartfelt. Even without specific knowledge to guide her, there could be no denying her feelings. Strengthened by what Taurik had inadvertently shared with her, Chen felt certain this was the right path.

Moving to her lavatory, she stared at herself in the mirror above the sink. She realized she already felt a bit better than just a few minutes ago. Carrying on in Taurik's stead despite not knowing exactly how to proceed had given her renewed purpose. Even with the pain she still felt, she could grieve Taurik's loss, along with those of Dina and even Rennan, while not letting it consume her.

She would persevere in their absence, and maybe come out the other side stronger thanks to their friendship. There was no better way to honor their memories.

Still studying herself in the mirror, Chen nodded with new resolve.

I won't let you down, my friends.

"We hear from our first classes at the Academy that service in Starfleet carries a risk. Exploring the unknown, encountering new lifeforms, pledging ourselves to the security of the Federation implies a potential cost not only to ourselves but also those we love. And yet, it is those very people and civilizations we hold dear that drive us to accept that risk."

Picard, standing behind a polished black podium atop a dais in the *Enterprise*'s main shuttlebay, looked out at the rows of assembled crewmembers. Behind him, a blue backdrop displayed the Federation seal. The memorial service was open to anyone, but there was an implicit understanding that duty came first. Stations and systems required their usual attention and oversight, and could not pause even for a moment's observance or reflection. Even so, he estimated nearly two-thirds of the crew complement was in attendance, requiring his remarks to be piped over the internal comm system to be heard here as well as throughout the ship. They stood silent, listening to him speak as he had for the past ten minutes, beginning with reading the names of those lost and continuing with his testimonial to the fallen.

"Those whom we lost today gave their lives in service to an ideal. They accepted risk to protect the rest of us: their shipmates, their friends. They did so without hesitation or reservation, they knew their actions were not needless or without purpose. Our responsibility to them—*our* purpose—from this time forward is to honor them by being worthy of their sacrifice. We must rededicate ourselves to exemplifying the principles they swore to uphold and protect. Those of you standing here with me, along with your crewmates listening across the *Enterprise*, are the finest representatives of those values. Our friends can rest easy knowing you will carry on in their stead. Dismissed."

Picard stepped away from the podium and down from the dais to an area behind the backdrop and cordoned off from the rest of the shuttlebay. He was alone only for a moment before he heard footsteps, recognizing the steps as Beverly's. His wife appeared from around the curtain, offering him a comforting smile.

"Very nice, Jean-Luc."

"I never know what to say." Though Picard long ago conquered his fear of speaking before an audience, doing so for situations such as this had always made him uneasy. As with so many other things, he learned to put aside personal feelings as required by his rank and station. The role of a starship captain was many things, and that included being an inspiration to those seeking guidance or simple poise in the face of tragedy. Six decades in the center seat had given him far too many opportunities to eulogize fallen crew, and he hoped never to be comfortable with it.

"Bridge to Captain Picard," called Worf over the ship's intercom. *"Sensors are tracking a quantum distortion beyond the limits of the Devidia system. We believe it is a vessel traveling via slipstream drive, on an intercept course with us, sir."*

"Starfleet?" asked Picard.

"The quantum distortions are consistent with a Vesta-*class starship, sir, but we won't be able to make a final determination until it drops out of slipstream."*

A quick turbolift ride from the shuttlebay returned Picard to the bridge. Picard emerged from the car, directing his gaze to the sleek, arrow-shaped vessel displayed on the main viewscreen. Narrow, streamlined, and compact, with its warp nacelles slung low and fully behind the ship's angular primary hull section, the entire design conveyed speed, in this case velocities far beyond even the *Enterprise*'s formidable capabilities.

"It's the *Aventine*, sir," reported Worf as he rose from the center seat. "Captain Dax is hailing us and requesting to speak to you."

The viewscreen shifted from the approaching ship to an image of Ezri Dax, sitting in her command chair on the bridge of her ship. She was in her early thirties, Picard recalled, but he could see in her still-youthful face the burdens of commanding one of Starfleet's most powerful vessels and the demands that placed upon her. Thin, almost imperceptible streaks of silver accented her short, dark hair, but the vitality behind her bright blue eyes also communicated centuries of wisdom thanks to the Trill symbiont, Dax, she carried within her.

Moving to stand at the center of the bridge, just behind the operations and flight controller stations, Picard nodded toward the screen. "Captain Dax, this is quite the surprise."

"*I only wish it were a pleasant one, Captain.*" Her expression softened. "*It seems you're no longer the only ship dealing with temporal anomalies. We're here to join the party.*"

Behind her, two figures stepped into view. Instead of Starfleet uniforms, they wore nondescript businesslike attire Picard would know all too well even if he did not recognize the people wearing the clothing. He could not help the feeling of foreboding that welled up within him at the sight of Meyo Ranjea and Teresa Garcia, agents from the Department of Temporal Investigations.

"*Captain Picard,*" said Ranjea, "*like Captain Dax, I wish I could say we're here under happier circumstances. We have a lot to talk about, and I suspect not much time to do it.*"

30

—◆—

Picard studied the containment unit now occupying space in cargo bay two. A single transporter pad of the sort he recognized from emergency units had been installed inside a transparasteel cylinder. At the end of the contraption was an interface module controlled by the nearby cargo transporter console reconfigured by Wesley Crusher along with Geordi La Forge and members of his engineering team for this purpose.

"Are you sure this will work?" asked Picard.

Standing at the transporter console, the top panel of which was open, La Forge replied, "I've run a half dozen tests along with computer simulations, sir. Everything checks out the way Wes said it would." He gestured first to Wesley, then the containment unit. "These emergency transporters have their own pattern buffers. We've added a second one, outside the unit itself and connected directly to the one inside. When we transfer the intruder's pattern to the main buffer, it'll pass through optical cabling to the buffer inside the unit before the materialization process kicks in, without having to raise or lower the transphasic shielding we'll have active the whole time. All power's being drawn from the warp engines, so there's no chance of a failure. Once they're in there, it's not going anywhere."

"That's pretty impressive," offered Captain Dax, who, along with DTI agents Ranjea and Garcia, stood to one side, out of the way of the work being done.

"Thanks, Captain." After closing the console's panel, La Forge turned to Picard. "We're ready to go, sir."

"Make it so, Commander."

The chief engineer keyed a sequence of controls and a force field flared to life around the cylinder. He then initiated a materialization sequence, which took a few seconds longer than the normal process owing to the extra safeguards the engineers had installed. A shower of energy inside the unit heralded the arrival of the humanoid, still unconscious from before, being transferred into the ship's primary transporter pattern buffer. The beam faded, leaving the figure cloaked in its dark robes and lying on the enclosed pad.

"And now we wait," said La Forge.

Stepping away from the containment unit, Picard gestured to Wesley to join him alongside Dax and the DTI agents. The *Aventine*'s captain continued to study the engineers at work while Ranjea looked to Picard and Wesley.

"You kept your guest in the transporter buffer?" asked Dax.

Wesley replied, "Given their abilities, it seemed the safest option until we could come up with a way to keep it under control. You don't want it getting out of that unit." He tapped the strap of the disruptor rifle slung across his back.

"Captain, Mister Crusher," said Ranjea, "I owe you an apology, and our thanks. It seems you were right all along. The evidence certainly points to the Devidians being somehow responsible for everything we've seen here."

"And elsewhere," said Wesley.

Ranjea nodded. "And elsewhere. Given what Captain Dax and her crew witnessed at Bezorek Station and the Axis of Time, we're at a loss to decipher their motives. If they're using artifacts like this and other methods of temporal travel, why destroy them?"

"There's a method to their madness." Wesley held up the Omnichron he had removed from his jacket pocket. "Destroying the Axis tracks with other actions they've taken. At least, the ones observed firsthand either by me or my future self. The Guardian of Forever, the Typhon Expanse, even the wormhole to the Delta Quadrant that *Voyager* found. These are all methods used for time travel, either deliberately or by accident, but we know the Devidians don't need them." He indicated Picard. "They have their own methods, which you've seen before and we saw today. But, they know we, or others like us, might seek out these artifacts and other temporal-displacement technology."

"And we might find some way to use it against them," said Dax.

"Exactly." Wesley returned the Omnichron to his pocket. "So they hunt them down and destroy them before we can get to them."

For the first time, Agent Teresa Garcia spoke up. "There's no way to know how many examples of such technology are scattered through the galaxy. Even the ones we know about or have under our control barely scratch the surface. I'm guessing the only reason we haven't been targeted is because we shield all such artifacts in our possession within redundant phase-discrimination fields. They're as isolated from spacetime as we can make them." Sweeping a lock of her shoulder-length dark hair away from her eyes, she glanced over to where La Forge kept watch on the containment unit. "The only thing we haven't tried is something like your chief engineer created."

"Captain," said La Forge, "it's coming around."

Wesley placed a hand on Picard's arm. "I'd like to talk to it first, sir."

"Of course." That made sense. Wesley had far more experience with these beings than anyone. He could prove useful so far as eliciting helpful responses from their captive. After verifying that Lieutenant Šmrhová and a security team were standing by in the event of a problem, he said, "Good luck, Mister Crusher."

"It's been a long time since I've heard you call me that."

Leaving Picard with a small, wistful smile, Wesley moved closer to the containment unit, whose occupant had risen to its feet and now regarded its surroundings.

"I've engaged the universal translator," said La Forge. "I incorporated everything we have about the Devidian languages, including what you gave us, Wes."

Wesley nodded before walking up to within arm's length of the containment unit's force field. "Can you understand me?"

"Yes."

Dax said, "Well, that was easy."

Focusing on the humanoid form, Wesley asked, "What are you? You're not Devidian, but we know you must be somehow connected to them."

"I am Devidian in all the ways that matter."

Reaching up, the figure pushed back the hood concealing its face, and Picard along with everyone else received their first look at the adversary Wesley Crusher had tracked across time and space. To him, the captive appeared almost like a mannequin. There were no developed facial features. There was no hair, no mouth. No eyes, or anything else resembling sensory organs.

"This vessel carries all that it means to be Devidian," it said. *"Traveling through space and time wears on our physical bodies, so we created these hosts to carry our consciousness on such journeys."*

"It's an avatar," said Ranjea. "An automaton. Organic instead of mechanical, but the same result."

Wesley said, "That explains why I couldn't pin down its biosigns. It's a life-form, but one created exclusively by and for the Devidians. It's not a sentient being in any real sense. Instead, it's just a repository for an individual consciousness." Of the avatar, he asked, "Is this a permanent state, or temporary?"

"I can return to my own body."

"Where are your people?"

"We no longer exist in this time period. Those who remain are elsewhere."

Stepping closer, Picard asked, "What of the creatures you sent to attack us? Are they like the ophidians you used to facilitate your travels through time?"

The avatar shifted its head as if looking at Picard. *"They are similar, yet like this vessel they were created for a different purpose. They protect us, but they also serve as hunters."* It returned its attention to Wesley. *"They search for those like you, who threaten us."*

"Threaten you?" Wesley shook his head. "I don't know anything about you."

"Like us, you can travel through time and space." The avatar gestured to Picard. *"Your ability to perceive time far exceeds these primitives, as does your ability to take action against us. We dispatch these servants to neutralize such threats."*

"Which threats?" asked Dax. "Who are we talking about?"

"Races like the Metrons, or even the Organians," said Wesley. "According to the O.C., my future self attempted to contact representatives of those races, but he failed. They'd all disappeared from their homeworlds or the regions of space where they were discovered. Whether they were destroyed or simply transitioned to another plane of existence, I don't know."

La Forge said, "I'm guessing the latter, or else this guy would be bragging about it."

"What of other races?" asked Picard. "The El-Aurians for example." So few of them even remained in the twenty-fourth century, and most were scattered to who knew where across the galaxy. Where was Guinan? It only now occurred to him that he had no idea where his old friend might be. Had she gone into hiding to avoid the threat the Devidians represented?

"What about the Q?" he pressed. Indeed, after so many years with no contact, it was unlike the bothersome omnipotent entity and Picard's one-time personal nemesis to not show himself. When at first the captain had thought this might all be one of Q's games, he had dismissed the possibility.

"I didn't have any luck contacting them either," said Wesley. "But it wouldn't surprise me if they just didn't care. I've even tried reaching out to the Aegis."

Garcia eyed him askance. "Please tell me you didn't."

"Not me. My future self."

"The Aegis." Picard knew the name. Centuries ago, the reclusive race harbored an obsessive interest in Earth, watching from the shadows as humanity navigated tumultuous periods of its own history.

"So far as we know," said Ranjea, "their interest in Earth began to wane by the mid-twenty-first century, after the Vulcans made first contact. The last known encounter with the Aegis or any operatives working in its stead occurred more than a hundred years ago."

"And then, there is you." The avatar seemed once more fixated on Wesley. *"Few of you endure, and you remain our greatest threat."*

"You mean the Travelers?" asked Picard. He looked to Wesley, whose expression had gone cold.

Wesley pushed closer to the force field. "How many of us have you killed?"

"Numbers mean nothing, so long as one of you persists." Pausing, the avatar cocked its head as if it were a real, living being scrutinizing Wesley. *"We know of your connection to one of your kind. He is no more, as you soon will be."*

"You killed them." It was a declaration. "You hunted them down and murdered them." Wesley turned from the avatar, and Picard saw the pain in the man's eyes. "I thought they'd gone into hiding, or died fighting as we learned more about the threat."

"Some of them live, but they are doomed. We have seen it." The avatar pointed to Wesley. *"Even you will fall to us. It is inevitable."*

Drawing a deep breath, Wesley released it in slow, deliberate fashion before returning his attention to the avatar. "Why? What do you gain from all of this?"

"Sustenance."

And just like that, it made sense to Picard.

"When we first encountered them," he said, "the Devidians were feeding on the neural energy from dying humans on nineteenth-century Earth. It stands to reason they'd eventually find other life-forms to provide similar nourishment."

Dax said, "Why settle for one planet, or just a portion of a planet, when you can have entire universes, anywhere, at any moment in time? In any reality?"

"They travel to different points in spacetime to feed on the neural energy of those who exist in those realities," said Garcia. "How has this not affected our timeline in some noticeable way? How can we not have detected this kind of activity before now?"

Looking to Wesley, Picard guessed his own expression of realization matched the other man's. "Because until now they haven't been feeding in this timeline. They've been preying on other ones; even destroying them."

Ranjea made no effort to hide his disbelief. "That's insane."

"Think about it," said Wesley. "It's all in the O.C. We know the Devidians started out by using different temporal phenomena as triggers for introducing branching points within an established timeline. Further, they're deliberately introducing instabilities into those timelines. The newer an alternate strand is, the more fragile it is, and this likely appeals to them because they can wreak havoc feasting on all the neural energy they can collect before that timeline collapses. This keeps them from effecting changes in other, more stable timelines." He extended his arms to indicate the space around them. "Like this one. And in theory, it keeps them from being noticed by anyone with an expanded perception of spacetime."

"People like you," said La Forge, "but also those with the resources to monitor timeline changes, like DTI agents."

"So much effort," said Picard. Something was missing. "Why go to such effort for so little gain? Create an entire branching reality, with the uncounted trillions of life-forms within it, only to collect whatever sustenance they can obtain by attacking a single world or a handful of starships? It doesn't make sense, not for a sentient people. Even if the Devidians view other life-forms as inferior, waste on such a staggering scale is inexplicable."

"Because what has happened is merely prologue."

Picard turned to face the avatar, whose utterly blank and unreadable face seemed to stare back at him. "What do you mean by that?"

"You are correct. It is a waste. Until now, each gathering has been but a test. We cannot wait for the universe to give to us what we need. To survive, we must take what sustains us."

"That's it," said Wesley. "I've had it all wrong. The Devidians aren't collapsing timelines just to cover up obtaining a limited supply of neural energy. Their goal is to collect *all* of the neural energy from *every living being* in a given reality. They've been testing it on recent, more fragile branches from existing timelines, but what happens when they perfect whatever it is they're doing? They could turn it on *any* timeline, including this one."

Dax said, "Energy on that scale? They can't feed on it all at once. They'd need a way to store it, wouldn't they?"

"Which means a construct of some kind," replied Ranjea. He pointed to the avatar. "It said the remaining Devidians were elsewhere. They have to be somewhere in spacetime. That could mean the distant past or the far future. Some other timeline, hiding somewhere we can't look."

Picard stepped closer to the avatar. "Where is your home?"

"Beyond your comprehension."

"No, it's not." Pulling the Omnichron from his pocket, Wesley activated the device and held it toward the avatar. "I think I know where this thing is from. I've been there." He looked over his shoulder to Picard. "I mean, my future self has been there. Will go there. Whatever. If I can lock onto the specific frequency of triolic energy this avatar used to get here, we can backtrack it to its origin point."

"You will fail."

Picard flinched as the avatar's body seized, its limbs locking up before it fell against the side of the containment cylinder and slid down to the transporter pad.

"What's happening?" he snapped.

Brandishing a tricorder, La Forge stepped closer to the containment unit. "I'm not picking up any neurological activity or other physiological function. It's completely inert, and doesn't even read as anything close to biological anymore." He looked up from the tricorder. "I think it's dead, Captain."

Garcia asked, "Dead? What killed it?"

"It was never really alive," countered Wesley. "Whatever Devidian consciousness was in there is gone; likely returned to wherever it came from. My Omnichron did register a minor triolic energy signature at the moment the avatar collapsed, but I can't tell if it was a signal or something else."

"If it was a signal," said Picard, "then the Devidians may know we're onto them. They'll be preparing, or coming after us."

"Meanwhile," said Ranjea, "without knowing from where in spacetime the avatar came, we have no idea where to even start looking for them."

"Maybe we do." Wesley tapped the Omnichron's outer casing. "I think I know where we need to go." His expression turned thoughtful as he regarded Picard. "In a way, you and I have already been there."

31

───•───

Sickbay was quiet at this hour. For that, Picard was thankful. It allowed him a brief respite during which he could set aside everything else weighing on him. For these few precious moments, he was not a captain; he was a father.

He stood next to René's bed in a private patient room. The lights were low, and the medical monitoring equipment had all been set to silent mode; if necessary it would transmit alarms to the staff on duty. It was in this quiet, comfortable setting that René slept. Someone, a nurse or orderly, had cut his hair and shaved his beard, giving Picard his first clear look at his boy's face.

Man, Picard reminded himself. René now appeared to be a young man of nearly twenty years. It was easy to see that his features carried faint echoes of both his parents. The lines of his jaw and the curve of his nose evoked his father, while high, delicate cheekbones honored his mother. His hair, deep auburn from his first days, now definitely reminded Picard of his own locks, long ago lost to time.

René twitched in his sleep. Though he did not awaken, a series of muttered, indecipherable syllables filled the room. Picard shifted his eyes to the monitor positioned behind the boy's head, but saw nothing out of the ordinary save a minor fluctuation in neurological activity. If he understood the indicators, they showed René was deep in REM sleep. What might he be dreaming about?

"I thought I might find you here."

Turning from the bed, Picard saw Beverly standing in the doorway. The patient room was a private affair, separate from the sickbay's main treatment and recovery areas and but a short walk down the corridor leading to Crusher's officer along with those of her medical staff. Beyond the open door, he heard the activity of those personnel on duty during this, the second of the *Enterprise*'s three duty shifts. It was early evening, ship time, but sickbay like other key departments always carried full staff regardless of time of day. Even if her son was not a patient, it was unsurprising to see Crusher here, still wearing her duty uniform long after her shift had ended.

"I wanted to see him before I left." Picard reached out to caress René's head. "Has there been any change?"

Crusher stepped farther into the room. "No. On the one hand, that's a good thing. There's no sign of the cellular activity responsible for his accelerated aging. As far as I can tell, he should age normally from this point forward."

"And on the other hand?" prompted Picard.

"We still have no way of reversing his condition." Studying René's sleeping face, Crusher sighed. "Physically, he's a healthy human male just entering adulthood. Mentally, he's still the same boy he was yesterday. If we can't return him to the way he was, in theory he could be taught to accept his situation, and there are therapies that can help accelerate his learning."

Though obviously grateful his son had been spared the same fate visited upon so many of his crew, Picard was not yet ready to accept René's condition as a *fait accompli*. "We can't give up all hope just yet, Beverly. There might be something—a piece of Devidian technology—that may help him." It was a long shot, he knew, but any chance was better than none. So long as there were avenues to explore, he would continue looking.

"He was talking in his sleep." Crusher nodded toward René. "None of it made sense. Names I didn't recognize. Places I'd never heard of. He must be dreaming, but at times I was sure he was talking at a level well above his physical age." She sighed. "I just don't understand any of it."

A shadow appeared in the doorway, and Picard looked over to

see Worf in the hallway outside the room. Excusing himself, he joined his first officer in the corridor.

"I apologize for disturbing you, sir, but you wanted to be advised when the *Aventine* was ready to depart, and I did not wish to use the intercom while you were with your son."

Picard offered a grateful nod. "I appreciate your consideration, Number One. Have all the preparations been completed?"

"Yes, sir. Commander La Forge and Mister Crusher have finished assisting the *Aventine*'s chief engineer with the modifications Mister Crusher requires."

After consultation with the captains and chief engineers of both ships, Wesley concluded the *Aventine* with its quantum slipstream drive made it the better vessel for effecting the transit to the far future, with him initiating the transfer and guiding the way using his Traveler abilities.

"Are they still aboard the *Aventine*?" asked Picard.

Worf replied, "Yes, and Lieutenants Cruzen and Chen, as well as Agents Ranjea and Garcia, have also beamed over."

It was a small team, with Ezri Dax and her crew providing additional security as well as technical expertise as required. Cruzen was in the unenviable position of replacing her colleagues Rennan Konya and Abby Balidemaj as deputy security chief under Lieutenant Šmrhová, and her presence on the team was in keeping with Worf's standing order that Picard have a personal escort during any away mission. As with anyone assigned to a ship's security detail, Cruzen understood the risks and accepted the tragedy that had befallen her shipmates. Likewise, and despite her role as the ship's contact specialist, T'Rryssa Chen had volunteered to take on the late Dina Elfiki's science-officer responsibilities. Though Picard regretted placing her in this position so soon after suffering such personal losses, Chen had assured him she was capable of carrying out her duties, and there was no denying she possessed greater field experience than most of the ship's other science officers. Indeed, there was something to the way she had requested his permission to join the team; an odd determination, perhaps to honor her friends' memories. Picard could respect that, and he also trusted her to conduct herself appropriately during the mission.

Worf said, "Respectfully, sir, I reiterate my request to accompany you." He had already volunteered—then insisted—he be allowed to go with the team. Picard knew the appeal was motivated largely if not solely by the Klingon's loyalty to him.

"I appreciate your persistence, Number One, but I need you here. Once we've departed you'll remain in orbit and continue scanning the planet in the event the Devidians have some sort of backup target site." He knew the ship's sensors had found nothing, but that did not rule out the possibility of the Devidians traveling here through another temporal vortex from some other point in time.

"And Admiral Riker, sir?"

"Contact him once we're gone and update him on our status. Transmit all our logs and relevant records to him so he can apprise Admiral Akaar. If we've not returned within twenty-four hours, rendezvous with the *Titan* and follow Admiral Riker's orders."

Worf drew himself up. "Aye, sir. Good luck, Captain."

"To all of us, Number One."

Once his first officer had departed, Picard returned to René's room. It was obvious from her expression that Crusher had heard every word of his exchange with Worf.

"Maybe you should wait for Riker and the *Titan* to get here."

Picard sighed. "I wish that were possible, but we don't know if the Devidian avatar's death triggered some message or an alert to its people elsewhere in time. We have to act now, in the hope we still have an element of surprise."

Crossing the room toward him, she pulled him to her. "Be careful." Noticing his eyes focusing on the still sleeping René, she added, "I'll take care of him until you get back."

With a last lingering look at his son, Picard kissed him and his wife before leaving them both. Later, there would be time for personal feelings. Now it was time to go to work.

And time, Picard reminded himself, *waits for no one.*

U.S.S. *Aventine* NCC-82602
Date Unknown

The spiraling, tunneling effect of slipstream travel was one with which Picard had little experience. Despite the *Aventine*'s inertial damping systems, he was sure he felt a twinge in his gut as the ship bored through the slipstream corridor. Standing near the turbolift alcove at the rear of the bridge, he sensed the reverberations coursing through the deck, consoles, and even the carpeting beneath his feet.

"It's normally not this rough," offered Captain Dax, swiveling her command chair so she could see where Picard stood with T'Ryssa Chen. "I'm guessing Mister Crusher's modifications are to blame."

"Rough, she says." Chen put a hand on her stomach. "I haven't felt like this since I tried that orbital skydiving class."

"How did you do?" asked Picard.

"I managed to make it to the ground before hurling."

Over the open intercom channel linking the bridge to the *Aventine*'s engineering section, Wesley Crusher announced, *"Coming out of slipstream in five seconds."*

"Everybody hang on," warned Dax's first officer, Commander Sam Bowers. "This could get a little bumpy."

"A little *more* bumpy, you mean," said Chen, low enough for her voice not to carry but not so that Picard missed it.

On the main viewscreen, the walls of the slipstream corridor dissipated as the *Aventine* flung itself into normal space.

"That's it," said Wesley over the link. *"We're here. At least, I think we are."*

"And where is that?" asked Dax. "How far did we travel?"

Seated at the bridge's science station, Lieutenant Commander Gruhn Helkara replied, "Positionally, we've come 728 light-years from the Devidian system. We're still well within the Beta Quadrant, beyond what should be the far boundary of the Romulan Empire." The Zakdorn looked over his shoulder toward Dax. "There are no Federation time beacons within sensor range, but even if there were, I don't think they'd still be working. According to the computer's estimate based on Mister Crusher's calculations, we've traveled over four thousand years into the future."

Picard watched on the viewscreen as the ship continued forward on impulse power. One star seemed to separate itself from the field of lights decorating the curtain of deep space, growing larger with each passing second as the ship continued its approach.

"K-type main-sequence star," reported Helkara. "Most promising for playing host to a system of habitable planets. Sensors detect six planetary bodies, four with at least one natural satellite. Due to the star's larger habitable zone, planets three, four, and five are capable of supporting life as we know it. Planets three and five are Class M."

"And planet five has some serious temporal activity happening on it." The report came from the ship's security chief, Lieutenant Lonnoc Kedair, from where she stood at the tactical station closest to Picard and Chen. "These readings are . . . they're off the scale, Captain. Waves of temporal distortion like I've never seen."

Helkara added, "There's some sort of dampening field active on the planet. From this distance it's impossible to get any reliable readings from the surface. The situation may improve as we move closer."

"Shields up. Go to yellow alert," ordered Bowers. "Conn, lay in a course for the fifth planet and take us in. Half impulse power."

Dax added, "I want to get the lay of the land before we enter orbit. Gruhn, are we alone out here?"

After a moment spent consulting his instruments, Helkara replied, "No other ships in the system or anywhere within sensor range, Captain."

"What about on the planet?" asked Picard. "Any life signs?"

"Inconclusive, Captain. Likely an effect of the dampening field."

Chen said, "It's a safe bet there's somebody down there. They're out here, in the middle of nowhere, four thousand years into the future. Stands to reason they prefer to be left alone. Meanwhile, for all we know, the Romulan Empire died out centuries ago, and the entire rest of this quadrant is empty. Maybe the Devidians took care of them too."

"Or, the Romulans are still around and their cloaking devices are even better now," said Bowers, "and we'll never see them coming until we're dead."

Neither officer's observations were invalid, Picard decided. There was no way to know what fate had fallen the Romulans, or the Federation for that matter. Indeed, the *Aventine*'s very presence here constituted a grave concern. He suspected Agents Ranjea and Garcia, currently belowdecks preparing for whatever away mission they ended up conducting, were likely having mild cardiac arrests at the very thought of the ship's crew acquiring insight into this distant future. Should they encounter Romulans or any other civilizations in this period, knowledge gleaned from those meetings taken back to the past posed a threat to the natural progression of future events. Picard knew their best course of action here and now was to accomplish their mission as quickly as possible and return to their own time, preferably without making contact with any indigenous populations.

"Entering standard orbit, Captain," said Lieutenant Tharp, the *Aventine*'s flight control officer. The Bolian studied his console's instruments before adding, "No indications of artificial satellites or any other potential threat in the planet's immediate vicinity."

On the viewscreen, a dull gray world dominated the image. At first Picard was put off by how uninviting the planet appeared. A thick blanket of clouds shrouded the atmosphere, blocking from view whatever landmasses and oceans the planet boasted.

Focused on his console, Helkara said, "The dampening field is definitely a factor with our sensors. The planet features three major landmasses and a variety of islands spread across its oceans. Scans are detecting a triolic energy signature from the surface. Though I can't get a clear reading, sensor returns indicate a massive structure at the center of the temporal distortions, located in the planet's southern hemisphere."

"But still no life signs?" asked Dax.

"Inconclusive, but if they're phase-shifting, then it's likely our sensors might not even pick them up."

Dax swiveled her seat to face Picard. "It's your show, Captain. What do you want to do?"

None of the information collected so far was useful, but it was not as though they could abandon the mission and come back another day. With everything at stake, there was only a single choice. Nodding to Dax, he indicated the planet on the viewscreen with the same gesture he made on his own bridge.

"Let's see what's down there."

32

———•———

The landscape was at once alien and familiar.

Peering through its forward port as the shuttlecraft *Daugava* descended through the clouds, Picard took in the desolation of the valley they approached. Barren, cracked soil broken by rock formations, craters, and fissures stretched in all directions toward the foothills of surrounding mountains. The sky was awash with dark, ominous clouds that blotted out all but the faintest hint of sunlight. Lightning crackled across the horizon though no rain fell.

"There's very little moisture in the air," said T'Ryssa Chen, seated at an auxiliary console behind the shuttle's pilot, Lieutenant Talia Kandel. "If these readings are right, there's been no measurable rainfall here for centuries."

Seated next to Kandel, Picard could believe Chen's report if the surrounding terrain was any indication. He saw not one sign of vegetation, let alone water to sustain it, or even evidence that anything had ever thrived here. It reminded him of Mars in the years after the process of terraforming Earth's planetary neighbor concluded in the early twenty-third century. At that point, the atmosphere remained unstable and even violent until more advanced environmental configuration systems were deployed to complete Mars' transformation into the Sol system's second habitable world.

"Still not detecting any life signs," said Kandel, leader of the *Aventine* security detail, consisting of herself, a human male, and a Zakdorn female. A Deltan like Meyo Ranjea, Kandel also had a head devoid of hair, and the cockpit's internal lights played off her smooth scalp. "Nothing in any direction as far as sensors can register in this mess."

"If they're anywhere, they'll be there."

It was Wesley, who had moved into the cockpit to stand behind Picard. He gestured toward the most prominent mountain in the area. Large and foreboding, it rose with improbably monolithic precision into the sky. Its base was not a gradual incline, narrowing as it ascended ever higher. Instead, the massif's upper tiers continued upward, forming a solid foundation with angles far too regular to be a natural occurrence. Picard was certain the entire edifice had been engineered to harmonize with the surrounding landscape. Even from less than two hundred meters away, he could see no cracks or crevasses marring its sheer face. Its summit appeared to be flat yet sloped at gentle angles, serving as the base for a massive structure. Crystalline columns extended from the peaks at precise angles, crossing past and through one another to form a complex latticework. The entire construct pulsed with energy, producing a medley of colors illuminating the clouds above the mountain.

"Welcome to my new nightmare," said Chen. "Scans show a massive fission reactor deep in the heart of the mountain, and what looks to be a sophisticated computer system overseeing everything. Whatever it calls software isn't like anything I've seen before. With the power the complex is putting out, it's no wonder transporters weren't an option. We'd never break through this background interference."

Assisted by Wesley and his Omnichron, Kandel selected an area of open ground fifty meters from the crystal structure, and less than ten meters from the edge of the mountain's summit. Within moments she brought the *Daugava* to a gentle landing, and the away team disembarked.

"My people and I will take point, sir," Kandel said, nodding toward the structure. Everyone carried phaser rifles that Wesley Crusher had adapted to fire at transphasic frequencies. The security team wore tactical vests with extra power cells for their weapons as well as holsters for hand phasers and tricorders. They also wore backpacks, which Picard knew contained personal emergency medical and survival kits as well as transporter pattern enhancers. There was no way to know if the devices would be sufficient to cut through the interference currently blocking the *Aventine*'s transporters, but as Kandel had stated during the pre-mission briefing, "There's only one way to find out."

Hefting his own phaser rifle, Picard nodded to the lieutenant. "I'll be right behind you."

"*We'll* be right behind you," said Lieutenant Kirsten Cruzen, the *Enterprise*'s security officer dispatched by Worf to shadow Picard. Like her counterparts from the *Aventine*, Cruzen sported full tactical gear and carried a phaser rifle cradled in the crook of her left arm, her other hand resting atop the weapon's stock. Her dark hair was pulled into a bun, keeping it away from her face. She exchanged a wry look with Picard. "I got the full rundown from Lieutenant Šmrhová, sir. *And* Commander Worf."

"We each carry our own burdens, Lieutenant."

Chen, holding a tricorder fitted with a phase discriminator, said, "There's no sign of life anywhere within the structure." Scowling, she asked, "Tell me I'm not the only one whose skin is tingling?"

"It's not just you," replied Teresa Garcia, who, along with her partner Ranjea, had opted for a tactical vest worn over a black jumpsuit in lieu of their standard DTI attire.

Ranjea said, "There's something else. It's almost like a . . . pull? Does anyone else feel it?"

Aware of the mild yet still perceptible tingling effect playing across his exposed skin, Picard also sensed a similar attraction. There could be no mistaking the source: the structure. To him, the latticework evoked comparisons to another vessel assembled with equal, unrelenting precision: a Borg cube. He felt a chill as dormant memories came rushing to the forefront, and he nearly flinched as the visions filled his mind.

Stop this, he chided himself. *The Borg are gone. Focus on the here and now.*

Forcing away the unwelcome thoughts, he fell in behind Kandel while she and her detail fanned out and started walking, providing a forward security perimeter as the team advanced on the structure. Rather than a dedicated entrance, the base of the lattice provided any number of avenues for proceeding toward its interior. A few paces to Picard's right, Wesley walked by himself, canvas satchel slung over his left shoulder and disruptor rifle strapped across his back.

"This is the place," said Picard, looking to Wesley. "Isn't it? From the vision we shared?"

"Yes." Wesley held up his Omnichron. "What I can't tell from the data records I've been able to access is whether my future self actually visited this place, or else learned about it via some other means. A lot of the information in here is locked out." He shook his head. "I understand why he set it up this way, but if I'm still being kept from seeing everything, you have to wonder what we don't know about."

The prospect of what unknowns might still lurk in their future was enough to give Picard pause. On the other hand, if Wesley's theory about his future self was true, and the Omnichron was revealing information only after other goals or milestones were reached, the progress they had made to this point might indicate they traveled a successful path.

I can only hope so, Picard thought. *For the sake of those we've already lost.*

As they drew closer, he became more aware of the pull as described by Ranjea.

"It's getting stronger," said Cruzen, keeping in step with Picard. "I can feel myself starting to walk a bit faster. What the hell is it?"

"Time," said Wesley, indicating the lattice. "Temporal distortions. I think this whole thing is a sort of lens, but instead of light it's refracting time itself. More accurately, it's a focal point for different time streams. Coming and going." He held up his Omnichron. "I'm detecting temporal distortions laced with triolic energy, but featuring hundreds of different quantum signatures. All of that is converging here before being shunted somewhere else."

Picard said, "If the Devidians are attempting to manipulate time in order to feed on the neural energy of all living beings within an entire reality, they would need the means to direct that energy to a central collection point. As there are no life-forms here, it stands to reason this might not be that final location."

Garcia said, "Whatever they're doing, it's obviously not something we can detect in the twenty-fourth century."

"According to the information I've unlocked so far, this remains a secret well after that." No sooner did he say the words than Wesley offered a sheepish look to his companions. "Sorry. Probably more than you need or even want to know."

"I'm guessing the Temporal Prime Directive is out the window at this point," said Chen. When Agents Ranjea and Garcia regarded her with matching quizzical expressions, she shrugged. "I'm just saying the time to worry about such things was before we shot ourselves four thousand years into the future. What are the odds it'll come up at the post-mission debriefing?"

Picard recognized her commentary for what it was, masking the pain she still felt over the loss of her friends. Given the circumstances, he could allow her a small degree of latitude, and he even agreed with her observations. The time for theories and rules created with the noblest of intentions might well be behind them in terms of time and space but also practicality. If that was true, then the extent to which it applied would in all likelihood be up to the Devidians and whatever they had wrought in this place.

Following Lieutenant Kandel and her security team, Picard moved past the threshold that was the closest thing to the lattice's entryway. He looked up at the crystal columns towering overhead, weaving together and past one another until they all became an indistinct blur high overhead. It was impossible not to feel the rhythmic pulse as the crystals channeled unimaginable energies. A low buzz permeated the air, audible enough to be slightly discomforting while not so loud as to be debilitating. Picard tried to put it out of his mind as he studied the structure's interior.

"It's like a maze," said Garcia, noting the overlapping columns of crystal that formed a web so intricate that it was necessary to examine each cluster at ground level to determine a path around them.

Chen replied, "Maze is right. As orderly and aligned as everything is, it's still a jumble. It'd be easy to get lost in here, so I'm recording our advance."

"Same here," said Cruzen, tapping the tricorder that was open and active while still held in its holster on her tactical vest. "So we can backtrack out of here if we need to. Can't be too careful."

Picard nodded. "Agreed."

Ahead of them, Wesley had moved in front of Kandel and her people, holding his Omnichron before him. "There's something in here. A smaller structure." He pointed deeper into the lattice's interior. "See it?"

Increasing his pace—with Cruzen moving to keep up—Picard now saw the large, dark shape nestled within clusters of crystalline struts, its angular design allowing it to sit cradled within the lattice, all but invisible amid the brightness cast off by neighboring supports. As they approached, Wesley's Omnichron began emitting a spasmodic tone.

"I think this is it," he said, stepping around another base of crystal beams crossing past one another until he was almost running toward the structure. An opening situated between two crystal struts offered entry to the alcove and Wesley disappeared into it.

"Captain!"

It was Cruzen, jogging to catch up as Picard plunged toward the entrance, phaser rifle at the ready. Pausing at the threshold, he aimed the weapon through the doorway and inspected the room only to find Wesley standing at its center. The compartment was at least twenty meters across and half again as wide. Lining the room's walls and surrounding Wesley were intersecting columns of flowing energy contained within transparent conduits stretching from the floor to the structure's high ceiling. A low drone filled Picard's ears, conveying the power feeding through this chamber.

"Wesley," he said, stepping into the alcove with Cruzen and Chen on his heels. "What is this place?"

Studying his Omnichron, Wesley said nothing. Instead, he moved closer to one assemblage of conduits. "I'm not sure. It's like a data hub, only ridiculously more complex." Releasing the device, he allowed it to drift from his hand, and it rose to hover above him. He extended his arms away from his body, and Picard watched him close his eyes. Then parts of his body began phasing out of view, replaced by swirls of energy as Wesley shifted from this continuum.

"What's he doing?" asked Chen.

"He's communicating," Picard replied. "Travelers like him have a unique relationship with space, time, and even thought. They're able to focus thought like a lens, as a means of better understanding the universe and their ability to move within it."

"That sounds like a fairy tale," said Ranjea.

Picard nodded. "For us, it may well be, but for someone like Wesley, with the unique gifts he possesses, it's something else entirely. I didn't believe it either; not at first. I'm a man of science, Agent Ranjea, but I've seen with my own eyes the power of a Traveler's thoughts to influence the universe around us. While I don't believe magic explains it, I'm absolutely certain there is an answer rooted in science that's simply beyond our current ability to comprehend. Perhaps we never will."

"Maybe it's better if we don't," offered Agent Garcia.

Wesley's arms dropped to his sides and Picard watched his shoulders sag as he turned to face them, eyes bloodshot and moistened from the strain of his efforts.

"Are you all right?" asked Picard.

Swallowing, Wesley reached up to wipe his face. "We were right. It's a form of transmission hub." He gestured to the room around them. "All of this, and the framework outside; it's just one connection within a larger network, designed to channel energy from hundreds, even thousands, of timelines. The whole thing is phasing between different quantum realities so fast we can't even detect the change. The lattice is the heart of this particular hub, drawing energy from the various realities and redirecting it . . . somewhere. I tried to track it, but the quantum shifting was too much. It just seems to fade between moments in time. I think it's their version of a data-encryption system. The endpoint could be anywhere in the past or future."

Ranjea gestured to the conduits with their chaotic energy flows. "You're saying this is energy pulled from different timelines?"

"There's information here too," said Wesley. "Staggering amounts of it. All your data storage facilities like Memory Alpha, Starfleet's quantum archives, and the DTI's protected repositories *combined* have nothing on this. You could spend a lifetime in here and never scratch the surface, and this is just one hub."

Examining the room with her tricorder, Chen asked, "How many of these hubs are there? I mean, how many would the Devidians need?"

"Enough to handle an unknown number of different timelines or alternate realities," replied Garcia.

Ranjea added, "Which in theory is an infinite number, with new ones being created all the time."

"And others being destroyed," replied Chen.

Wesley nodded. "Exactly." He turned to regard the intricate web of conduits. "However, the key to understanding what they're doing, and how we might stop them, is here, somewhere. We just have to find it." Holding out his hand, he retrieved the Omnichron and began adjusting its internal components. "We also have to be careful. In a manner of speaking, this hub is perched at the intersection of thousands of timelines, acting like how a stream gauge monitors the flow of water along a river. I don't know that it has any direct control over the flow itself, but instead communicates with other locations in spacetime."

"Without knowing more about how it works," said Garcia, "any interruption in that flow could be catastrophic, with repercussions across an unknowable number of alternate timelines."

Wesley sighed. "Even attempting to access the system overseeing the process could be dangerous. We need to be extremely careful here."

An abrupt warble in the hum of the energy saturating the room startled everyone, punctuated by the shifting of colors within the overlapping conduits. Picard and everyone else were still reacting to the sudden shift when shouts of alarm from outside echoed through the alcove's open doorway. Then came phaser fire, just before Lieutenant Kandel's voice erupted from Picard's combadge.

"Kandel to Picard. We've got company."

Picard looked to Wesley. "We may not have time to be careful."

33

"Red alert! We've got incoming!"

Lonnoc Kedair's warning came only seconds before an impact against the ship's deflector shields set off every alarm indicator around the bridge. Warning symbols flashed across every console and the strips of accented illumination flared harsh crimson. The strike was hard enough to lift Ezri Dax off her chair and slam her back down again. She grimaced in shock more than pain, quickly scanning the bridge for signs anyone might be injured.

"Evasive!" she snapped. "Emergency starboard!"

At the flight controller station, Lieutenant Tharp stabbed at his controls. Ezri watched the planet shift to the left and out of frame on the viewscreen as the Bolian maneuvered the ship out of orbit. The move was not fast enough for her to avoid seeing a massive, dark slithering mass gliding past the screen, only for it to recoil and drift away after striking the *Aventine*'s forward shields. Energy sputtered at the point of attack while the creature seemed content to retreat.

"Computer, discontinue audible alarms!" shouted Sam Bowers over the din.

The abrupt silence was enough to make Ezri blink in surprise. Even without the sirens, it was evident the ship was still under attack. New collisions against the deflector shields registered on her chair's status panel. Too many of the indicators flashed red instead of green. She looked to where Kedair held on to her console with one hand while continuing to oversee her instruments.

"Kedair, what are we looking at?"

The Takaran replied, "Eight Nagas. Varying in size, but all attacking the shields at different points around the ship. We were ready for them this time, Captain. Lieutenant Leishman reports engineering is channeling power directly from the slipstream drive."

"Shields are at eighty-seven percent," reported Lieutenant Oliana Mirren from ops. "But we're already straining the primary shield generators."

Kedair said, "Leishman is working the problem, Captain, with the assistance of Commander La Forge."

Feeling a slight surge of relief, Ezri pointed to the viewscreen. "Conn, get us some maneuvering room. Kedair, target those bastards and fire as soon as you get a shot."

"Phasers and torpedoes on standby," replied the security chief.

At the science console, Gruhn Helkara said, "The Nagas are continuing to shift in and out of our spacetime continuum as they attack the shields. We've got fluctuations in the deflector frequency harmonics. This is not something we encountered at Bezorek Station."

Bowers asked, "Are you telling us they've learned new tricks?"

"It would seem so, Commander."

A new strike against the shields was enough to make the entire ship tremble and Ezri grip her chair to avoid a repeat of the previous episode. Still more warnings flashed across the bridge, and this time Mirren was thrown from her seat to the deck, landing hard on her side. Bowers lunged forward, crossing in front of Ezri to assist the lieutenant, who was already pushing herself to a sitting position. Mirren winced in pain as Bowers knelt beside her.

"You all right?" he asked.

The ops officer nodded, grimacing as she let him help her to her feet. She pressed her free hand to her left cheek, which Ezri could see was already red from where she hit the floor.

"I'll live, sir."

Moving out of the way so Mirren could resume her station,

Bowers took the opportunity to check her console while she situated herself. "Shields are at sixty-eight percent, Captain, and the fluctuations in the shield generators are increasing. Routing power from the slipstream drive is overtaxing the entire system. We risk losing everything if it overloads." Another impact to the shields served to emphasize his point, and it was only fast reflexes that let him grab onto the back of Mirren's chair, preventing him from tumbling to the deck.

"Shields at fifty-three percent," reported Mirren.

From the tactical station, Kedair called out, "Target acquired. Firing phasers."

Ezri looked to the viewscreen to see a pair of orange-white energy beams lance outward from the phaser cannons along the underside of the *Aventine*'s primary hull. The beams tracked to their target in seconds, striking along the flank of a Naga sailing past the screen. Modified to employ transphasic frequencies, the weapons scored on Kedair's first attempt, cutting through and destabilizing the creature. The Naga's immense body dissipated in the face of the onslaught as Tharp guided the ship into its next evasive turn. Even as the ship banked to its left, two more strikes against the shields raised more alarms.

Maintaining his position over Mirren's shoulder, Bowers reported, "Shields at forty-one percent and dropping."

Kedair said, "Captain, we are being hailed by the away team."

Tapping the communications control on the pad set into her chair's armrest, Ezri said, "Picard, we're taking fire up here. What's your situation?"

Filled with static, the channel buzzed and popped, slicing into the *Enterprise* captain's voice as it burst from the bridge speakers.

"We're under atta . . . eed . . . gency beam . . ."

Standing at the hub's entrance, Picard fired his phaser rifle into the maze of overlapping crystal columns supporting the temporal hub's immense lattice. His shot missed the Naga drifting in and around the clusters of support struts, and he watched the beam twist up and away as it was pulled to a nearby column where it impacted without any apparent harm.

"Please tell me hitting the beams won't blow us up," said Chen. She had taken up position across from Picard at the entry, and together they covered each other's blind side. Standing a pace behind them, Kirsten Cruzen aimed her phaser rifle over their heads.

"We can't stay here," she said. "They'll trap us."

Over the open communications frequency he had enabled with his combadge, Picard heard the broken, static-filled voice of Captain Ezri Dax. *"We can't . . . shields. Nagas are atta . . . ying to lock . . . hancers."*

"Nagas," said Agent Ranjea, from where he stood just behind Chen. "They can't beam us out of here with their shields up, even if they are getting a lock on the pattern enhancers."

Picard peered through the doorway to where Lieutenant Kandel's security team had deployed the trio of transporter pattern enhancers. Two of the units were set against the hub's forward wall, with the third five meters straight out from the entry. The idea was simple. Once activated and working together, the devices sent an extremely powerful signal up through the interference generated by the lattice structure around them as well as the atmosphere, where the *Aventine* would hopefully be able to lock onto the signal and beam up any life-forms within the enhancers' perimeter. Providing cover for Picard and the others, Kandel and her team had positioned themselves at the outward edges of that boundary, searching for any Nagas moving within the latticework. It appeared even these smaller creatures were still too large to navigate many of the gaps between clusters of angled crystal columns, offering the away team a saving grace from their current predicament.

For his part, Picard was torn between positioning himself outside the hub and alongside Kandel or remaining here covering Wesley while he worked. Glancing over his shoulder, he saw Wesley standing alone before the wall of conduits as the hellish energy pulled and dispersed through time itself. The room's omnipresent hum had increased in pitch, suggesting greater demands placed on whatever control system oversaw the immense construct. Seemingly oblivious to everything else around him, Wesley held his arms out to his sides, his eyes closed and his body once again phasing in and out of view. Picard could not begin to fathom whatever communication the other man might be effecting, reaching out through space and time with the power of thought while seeking connection with this mechanism.

"Incoming!"

It was Kandel, pointing with her free hand to where a Naga was approaching from Picard's left. The lieutenant, wasting no time, leveled her phaser rifle at the incoming attacker and fired, with her two security officers joining her along that section of the enhancers' perimeter. A trio of phaser beams lanced toward the creature as it banked around a crystalline column, halting its advance as Kandel scored a hit. Acoustics carried the Naga's pain-racked cry through the latticework. It bumped into the column, arresting its movements long enough for the three officers to concentrate their fire. The modified weapons found their mark, quickly disintegrating their target.

Movement from the corner of his eye made Picard flinch, and he pushed back from the doorway, grabbing Chen and pulling her with him as a black mass drifted within two meters of the door, *inside the perimeter.*

"Look out!"

His warning was too late, as the Naga rammed into the two junior security officers. They disappeared in dual explosions of ash. Picard recoiled in horror, remembering they had pledged to protect him without his knowing their names. Kandel pivoted toward the new threat, firing her weapon at the Naga as it drifted out of view, concealed by the lattice.

"I'm going outside," said Agent Ranjea, hoisting his phaser rifle. "She needs backup."

"Agreed." Picard moved to follow. "So do you."

"You need to protect Crusher," Ranjea countered, nodding back to where a phase-shifting Wesley remained still. He nodded to Garcia. "We've got this."

"We can protect the entrance from outside, while providing better covering fire." Picard stepped out of the hub. No longer would he allow the others to risk their lives defending him. "Chen, you take position next to the door. Watch our backs, and Wesley's."

Along with Cruzen, Ranjea, and Garcia, he assumed a defensive position near the hub wall, checking to ensure everyone remained within the enhancers' perimeter. If the *Aventine* managed to get a transporter lock, they could beam the team out in seconds. As for Wesley, Picard grimly conceded he almost certainly had a better chance of escaping the situation on his own.

"I don't know how much longer we can stay here, sir," said Kandel, who was already replacing her phaser rifle's power cell. The configurations to support transphasic frequencies were draining the weapons much faster than normal. Her face was taut, her jaw clenching as she forced herself to bury her reaction to the loss of her people and focus on the mission.

She was still inserting the fresh power cell when another Naga appeared above and behind her, arcing up and over a nearby column to strike her in the back. Kandel vanished in an expanding trail of dust as the creature banked to its left, away from the hub and toward Ranjea. The DTI agent was still raising his weapon when the Naga slammed into him, wiping him from existence before Cruzen could fire her phaser. Her shot hit the creature across its back, causing it to spasm and buying time for Picard to add his weapon to the counterattack. Garcia and Chen joined in, the four weapons inflicting enough damage to bring down the Naga. It faded into oblivion, leaving the remaining team members reeling.

"What about the shuttlecraft's transporter?" blurted Chen. "It's only one pad, but—"

Propping himself against the hub wall, Picard shook his head. "We have to hold out until Wesley's finished." He cast a look over his shoulder to where Wesley remained in communion with the hub.

Whatever you're doing, Wesley, do it faster.

Holding on to the nearest console as the *Aventine* shuddered around him, Geordi La Forge watched the shield status indicators shift from orange to red.

"Down to twenty-four percent," said Lieutenant Mikaela Leishman, the ship's chief engineer. Wiping sweat from her face, she brushed aside a lock of her dark hair as she consulted her workstation. "Another couple of hits and that's it for the shields." She looked to La Forge. "Unless you can conjure another of your famous *Enterprise* chief engineer miracles."

Studying the master systems display above Leishman's console, La Forge asked, "What about bypassing the damaged flow regulators and channeling power directly from the slipstream drive? The shield generators have their own compensators to prevent overload. We run the risk of a surge running back to the drive, but it'd buy us time to run a bypass to backup regulators."

"If we got a power surge while we were doing that, the slipstream drive would be history." Leishman tapped the display. "It's a lot more sensitive than warp drive. On a good day, you have to charm it, flatter it, do a dance, and offer up a firstborn as sacrifice to get it to work right. We already pushed our luck with the modifications to get us here, and it's our only way back home. And we'd lose the shields on top of everything else. We'd be sitting ducks for those things."

Memories of lost friends still fresh in his mind, La Forge sighed in agreement. "Yeah."

So far, evasive maneuvers, effective weapons fire, and no small amount of luck had spared the *Aventine* the worst effects of direct attack by the Nagas. At last report, three of the original eight creatures had been dispatched, but the remaining five continued to wreak havoc. It was only a matter of time before they slipped past the fancy flying and Lieutenant Lonnoc Kedair's masterful weapons acumen and overwhelmed the ship's deflector shields.

"What about reconfiguring the phasers to emit a wide-beam effect?" Leishman tapped controls to bring up schematics for the *Aventine*'s weapons systems. "Kedair wouldn't have to be so precise with her targeting."

Studying the schematics, La Forge replied, "I think I've got it." He ran his fingers over the specs, tracing lines while calculations took shape in his mind. "We program the shield emitters to simultaneously transmit a broad-spectrum transphasic pulse. Those arrays are as powerful as phasers, and they're designed to operate across a wider range of random frequencies. So, we send a signal to all the emitters at the same time and basically spin the frequency dial. That should be enough to disrupt their own phase-shifting. Might even push them out of our continuum."

Leishman ran her hand across the schematic, mimicking La Forge's movements as she pondered the idea. "Even if it works, pushing this amount of power through the emitters means we get one chance at this, maybe two, and if we're lucky we won't fry the slipstream drive."

"If we don't try something, they're going to get in here."

Blowing out her breath, Leishman rapped the console with her fist. "That's what I like about having only one choice. Makes it simple. Let's get to work."

34

Wesley remained still. His Omnichron hovering above his head as though standing watch, he stood with eyes closed and arms extended, seemingly at peace with himself and whatever universe— or universes—he occupied while all hell broke loose around him.

Concentrating their phaser fire, Picard along with Cruzen, Chen, and Agent Garcia dispatched another Naga. With practiced ease while the others covered him, Picard dropped his rifle's spent power cell and inserted a new pack while trying not to look at the discarded units lying on the ground around him. Instead, he returned to his crouching position near the hub's open entry, bracing himself against the alcove's smooth wall. Resting the phaser on his knee, he searched among the web of crystalline stanchions for approaching threats. With the incessant drone of the hub behind him, it was impossible to listen for anything moving their way, and tricorders had proven less than helpful in here, given the Nagas' ability to phase-shift.

The creatures were circling, like sharks sizing up their prey before moving in for the kill. Other than the one rogue attack responsible for the deaths of Kandel, her security team, and Ranjea, they seemed leery of weaving between the conduits toward the hub. Their own bulk, along with the close quarters, offered little room for maneuvering. So long as the team could keep their assailants in sight, they stood a small chance of holding them off.

Another of the Nagas appeared, drawing fire from Cruzen and Agent Garcia as it glided between stanchions. Chen fired at a second Naga as Picard moved to join her, dropping to one knee and firing at the serpent's tail before it moved out of his line of sight. Grunting in frustration at the missed opportunity, he shifted his aim to help Cruzen and Garcia, their efforts also coming up short as the creature drifted out of view.

"I don't get it," said Cruzen as she and Garcia adjusted their positions so they each could keep watch along a different avenue of approach. "They can phase-shift through our hull and other solid matter, so why aren't they just charging us head-on?"

Chen replied, "Something about the temporal distortions in play here? All of that energy being directed through this place." She looked at the latticework towering above them. "That might just be it. They're phasing in and out of spacetime, and these beams are literally channeling energy drawn from multiple timelines? Maybe it's dangerous for them to interact with them that way."

"Wouldn't that presuppose they're sentient?" asked Garcia, splitting her attention between the conversation and scanning the lattice for signs of danger. "I thought they were basically bred and trained as hunters against people like Wesley. Without blindly running into the conduits, how would they know what to avoid?"

Picard pushed himself to his feet, lifting his phaser rifle and aiming it at the answer to their questions, which now approached them. "The Devidian avatars. They're controlled by the avatars."

The humanoid stepped into view, and in response to its arrival the two Nagas moved off, disappearing between columns and deeper into the lattice. Like the one they had captured aboard the *Enterprise*, this avatar was dressed in dark robes that concealed its figure, though its hood was back far enough that its smooth, featureless face was visible. Picard blanched as a blast of cold, rancid air seemed to herald the avatar's arrival.

"Your effort is wasted. You cannot hope to understand that which overwhelms your limited intelligence."

Despite the urge to fire, Picard held the phaser aimed at the avatar but did not press the trigger. "There must be some way to provide you the sustenance you need without such wanton destruction. We can help you if you would allow it."

"You are beneath us. You are insignificant. What has been set into motion cannot be stopped. We will endure."

"And what about the rest of the universe?" asked Garcia. "Uncounted realities, uncountable lives, all sacrificed so you can survive? Why do that if another way can be found?"

The avatar turned its head as if to regard the DTI agent. *"There will always be life. So long as we endure, others can thrive."*

"But only in service to you," said Picard, feeling his anger intensifying. "Livestock, awaiting the slaughter. That's what you want. That is all you require. Your existence is without purpose. You're a blight, a cancer on the entire universe, and you need to be removed."

"The universe belongs to us. All realities belong to us. You are nothing. You are less than nothing. You offer nothing, but the momentary sating that comes from your passing and your essence transferring to us." The humanoid raised its hand, palm toward Picard. *"Once you are gone, there will always be others to rep—"*

Cruzen's phaser beam caught the avatar in the center of its face. The humanoid staggered back as Garcia fired, striking it in the chest. Both women kept their weapons trained on the avatar until the rush of orange energy washed over it and it faded from existence.

Stunned by the abrupt execution, Picard turned to Cruzen only to see one of the Nagas coiling out from behind one of the crystalline struts. He aimed his phaser rifle at the new threat, but the lieutenant was already ducking and rolling out of the way. The creature kept coming and Picard fired, his weapon's beam striking it across the top of its head. It was not enough to alter the Naga's attack and Picard backpedaled, searching for retreat.

"Captain!"

Something slammed into his right side, driving him toward the hub. He barely had time to tuck and absorb the fall before he struck the floor. Grunting in pain as he landed, he felt the weight of something on his legs and jerked his head around to see the Naga lumbering past the entrance, phaser fire from two weapons, Cruzen's and Garcia's, tracking it as it disappeared from view.

Then he heard the tormented moan.

Crumpled on the floor just out of arm's reach, Chen's body was racked with spasms. She curled into a ball, her hair now gone, her skin turning ashen, withering and tightening as she aged decades before his eyes. Her uniform had already decayed and fallen apart, leaving her bare and frail.

Despite all of this, she was still alive.

"Oh no." It was Cruzen standing at the entrance, her face a mask of revulsion as she beheld her shipmate. Then training snapped in and she tapped her combadge. "Cruzen to *Aventine*. Medical emergency! Beam us up, *now!*"

Ezri Dax winced at the away team's call, at the sound of Lieutenant Cruzen's anguished plea for help. There was nothing she could do.

"Bridge to engineering. Give me good news."

Over the intercom, Lieutenant Leishman replied, *"We're almost there, Captain! Just two more minutes!"*

"We don't have two minutes! The away team's calling for emergency transport."

Yet another strike against the shields rocked the ship, this time in much more violent fashion. Anyone on the bridge not seated or holding on to something was thrown to the deck. Commander Bowers rolled to his left, almost tumbling out of his chair and into Ezri's lap. Over her left shoulder, Ezri glimpsed Lieutenant Kedair falling backward from her tactical console, landing hard on her right side. The impact came as new alarms filled the air, including the one warning Ezri most dreaded.

"Our shields are down!" called Commander Helkara. "Shield generators overloaded. They are cycling. Forty-two seconds to restart."

"Our evasive action is helping," said Kedair, who had pulled herself back to her station. "But there are still five of those things out there. Unless we leave orbit entirely, the creatures will inevitably catch up to us."

Ezri said, "Conn, continue evasive maneuvers. Mirren, are we in position to beam up the away team?" With the shields down, she reasoned, at least that opportunity presented itself.

Without looking up from her controls, Lieutenant Oliana Mirren replied, "Yes, Captain, but sensors are detecting only one biosign within the pattern enhancers' perimeter."

"Beam that person directly to sickbay now." Ezri had no idea who it was, or why they might need transport, but right now every chance to retrieve the away team had to be exploited. Details could be sorted later.

Over the intercom, a voice said, *"Sickbay to bridge. Lieutenant Chen from the* Enterprise *has just arrived."* It was Lieutenant Simon Tarses, the *Aventine*'s chief medical officer. *"Her condition is . . . critical, Captain."*

"Do what you can for her, Doctor," replied Ezri. "We're working to bring up the rest of the away team. There may be more casualties." She had no idea as to the status of Captain Picard and the rest of his group on the surface. "Mirren, keep an eye on the beam-up site. Any chance you get to retrieve someone, you do it."

Kedair said, "Captain, three smaller Naga life signs are approaching the hull. Two toward the primary hull, the other near the engineering section. I think they may be too close to shake."

Jumping up from his chair, Bowers retrieved a phaser rifle from under his seat. With his free hand he tapped his combadge. "Bridge to all personnel. Expect hostile intruders to breach the hull. Prepare to defend yourselves and the ship!"

After Wesley Crusher's briefing about the Nagas and their handlers, the Devidian avatars, and the danger they posed should they breach the ship, hand phasers and the larger rifle variants, all reconfigured to fire at transphasic frequencies, were issued as far as they could go, arming more than two-thirds of the ship's 750 personnel. The *Aventine*'s security detachment was at this moment deploying to every deck, ready to support their shipmates with extra power cells and personnel to see that the ship's vital areas could be defended. Here on the bridge, every officer carried hand phasers, with Bowers, Helkara, Kedair, and Ezri armed with phaser rifles.

To everyone on the bridge, Bowers said, "Listen up, people. Whatever happens next is likely to be fast and vicious. Be ready for anything. We've still got a team on the surface that needs our help, so right now our mission is keeping the ship out of trouble long enough to get them up. Understood?" He was answered by a chorus of affirmative responses, after which he turned to look at Ezri. "Showtime, I guess."

Ezri nodded. "I guess."

The sound of an alert indicator from the science station drew Ezri's attention. Studying the litany of information being fed to his station from the ship's external and internal sensor arrays, Helkara said, "Naga life-forms have breached the hull. Decks twenty-one, thirteen, and two. They're inside the ship, Captain. Sensor readings are indistinct, but they appear to be moving between bulkheads and decks. With their ability to phase-shift, they can reach any part of the ship within seconds. I highly advise that all—"

Energy crackled across the console just before a massive, dark head emerged from behind the array of displays and a Naga pushed through Helkara's head and upper chest. The Zakdorn disappeared in a cloud of ash as the creature shifted through the workstation and the adjacent bulkhead.

Ezri was the first to see the science officer's appalling death and lunged from her chair, bringing up her phaser rifle. Lieutenant Tharp beat her to the punch, twisting around in his seat and raising his hand phaser to fire at the creature. The modified beam was enough to draw the Naga's attention to the Bolian; he and Mirren vacated their consoles and scrambled out of the command well. From across the bridge, Kedair fired her rifle at the creature. Despite its size, it moved with startling speed, coiling up and around the bridge overhead and taking the brunt of the security chief's attack with little effect.

"Combine our firepower!" shouted Ezri, getting off a quick shot as the Naga twisted its body and dropped from the overhead straight at Tharp. The conn officer had no time to react before the creature slammed into him, and he vanished, the dust of his remains spattering Mirren, who screamed while rolling out of the monster's path.

Kedair's next shot caught the Naga along its flank, causing it to jerk in her direction. Mirren added her hand phaser to the mix and Bowers followed suit. Ezri watched as they succeeded in aggravating the creature. Its body snapped to the left to face Bowers, who was already trying to adjust his aim with the thing's yawning, tooth-filled maw less than three meters away. Firing her own phaser rifle bought her first officer the extra second he needed to dive across the ops console and out of the creature's path.

"Sam!"

Ezri waved her rifle, indicating for Bowers to get clear before opening fire again. This time the creature's hide rippled in response to the attack and it jerked and curled over on itself. Kedair and Bowers took aim, their phaser beams converging at a spot near the serpent's head. Now in obvious pain, the Naga convulsed and its cry of suffering filled the bridge. Sidestepping to stay clear of the creature's movements and sensing it must finally be succumbing to the counterattack, Ezri corrected her aim for one more shot at its head. The Naga's body wrenched around once more, this time coming close enough to Ezri that she felt air displaced by its passage.

Then she felt another sensation taking over, an odd tingle beginning to play across her skin. She was vaguely aware of alarmed shouting, but all of that was lost amid the sudden rush of emotions and other sensations as the Dax symbiont reacted in obvious distress. The color faded from her vision and her surroundings—the bridge, Sam Bowers and Lonnoc Kedair continuing to fight the Naga, Oliana Mirren scrambling toward her—all lost substance, turning indistinct in the face of a brilliant white light intensifying to wash away everything.

35

"Bridge to all personnel. Intruders on decks ten and twenty-two, with others still trying to breach the hull. Hostiles continue to be resistant to phaser fire. Avoid direct contact and engage with multiple weapons. Do not shoot to disable. Repeat: Do not shoot to disable."

Listening to Commander Sam Bowers over the intraship comm system, Geordi La Forge heard angst and fear in the first officer's voice despite what sounded like the man's obvious attempt to keep his emotions in check. Turning from where he worked to input another set of reconfiguration requests for the ship's deflector shield emitters, he glanced to Lieutenant Leishman only to see the *Aventine*'s chief engineer regarding him with a worried expression.

"He sounds shaken," she said. "Something's happened. Something bad."

Like everyone else on the ship, La Forge and Leishman had heard the initial intruder warning, with reports of three breaches. He had not missed the implicit meaning of the alert about deck two, given its obvious proximity to the bridge. At the same time, he and the rest of the engineering team had their own problems: at least one of the intruders was in the secondary hull, which meant it was close enough to present a threat to them. In response to that danger, security teams were already on station inside engineering, both on the main level and the catwalk serving the room's upper tier. Everyone was armed at least with a hand phaser, though several also wore rifles slung over shoulders. Leishman had ordered her people to secure the warp core, slipstream drive, and other vital areas. La Forge's assistance came in from lessons learned from the *Enterprise*'s previous and very costly encounter with the Nagas.

Taurik and the others saved us, he reminded himself. He was determined his colleagues' work and sacrifice would now save more lives.

"I've finished adding the new program to the emitter arrays," said Leishman. "You ready with the power transfer?"

La Forge patted his console. "Yes." He scrutinized the master systems display, noting the *Aventine*'s deflector shield generators had completed their cycling after the overload. The shields were already back online. "Shield strength is increasing. Hopefully, that'll keep any more of those things from getting in here."

"Unless we blow out the generators again with this stunt of ours."

"Well, there is that."

"Warning," said the *Aventine*'s main computer. *"Intruder detected in engineering section eleven beta."*

Leishman looked away from the workstations toward the overhead at the center of the room. "Deuterium storage. That's one deck above us. We may not have a lot of time." She tapped her combadge. "Engineering to bridge. We're almost ready to go with the emitter pulse."

Instead of Captain Dax, it was Bowers who replied. *"As soon as you're there, punch it."*

"We don't know what this will do to the shields, Commander."

"If it doesn't work we'll break orbit, but if we don't get Picard and his team up, this whole thing is for nothing. Do it!"

Any reply Leishman might have made was lost as La Forge heard phaser fire from the engineering room's upper tier. He looked up to see two *Aventine* security officers brandishing phaser rifles and aiming them at the Naga that was still phase-shifting through the room's overhead, like a shark emerging from the ocean depths in search of prey. Proximity to the ship's warp core made it strike the transphasic containment field configured by La Forge and

Leishman. Energy crackled and sparked as the creature brushed the field with its left flank before it angled itself toward the main level. Three more *Aventine* crewmembers moved to engage, their phasers catching the Naga head-on. Again the creature recoiled from the attacks. No sooner did they start firing than La Forge noticed more movement farther back in the room. A dark, hooded figure stepped into view from the warp core's far side, its right arm raised.

An avatar.

"Mikaela!"

A foul odor filled La Forge's nostrils and he felt a chill across his exposed skin as he beheld the intruder. Grabbing Leishman's arm, he pulled her away from the console just as the avatar released pulses of silver energy from its hand, sweeping its arm across the engineering section and catching the three security officers in its path. All three crewmembers vanished in clouds of ash while the salvo continued through them to strike Leishman's workstation. The bank of displays exploded from the strike while the avatar un-leashed more fury, this time catching a human woman and a male Tellarite. Neither even had a chance to bring their weapons to bear before they disappeared.

As Leishman grabbed the phaser rifle she had positioned near her console, La Forge unholstered his hand phaser while at the same time stealing a glance at the status indicators on his own console. The power readings were as good as they were going to get, and a single illuminated control flashed the command he was waiting for: "Execute." He looked back to see the avatar advancing across the main floor. Behind it, the Naga twisted its body in the act of dispatching two more *Aventine* crewmembers before turning to follow its master as the humanoid walked slowly toward them. Leishman fired her phaser rifle at the avatar. The beam drilled into the intruder's chest, halting the figure's advance but not stopping it. In response, the Naga glided over the avatar and set its sights on the two engineers.

"Do it!" shouted Leishman before she fired again, hitting the Naga, which kept coming.

La Forge hit the control.

He had no idea what the effect looked like outside the ship, where several of the Nagas must have been continuing their efforts to penetrate the shields and the hull, but in engineering the effect was immediate. Erupting from the containment field emitters protecting the warp core and the slipstream drive, a transphasic pulse rippled across the room, distorting everything in La Forge's line of sight. It struck the Naga and its avatar, sending both intruders into a fit of frenzied spasms. He watched as their bodies stretched, warped, and phased in and out of sight before fading away altogether.

At the same time, numerous alarms wailed as system indicators flashed status alerts. Doubtless still reeling from the attack they had just endured, members of Leishman's team moved toward various workstations. La Forge watched as their experience and training took over.

With the sirens muted and her own console destroyed, Leishman consulted La Forge's station before tapping her combadge. "Engineering to bridge. We've got blown power relays and shield emitters all over the ship, but all vital systems are still online. Tell me that worked."

"It worked, Mikaela," replied Bowers over the open channel. "Well done. Are transporters still functional?"

Relief washing over him, La Forge said, "Up and running, Commander."

"Good." Bowers sounded tired, if not defeated. "Let's hope we can get our people off that damned planet."

From where he crouched inside the entry to the hub, Picard fired his phaser at yet another Naga. He counted five of them drifting among the towering lattice. Without their handler they were getting bolder, seemingly operating on instinct. They circled the hub, their movements bringing them into contact with the structure. He watched as they brushed various crystal supports, reacting to the touch and the resulting release of energy before changing direction only to do it again. More than ever, they were primitive animals—hunters that knew their prey was cornered—and they were waiting for an opening to move in for the kill.

"I'm down to my last power cell," said Agent Garcia from where she knelt across from Picard on the entry's opposite side. He watched her insert the pack into her phaser rifle before he checked the status of his own weapon. Less than half a charge remained. Based on what they had experienced so far, the rifle would be exhausted before they succeeded in dispatching the remaining creatures. Kneeling between them so she could cover any direct approaches on the entrance, Lieutenant Cruzen reached to her tactical vest and retrieved her last two power units, placing them on the floor where Picard and Garcia could reach them.

"No more where those came from," she cautioned.

Looking over his shoulder, Picard saw that Wesley Crusher remained locked in his odd trance, still communicating with whatever lay at the heart of this immense mechanism. Whether he was interacting with an intelligence or simply finding his way within a vast, sophisticated computer system, Picard did not know. Hovering around him was the Omnichron, an audible hum emanating from its interior.

"Move it, Wesley," he said, low but still loud enough for Cruzen and Garcia to hear.

At some point, would they have to accept that Wesley's efforts were in vain and there was nothing to be gained from staying here any longer? The cost exacted just to get to this point was already too high. Fighting back rage and despair, Picard could not shake the vision of T'Ryssa Chen that now tormented his thoughts. Frail and broken, whisked back to the *Aventine*, where he knew that ship's medical staff was at this moment doing everything in its power to save her, but what could be done?

"Incoming!" It was Cruzen, raising her phaser rifle to fire at another Naga that had finally chosen to attempt a frontal assault; passing the last columns of crystal barring its way, it sprang toward the entry. She fired, hitting the creature just below its mouth. It jerked to its left, starting to bank away before Garcia and Picard fired their own weapons. The combined attack was enough to send the Naga dissolving into nothingness.

Wesley Crusher chose that moment to emerge from his trance. Opening his eyes, he blinked several times before he noticed his companions.

"I've got it. At least, I think I do." He looked around the room. "Where is everyone?"

Garcia said, "It's a long damned story, and I really don't want to tell it here. What do you think you found?"

"The key to everything." Wesley reached out, retrieving his Omnichron. "What the Devidians are doing. How, and why. I couldn't record everything because the amount of information is staggering, but I got enough. Besides, we really need to go. I managed to convince the computer intelligence overseeing the reactor to deactivate its cooling systems. We've got about ten minutes before this whole mountain goes up."

"Maybe run that by the group before you go rogue, Traveler," said Cruzen, irritation lacing every word before she looked to Picard. "We can make it to the shuttle, sir."

Garcia replied, "There are still who knows how many of those things out there. To hell with the shuttle. They can build a new one."

"Agreed." Picard tapped his combadge. "*Aventine*, we're ready for transport."

Static filled the open connection, not quite drowning out a male voice. "*Captain Pic . . . eady to trans . . . ock . . . hancers.*"

Leading the way out of the hub with his phaser at the ready,

Picard entered the area covered by the pattern enhancers, with the others following close behind. To his great relief, columns of transporter energy found them within seconds and he watched the alien latticework fade away.

Leaving Cruzen and Garcia to handle any debriefings, Picard made his way from the *Aventine*'s transporter room to sickbay. It took him a moment to orient himself to the unfamiliar layout before proceeding to the trauma ward.

The room was a hive of activity, with three people moving around a treatment bed, each wielding medical scanners, tricorders, and other devices Picard did not recognize. At the center of their attention was T'Ryssa Chen, impossibly aged and looking even more brittle than when he had last seen her. She was almost invisible under the sheet covering her from the shoulders down, except for her arms, which lay at her sides. Despite pale, wrinkled skin and deep lines in her face along with the lack of hair that accented her delicately pointed ears, Picard still recognized her features even with the mask covering her nose and mouth to provide oxygen. Her eyes were closed and her expression was almost peaceful, and for a moment he feared he was too late. Then his eyes took in the medical status monitor behind Chen's head and he noted her life signs. Respiration, blood pressure, body temperature, brain activity. All were active despite being at critical levels.

"Captain Picard," said one of the doctors on duty. He was a tall man with dark hair, upswept eyebrows, and ears that, while not quite pointed, still were not round like a human's. It took Picard an extra moment to recognize the man.

"Doctor Tarses." Picard regarded him with awkward sympathy. Formerly a medical technician assigned to the *Enterprise*-D under Beverly Crusher, Tarses had faced a great deal of legal trouble nearly two decades earlier when it was discovered he had falsified his entrance application to Starfleet. Not disclosing his Romulan heritage by virtue of his paternal grandfather had nearly scuttled his medical career, but Picard was gratified to see Tarses had weathered those challenges. "How is she?"

With a heavy sigh, Tarses shook his head. "I'm sorry, sir. There's nothing we can do. The accelerated aging was too much too fast. Her internal organs are shutting down, her cells are breaking down at a subatomic level. We've managed to arrest that decay with a stasis field and we have her on full life-support, but it's prolonging the inevitable."

"Is she in any pain?"

"No, sir. We've blocked that. She won't feel anything from . . . from now on."

Picard fought to maintain his bearing. Years of discipline and command presence made that second nature along with the emotional shield he had developed to endure the tragedy of losing someone in his charge. He had experienced that far too often during his career, but all of these tools were failing him.

"I'd like to talk to her."

"Certainly, sir." Tarses stepped aside, before gesturing to his people to give Picard a moment of privacy.

Even with what he guessed had to be a significant amount of sedation to keep her comfortable, Chen seemed alert. Her eyes moved in response to Picard as he approached her bed. Instinct made him reach for her hand, only to be stopped by the stasis field surrounding her.

"Captain," she said, her voice low and weak.

Picard held up his hand. "Save your strength, T'Ryssa." In spite of his plea, she managed to raise her hand, her palm facing him. He moved his own hand to mirror her movements, though they remained separated by the stasis field.

"Did . . . did we do it? Wesley?" Every word seemed to drain her even further.

"We did. Wesley found what he was looking for. We know what to do." Picard actually had no idea what Wesley's efforts might reveal. None of that mattered now. It could wait, at least just these few minutes.

He leaned closer, his voice softer. "You saved my life. Thank you."

It was not even the first time she had done so, considering previous actions she had taken to protect the *Enterprise* and its crew at great risk to her own personal safety. That truth only served to make this current reality so much more painful.

Drawing her hand back, she rested it on her chest.

"Thank . . . you. For . . . every . . . thing." Then T'Ryssa Chen closed her eyes forever.

36

Picard steeled himself at the sound of his ready room's door chime. Conversations of this sort were as unpleasant as they were necessary. He had already allowed too much time to pass, though in fairness, matters of greater importance required his attention. Those were addressed, at least for the moment, leaving him a brief window of opportunity to carry out a more somber yet still crucial task. While he would have preferred to be alone, to dwell in the privacy of his own thoughts and feelings, duty demanded Picard set aside his personal grief and focus on those looking to him for leadership and guidance.

"Come."

The doors parted to reveal Commander Bowers. Now the *Aventine*'s acting captain, the man already appeared to have aged just in the precious few hours that had passed since the ship's return to its proper place in time.

"Captain," he said, offering a small nod of greeting.

Rising from his seat, Picard gestured to Bowers. "Commander. Please, come in." His guest took one of the chairs before the captain's desk, sitting ramrod straight. "I'm sorry we didn't get a chance to talk before now."

"I understand, sir." Bowers cleared his throat. "There's a lot to deal with right now."

"Yes." It was a quiet reply, offered as Picard returned to his seat. Neither man needed to elaborate, he suspected. The journey home from the distant future was a blur, preceded by the recovery of the shuttlecraft *Daugava* and observing the destruction of the Devidian temporal hub thanks to Wesley Crusher's actions. As with the *Aventine*, the *Enterprise* crew was still processing the events that had transpired and their dreadful impact on both ships. A memorial service was scheduled for later this evening in the *Enterprise*'s main shuttlebay. Picard would speak at the ceremony, to commemorate Lieutenant Kandel and her team for their sacrifice on the planet's surface, and T'Ryssa Chen. Bowers would memorialize his captain and the fallen members of the *Aventine*. The service would also remember Agent Meyo Ranjea.

"I am truly sorry for the losses your crew has suffered," said Picard. "And I sympathize with your personal situation, though I also commend you for how you've comported yourself in the wake of such tragic circumstances. I can think of no finer way to honor Captain Dax."

His expression sullen, Bowers replied, "Of course I've always wanted to command my own ship one day, but not like this." He cast his eyes to where his hands lay folded in his lap. "I wonder what she'd think of this. She'd probably find a way to joke about the irony, considering how she earned her own command."

Picard knew the story quite well. Assigned to the *Aventine* as its second officer when the Borg invaded the Alpha Quadrant six years earlier, Dax found herself forced to assume command during that vessel's first combat action in the Acamar system. While defending the system from the Borg's advance, the *Aventine*'s captain and first officer were killed, leaving Dax as the senior surviving officer. Less than a week following that battle, Starfleet Command issued her a field promotion to captain and command of the *Aventine*.

"It's funny," said Bowers, a small smile teasing the corners of his mouth. "When she first took command and made me her number one, Ezri struggled with self-doubt. She confided in me that she wasn't sure she could pull it off. Given what we were facing against the Borg, I think we were both just scared, but we figured it out pretty quickly. There wasn't really much choice at the time." He returned his attention to Picard. "I suppose if there's anyone who can understand any of this, it's you, sir."

"Indeed." His own ascendancy to the *Stargazer*'s center seat had come following circumstances not dissimilar to those inflicted upon the *Aventine*. He had faced the same doubts, the same questions about his own competency to lead at a critical juncture, with so many lives counting on his making the correct decisions.

"Although we train for the day when we might be given such responsibility," Picard said, "I believe having it thrust upon us without warning tests us in a manner unlike any other challenge we're ever likely to confront. Ezri Dax faced such a test, and she validated Starfleet's trust in her. I have no doubts the same will be said of you, Commander."

Bowers's expression softened. "Thank you, sir. I appreciate that. I know what's expected of me. I can keep her seat warm, but I can't replace her. I can't even imagine trying. She wasn't just our captain and my friend. It's so much more than that." He sighed. "I mean, the death of so many good, dedicated people is a tragedy. No life is replaceable, but her loss is something else altogether, not just for us but for the entire Federation. Trying to fill shoes like that is just not something I ever envisioned trying to do."

Once again, Picard sympathized with the younger man's feelings. The promising life and career of Ezri were cut far too short, and the passing of the Dax symbiont was almost too great a tragedy to express. A living repository of knowledge and experience, Dax had been a firsthand witness to nearly four centuries of history, as conveyed through the lives of those nine fortunate souls chosen to be the Trill symbiont's host.

"The bond between a captain and their first officer is unique, Commander. Ezri Dax placed her trust in you. She *believed* in you. Honor her sacrifice not by trying to replace her, but instead being the captain she knew you can be. Your crew needs you to do that, particularly now."

Nodding, Bowers asked, "To the bitter end, sir?"

For the first time, Picard smiled, recalling a similar question posed to him long ago by Will Riker. "Nothing at all bitter about that, Commander."

Holodeck three was in its default state, entirely black and covered with a field of yellow gridlines. Only the arch with its computer interface, positioned before the room's entrance, broke the monotony surrounding Picard along with Beverly and Wesley Crusher, Geordi La Forge, and Agent Teresa Garcia.

"Wes was right," said La Forge. "His Omnichron's storage capacity was completely depleted by the time he disengaged from the Devidian system. It's even taxing our own data storage, so we've modified the interface between it and the main computer. We're treating the Omnichron like external storage, from which the computer can access and retrieve information just like it would with one of our own data cores."

"It could take weeks to sift through it all," added Wesley, holding up the Omnichron. "So we're building search algorithms to narrow things down." He exchanged looks with La Forge. "What we've found isn't good news. At all."

He released the Omnichron and it moved to hover at the center of the room. Within seconds the holodeck activated, generating a scene with which Picard was familiar: the hub inside the Devidian lattice.

"It's like we surmised," said Wesley, indicating the conduits with their flowing torrents of energy. "What we found in the future was just one component within a vast network of similar junctions, scattered through different points in space and time. The whole thing is apparently designed to channel temporal energy outward from a central nucleus and through hubs like the one we found." As he spoke, the scene shifted, reducing the hub and its supporting lattice to a single white dot on an immense black field. More dots appeared, reproducing faster than Picard could count. A larger icon appeared at the field's center, and from that point lines began crossing the field to connect to each of the uncounted dots.

"Energy from a central location in spacetime is being directed toward multiple timelines?" asked Doctor Crusher.

"At the same time," said La Forge, "neural energy harvested from living beings within a timeline can be directed through the same network back to that nucleus. Remember, this is just a simplified representation. The actual network is so much bigger, it's almost impossible to visualize."

Wesley indicated the diagram coalescing in the space before the group. "That's pretty much it. Based on what I've been able to extract from the data, the Devidians were a dying race, limited by the energy they could find to provide sustenance. Expanding on their smaller-scale approaches to harvesting neural energy from living beings, they moved their entire species to an unidentified point in time. Whether that's the future or the past, I don't know, but it allowed them to expand on their initial methods of deriving neural energy to an operation on a much larger scale. We're talking orders of magnitude. Instead of their species dwindling to the point of extinction, they thrived."

"So, somewhere in the far future," said Garcia, "or maybe in the past, the Devidians are seizing on instabilities found in various time streams so they can extract neural energy from living beings within those realities." She pointed to the larger circle at the center of the presentation. "And this thing, this nucleus, is behind it all."

La Forge replied, "With the hubs doing most of the heavy lifting. At least we think that's the case. We also don't believe this is something that started with the Devidians. From what we know based on prevailing temporal theory and our own experiences with temporal phenomena, time itself is always fracturing into an ever-increasing series of branching realities. These in turn spawn their own branches, and successive deviations are more fragile than their predecessors as they divide and extend outward, farther and farther from their original fracture points. It's like a rock cracking a window. Left untreated, that crack spreads out, splitting and dividing with each new crack smaller and thinner than the last until you run out of window."

Or time, thought Picard.

Agent Garcia said, "Time travel can be that rock making a crack in the window. Every time someone travels to the past, if they alter an event, a new reality branches off from that point, and the process repeats itself over and over. It can happen by traveling to the future too. After all, our future is someone else's past." When no one said anything in response, she added, "Now you know why the Department of Temporal Investigations is so uptight about such things."

Studying the representation of the network, Picard said, "You believe the Devidians have found a way to exploit what the universe is doing naturally."

"That's our best guess, based on what we've been able to extract from the data," replied Wesley. "The Devidians either take advantage of fractures introduced into an existing timeline, or they simply make their own, then use these hubs to collapse those timelines and draw the neural energy from living beings within those realities. The more fractured or extended a branching timeline is, the more fragile and susceptible to this process it becomes. At first they seemed content to feed on timelines closer to their point of origin or branching, perhaps as a way to minimize changes to the more stable timelines or what I've taken to calling 'parent realities.' Think about a tree branch. You trim off smaller branches, either because they're dead or diseased, or to keep the larger branch from buckling under too much weight."

Doctor Crusher said, "So that's what the Devidians are doing? Trimming dying or inferior branches from a tree?"

Wesley waved his hand toward the Omnichron and the scene shifted once again. This time the representation did resemble a crack in a windowpane, propagating and expanding in all directions as it spread across the black field.

"For them, we think it's simply about the sustenance they can derive from the process," he said. "A fragile, corrupted timeline offers an easy ability to consume the neural energy from all of the life-forms residing within it. This in turn fuels their ability to go after more stable, established realities. It's an escalating process, with the Devidians working their way from weaker branches to stronger ones, but their appetite for the neural energy that sustains them has grown out of control. There's plenty of it out there, in the form of countless, limitless timelines and alternate realities, but it'll never be enough."

"They are in an unwinnable race against their own avarice," said Picard, "and it's the universe that will suffer for it."

Wesley gestured to the spiderweb of timelines branching across the display. "While some timelines are more fragile than others, they all have one thing in common: an apex, or a point at which balance is lost and the entire reality slides toward entropy. There are timelines that can't be saved due to the nature of their creation, or the universe doing its own kind of housekeeping."

"Here's the bad news," said La Forge. "The Devidians have been working their way toward the more stable timelines, ones that don't feature a lot of deviations or branches. If we don't stop whatever the Devidians are doing, the damage won't just be limited to our reality. The effect will just keep cascading farther and farther, until eventually the Devidians chew all the way through to the trunk of the tree, the original reality from which everything else originated."

"How much time do we have?" asked Garcia.

Wesley's expression grew somber. "A few weeks, a month at the outside, at least as we perceive time in this reality."

Picard took in everything being said and played it against his recollection of what he and Wesley had seen in the vision they shared of the future. He felt a sense of dread beginning to settle upon him; a certainty that there might be no solution to this crisis. No action that could be taken to stave off oblivion. On the other hand, doing nothing almost certainly guaranteed annihilation, not just for this reality and everything in it, but anything connected to it through the wonder of infinite planes of existence. He knew he could not stand by, doing nothing, while there existed the faintest, even unlikeliest chance of stopping the Devidians.

Crusher said, "We keep talking about branching timelines, unstable timelines, even corrupt timelines. Now you say there are timelines that might need to be 'trimmed' in order to save other realities. How do we know which timelines are 'right' or 'wrong'?"

"It's not about right and wrong," replied Wesley. "It's about how stable a timeline is after it branches from an existing reality. The more recent the point of divergence, the more fragile it is. The easier it is to disrupt. The Devidians have figured out how to feed on the neural energy of beings living in an unstable timeline reality. They don't have to conquer an entire alternate reality, but instead they pull just enough energy out of it to cause it to collapse in on itself." He sighed. "I've watched it happen."

"We know that not only are there multiple timelines," said Garcia, "but sometimes timelines cross one another, converge, then split again. This might explain why the same events happen across different realities, even if it's accidental. Still, we believe those to be divergence points, and if Mister Crusher is right, those then contribute to the corruption of even stable timelines, making them perfect targets for the Devidians." The DTI agent looked to Picard. "For example, there's the Raqilan weapon ship you found last year. The information Commander Taurik retrieved from that vessel— and quarantined before we debriefed him—included sensor logs recorded just prior to its time jump from the late twenty-fifth century. Their long-range scans detected the presence of a large spacecraft entering its home star system. It was a Borg cube."

A knot formed in Picard's gut. "You're certain?"

"Absolutely." Garcia's expression softened. "According to the theory he shared when he was debriefed by DTI, Taurik believed the Borg ship may have been drawn by the experimental weapon ship, which the Raqilan built by reverse-engineering a prototype planet killer they found crashed on an asteroid in their home system. Taurik also discovered the ship and its crew had a quantum signature different from ours, proving they came from a future where the Borg were not overcome six years ago. Their attempt to time-travel into their own past somehow brought them to ours. It was specifically this information that motivated Taurik to quarantine the ship's computer data and protect you all from potential Temporal Prime Directive violations."

Garcia said, "This suggests that by traveling into our past instead of its own, they introduced an instability into this timeline that the Devidians can now exploit."

"I think this is what my future self was investigating," said Wesley. "He was hunting for information about this for decades. Everything's in the O.C. For all I know, I've died a half dozen times but an alternate version kept picking up the baton and continuing the search."

"There's more," said La Forge. "Wesley—the future Wesley—wasn't the only one working on this. We can guess other Travelers were trying to find answers, but Starfleet in the future was also investigating. According to the data he stored, they knew something was building five hundred years from now, but also stretching from their future to our past. The instability was there, the whole time. They tried to fix it, but those were stopgaps at best, and the more corrupted our timeline gets, the more interest it draws from the Devidians."

Her gaze fixed on the map representation, Crusher said, "One thing's for sure. The Devidians have to know we're onto them. You may have destroyed that hub four thousand years in the future, but it's just one. It makes sense there would be multiple such hubs within a given timeline. The only way to stop the Devidians is to find this nucleus: the heart of their network."

"And that will be the trick," said Wesley. "So far, I've found nothing in the data I retrieved that offers a hint about that location. It's most likely in another timeline. It might even exist outside time itself."

"Outside time itself?" asked Garcia. "How is that even possible?"

Wesley offered a grim smile. "I've been around the cosmos enough to know that just about anything is possible."

"But what about this timeline?" asked Crusher, her expression anxious. "Can we save it?"

"Possibly." Wesley gestured to the map of timelines before them. "Right now, this reality is something like a diseased tree branch. It's sick, and if we can't treat our infection, the only cure is to sever the branch in order to save the rest of the tree."

This, Picard knew, was bigger than one ship and crew, even one so capable as that of the *Enterprise*. If Wesley was right, then this entire reality was at risk. Indeed, a haunting realization was beginning to take root in Picard's consciousness: it might well be necessary for this timeline to die to prevent the disease from spreading, contaminating all of time throughout this universe and countless others. If he and his crew were to have any hope of stopping such a catastrophe from coming to pass, they would need help; all the assistance they could find. Armed with this sudden apprehension, he tapped his combadge.

"Picard to bridge. Set a course for Earth and engage at maximum warp. Also, dispatch a subspace message to the *U.S.S. Titan*. Extend my urgent request to Admiral Riker to join us."

37

His eyes snapped open, and Worf caught a glimpse of the overhead above him before pushing himself out of bed. Shaking off slumber, hands up and ready to strike before his bare feet touched the carpeted floor, he scanned his bedroom for intruders or some other threat. There were none.

"Computer, lights!"

The illumination increased, bringing the room into full relief. He made short work of inspecting every corner of his quarters. Only after he entered his main sitting area did he realize he had not shaken a sensation of unfamiliarity. These were his quarters, and yet they felt like those of a stranger. Even with mementos and other possessions he recognized as belonging to him, he could not shake the idea he was somehow intruding.

It was the dream. *Again.*

Grunting in frustration, Worf moved to his desk. He reached for the computer interface and tapped a control.

"Personal log, supplemental. For a second time, I have experienced an odd dream. Bits and pieces of it tease me, lurking in the shadows of my mind and defying my every effort to drag them into the light. The parts I *do* recall feel as vivid as any other memory, even though I know I have never taken part in the events the dream depicts. Even more bothersome is how *very real* it all feels. The corridors of the old *Enterprise*. Outdated uniforms and weapons. Bodies. The woman crewmember reaching out to me and calling for help." He struggled to remember more. "Flashes of energy and then above it all—*beyond* it all—something else here. *Another presence.* I felt it. Whispers teasing my ears, but when I turn to find the source, there is nothing. I am alone, and yet I'm not." What was he not seeing? At the fringes of his perceptions lay an unseen, unknown enemy.

Wait, he realized. *Not unseen. Not unknown.*

"The Nagas," he said. "And their avatars." Given recent events, it made sense that he might dream of them now, but it did not explain the earlier instance. It was unlike him to experience the same dream more than once except on very rare occasions, but this was altogether different.

Worf began pacing the room, lost in thought. "Has my mind merely inserted the Nagas and their Devidian masters into an existing fragment of my subconscious, or is something else at work here? How can I know?" With everything that had happened over the past few days, he could not discount the effect of those events on him. Perhaps this, coupled with simple fatigue, was responsible for the havoc on his sleep. It was a reasonable explanation but at the same time, uncertainty nagged at him.

"I should report this to Doctor Tropp."

Reaching the entrance to his sleeping area, Worf turned back to face the desk. "Computer, pause recording." He considered his previous discussions with the physician, who, after listening to his explanation of his previous episode of disturbed slumber, gave his pledge of confidentiality. That agreement required Worf to keep the Denobulan apprised of future dream incidents. His duties as the ship's first officer, to say nothing of his personal honor, demanded he contact Tropp. At the same time, something—almost a voice at the edge of his awareness—seemed to be imploring him to take no such action.

"Wait," he said. "Could my subconscious somehow be trying to warn me?" It was the first time he had considered that possibility. Might he be experiencing premonitions? Was it even possible that, for reasons unknown, he somehow had traveled through time? It would not be his first experience with inadvertent temporal phenomena. He knew firsthand the sensation of shifting from one reality to another, each one feeling as familiar as the one before it, yet all of them undeniably alien to him. Could something similar be happening now?

"Computer, scan me. Are there any indications of temporal displacement?"

"Negative. No residual tachyons or chronitons, or other known elements that might indicate such a transition."

He knew this was not conclusive. There could be any number of methods for moving him through time undetectable by the ship's sensors. A neural scan might indicate an abundance of recent memories for which he could not account, but that would require reporting to sickbay, and he was not yet prepared to do that.

"Computer, resume recording," he snapped. "So far, the dreams have not impacted my ability to carry out my duties. Captain Picard needs me. I cannot allow myself to become compromised. I will not permit that to happen, though I do have several more questions requiring answers. For now, I will seek those answers by myself. End recording."

The desktop terminal's screen went dark, the log now committed to the computer's main data storage banks. It could only be accessed by him, although Captain Picard and Doctor Crusher could override the personal lockouts with their respective command codes. That did not concern Worf. If circumstances reached a point where such an action was necessary, there would be far more serious problems demanding attention.

Was he making a mistake?

The sensation of his head falling forward roused Picard from fitful slumber. He sat up in the chair, blinking himself awake as he regarded his surroundings: René's room, with Picard occupying a soft chair in one corner near the bed.

In the bed, René slept.

Slow, steady breaths indicated deep slumber, for which Picard was grateful. The boy needed the rest, if for no other reason than it gave him a brief respite from the challenges he now faced.

He's not a boy, Picard argued with himself.

But he is, in all the ways that matter. He's still a child, and he needs your help. He needs you to be the same father you've always been. You have to be strong. There can be no wavering. No indecision. No regrets. For his sake, and yours.

Watching René, the bedcovers pulled up to his chin while his right foot stuck out from beneath the blanket, Picard weighed leaving him to his slumber and heading to bed himself. In the bedroom he shared with his wife, Beverly Crusher had finally found solace in sleep. He told himself she needed the rest more than he did. It was not quite a lie, but rather it was denial. Sitting here would do nothing to help René, and the simple truth was Picard knew the longer he avoided sleep, the better the chances he might avoid dreaming. Would he be haunted by the faces of those lost during this mission? It was a possibility, if a remote one.

Not that it mattered, as even in full wakefulness he sensed their presence. They were here, hovering just out of sight and yet close enough he imagined he could feel them. He wished they could speak. There was so much to say; so much he should have said, yet never did. There was supposed to be time for such things. No more.

Movement near the door caught his attention, and he looked up to see Wesley Crusher standing at the threshold. The other man offered a contrite expression.

"I'm sorry to disturb you, Captain. I just wanted to check on René."

Picard had not heard the doors to his quarters open or close. He opened his mouth to ask how he had gained entry but opted against it. Surely a secured door was no match for a Traveler.

"He's been asleep for a few hours. Your mother gave him something to help with that." On those few occasions René had been awake, he acted as if delirious, which brought with it panic. To that end, Doctor Crusher had opted for gentle sedation. If nothing else, the old adage of rest being an effective treatment prevailed.

Once the *Enterprise* and *Aventine* returned to Earth, her intention was to consult with colleagues at Starfleet Medical, hoping some obscure remedy lay waiting to be discovered in that organization's vast library of interstellar medicine.

Shifting in his seat made Picard remember the book on his lap, which had fallen open at some point. He lifted it so that the small reading lamp next to his chair illuminated the book's pages and the words printed on them. He closed it, running his fingers across its imitation leather cover with his fingertips.

"I can't remember the last time I read a real book," said Wesley, his voice low. "Or any book, for that matter."

Picard cleared his throat. "I wasn't really reading. It was . . . it was something I gave to Lieutenant Chen as a gift after she did a most thoughtful favor for me. Your mother returned it to me earlier this evening." He smiled, recalling the occasion. At Doctor Crusher's request, Chen had undertaken the task of restoring to working order his Ressikan flute, damaged during the Borg Invasion. He could not part with the treasured memento no matter its condition, but being unable to play it wounded him. Chen had fixed the irreplaceable instrument, thus restoring to him a precious measure of inner peace. In return, he offered her the book.

"May I?" Wesley extended his hand and, after taking the tome, opened its front cover and found the inscription Picard knew was there. "To T'Ryssa Chen: Things aren't always as they seem, and sometimes they surprise you. Thank you. JLP." He closed the book. "I'm sure there's a story here."

"It's historical adventure fiction, written over a century ago," said Picard. "It offers an 'alternative account' of humanity's first contact with the Vulcans. Needless to say, its version is very much at odds with the actual events." He smiled again. "You can take my word for it."

Wesley regarded the book. "Not your usual taste in leisure reading."

"Riker gave it to me, following our little excursion to twenty-first-century Earth, where we got to observe the actual first contact. After we saved history from Borg assimilation. It's a bit of whimsy, I grant you, but in recent years I've come to remember embracing that every so often isn't necessarily a bad thing. T'Ryssa Chen helped me with that."

Though he'd harbored doubts about her when she reported to the *Enterprise* for duty, it had taken her little time to make a lasting impression. At first put off by her jovial, even rebellious if not insubordinate demeanor, Picard conceded he saw much in her that reminded him of himself at that age. Young, new to Starfleet, and with her whole life ahead of her, ready to explore the galaxy. She had proven herself an invaluable addition to the *Enterprise*, and he enjoyed the sort of unexpected mentoring relationship that had evolved between them. He liked to think she had gained from him an even greater appreciation for duty and loyalty to ship and crew. From her, Picard acquired a renewed outlook on life, remaining mindful that simply living life was not nearly so rewarding as experiencing and *enjoying* it. The demands of duty in recent years had seen him forget that sentiment.

Cherish every moment, because they'll never come again. He recalled what he told Will Riker years ago, and which he recently began taking to heart once again. *What we leave behind is not as important as how we've lived.* He wondered if there was a reality where he had found the time to share with her—and others, lost during this mission—how much their being in his life meant to him. He hoped that was the case.

Thank you, T'Ryssa.

Moving with care, Wesley sat on the corner of René's bed, mindful not to wake his younger brother. With hands clasped and resting in his lap, he turned so he could study the boy—*the man*—sleeping before him. In that moment, Picard saw the weight not just of worlds on his shoulders, but the entire universe. Time itself. What had he seen in his travels? What secrets did he carry? What knowledge was he unable to share?

Picard felt that same burden of responsibility. Did the moments lived to this point have any real meaning, or were they fated to be casualties to the coming storm? Could all of reality be saved without sacrificing this timeline, or was doing so the only key to victory? Was it *his* destiny to vanquish preordained expectations, or was he condemned to an inevitable, inviolable fate? How many moments were left, not just for him but for René, Beverly, Wesley, and indeed an entire reality?

"Wesley," he said. "Do you believe we can succeed? What does success even mean? How do I lead this crew without some idea of what we're facing?"

After a moment, Wesley drew a deep breath. He looked away from his brother, meeting Picard's anxious gaze.

"I don't know."

END OF BOOK I

STAR TREK™
CODA

will continue in

BOOK II

THE ASHES OF TOMORROW

AFTERWORD

"The past is written, but the future is left for us to write."
—Jean-Luc Picard, 2399

"Dude. It's so much worse than you think."
—Dayton Ward, July 2019

The genesis of what ultimately became the *Coda* trilogy, of which you've just read the first book, came about in the spring of 2018. That's when Kirsten Beyer—longtime friend and fellow *Star Trek* novelist, who at the time was working as a writer on *Star Trek: Discovery*—contacted me. She was calling with a bit of news I was obligated to keep to myself for the foreseeable future: Sir Patrick Stewart would soon return to our television screens as Jean-Luc Picard in an all-new series for CBS All Access (now Paramount+).

After I picked my jaw up off the floor, I started asking Kirsten questions in rapid-fire fashion. When would the show be set? What would it be about? Would the rest of the *Star Trek: The Next Generation* cast be returning as well? Details were very, very scarce at this early juncture, but Kirsten was able to tell me the new series would be set many years after Picard's last appearance in the 2002 feature film *Star Trek Nemesis*.

Uh-oh, I thought.

From that moment, I was sure of one thing: the *Star Trek* novels published by Simon & Schuster—specifically, the post-series stories featuring the casts of *Star Trek: The Next Generation*, *Star Trek: Deep Space Nine*, and *Star Trek: Voyager*—would be impacted in some fashion. Dating back to 2001, these novels had been telling tales of the characters set after the events of their respective television series. With the television shows and feature films concluded—for the foreseeable future, at least—the editors and authors enjoyed a tremendous degree of freedom to explore the characters in ways that could never be done while the series were in active production. Events unfolded that permitted characters from one series to work with those from another, telling stories with repercussions carrying forward into future novels. The continuity between the novels became much more intertwined, evolving and deepening with each new story. Characters from any of the series could appear anywhere, either as "guest stars" or even semipermanent reassignments depending on the needs of a particular story. Some even "starred" in series of their own.

In addition to allowing for the development of core characters from *TNG*, *DS9*, and *VGR* beyond what would have been possible while each of those television series was still in active production, the *Star Trek* novels introduced characters to fill gaps left by those who had been given new assignments or simply opted for some other life path, or had died, or who were presumed dead. This is *Star Trek*, after all. Further, the developing novel continuity eventually grew to include tales told under the banner of several spin-off novel series. In addition to *Star Trek: Titan*, there also was *Star Trek: New Frontier*, *Star Trek: Corps of Engineers*, *Star Trek: Klingon Empire*, and *Star Trek: Department of Temporal Investigations*.

While these series tended to unfold alongside and eventually after events shown in the latter *Star Trek* feature films and television series set in the twenty-fourth century, this interwoven future history didn't forget other eras. Novels set in and around the original *Star Trek* series and after the events of *Star Trek: Enterprise*—though largely containing their adventures to, respectively, the twenty-second and twenty-third centuries—still found links to the "expanded universe" continuity. It had almost become a living, breathing thing, enticing readers to dig ever deeper into the mythos being augmented with each new book while demanding the editors and authors keep track of an ever-increasing amount of information. With no new television series or films on the horizon, those of us privileged to write and publish the novels enjoyed a freedom rarely offered within the realm of media tie-in publishing. Within reason, and so far as we did our best to remain true to the same principles that had guided those TV series and movies, there were no limits to what we could do. At the same time, each of us was motivated by a sincere desire and, dare I say it, responsibility to do right by *Star Trek*, and therefore justify the trust placed in us by its guardians. It was daunting and yet exhilarating all at the same time. Looking back at what we were allowed to do thanks to the good graces of the licensing offices at CBS, I'm honestly floored, even after more years than I care to count out loud.

Then, as often happens these days when we're talking about any entertainment property with any sort of legacy, *Star Trek* "woke up" again. Except for the three feature films released between 2009 and 2016, the franchise had been dormant on screen since 2005 and the final episode of *Star Trek: Enterprise*. 2017 brought us *Star Trek: Discovery*, a prequel to the Original Series, which carried with it the potential to lay claim to an area of storytelling that had largely been left to novels, comics, games, and other expanded media. Next came that call from Kirsten Beyer in early 2018, alerting me on the down low that *Star Trek: Picard* was in the earliest of planning stages.

As months passed, Kirsten would keep me updated, and as bits of information came my way, I started to see at least some of the potential impacts to the ongoing storylines being told in the novels. I jotted down a few preliminary notes, but Kirsten and her fellow writers were still figuring out the important things. Where to set the series relative to the other shows and films? How to explain what happened between Picard's last on-screen appearance in *Star Trek Nemesis* and the new storyline? What other familiar characters might appear?

In April 2019, Kirsten sent me a document she'd written as something of a primer for writers new to the series and indeed *Star Trek* as a whole. It laid out the relevant high points of *Star Trek* "history" in chronological order; not just those facts established by previous series and films, but also pieces of internal backstory that would inform *Picard*'s first season. It was exactly the boost I needed to kick-start my own thinking, because now I knew exactly how and to what degree the new series would affect what had been laid down in *Star Trek* novels and their shared continuity dating back nearly twenty years.

By this point, there already was preliminary discussion about how the books might adapt to what soon would become the new status quo of canon *Star Trek*. As writers and most readers of such works know, tie-in novels exist to support the parent property. The books we'd been writing these past several years would have to alter course in order to better complement what was once again a very active *Star Trek* production cycle. Each new show would be adding to the franchise's already vast mythology and attracting new fans, compelling tie-ins like ours to be accessible to new readers. Given the lengthy history of *Star Trek* novels and their ongoing continuity, this presented a huge challenge, as we also wanted to honor the readers who had taken this journey with us.

Many of you reading this right now likely are aware of what happened after Disney purchased Lucasfilm and the rights to the *Star Wars* franchise and began production on what would become the seventh *Star Wars* film, *The Force Awakens*. After hearing for decades that novels, comics, games, and other narratives were a form of *Star Wars* canon held to strict consistency not only with one another but also the films and television series, it was announced in 2014 that everything contributing to the *Star Wars* Expanded Universe now were considered "Legends." Generally speaking, these tales would not inform new films, TV series, or even books, comics, and games going forward. Fans of this material felt betrayed, as though all the time (and money!) they'd invested in these products over the years had somehow been wasted. Though the challenge we were facing with the *Star Trek* novels was not on that scale, my feeling at the time was that I very much wanted them to avoid a repeat of the *Star Wars* situation.

It was a sentiment shared by my editors, Ed Schlesinger and Margaret Clark, and also John Van Citters at CBS Licensing. All three were on board with the idea of us doing something within the novels to acknowledge this latest evolution in the *Star Trek* brand without simply scrapping everything that had come before. Skip ahead to July 2019, when I sat down with friend and fellow *Star Trek* novelist David Mack at the annual Shore Leave convention we both attend every year. It came as no surprise for me to learn he'd heard some things about the new *Picard* series and was also considering what to do about the impact to the novels. Like me, he also was concerned about respecting the loyal readership who had stuck with us all these years. He'd recently met with our colleague James Swallow and discussed ideas with the intention of pulling me into their conversation. They had a rough plan in mind, which in some ways mirrored much of my own thinking . . . right down to Dave and me more or less coming up with the same ending. However, unlike me, he and Jim had not been privy to information from Kirsten Beyer and the still developing *Picard* series. Once Dave laid out his and Jim's basic idea and the challenge that came with reconciling the novel continuity with the show's and indeed the entire franchise's new paradigm, that's when I had to drop the bomb.

"Dude," I said. "It's so much worse than you think."

I said it mostly as a joke, but the truth was we had a big job ahead of us; so Dave, Jim, and I got to work. Starting over. Brainstorming. Idea tossing. Emails. Skype calls. Notes passed back and forth. Over the course of several months during late 2019 and early 2020, we figured out a storyline to unfold across three books: the plotlines that would run through this trilogy but also the beats that would inform each novel while supporting its companions. We tossed ideas between us like poker chips. Things that at first sounded good for one book found a better home in another, and so on. All the while, we tried to remain conscious of our primary mission: honoring what had come before while helping transition to what lay ahead. It was a spirited collaboration from start to finish, and I enjoyed every minute of it.

Which brings us to you, Welcome Reader. You hold in your hands just the first piece of what we hope comes across as a work of sheer love, not just for *Star Trek*, but also the *Star Trek* novels and the fans who've read and supported them. Whether you've been with us on this journey for years or are just coming aboard to see what the fuss is about, we're glad you're here, and we hope you'll stay with us as we turn yet another page . . .

ACKNOWLEDGMENTS

First, many thanks to my co-conspirators in this bit of literary mischief, David Mack and James Swallow. This isn't our first collaboration, but I daresay it's been the most challenging, and undertaking it with my fellow ne'er-do-wells made it more fun than should be allowed, or maybe even legal. It's even inspired us to start our own metal band, "Wormhole Death Canon." Stay tuned for announcements about our first album and upcoming concert tour.

A truckload of thanks to our editors at Gallery Books, Ed Schlesinger and Margaret Clark. When we first proposed the initial idea that ultimately morphed into this mammoth story of which *Moments Asunder* represents merely the first third, their instructions to us boiled down to a simple directive: "Swing for the fences." Not simply my editors for more years than any of us might want to admit, they've also been mentors and friends. Throughout this project, they've been nothing less than unwaveringly supportive, and there's simply no way something like *Star Trek: Coda* gets done without their guidance and trust.

Thanks also to John Van Citters, Vice President of *Star Trek* Brand Development within the larger realm of ViacomCBS Global Franchise Management. John's been a servant and protector of *Star Trek* for about as long as I've been writing *Star Trek* novels. I've never doubted his devotion and commitment to the property, and he's always been a source of great counsel and inspiration. Like Ed and Margaret, John was nothing but encouraging and enthusiastic as we labored to navigate this latest curve in the long, winding road of *Star Trek* publishing.

I think it's also way overdue that I call out and salute Scott Pearson, friend and fellow author who also for the past several years has served as the primary copyeditor for the *Star Trek* novel line. Scott's deep knowledge of the series' canon and continuity along with his keen eyes and editorial prowess have saved our butts on uncounted occasions. A project like this demanded he level up his already considerable game, and while I know he probably cursed Jim and Dave and myself more than a few times while pushing through these three manuscripts, I'm sure his calls for our painful sacrifices to some heretofore unnamed deity were made from a place of love.

I offer a special acknowledgment to the late Margaret Wander Bonanno, who passed away in April 2021, while I was in the midst of finalizing this novel. I became a big fan of her writing in 1987, when I first read her novel *Strangers from the Sky*, which remains one of my very favorite *Star Trek* tales. Margaret was always a source of inspiration, up to and including the writing of this book, and I'm honored she saw fit to call me her friend.

You know I can't write any set of acknowledgments without mentioning Kevin Dilmore, my best friend and frequent writing partner. Even if he's not actively working with me on a project, he's still my principal collaborator. He's my sounding board, offering time and again a width and breadth of knowledge that far exceeds my own along with his humor, love of *Star Trek* and storytelling, and ability to see things that simply confound or escape me.

And then there's you, Reader of the Book You Currently Hold in Your Hands. From the moment it became apparent the current line of post–TV series *Star Trek* novels set in the twenty-fourth century would now be out of step with the official, canonical future histories of Jean-Luc Picard and the crew of *Star Trek: The*

Next Generation in particular, we had one idea: give fans who've supported us throughout all these many years and so many stories something we hoped might serve as a worthy transition to the "new reality." Whether we did that is ultimately for you to decide, but I can't overstate how much you factored into our thinking every step of the way.

Hailing frequencies closed!

ABOUT THE AUTHOR

Dayton Ward understands and forgives readers who skip over these "About the Author" pages. It's easy to gloss right past them. Besides, a lot of them can be kind of pretentious, with the author listing everything they've ever written along with the names of every cat they've ever rescued from a tree. Dayton hates being that guy, even though he truly digs cats.

What Dayton can tell you is that his first *Star Trek* "expanded universe" story was written in the early 1980s, and you'll be thrilled to know it remains unpublished. Indeed, the story itself doesn't even exist anymore. All copies have been burned, and all witnesses have been silenced. You're welcome.

If you've made it this far, let Dayton know by visiting him on the web at **DaytonWard.com**, where you can read about all the stuff he's written and thank him for sparing you the pain of yet another long, drawn-out "About the Author" page.